ALSO BY WILLIAM BAYER

*Pattern Crimes*

*Switch*

*Peregrine*

*Punish Me with Kisses*

*Tangier*

# Blind Side

# Blind Side

## WILLIAM

## BAYER

### WITH PHOTOGRAPHS
### BY THE AUTHOR

*Villard Books · New York · 1989*

All rights reserved under International and Pan-American
Copyright Conventions. Published in the United States by
Villard Books, a division of Random House, Inc., New York,
and simultaneously in Canada by Random House
of Canada, Limited, Toronto.

Grateful acknowledgment is made to Chappell & Co. for
permission to reprint lyrics from *Can-Can* by Cole Porter.
Copyright 1952, 1953 by Chappell & Co. (Renewed).
All rights reserved. Used by permission.

The author wishes to thank the following for assistance and/or advice:
Neil Lukas, photographer; Bill Jay, photographer, teacher and
photographic scholar (whose advice on construction of the gun-camera
was invaluable); Peter Gethers, editorial director of Villard Books. He
would also like to thank his models: Nick Bayer, Beth Litchfield, Alex
Szogyi, and, most particularly, Eugenia Martino for her patience,
endurance and for giving such good "dead-eye." Needless to say, they
bear no resemblance to the characters in the book.

Library of Congress Cataloging-in-Publication Data
Bayer, William.
Blind side.
I. Title.
PS3552.A8588B55   1989        813'.54        88-40611
ISBN 0-394-57257-2

Manufactured in the United States of America

9 8 7 6 5 4 3 2

First Edition

Book design by JoAnne Metsch

*For BATO and LEILA*

# One

The camera is an instrument of detection. We photograph not only what we know but also what we don't know. When I point a camera at a subject, I am asking a question. Sometimes the photograph is the answer; I am the one who gets the lesson.

—Lisette Model

THE FIRST TIME I SAW HER MY VISION WAS BLURRED—
not surprising, since I was peering through a view camera. She
stepped into my frame, then stood there out of focus. It was a while
before I could make her out.

But even when I did, when I thought I knew who she was and
who she wasn't, my vision was still blurred. It took me a long time
to discover that. And then it was too late.

It had been a steaming hot July day, the kind of bad day of high
humidity and noxious fumes you get in Manhattan in the summer
months. Then it rained in the early evening—a hard, fast summer
rain. A little after midnight, unable to sleep, I went out looking
for something to photograph. The streets were wet and smelled of
iron, and there was a scent of dead flowers in the air.

I set up a couple of times in the lower reaches of Soho, executed
two nightscapes ("Urban Nightscapes by Geoffrey Barnett"). But
even as I was taking the exposures, and they were long, I knew
pretty well I was wasting my time.

I headed west then, into Tribeca, prowling a neighborhood near the river, dark lonely streets of old five-story warehouses. The buildings were dark, except for an occasional loft converted into a residence, and when I spotted one of those from down on the street, I could tell the people who lived up there had built themselves a little paradise—I saw lights hanging from ceiling tracks and the tops of huge paintings mounted on the walls.

It was on Desbrosses Street, around 2:00 A.M., that I finally found something that I liked: a brick-building wall on which the silhouette of a man, ecstatic and spread-eagled, had been painted with some kind of tar.

I recognized the style. It was the work of an anonymous environmental artist whose paintings had begun during the winter to appear on walls downtown. Arms flailing, torsos twisted, his figures seemed to be pinned against the bricks by fusillades of bullets.

But there was more than the painting that drew my attention to that particular stretch of wall. A gleaming white stretch Cadillac limousine was parked just in front. There was a driver inside. I couldn't see his face; the glass was the kind that's black and opaque. But I knew he was there because I could see the smoke from his cigarette curling out of an open inch of window.

I liked the vision: that long sleek white car, ghostlike beneath the streetlamp, set before that painting of the executed man. And as I stared I knew just how I wanted to shoot it too: straight on, from across the street, the car off-center, the harsh painting strong on the right. It was so good it could have been my trademark shot— a mysterious, menacing vision of an empty city street at night.

I set up my tripod, put a 120mm. on my Deardorff, pulled my focusing cloth over my head, and began to frame and focus. I had everything composed about the way I wanted it, when I was confronted by the face of a young woman who had wandered into my frame.

4

She stood there staring at my lens. "Are you an alien creature?" she asked.

Since I was focused on the wall, I couldn't make her out. "Mind moving, please? You're blocking my shot."

"You look pretty funny," she said. "You seem to have five legs."

"You must be the local comedian?" I said. She moved closer, taking up most of the frame.

"Thanks," I said. "Do you think you could get even more in the way?"

Still she didn't move. "Car's great, isn't it? Belongs to the people I'm with. I've heard about the guy who does those wall paintings back there. They call him the Shadow Painter. Frankly I like the shadows better than the paint."

"*Please.*"

"What? Oh! Sure." She finally moved. "You here on account of Lil's?"

"What's Lil's?" I was checking my edges.

"Thought *everyone* knew that."

"Not me." I couldn't wait to get rid of her. When you're working on the street, curious civilians can be a real pain.

"It's a club. See the door down the block? I just thought—you know, lots of famous people going in and out . . . Can I look?" She was standing beside me now. I smelled her perfume, dark and musky, as she crowded in to peer.

"Don't touch the camera," I warned her, then stepped back and studied her as she bent forward. Her figure was good. Her skimpy black dress, damp from the exertions of dancing, clung tightly to her back. Her ringlets of light tawny hair were wet where they touched her neck.

"It's upside down."

"That's the way it looks through a lens."

She turned to me then, and for the first time I saw her face: young, clean features as perfect as a model's, but more giving, more sultry, perhaps the face of a young actress, I thought. Her cheekbones were high, her eyes were almost feline, her mouth was slightly open and her lips were beautifully carved. I thought of the young Lauren Bacall; she had that same handsome smile.

She didn't act wacky, though, not like the multitude of lost, stoned, punked-out girls who wander through the downtown clubs snorting coke and dancing until the dawn. So much free-floating powder in the clubs, I'd heard, you snort the stuff just breathing in the air.

"What are you shooting?"

"A chunk of time."

"Hmmm. Enigmatic," she said. "How big a chunk?"

Something about the way she phrased her question changed my feeling about her. Suddenly I didn't want her to go away.

"About twenty-five minutes," I said. "I'll close down the aperture, then strobe the wall."

"Too bad. The car'll be gone before you're finished. It's leaving as soon as my friends come out." She was telling me I was about to lose my picture. "A chunk of time—I *like* that." She laughed, and I took another hit of her intoxicating perfume. "And I like you, Mr. Enigmatic Photographer." She gazed at me, waiting for a response.

"Well, that's nice," I said. "Maybe if I got to know you better, I might get to like you too."

"Maybe you could get to know me better."

"Maybe I could."

"You're a photographer. I need some head shots. Would you shoot some for me?"

What she was asking was impossible, of course, but I wasn't prepared to tell her so. "Maybe. I don't know . . . ." I said.

She nodded. "How do I get in touch?"

I pulled out my wallet and handed her my card. She studied it. "Geoffrey Barnett. Sounds familiar. Have I heard of you?"

I shrugged; she'd asked my least favorite question.

"Hey! Kimberly!"

She turned. Four young people were clustered by the Cadillac. She waved to them. A young man with a geometric haircut waved back. Two girls and a second boy climbed inside the limo.

"Come on, Kimberly. Time to go."

"Be there in a flash." She turned back to me, eyes focused, earnest. "I'll call you tomorrow." She gently waved my business card. "Know something? I *have* heard of you. Good night, Mr. Geoffrey Barnett. . . ."

She gazed at me, smiled, and then, in a single flowing movement, turned, crossed the street and stepped into the car. Moments later the big white Cadillac pulled away from the curb leaving tiny ripples in the puddles on the street.

I hung around for another quarter of an hour, trying to take some kind of photograph. But even with the shadow painting strong on the wall, the scene felt forlorn without the car. So I gave it up, packed up my stuff and headed back to Nassau Street.

Walking home I gave some thought to the handsome girl I'd met, how she was young and bright and full of life and how nice it would be to get to know someone like that. She'd given me just the right entrée too. Photographers are always approaching attractive girls on the street. Tonight a very attractive girl had asked to pose for me, and I couldn't accept for reasons I didn't want to have to explain.

So . . . another missed opportunity. I had no idea then that soon she would enter my life.

She called the next afternoon. I was in a rush to go out, so I guess I was pretty abrupt.

"Geoffrey, it's Kim. Kimberly Yates. We met last night. Remember? I'm calling about those head shots we talked about. You said you might do them for me."

*Damn!* "I don't do head shots," I said.

"Then why did you say—"

"I didn't promise anything."

"I didn't say you 'promised,' Geoffrey. But I thought you more or less agreed."

I took a breath. There was only one way out of this. I'd have to be blunt. "I was busy. I wanted you to go away."

"But why would you want me to do that?" She sounded hurt.

"So I could concentrate on my work."

There was a little pause then. "Funny. I don't remember it that way at all."

"Well, that's the way it was. I'm sorry," I said.

"I was serious."

"I wasn't."

She paused. "That's it, then?"

"Pretty much," I said.

"I see." She paused. "Well, maybe next time I'll catch you in a better mood. . . ."

I glanced at my watch as I put down the phone. I was running late. I didn't wait for the elevator, just grabbed my portfolio and tore down the stairs. I had an appointment with Jim Lynch, photo editor of *Life*. When you're summoned by a guy like that, it's not good practice to be late.

In the taxi on the way uptown I thought about Kimberly again. I was forty, I didn't have a girlfriend, and she had the aura of a girl who was available. Shooting her portrait, getting to know her— that could be a lot of fun. Maybe if I just picked up my camera, casually pointed it at her, and tripped the shutter sort of by accident.

. . . But I'd tried that before and it hadn't worked. I had a hunch it also wouldn't work with her.

It was too depressing to think about what might have been, so I turned my attention back to Jim Lynch. I'd known him well in Vietnam but it had been a long time since we'd talked. He'd risen mightily since we'd been photojournalists together. I, meantime, had sunk out of the profession.

Seeing former colleagues wasn't easy for me. The encounters had a way of turning awkward. Photojournalists, packing Leicas, just back from the latest war, don't have a hell of a lot in common with a guy who trudges lower Manhattan at night, hauling a tripod on his back.

I gathered I didn't rate very high with Jim either; he hadn't asked me to lunch. "Got a proposition," he'd said when he'd called. "Come on up. Bring your portfolio. Want to see your latest stuff." Would he really consider running my nightscapes? The fantasy was exhilarating—perhaps too good to believe.

Standing in front of the Time-Life Building, I started feeling the old anxiety. That glass concrete slab had once been the high temple of photojournalism. In the old days to be a *Life* photographer was to be a member of a special caste. You earned big bucks, traveled the world, and when you said "I shoot for *Life*," all doors opened fast. You also ate a lot of shit: you laid out *your* story—they ran *their* story; you shot—they cropped; you were an employee—they were gods. *So what am I doing here?* I asked myself. *Haven't I given this up?*

Now all the excitement was gone; *Life* had become a boring monthly. Yet I still felt the stress, bred out of memories of impossible deadlines, peer competition, struggles to get pouches of film onto planes, and the heat of battles with the layout editors, battles you could only lose, losses that filled you with scorn and self-contempt.

And so I entered the portals with a wishful thought: Jim wouldn't have called me here unless he *did* want to run some of my recent work.

It had been a decade since I'd last seen him, but he looked pretty much the same. His hair was grayer and he sported a brush mustache, instead of the bushy beard he'd worn in Vietnam. He sported a pair of horn-rimmed glasses too, and a pair of snazzy striped suspenders over his form-fitting Italian shirt. He looked lean and fit, like a guy who worked out. Probably had a corporate membership in a gym, along with the sterling-silver health plan, and the solid-gold retirement deal.

He looked through my portfolio, attentive to every shot, gazing, squinting sometimes, as if using his eyes to photograph my photographs. The process didn't take long. "Nice, nice . . . ." he muttered, moving quickly from sheet to sheet. Jim knew how to look at pictures—it was all he did, all day every day, and he did it very well.

"Outstanding," he said when he finished. "Got a real look. Not derivative like a lot of stuff I see. Congratulations, Geof—you've forged yourself a style."

He glanced at me over the tops of his horn-rims. "Especially like the black-and-whites. Clean. Hard-edge. Nice, very nice. And the color work's lush. Those nightscapes: haunting quality there. The absence of people—interesting. Considering what you used to do. It's what's *not* there that makes them work for me. Like what they say about music—it's not just the notes, it's the silences in between. Here it's the voids." He did his horn-rim number again. "What do you think?"

"I think you're making me feel great," I said. "You must be softening me up."

He laughed. "Making money? I know selling prints is rough."

"I eat. Sometimes pretty good. I also pay the rent."

"Still got that great studio? Nassau Street, isn't it?"

"I live there now."

"Sure. Figures. Sleep in the same room as your cameras. Yeah, I can relate to that." He leaned back in his swivel chair. "You're wondering why I called?"

"I was," I said.

"Like I told you on the phone, I've got a proposition."

"So propose." I settled back myself.

He nodded. "First I want a promise. You'll give what I say a little thought. Think before you react."

"I always think."

"No flying off the handle?"

"Promise. Now what do I think about?"

"Beirut."

"Hey! You can stop right there!"

"Hear me out, Geof. I'm talking three, four weeks. Twenty grand plus expenses. Pretty good bread."

"Sure, it is. If I don't get killed."

"You're not the type who gets himself killed."

"That's what everyone who died there said before he went."

"You're different. Know how to operate. You'll stay safe and bring back the goods."

"Why Beirut? Nobody gives a shit. The place has looked the same for years."

"You can make it look different." He tapped the top of my port-folio case.

"Expect me to take a view camera? You must be nuts!"

"Don't get it, do you? I don't care what camera you take. I'm talking about your eyes. You'll see it differently. That's why I want you. When you shoot it, it *won't* look the same."

"No way!"

"You said you'd think about it."

"Forget it, Jim. I'm not going to Beirut."

He stared at me. Up to then he'd been coaxing; now I could see a little glimmer of meanness in his eyes. "Turned yellow, huh?"

"If it makes you feel better, think that, go ahead." I stood, ready to leave.

He looked at me curiously. "Why? Tell me. Why the fuck not? What makes you think you're so goddamn special?"

I started to turn but he grabbed my arm. "I know you're not yellow. That was a cheap shot. I'm sorry." We stared at each other. He looked sincere. I sat down again. "Tell me what's bothering you, Geof. I really want to know."

"It's simple, Jim. It's a lousy assignment."

"Funny, I think it's the best assignment in the world."

"Lunatics firing at one another. Bodies in the streets. I'm not interested in that."

"You were plenty interested in that in 'Nam."

He was right. I'd been intensely interested. Fascinated. Nothing on earth had intrigued me more. "I was an asshole in 'Nam," I said.

"So who wasn't?"

"Maybe I don't want to be an asshole anymore."

"Damnit, Geof. You shot that fucking Pietà."

I'd known, even when I came in, that sooner or later he'd bring that picture up.

". . . you, Eddie Adams, Nick Ut . . . master images . . . made history . . . changed our perceptions of the war." He glanced at my portfolio box. "Forget this arty crap. Sleeping with your cameras, squeaking by—that's no kind of life. Stick to what you know, what you do better than most anybody else. Like it or not, Geof, you're a photojournalist." He peered at me shrewdly. "If it's the money . . . Look—I'll try to get you twenty-five."

"It's not the money."

"What is it, then?"

"I'm no longer a photojournalist."

I must have been convincing; from the way he looked at me I could tell my message was finally sinking in. He sat back, shrugged, and then he whispered, "Then you don't really belong here, do you, Geof? You probably shouldn't come in here anymore."

I smiled. For a moment he seemed confused. Then he smiled too.

"Yeah! I called you. You didn't come up to sell me. Shit, I'm so used to guys trying to hustle me for jobs . . ." He stood up. "Come on, let's get the hell out of here, go get ourselves a drink." He slipped on his jacket. "They got this phony English pub downstairs."

On the way to the elevator he slapped me on the back. "Respect you, Geof. Really do. Wish I had your guts. Hundred guys I know'd give their left ball to do what you did—say to hell with it, give it up."

Downstairs in the bar he continued in the same vein. By the third drink his eyes began to mist. "Boy, you really did it right. Got off the old treadmill while you still had something to say. Became an artist. Confronted photography. Used it to discover who you are. Your work's solid, Geof. Better than that. It's damn fuckin' good. I envy you. And you were right to turn me down. But making it pay—isn't that the trick?"

It was past midnight when I finally stumbled home, full of rare steak and expensive Scotch, and in an awful self-pitying mood. That's always the problem when you drink with guys like Jim; they spread it around like a disease.

There wasn't anyone to come home to either, just a couple of disconnects on the answering machine, and my big view camera parked in the middle of the room. I stared at the lens opening and it stared back, one big reproachful eye.

13

I splashed cold water on my face, then turned the camera to the wall. I didn't want it to see the way I felt. Jim didn't know it, but it hadn't been on principle that I'd turned him down. Three weeks' work for twenty grand—I'd have done almost anything for that. The truth was I *had* lost my nerve, though not the way he thought. It wasn't the madmen's bullets that scared me off Beirut, or the danger in the streets, or the possibility of being kidnapped, though all that was real enough. It was the certain knowledge that I couldn't carry out the assignment, because the assignment involved photographing people.

You see: it had been three years since I'd shot a human face.

The next morning I was still in bed, hung over, feeling bad, when the phone rang hard against my ear.

"Hi! It's me—Kimberly. Getting you at a bad time?" And then, before I could answer: "I'm just downstairs and around the corner. I was wondering . . . could I pop up?"

"What time is it?"

"Quarter past ten. Didn't wake you, did I, Geoffrey?"

"Where are you?"

"Corner of Nassau and Ann."

I wrapped a sheet around my waist, then carried the phone to the window. She was standing in the booth on the corner in front of the bronze plaque embedded in the building wall that says Edgar Allan Poe wrote "The Raven" on that very spot.

"What are you doing downtown so early?"

"Early audition," she said.

"Get the part?"

"They turned me down. I didn't want it anyway."

I didn't believe a word. There are no auditions, early or otherwise—not in my part of town. But she was looking pretty good down there in her New York actress-model garb, chest straining against the fabric of her T-shirt, rear stretching the bottom of her tight and beltless jeans. She was sexy and she knew it, and it seemed she'd worked up some kind of crush on me too. Why else come around after the way I'd talked to her the day before? She actually seemed to be panting as she waited for me to speak. Yeah, she was looking good, full of life, and I needed something good just then. Something fresh, warm and alive. Maybe, I thought, somehow, there might be a way. . . .

"Tell you what, Kimberly—why don't you go around the corner, get yourself some coffee. Give me about twenty-five minutes. Then come back and ring the bell."

I recall my first thought when she came through the door, that she was even better-looking than I remembered. A little older too—closer to twenty-five than twenty-one. There was an appealing sultry eagerness about her that made me sorry I'd been rude. To anyone. Ever. That's how attractive she was.

"Hi!"

"Hi!"

"So this is where you live?"

"Live and work," I said.

She glanced at the walls. "Nice. Mind if I look around?"

I shrugged. "Help yourself."

I watched her then as she began to scan my pictures. She stopped before a print.

"This one isn't yours."

"No, it's by a friend. He shot it in New Mexico."

"Nice," she said. "And this?"

"That's by Edward Weston," I said.

" 'Pepper No. 30,' isn't it? The print by Cole." I nodded. She knew her stuff. "You must like it. Tell me why?"

"It reminds me of something," I said.

15

"What?"

"That it took Weston thirty tries before he was satisfied he'd seen a pepper right."

She smiled. "Good reason." She pointed at my Pietà. "And this—?"

"That one's mine," I said.

She turned toward me. "You're kidding!" I shook my head. She looked confused. "You shot this! You have no idea! As a little girl . . . God! I was haunted by this."

I stood silent. People had said things like that to me before, and I'd never figured out how to respond. The Vietnamese mother, face in torment, staring at my lens while embracing the bloodied naked body of her son—it touched some chord, spoke of love, despair and the total agony of war. And the men standing around her, the men who'd killed her boy, smiles twisted by shame at what they'd done—they too were victims. That was what the picture said.

"Can't believe I'm standing here with a person who made something that . . . that changed my life. Course, I was only ten years old."

"Changed mine too," I said. "And I was only twenty-five."

"Didn't you win a prize or something?"

"That was the good part," I said.

She studied me, nodded and turned back to my wall. "What you're doing now—it's completely different. Like you're another person altogether."

"Well, I hope I am."

"I definitely think so. You're in a completely different place. But there're still times you'd like to become the person you were back then. Trouble is, you don't think you can." She nodded, as if to herself. "Actually, I think it's possible—if you really wanted to do it, you could. But you don't. Not really. You just tell yourself you do. And less and less as time goes on . . ."

"What are you?" I asked. "Some kind of witch?"

She smiled. "Do I read you right?"

"A lot better than some therapists I've been to see."

"Maybe they tried too hard. See, I think the trick is not to try, just to feel and understand." She gazed again at my Pietà. "You don't like to talk about it, but still I'd like to hear . . ."

We sat down, and she began to talk. She told me about a friend of hers, a girl in her fourth-grade class, whose older brother had been killed in Vietnam. On account of that the girl hated all Vietnamese, and, Kim, being her friend, hated them too. Except one day her homeroom teacher showed the class my picture, and after that Kim changed her mind.

"I realized they were people too, and that it was the war, not the people, that was bad. I lost my friend on account of that. She'd been hurt too badly. She couldn't change. But I could. So I'm grateful to you. To my teacher too, of course. But especially to you, for taking that incredible photograph."

She asked me about the circumstances that had led up to my taking it. I told her the story, and even as I did I was amazed. I was exposing myself to a girl I didn't even know, some kid who'd wandered in, said a few sensitive things, and was now soliciting my intimate thoughts.

". . . it was a fine moment. Ugly. Brutal. In its way even superb. And I was there, and lucky enough to have the right tool in my hands. So I trapped it. *Click!*"

"Then?"

"A couple of days later it hit. Seen around the world. That's every photojournalist's dream. Made me famous for a while."

"And now?"

"I don't shoot events. It's light that moves me, captured in long exposures."

" 'Chunks of time.' "

I nodded. "Now I'm looking at the silent undercurrents, not the violent waves."

"How about people?"

"Don't shoot them much."

"Why not?"

I shrugged. "Too difficult, I guess."

"Too much trouble—isn't that what you mean?"

I glanced at her. "Maybe something like that." I felt uneasy. Our conversation was taking an awkward turn.

"So what *do* you shoot these days?"

"Streets. Buildings. Walls. Night stuff mostly. Anything that's—"

"Still?" she asked.

"Yeah—still. But that wasn't what I was going to say."

"What were you going to say?"

"Quiet," I said. "Anything that's quiet."

"Right. . . ." She nodded, stood up, and began to scan the walls. "You were very good with people. I can see you were. Know something? I've seen your stuff before."

"The Pietà."

"Not just that. Other stuff too."

"Like what?"

"Portraits. Actors, writers, athletes. In magazines. Maybe three, four years ago, when I first came to New York. I saw them." She turned and faced me. "I thought they were pretty great."

I thought they were pretty great too. Unfortunately I couldn't shoot them anymore. "Well," I said, "like I told you when you called, I no longer do that kind of work."

"Maybe you should start again."

"Think so?"

She nodded. "See, I think maybe if you started shooting people, you wouldn't sound so sour the way you do."

I stood up. She was right, of course. But still I wanted her to leave. "Do I really sound sour, Kim? I'm sorry. I wish I didn't."

"Maybe if you went back to shooting people," she said, "you'd give up all this . . . boring malaise." She waved her hand at my most recent prints.

I stared at her. She stared straight back. I expected her to apologize, but she stood her ground, and that made me mad.

"Now, that's a clever little speech," I said. "And you're a clever little girl. Sashay your way in here, toss a few compliments, fake up a little profound analysis. Then, when you see that's not going to get you what you want, try some rude insults to see if maybe that'll turn me around."

"What is it you think I want from you anyway?"

"You want glamour head shots, right?"

"It would be a privilege to have my portrait taken by you. But that wasn't why I said it."

"So why did you say it?"

"Because I felt it. I think it's true, and I think you need to hear the truth."

Christ, I thought, just what I don't need: a girl who wants to level with me, straighten out my life.

"Okay," I said. "You're very nice. You want to help. You're full of good advice. You'd even rechannel my career if I'd let you, steer me in the right direction, help me fulfill the promise of my talent. I really appreciate your sincerity, Kimberly." I paused, and then I lied. "Trouble is I like what I do. Believe it or not, I even like myself."

"I'm sorry," she said.

"Doesn't matter. I think now it's time for you to go."

She stared at me, eyes perplexed.

"The door's over there," I said.

She stared awhile longer, then I saw her anger rise. I could actually see it come, roll slowly up her face, the way it sometimes does in a great actor at a crucial juncture in a play.

"I know where the goddamn door is." She started toward it. "I don't know why I came down here anyway. After the way you talked to me yesterday, like you thought I was some kind of dumb club slut or something. But still I liked you. Thought we could be friends. I see now *that* was a mistake." She paused. "You really are a nasty jerk, you know. So—best of luck, Barnett, with all your turgid photographs of empty streets."

She had the door open, was about to step out, when suddenly I changed my mind.

"Shut it."

"Don't worry. I don't slam doors."

"Come back inside and shut it. Please."

She glared at me, stepped back in, then stood with her back against the door. "Okay," she said, "what do you want?"

"You still want a portrait?"

"Damn straight I do."

"Then maybe I'll shoot one for you," I said. "Maybe then we'll find out who you really are."

"I know who *I* am."

"Do you? You're an actress, right?" She nodded. "That's why you want the head shots. Tell you something—I don't think much of actress photographs."

"Neither do I," she said. "That's why I came to you."

"So tell me—how you feel about acting?"

She thought a moment. "It's the only thing on earth I really care about."

"Gee whiz," I said, "I think I've heard that corny line before."

20

She laughed. "Guess I deserve that. After what I said to you."

"Your manipulations were too transparent. But your angry moment at the door—I believed in that. The thing is, Kimberly, when I take a portrait, I don't let the person act."

"How do you stop them?"

"There are ways."

She smiled. "I know what you're trying to do."

"What am I trying to do?"

"Scare me off."

She was right, but I wouldn't admit it. "Now, why would I want to do a thing like that?"

"Maybe because you're afraid yourself."

"Of what?"

"Taking my picture." And then, when I scoffed: "Well . . .?"

There was something taunting in her expression then, as if she were daring me to show her she was wrong. What she didn't know was that she was the second person in twenty-four hours to accuse me of photographic cowardice, and I was getting pretty sick of hearing that and knowing it was true.

"Come back this afternoon at three o'clock," I said. "But I warn you—it's no picnic modeling for me."

"I'm willing to work for it."

"You'll work, all right."

"Anything special you want me to wear?"

I shook my head. "No makeup either. Show up on time, bring your face and call if you change your mind."

"A portrait session with The Great Photographer!" She smirked. "I wouldn't cancel that in a million years."

It was after eleven when she finally left, which meant I had less than four hours to psych myself up. One solution would be to shoot

21

her without loading in any film. I could lie to her later, tell her the rolls got ruined at the lab.

But that was too easy. The real answer, I knew, was to actually take her portrait. My ability to do that, however, was dependent on whether she was the angel I'd been waiting for—the saving angel with the secret key who could unlock the blocking door.

I hoped desperately that she was, but I had little faith.

At two-thirty my hands began to shake. By a quarter to three I started to shiver. Then I looked out the window at the public thermometer across the street and discovered to my shame that it was 82 degrees.

What the hell was the matter with me? I was tired of panic attacks, tired of having to turn down beautiful women who begged me to take their pictures. I'd had it. Today was the day. No matter what it cost me, today, I resolved, I would beat down the blocking door myself.

At 3:00 sharp my downstairs buzzer rang. *Okay*, I thought, *here we go*. I left my front door open a crack, then retired into my loft to wait.

She announced herself with a fanfare. "Ta da!" she said, striking a pose just inside.

Against my instructions she'd dressed up. She was decked out in a kinky downtown outfit, short black skirt, leather jacket and top, textured stockings and exaggerated spike-heeled shoes.

"Great entrance," I said. "Great outfit too. Now take it off. All of it."

She stared at me.

"Go on," I said. "Get undressed."

"You're kidding!"

"Uh-uh. Hurry up. Everything but your underwear."

"Hey, Geoffrey! I'm here to get my portrait shot."

22

"You'll get your portrait shot, but without any armor on."

She plucked at her jacket. "You call this armor?"

"Look, kid—don't waste time. We'll do it my way, or we won't do it at all." I paused. "Unless, of course, you're afraid to show yourself."

She looked hard at me. "*I'm* not the one who's afraid."

"Prove it."

She hesitated. Then she smiled to herself. Then she obeyed. She undressed with marvelous nonchalance, taking off her garments piece by piece and dropping them into a heap on the floor.

I'd told her to stop at her underwear. As I suspected, she didn't wear a bra. I never intended that she strip herself naked, but she surprised me—that was exactly what she did.

She peeled off her stockings, gave me a smile, then stepped out of her panties. Then she bunched them up and tossed them carelessly at my face.

Just in case she thought that gesture was but a prelude to a screw, I made a point of quickly disabusing her. I turned off the air conditioner, pulled down a white background shade, placed her in front of it, then poured hot light on her—lots of it—to make her sweat. I rolled up my big 8 × 10 Sinar to intimidate her. Then I grabbed my motor-driven Leica, stood before her and prayed for courage.

"Well?" she asked, with the same taunting smile she'd showed me in the morning. I was annoyed, but I had to admire her. Even standing naked, she had incredible poise.

"Let's see you move," I said.

"Let's see you shoot."

"I'll shoot when I'm ready to shoot. Do your stuff. Show me who you are."

She placed her hand on her hip and struck a pose.

"Phony," I said. "Try something else."

She spread her legs, then wrapped her arms about herself as if to protect her breasts.

I circled her, shook my head.

"I'm not used to this," she said.

"Forget you're nude. I'm only looking at your face."

"Can I sit down?"

"Not yet. Show me something real."

"I don't know what you want exactly."

"Speak to me with your body, Kimberly. Say: Here I am, with nothing to hide."

She tried another stance, then shook her head. "I can't do it. Help me, Geoffrey. Please."

"You said you were an actress."

"I *am* an actress!"

"Then take direction."

"I can't!"

"What you're saying is you want to control the session, and if you can't control it, you aren't willing to work."

When she looked to me again her expression was helpless. "Okay," she said. "I give you control."

"You're sure?"

She nodded. I raised my Leica. And then I started ordering her around.

"Stand straight. Arms at your side." *Whap! Whap!* "Now put your hands behind your head." *Whap!* "Wider. Now spread your legs. No! Too much. There—stay like that." *Whap! Whap! Whap!*

Six shots! A sixth of a roll! I'd started. At last!

"What's with all this physical-obedience crap?" she asked. "I don't understand what you're doing at all."

"Shut up! You don't have to understand. Now get down on the floor." She hesitated. *Whap!* "You heard me—I want you down."

24

She got down. "Now look up." *Whap!* "That's it, but not so angry. Yes. That's better." *Whap! Whap! Whap!* Eleven shots! "See, Kimberly—your face looks different now."

"Really? How?"

"Not so haughty, not so proud. You're loosening up. And there's lots more you're going to do for me." I lowered the camera. "Unless, of course, you want to quit."

She looked outraged. "I'm not a quitter."

"You can always leave, you know. Any time."

"No way," she said. "I'm seeing this through."

"Good," I said, shooting directly down. "I like a girl who can stick it out. Now on your belly. That's right." *Whap! Whap! Whap!* Fourteen shots! "Now writhe, and then look back at me. . . ."

She writhed. I stood astride her continuing all the while to shoot. I felt like an animal trainer standing over a tigress. She was recalcitrant; my camera was my whip.

For a good twenty minutes I ordered her around. Do this. Do that. All the time firing away. Sweat began to rise on her body; it frosted her back, gave a sheen to her flesh. A heady aroma started to come off her too, perspiration mixed with her perfume. I liked it. The smell excited me. But I tried hard not to let on. For all my excitement I continued to treat her like a thing, acting bored with her, preoccupied with problems of technique.

I wanted, you see, to take her through a full spectrum of emotions, to get to know her face when she was cross, petulant, angry, unnerved. If there really was something in her, I wanted to bring it out. And I wanted to punish her too for her remark about my "being afraid," humiliate her, make her surrender and give up. Then, even if she did decide to quit on me, I could throw her panties back in her face and laugh as she stalked out.

She was tough. She resisted. And the more I pushed her, the more defiant she became.

"Used to being treated like this?"

She grinned. "Like what?"

"A piece of meat."

"Oh, that." She laughed. "I've been through worse in acting class."

"So maybe you like it."

"So maybe I do." She shrugged.

"That's okay," I said. "I can use that too."

"Sure. Use it. Use everything. That's what I'm paying you for."

I stood back from her, amazed: she actually thought I was in her employ. "Think you can afford a session with me?"

"Is it really so hard to take a girl's picture?" she asked. "The way you act, you'd think it was torture."

I stopped then, ostensibly to reload, but really to gasp at what she'd said. Because I *was* shooting her, for twenty minutes I'd been taking pictures of her face. And I hadn't even thought about the implications of that; I'd been so angry, so wrapped up in my anger at her taunts, I'd banged away at her, and my hands hadn't even shaken.

So—she'd won. She'd tricked me into a portrait session, forced me into breaking through my block. All the time I thought I'd been controlling her she'd been controlling me.

Suddenly I wasn't angry anymore. How could I be? She'd done what no shrink had been able to do: freed me, temporarily at least, from my three-year block against photographing the human face.

When I resumed shooting I was a lot less hostile, and she must have picked up on that, because she finally started to give me something back. It wasn't much. I burned a lot of film. But it was a beginning, a glimpse at who she was.

"At last," I told her, "you've dropped the mask. Get dressed and take a break."

"Then what?"

"We're going out. We're about at the point where we begin."

I burned two more rolls out on the street, posing her against pedestrian crowds, then telling her to stand sluttish but proud against a harshly sun-lit graffiti-scrawled brick wall. I liked the way she raised her arm to shield her eyes from the sun. Finally, I thought, we're getting somewhere. For one thing, she was cooling down.

"You say you're an actress. What have you done?" I asked.

"A few workshops. Some soap operas. Walk-ons mostly, but I've been up for a couple of decent parts."

"How do you make a living?"

"I model a little. Waitress sometimes too."

"You really want to make it, don't you?"

"Yes, I really do."

"I've heard that before. Lots of girls here say things like that."

"I'm not 'lots of girls.' I'm Kimberly."

"Yeah, Kimberly . . ."

She nodded.

"And that makes you special."

She nodded vehemently.

"I'll say this for you—you're persistent enough."

"Pays off sometimes. Like here we are."

"Yeah," I said. "Getting tired? Want to quit?"

"You kidding?"

"We've just started, you know."

"So let's cut the talk and get back to work," she said.

Oh, she was hard-ass! Going to show me how tough she was. That she could take whatever I wanted to fling at her. That I could *whap! whap! whap!* her a thousand times, and still she'd come back for more.

And there was something else too, this notion she had that somewhere along the line she'd *commissioned* me to take her portrait: that though I could strip her, order her around, I did all that with her consent; that in the end I worked for her because she was the one who was going to pay the fee.

That wasn't the way I looked at it, but it was something to work with—this battle of our wills. We'd gotten through the first level of hostility, were approaching something deeper now. I wasn't quite sure what it was, but felt I could make it work.

When we got back to the studio and she started to take off her clothes, I told her to stay dressed. Then I perched her on a high stool in the middle of the room, lit her carefully, and went to work with the 8 × 10.

That's a slow examining camera, a camera with a presence. It says to the sitter: "I'm as big as you and I've got this big eye and I can see deep inside your brain. So don't try to fool me because you can't. And maybe, if you show me who you are, I may decide to treat you nice. . . ."

I was working seriously now, looking closely at her, looking to see who she really was. And I saw a lot more than I expected, vulnerability of a special sort. Perhaps some injury suffered in the past had hardened the surface of her, giving her the strength to take the treatment I'd been dishing out. But there was a place, I sensed, somewhere deep inside, that was soft and easily hurt. That was the place I wanted to reach.

There's a lot of misunderstanding about serious portrait photography—people think photographers want to strip their subjects bare. Some do, but for me it's not so simple. I'm interested in showing the tension in my subject, the war between the face he shows the world and the hidden face within.

It's that tension, crystallized in a kind of reflective expression, that can give a portrait real depth. The hyped-up magazine portraits, the ones of the rock stars staring meekly from the welter of rumpled sheets, or the comedians looking sad beside the urinals— for me they're attitudes, much too easy, much too glib. I feel the same about the so-called cruel portraits of Avedon, portraits that say, No matter how high this person's status, inside my studio there'll be no flattery. That's a message that tells me a lot about Avedon, but very little about his sitters.

That afternoon, as I began to take my first serious pictures of Kimberly, I gave up the last remnants of my disdain. I was interested in her now, interested in the problem she presented. This, I thought to myself, is a girl who has a secret.

I got caught up as I exposed frame after frame of sheet film, working slowly, trying, with each exposure, to edge closer to that tender place inside. I forgot about time. It was after nine when I finally stopped. She looked at me curiously when I told her we were finished for the day.

"We're not done?" she asked.

"Just with the first session. We've still got a ways to go."

She stretched. "How many sessions are there going to be?"

"As many as it takes. Come back same time tomorrow afternoon. Be prepared to work till eleven or twelve."

She kissed me briskly on the cheek, then headed for the door. When she reached it, she turned. "I learned something today."

"What was that?" I asked.

"Two things actually. First, don't ever dress up for Geoffrey Barnett. Second, beneath the nasty exterior the guy's a pussycat."

She gave me her handsome smile, then disappeared.

Later that night, still excited about what had happened, I phoned my closest friends to tell them the news. Frank Cordero and his Vietnamese wife, Mai, lived in Galisteo, New Mexico. He was ex-

Special Forces, now a photographer. She was a sculptor. I was in love with her once.

"Well, it finally happened!" I told Frank.

"You took a portrait?"

"What else?"

"Oh, Geof—that's terrific!"

He put on Mai to congratulate me too, then came on again. "It was a 'she,' wasn't it?"

"It was a 'she,' all right." I told him about Kimberly, as much as I knew, and how she had even admired the print of his I have hanging on my wall.

"Thing is," I said, "I don't know how well I did. Or whether I can do it again. I want to keep working with her as long as I can, see how far I can take it. Then, if the results are good, I'll try with someone else."

"Stick with her, Geof," Frank advised. "Don't give that girl up. She may have changed your life."

My sessions with Kim continued. The city got caught up in a heat wave, the humidity was terrible, the air turned stagnant and suffocating. But no matter the physical discomfort, she always showed up on time.

When we worked outside, I'd usually pick the location. But when she'd suggest a place, I was happy to go along. Mostly we worked in my studio, and then usually with the view camera. The pace slowed down, sometimes to one or two exposures an hour.

When we'd finish I'd let her use my shower before I sent her home. Then, after she'd leave, I'd feel a certain emptiness around the loft.

There was an ideal portrait I was working toward. Though I couldn't visualize it yet, I felt that eventually it would come. Kim was a challenging subject. I was determined to shoot until I got her right. And she was there for me, helpful, obedient, patient when I stood before her, sometimes afraid.

I tried hard not to reveal my fear to her, and if she sensed it, she kept her feelings to herself. I wasn't sure if she understood what we were doing, how important her presence was. But then the best nurse is always the one who refuses to acknowledge that you're sick.

I was working toward a major breakthrough, my return to the human face; I wanted to produce a picture that would be better and deeper than any portrait I'd made before. It was madness, of course. I'd never spent so much time or film on a single subject. But on the third day, when I realized I was not at all eager for the sessions to end, I felt fortunate to have found a sitter so receptive, and apparently oblivious of time.

Not that she didn't rebel. She did. Her first attempt came near midnight, toward the end of our third session. She'd been glaring at me angrily for half an hour, while I sat watching her, refusing to shoot.

"Grimace as long as you like," I said. "I'm patient. I can wait you out."

"Fuck this shit! I'm going home!" She hopped off her stool, looked up at the ceiling, opened her mouth and screamed.

"Oh, that's nice," I said. "Do that again." She cursed me. "Like I said," I told her, "you can go home anytime."

"It's so *enraging* when you say that! If I quit now, it's over, right?"

"If you walk out before I dismiss you, it's definitely all over," I confirmed.

"Do I get my glossies?"

"You get them when I give them to you. I only give them to you when I'm done."

She stamped her foot, returned to her stool, glared at me, then relaxed, grimaced, grinned, shook her head furiously, moaned and slumped. When she glanced up to see how I was taking her little tantrum, I caught a glimpse of something mischievous, and squeezed off a shot.

"Thanks, that was nice."

"Bastard!" she hissed.

But I was extremely pleased. That encounter made me feel powerful. I was amazed at the speed of my recovery. I was no longer merely pretending to be in control; I felt that at last I was.

It was 2:00 P.M. on the fourth day when, without my contrivance, she finally broke down. I'd been circling her slowly, catlike, while she sat in her usual erect position on the stool. Suddenly she began to cry.

I stopped my stalking. "What's the matter?"

"You're violating me." Her voice was raw.

I handed her a lens tissue to wipe away her tears. Then I helped her from the stool.

I led her to my bed in an alcove off the studio, where I keep a ceiling fan. I turned it on. I told her to lie down. "Rest awhile. You'll be okay." I patted her head, then left her alone.

I went into my darkroom. *What the hell are you doing?* I asked myself. It was as if I thought that by photographing her so extensively I could somehow take her in, that film was blotting paper I could use to absorb her, capture her image and thus make her part of myself.

Half an hour later I came out, half expecting to find her gone. But she was ready to go back to work.

"Sorry," she said, smiling. "Sorry I acted that way. All part of the process, I guess. . . ."

I treated her more tenderly after that.

· · ·

33

We didn't chatter when I photographed; all our talk took place during breaks. She asked me questions about photography and I gave her my views. When I asked her about her life, she happily filled me in.

She was from Cleveland. Her father was a doctor. Her mother was a violist who taught at the Cleveland Institute of Music. She had started studying music herself at Oberlin, hoping to make a career as a pianist, but after her second year she switched to acting, then quit college and moved to New York.

At first it had been a struggle; she'd taken advanced classes, supporting herself by working as a waitress. But lately things had been picking up. Her goal, she said, was to become a star. "Not a movie-type star," she explained. "An actress who can play great parts greatly on the stage."

Such a dream! It must be shared by a good ten thousand girls in the city at any given time, and the denouement for most of them is predictable too: a little spurt in their careers before the inevitable failure to connect. Except, Kim assured me, it wasn't going to be that way for her. *She* was determined; *she* had "the sacred fire"; *she* would *never* give up. And that was why *she* was going to make it. Couldn't I see the determination in her face?

"Oh, sure, I see it all right. Trouble is—it isn't you."

"Then who the hell *is* me?" she demanded to know.

"When we discover that," I said, "we'll finally have our picture."

On one of our breaks she questioned me: "What's this thing you've had against shooting faces?"

"Sorry, Kim, it's not a 'thing.' "

"What is it, then?"

I shook my head.

"Be fair, Geoffrey. Tell me about yourself. You're always making me expose myself to you."

I agreed she had a point.

"So what was the problem?" she asked.

I shrugged. "Don't really know. Happened one day in the middle of a session. Got the shakes. Couldn't go on. Canceled. Sent the sitter home. Then it kept happening, always when I was shooting people. Suddenly I was stymied in my work. I'd read about stuff like that, phobic reactions—pianists losing control of their right hands, singers whose teeth chattered, runners fainting at the starting line. So I started going to shrinks. Spent lots of money, got lots of interpretations: I was afraid of being successful, afraid of relationships; I had 'survivor's guilt' about the Pietà and all the money I'd made from it. My girlfriend at the time told me I'd grown *cold* to people—including to her, she said. Shortly after she made that observation she packed up her bags and left. Then a new girl came along who told me I was 'wounded' in 'my spirit.' She, in Catherine Barkley fashion, would salve my wound and nurse me back to health. Unfortunately our eye contact was bad, so we never got our relationship off the ground. Eyeball to eyeball—see, that was the problem. When I worked I couldn't look people in the eye. Can you imagine a photographer with a problem like that? So I fell back on nightscapes. You know—my 'turgid empty streets,' my 'boring malaise.' "

"Oh, Geoffrey—you know I didn't mean any of that."

"It's all right. You've been long forgiven. Anyway, I like my nightscapes. But how many do I want to make? You could have asked the same of Ansel Adams: 'How many of these gorgeous, pristine and totally empty grand landscapes do you want to shoot, Ansel?' He wouldn't have understood—they were his lifework. I don't feel that way. My nightscapes are a project. But, unfortunately, there isn't much else I can do these days."

"You miss the people?"

"That's just the point. That's what my 'boring malaise' is all about. All my night streets are empty. They cry out for people. The way I cry out. But I can't seem to put them in."

She studied me. "Not true."

"What do you mean?" I asked.

"Don't you see, Geoffrey? You're shooting me. So now, obviously, you can."

On the fifth day I was seized by a strong desire to photograph her nude. Not to take pictures of her face when she was naked, as I had the day we'd started, but to make serious full-length nude studies of her body, with her features concealed, or at least not clearly seen.

"But why?" she asked. "I thought we were working toward a portrait."

"We are," I said. "This is another approach."

She raised her eyes to the ceiling. "If I'd known it was going to be like this!"

"Look, Kim—"

"Yeah, I know—I can quit anytime. Well, fuck you, Geoffrey Barnett! Shoot your goddamn nudes!"

The nude sessions were trancelike for me. I'd study her, light her, move my camera in and shoot. Then I'd have her turn a different way, or I'd try a different lens, or I'd apply a different kind of light, then shoot her again. As I exposed each sheet, I'd feel an increasing need to expose another. Even as I worked I knew I was obsessed. But still I couldn't stop.

Was it Kim, or the project of shooting her, that obsessed me? I wasn't sure and grew confused. I realized I was exhausting myself, considered the possibility I was losing my grip. But still I worked on, in search of . . . I knew not what. Just mystery, I kept telling myself, the mystery in her, which I felt a need to capture, and by so doing to understand. But why? Why did I feel the need? What *was* it about her? I agonized.

When I explained to her my conviction that it was a prevailing sense of mystery that always characterized the best photographic portraits, she asked why this was so.

"It's mystery that makes a portrait fascinating," I explained. "Without it a photograph is merely a picture. With mystery it becomes something else."

"What?"

"Sounds pretentious when you say it."

"Say it."

"It can become art."

"So is that what you want to do—turn me into art?"

"Wouldn't be so bad if I could bring it off, would it?"

"Am I really so fascinating, Geof?"

"To me, right now, you are."

"Is that why you like to photograph me all the time?"

I thought a moment. "Maybe I do that because you're safer for me that way?"

She smiled. "Safer?"

"Framed and packaged. Still."

"Under control—isn't that what you mean?"

I didn't answer her, but I knew she was right, because I think then I was still a little bit afraid of her. She was so alive, attractive, so fascinating to me in the flesh. She was much safer on film, arrested in abstract black-and-white.

I glanced at her. She was looking at me with interest and curiosity. And then with a growing confidence—I saw the transformation in her eyes.

"You're obsessed with me, aren't you?" she asked, quietly. I turned away. "Aren't you, Geoffrey?"

I shook my head. "You know I am."

"And maybe more than that. I've felt something else these last few days."

"What's that?" I asked, thinking I knew what she was going to say.

She smiled at me. Again I turned away. "Hey, look at me! Why do you act like you're suffering so much?"

"Don't pity me, Kim." I spread my palms. "It's over. I give up." I started toward the darkroom.

"What do you mean: 'give up'?"

"Take the proof sheets, mark the shots you like. Mail them back and I'll make you prints."

She rushed to me. "I don't pity you, Geoffrey. God! Can't you see? The attraction I feel. I can't keep away from you anymore." She laced her hands behind my neck. "I want you. *Want you.*" She pulled my face down and kissed me gently on the lips.

Suddenly all my tension eased away. I no longer had to rule, no longer had to be in control. We could become lovers, not merely model and photographer. The game between us had finally been resolved.

There was a storm that afternoon. The sun, which had been broiling the city through the day, disappeared behind a cloud. A few minutes later thunder rumbled. We made love as the rain beat upon the windows, sheets of it sweeping in from the Jersey side.

Again I felt I was in a trance. It was strange and marvelous to finally touch this person I had been examining so closely for so many days. Her body was familiar, as were her eyes, her smile, her scent. But still I didn't know her. As I reached to touch her I hoped her secret would be revealed.

Our first caresses were tentative, as if, like lovers who had yearned too long, we dared not move too fast. A moment later we were tearing at each other, licking, hungry, selfish. We clawed and feasted like rutting strangers, caring only to satisfy, devour.

Rivulets of sweat ran down our bodies. Afterwards, when we were done, we lay together beneath the ceiling fan, panting, slick and sweet from sex. She placed her palm upon my chest and smiled the smile of discharged desire.

"I don't usually go to bed with my models," I said.

"We've been much more than photographer and model, haven't we?" She stroked me. "Poor Geoffrey, you thought you were looking for mystery, and all the time you were just wanting to be loved."

Later she asked me if, during all the days of shooting, I had had fantasies about taking her to bed.

I shook my head. "I was looking at you. But I was working out something inside myself."

"Well, I had fantasies about *you*," she said. "Even from the start."

"Tell me."

She giggled.

"Please . . ."

"All right." She licked her lips. "Those first few minutes, when you made me strip and crawl— I obeyed, but inside I was fighting you very hard."

"I knew that."

"I had to, to protect myself. But I was also very turned on. So I developed all these lewd fantasies—jumping you, shredding your shirt, pulling you down to the floor, stuff like that."

"Sounds like fun."

She laughed. "I had this one where I climbed on top of you, sat on your cock and rode you till you came. Then I took one of your cameras and pointed it at you as you shriveled down."

"Oh God!"

"Yeah! I wanted to take pictures of your diminishing cock, laugh at you as I did. I wanted to demean you sexually. That would be my revenge."

"You were really angry."

"Oh, I was angry. Yes!"

"Now?"

"Not now. Now I've got what I want, wanted all the time." She kissed me. "Got you, Geoffrey boy. But still"—she showed me a look of greed—"you'd better watch out."

It had been a long time since I'd felt so alive, perhaps not since the day I'd shot my Pietà. There was the same feeling of irrevocable destiny, of having arrived at an intersection that had somehow been ordained.

There was a heap of negatives in my darkroom, showing the thousand faces of Kimberly Yates. But now I held her actual face between my hands. Examining her, peering into her eyes, I grew dizzy with fascination. Grasping her to me, pressing her against my chest, I felt the beating of her heart.

My sense of being in a trance continued through the night, as did my feeling that what had happened between us was, in some way, unreal. I hadn't counted my exposures, but I had gone many hundreds past Weston's thirty. The question was: Had I seen Kim right, as Weston had seen that humble pepper, and, by his seeing, immortalized it forever?

When she left in the morning to go home, change, and attend an audition, I set to work in the darkroom to see what I had wrought. I spent the entire day making prints, not bothering to eat or answer the phone. When she returned at seven, I had eighteen big 16 × 20s and another ten 11 × 14s tacked up on the walls.

When she walked in and saw them, she was stunned.

"Wow!" She gazed around.

I kept quiet; I wanted her to look. I watched as she examined them, noting at first how surprised she was, and then how pleased by their cumulative effect.

They weren't finished exhibition prints—just good work prints, good enough to show the potential of the negatives. I'd organized them, placing eight of the nudes together on one wall, ten of the big view camera portraits on another, and a third grouping, a selection of the many exteriors I'd shot when we'd worked outside with just the Leica.

When she finished looking, she turned to me. "Oh, Geoffrey! They're wonderful."

That felt good. "Anything else?"

"Well, since you ask"—she looked at me slyly—"I think there's something more in them. Perhaps something even you don't see."

"What's that?"

"Maybe love," she said. "Love and admiration."

"Yes . . . maybe. . . ." For I had seen that too, even in the proofs: that all my shots of her together were nearly as filled with obsessive love and awe as the famous paintings by Andrew Wyeth of his model Helga, or maybe even (and the thought was very humbling) the series of photographs taken over many years by Stieglitz of Georgia O'Keeffe.

"But still . . ."

"What, Geoffrey? What don't you like?"

"Oh, I like them. I know they're good."

"Then what's the matter? There is something. Tell me."

"I keep thinking there's something missing," I said.

"What? What *could* be missing?"

I thought about it. "Maybe that final, single, powerful image. You know, the definitive portrait. The one that reveals—everything."

. . .

41

Over the next few days we burned white-hot, even as we fell into a routine. I'd spend my days alone in the darkroom, working up prints for the series, while she went out about her business, visiting modeling agencies, attending classes and auditions.

In the early evening she would come back to the studio, then we'd order in food or grab a simple meal in the neighborhood. Afterwards we'd talk awhile, perhaps listen to jazz or watch one of my old *film noir* videos.

She adored these old movies of trapped men and cunning women ensnared and made mad by passion, acting out stories of crime and punishment in dark forbidding cities. The strange monotone performances, the masklike faces, the chiaroscuro lighting and the mazes of deception in which the characters moved—all these things fascinated her, she asked me endless questions about them, and she had her own quite particular views:

Re *Double Indemnity*: "When do you think Barbara Stanwyck knows she's going to get Walter Neff to kill her husband?"

"Sometime between his first and second visits," I suggested.

Kim shook her head. "I think she knows the minute Neff walks into her house."

Re *The Big Sleep*: "That camera hidden in the Chinese head— could something like that really work?"

"Sure," I said. "If the lens were wide enough, and there was some way to trigger the shutter by remote control. Then you could photograph all the bad stuff taking place across the room."

She nodded, she understood, but she didn't think the blackmail material was strong enough. "The trouble with that movie is that the pictures aren't really incriminating. So I don't believe General Sternwood would feel forced to buy them back."

"Has your body ever felt so good?" she asked, curling against me one night after we had made intoxicating love.

"You *are* a witch, aren't you?"

"Yes, I think I am. . . ."

I was forty years old, I'd traveled the world, I'd had numerous girlfriends, and, in my hotshot photojournalist days, had enjoyed my share of one-night stands. I'd lived with several women and been married once. But none of the women I'd known was as good in bed as Kim.

How to justify such a claim? Her skills went way beyond technique. It was the way she anticipated, sensed my every need. Yet everything she did seemed effortless and every time she touched me it was in a different way.

She took over some part of me, some passionate aspect I hadn't known since adolescence, toyed with it, then seized it and used it to make my body sing. Gentle or rough, rushing me or torturing me with pleasure over many hours, the sheer power of her lust would take me over, causing me to ache with desire. Then I was hers, wanting only to satisfy, to make her come and come again. But even as she induced me to race her toward her climax, she always paid me back tenfold.

Sex made me mad for her—and hungry for her all the time.

Fearful too, sometimes, for even as I gave myself up to her, the feelings were almost too strong to bear. I wondered if I could sustain them, if there was danger in such abandon. But I ignored my fear, yielded to my passion, and, to keep sane, continued to photograph.

*Photography*: that was an important part of it. I could not stop taking pictures of her. Not that I ever wanted to. My obsession didn't lessen after we became lovers; rather it seemed to grow.

What was I after? I know better than to think there can be such a thing as a perfect portrait. Looking back, I believe it had to do with mystery, because something in her refused to be caught. The mysterious quality I kept talking about, that I said I wanted to evoke around her in a portrait, was actually the mystery I already saw in her, and desperately needed to solve.

So I photographed her, hoping to solve it. In the early evening, when the light was sweet, she'd choose an area of the city, we'd go to it, I'd shoot a roll, and then we'd go on to dinner. Later I might pose her in the studio, squeeze off several shots of 4 × 5, and the same again in the morning before we parted for the day.

From one of those early morning sessions I produced a picture I liked very much: a long shot of her, nude, seated on a stool, staring off dreamily into space. Plenty of mystery in that picture, for it raised many questions: Who is this woman? What is she thinking? What is her relationship to the photographer?

In the background, barely visible, were the photographs of her I'd tacked to the walls, and the whole room was captured too, filled with sunlight broken by the windblown blinds. Some of these bars of light were palpable, each holding a suspension of sparkling dust, while others striped her naked flesh, creating a pattern like a net or web.

One night, after making love, lying with my head by her feet, I discovered, fondling her, a small tattoo. It was on her ankle.

"Now, what have we got here?" I asked.

To make her move so I could see it better, I ran my finger along the bottom of her foot.

"Hey! Quit that!" She grabbed my arm, laughed as she tried to twist away.

"Stay still!" I commanded, wrestling her leg back to the mattress. "I want to read what this damn thing says."

We were at that joyful early stage in a physical relationship where the reactions of the beloved's body are still unknown. Lately we'd been playing with mock-hurting each other—one of us bending the other's fingers or biting the other's ears to see if he/she could make him/her beg for mercy and cry out. Kim introduced me to that form of play, which aroused me much more than I would have thought. Momentary exchanges of power, mild forcing, pretending to submit—when Kim discovered that such activities had an exponential effect upon my excitement, she began to introduce them frequently.

"Where'd you get this?" I asked. There were two linked circles etched in blue, each containing a letter. The letters were pink. I made them out, the initials *K* and *G*.

"Oh, that old thing," she said. "In Florida. A weird Oriental tattoo artist did it. She was almost a dwarf."

"K is for Kimberly," I said. "So who was G?"

She wiggled her toes. "Another person. . . ."

"A lover?" I bent her foot again.

"Ouch! Maybe. . . . Yes! A lover. Stop that, Geoffrey! Yes!"

"Someone I should know about?"

She pulled her foot free, smiled mysteriously. "Just a youthful error," she said. Then, like a cat, she showed her teeth, and with a hiss attacked my neck.

She had a roommate, who, she said, was a successful model— at least in certain downtown circles where she'd won the hearts of several young designers.

"Her name's Cheryl Devereux," Kim explained. "But everyone calls her Shadow. She's famous for having once slapped a photographer who dared to call her 'candy ass.' She's black, from New Orleans, a dusky beauty. It's because of her I haven't had you up to my apartment."

Though I had dropped her off several times at her building, she had never invited me up because Shadow had a "beau" who often slept over in her room. But still, I said, I would like to meet her friend, so late the following afternoon Kimberly brought her down on the pretext that I would shoot her portrait.

I didn't think much about it until the two of them walked in. Then I grew worried. Yes, I'd been able to photograph Kimberly. But had I really broken through my block?

Shadow was stunning, almost six feet tall, thin, angular with a gorgeous café au lait complexion. Her voice was soft, classy-Southern, but her hair was very downtown—cut into a geometric shape, it resembled a modified obelisk.

The three of us talked awhile. Shadow was most admiring of my photographs. She said she thought the ones I'd taken of Kim were among the best portraits she'd ever seen.

"Geoffrey didn't like me when we started out," Kim told her. "The first thing he did was tell me to undress."

Shadow smiled.

"He meant just down to my underwear. But then I fooled him—I took off everything."

Shadow's eyes enlarged. "Then what happened?"

"The poor man was totally embarrassed."

Shadow was amused. "Is that true?" she asked me.

I nodded. "It was a good move for both of us."

"I'd love it if you'd photograph me," Shadow said. "The guys I usually work with use me for a prop."

I was hesitant.

"Go on, Geof," Kim urged. "Why don't you give it a try?"

I looked at them. They were both staring at me, waiting for a response. I nodded, crossed the room and started to load my Leica. My hands weren't shaking, but they weren't all that steady either. Then, when I heard Kim urge Shadow to take off her top, I turned around. "That's not necessary," I said.

"No, I'd really like to," Shadow said. "I think it would loosen me up."

She stood and pulled off her jersey. She turned to me. "You don't mind, do you?"

I shrugged. She bent and took off her skirt. When she straightened up she looked fabulous, in her all-black lace bra, garter belt and stockings. Self-assured, totally elegant, the very opposite of "candy ass."

As I set up the lights she and Kim joked around. Their girlish banter made me envy them their youth.

I started slowly, working my way around Shadow, not giving commands as I had the first time with Kim. I liked her immediately. I could see she had a way with photographers, knew how to establish a fast rapport, and that she had the kind of face the camera loves, strong sculpted features and skin that can model light. She was a pro. Her moves were good. But I couldn't shoot her face. The only way I could photograph her was to cut her off at the neck and at the knees.

I bluffed the scene out. My hands didn't shake and I managed by pretending I was shooting an advertisement for lingerie. I didn't think Shadow could tell I was avoiding her face, but I was badly disappointed. Though I had gotten to the point where I could shoot intimate pictures of Kim, I realized I was still a long way from being cured.

After half an hour, when I put my camera down, the three of us went out to eat. Shadow led us to a crazy place in Tribeca, a hangout for models and photographers. Here plastic Madonnas, model Statues of Liberty and other souvenir-shop knickknacks were mounted on pedestals and carefully lit. The point, I gathered, was to proclaim that if junk can be presented as art, it must therefore follow that art is junk.

Shadow was a regular there. People greeted her when we came in. Kim was greeted too, by a heavyset man at the bar with big sad eyes and gray wavy hair. She shrugged when I asked her who he was.

"Just one of your own, Geoffrey. Another photographer."

After we ate, Shadow excused herself. She had a late date, and had to go home to dress. When she was gone, Kim suggested we go on to one of the downtown clubs.

"I feel like dancing. For hours," she said dreamily.

"Maybe it's the age gap," I said, "but I hate those places. I really do."

"Oh, don't be such a stick, Geoffrey. It's time we had some fun."

"It wouldn't be fun for me," I said quietly.

"Something's the matter, isn't it?" She was staring closely at my eyes. I shrugged. "It didn't go well—the session, I mean." So she knew.

"No," I said, "it didn't go well."

"You looked like you were getting into it."

"I shot her body. I couldn't shoot her face."

"Well, that's a start at least. Next time it'll go better. It will. You'll see."

"Maybe if she hadn't gotten undressed," I said. "I think that distracted me."

"My fault, Geoffrey." She took my hand. "I was worried when I saw you hesitate. I thought you needed a distraction. I'm sorry. I really am."

I think that may have been the moment that I fell in love with her, consciously at least. She was so sincere, solicitous, so sensitive to my needs. She'd seen I was in trouble and had tried her best to help.

"I'll tell Shadow you weren't satisfied," she said. "I'll tell her you don't like to show work you don't think is good. She'll understand.

She'll respect you for it. Next time, and there *will* be a next time, Geoffrey, I'll bring her down and you'll do it like nothing was ever wrong at all. . . ."

In the taxi on the way back to my loft she told me she'd been invited to a dinner party by a painter friend and his wife. "It could be amusing, but I don't want to go alone. I'm going to turn them down. Unless . . . well, if I could get you invited too, as my date"—she smiled—"would you come? Would you, Geoffrey? *Please.*"

I told her that of course I'd come, and that I'd love to meet her friends.

She kissed me, and when we got home she asked me to put on *Double Indemnity* again. She wanted, she said, to define for me the very moment when Barbara Stanwyck makes her decision to seduce and recruit Walter Neff.


The next hot, sticky Sunday I took her on an afternoon tour of Soho galleries. I wanted to see the work of various up-and-coming young photographers whose pictures had been touted lately as "photographic art."

I hated everything, and by the time we reached the last gallery I was so annoyed I swept her by the pictures fast.

She chased around after me. "Hey! Stop! Let me look."

"Nothing here worth looking at," I muttered, guiding her to the door.

When we were out on the street, she turned to me, mad. "What's the matter? I liked that stuff."

"All those perfect prints of sodomy!"

"Well, I kind of liked the style of them," she said.

"Sure, they're pretty. What he does, he applies 1930s fashion-glamour style to sleaze. The idea is to make ironic comment on the meaning of glamour. Assuming anyone's interested."

"Well, okay." She pouted for a moment. "Whose work *do* you like? What about that Susan Kaufman's?"

"Her stuff's okay, but awfully easy. Take pictures of yourself standing in weird positions, then inscribe feminist slogans across the tops."

"Stan Kesten?"

I curled my lip. "Hang out at beaches, airports, amusement parks, shoot snapshots while allowing yourself to be pushed around by the mob. All based on the no doubt sincere belief that by this false-naive technique you'll record the frantic rhythm of contemporary life."

"You're cruel, Geoffrey."

"Am I? That's what I'd call Johansen, the one *Artforum* says is such a comer. For me he's the most sinister."

"*Sinister?* Why?"

"On account of his approach, the smarmy way he goes into a suburb, then uses his camera to coldly trap the residents. Their hideous houses, gilded furniture, polyester clothing, overcooked food and mottled skin—all evidence of their pathetic aspirations, their mean and vulgar taste. Back in the darkroom he deliberately slops on chemicals to make his prints look ragged and handmade. He makes one print of each shot, destroys the negative, then encases the print in an incredibly expensive frame. The idea, you see, is that what is tasteless in someone else's house can be turned, by being photographed, into a precious tasteful artifact. The person who buys a Johansen buys cultural superiority. And by making each print unique, Johansen negates one of the great strengths of photography, which is that a photograph is endlessly reproducible."

She raised her eyebrows when I finished my tirade. It was a while before she spoke.

"Maybe you're right, Geoffrey. I trust your taste. But I worry about you when you talk like that. You sound bitter and ungenerous, as if you feel the success of younger artists takes something away from you. Thing is, I bet those kids consider you a hero, and I don't mean just for the Pietà either. For your nightscapes, your portraits, the pictures you've been taking of me if they could see them. You've told me art isn't a zero-sum game, that there's room in the galleries for anything that's good. You *are* good, Geoffrey. You know it too. Maybe you lack the ruthless streak it takes to make it in New York these days. But I think that's something I might be able to help you with. . . ."

*God! She knew how to make me feel good!*

She got me an invitation to her dinner party, and when we got there and I discovered who was giving it, I was surprised—I hadn't known she moved in such exalted circles.

Our hosts were the painter Harold Duquayne and his society wife, Amanda. Duquayne was famous, one of the young "New York heroics." It was alleged that he and Amanda were possessed by an insatiable craving for publicity. Certainly one read about them frequently enough. I had seen numerous photos of the pair, including one on the cover of *New York* that showed Duquayne, intense and bearded, clothing spattered with paint, glaring at the viewer while Amanda, wearing a black leather jumpsuit, gazed at him with sorrowful longing.

A recent Duquayne painting filled the background, instantly recognizable because all his work looked pretty much the same. He painted on an enormous scale, but his drawing was not very good, with the result that his canvases usually looked better in reproduction—a point made by several critics when they reviewed his mid-career show at the Whitney.

His stylistic trademarks were borrowed from painted icons of the Eastern Orthodox Church: gold leaf applied to the backgrounds and the heads of his figures surrounded by halos. However, Duquayne's figures were never engaged in spiritual pursuits but in the most mundane contemporary activities: housewife vacuuming a flight of stairs; high school kid in prom dress greeted by her date, etc. The contrast between these trite actions, the mannered postures, and the disks of radiant light surrounding the figures' heads created a strange and troubling effect.

The Duquayne loft took up an entire floor of a cast-iron building on Spring Street. The moment we entered I was struck by its luxury: chairs and sofas upholstered in glove-soft leather, and superbly lit large-scale contemporary paintings on the walls. I counted a Schnabel, a Fischl, a Bacon and a very good Kitaj. There was also a collection of framed photographs, vintage prints by Arbus, Outerbridge, Mapplethorpe and Man Ray.

Amanda Duquayne greeted us warmly. She and Kimberly embraced like very close friends. Harold Duquayne turned out to be stocky and short. He spoke in a gravelly whisper, and twitched his nostrils the way cocaine users like to do.

The other guests were the distinguished and elderly art critic Philip Treacher; his sluttish student-lover, Ivan somebody; and a husband-wife writing team, specialists in cooking and luxury, whom I recognized from the photo on the front jacket of their book *The Good Life: Entertaining with the Vanderkamps*.

With the arrival of the soup course, a California version of mulligatawny, the Vanderkamps launched into a vicious attack upon a well-known restaurant critic.

"Have you seen her lately? She must weigh two hundred pounds."

"She loathes salt. She adores desserts."

"We hear she takes bribes. Don't quote us, of course."

"No other explanation when she gives four stars to that fraud Desforges."

Philip Treacher interrupted. "We ate at Desforges the other night. Thought it was pretty good."

The Vanderkamps exchanged a look.

"He uses bottled Maggi instead of stock."

"I didn't know that," Treacher said.

"He says, 'Zee Americans don't know zee difference.' "

"All these French chefs—when they come over here they think they're slumming."

"And meantime," added Mrs. V., "they make carloads of money!"

The Vanderkamps continued to interrupt each other, each vying to make the better bon mot.

"Course they're all hypocrites. Only decent places left to eat are in Chinatown," Mr. V. proclaimed.

"Except for a certain divine little Mexican bistro tucked away in Chelsea. We use it as our local canteen."

"What's it called?" I asked.

Mr. V. brought his finger to his mouth. "Can't tell you. Word'll get out and the place'll be ruined."

I looked over at Kim. She smiled and rolled her eyes.

"Well, I like greasy hamburgers," I said.

"And *I* love greasy anything," Ivan added, turning to Treacher, running his tongue across his upper lip.

With the pasta course, borne by a beaming Hispanic woman, the conversation turned to the current art scene, about which Harold Duquayne made a little speech, the gist of which was that the new painters, the ones still in their twenties, had no guts because they had no appetite for money.

"They rebel against my generation by tightening down their scale. The latest fad is to paint small and be trivial. And they try to make a virtue out of being noncompetitive. They call us 'overblown,' say we're consumed by money, fame, rivalry and envy."

"But you are, dear boy!" Treacher said.

Duquayne laughed wickedly. "Stick it up your ass, Philip. You know more about envy than anyone in the room." He turned to me. "What do you think, Barnett?"

"I think you've got a point," I said, not wanting to tangle with the little tyrant.

"Isn't it the same in photography? The way the level of ambition keeps dropping? Just wait—in a couple of years you'll be grateful for anything that isn't a Polaroid."

"I noticed your collection," I said. "Who do you like in photography?"

"No one. I detest photography. I collect only for investment. No tactile experience. Everything's glossy and small. To me the talent of Arbus was in finding all those freaks. Then it was just stick it in their faces and 'Pretty for the picture!' "

He was taunting me. I glanced again at Kim, who encouraged me with a nod. When I turned back to Duquayne and saw his smirk, I decided to take him on.

"If it weren't for photography," I told him, "you wouldn't have anything to paint."

He flushed. "What the hell're you talking about?"

"All those little scenes you blow up so big—the girl mashing down the lever of the toaster, the father barbecuing hot dogs on the patio. You got those images from print ads in magazines. In other words—*photographs*."

For a moment he looked stunned. Then he said, "But look what I *do* with them."

"You gussy them up with ideas you got from looking at *photographs* of Greek and Russian icons."

"Well said, lad." Philip Treacher beamed. He and Ivan were holding hands.

"I think you're being a little hard on my husband, Mr. Barnett." We all turned. Amanda had been quiet till then.

"Well, isn't that the essence of New York?" I said. "We warm up tearing into the latest eateries, then go on to tearing up each other?"

"Hey! That's it, man!" Duquayne liked me now. "You're okay. Glad you could come. When Kimberly called and said she had this photographer friend—we didn't know what to expect."

"Kimberly has brought around some of the oddest men," Amanda said. She smiled at Kim. "Haven't you, dear?"

"Guess that depends on what you mean by odd. They always seemed to fit in here," Kim said. Something about the way she and Amanda smiled at each other suggested an undercurrent, some kind of complicity.

With the main course, a platter of rabbit sausage and *al dente* vegetables, the conversation turned back to painting. Big sums of money were mentioned, gallery owners' seductions were analyzed, collectors were mocked, and half a dozen major artists were exposed as frauds. With the salad we dissected some current films, and with dessert the subject returned to food, a discussion again dominated by the Vanderkamps, who decreed that no matter what famous restaurant one went to in New York, one was doomed to disappointment.

Outside the air was sticky and thick. Kim and I quarreled the moment we hit the street.

"How do you *know* such people?"

"Harold and Amanda—I think they're kind of cute."

"Yeah. Like a couple of vipers."

"You seemed to be enjoying yourself."

"How *do* you know them anyway?"

"I just know them, okay?" Her forehead was glossy. "What's the matter, Geoffrey?"

"It was a wasted evening."

"Why use that word?"

"Their unearned opinions, clever put-downs. I hated the whole thing. Everyone was repulsive."

"Maybe they were. But why do you have to be so sour all the time?"

"You said that to me once before."

She glared at me. "And now it seems we have the proof."

I was offended. I knew she was right, but I didn't want to hear it.

"Maybe we're seeing too much of each other," she said. "Maybe we need a little rest."

"I'm sorry you feel that way. Until just now I thought we were getting along pretty well."

"Did you?" She gave me a withering look, then stepped into the street and raised her hand to flag a cab.

"Hey! Wait! Not so fast!"

"No, Geoffrey. I think we need a break." The cab pulled up. She opened the door. "Time I slept in my own apartment for a change. . . ."

She got in the cab and slammed the door. Then she looked straight ahead. I called to her, but she wouldn't turn. When the light changed, the cab sped uptown. I stood watching until it disappeared.

I couldn't sleep that night. I missed her. I hadn't expected her to walk away. For a long time I'd lived alone, reclusive, turned inward, in a kind of somnambulant state. Then she came into my life and I woke up again. Now, alone in my bed, I felt frightened of slipping back.

I got up at 3:00 A.M., dressed, packed my tripod and Deardorff, and went out to prowl the streets. The air was dense, still and humid. Within minutes my clothes were soaked.

I never got around to setting up my equipment, just roamed and felt the city's emptiness. Around 4:00, I wandered over to Desbrosses to find that stretch of wall where she and I had met. The phone booth on the corner was empty as a coffin, Lil's was closed, and there was no one around. The figure in the shadow painting looked as if he'd just been executed. I stared at him, felt wretched about myself. Then, without taking a single photograph, I shuffled my way back home.

I phoned her early in the morning.

"Who's this?" Her voice was groggy. Unlike me, she had slept very well.

"Look, Kim—I'm sorry. You were right. I promise I'm going to lighten up."

"Oh, Geoffrey—it's you. What time is it anyway?"

"Of course it's me. Who else did you expect?"

"I thought we were taking a break."

"Come on, Kim—forgive."

There was a pause. I held my breath.

"Sure. I'm crazy about you. Didn't you know?"

She was busy. Saturday was her day for errands, and she and Shadow had a modeling appointment in the evening. She thought she'd be too exhausted to come by afterwards, so she proposed we meet the following day for a reconciliation brunch.

When I put down the phone I was happy once again, though I wondered how I'd make it through another night alone.

As it turned out I didn't have to. She woke me up at 2:00 A.M.

"It's me. On the corner. Can I come up?" There was an edge to her voice. She sounded out of breath.

"What's the matter?"

"Damnit, Geoffrey! Can I come?"

"Of course. I'm sorry. . . ."

A minute later she rang and I buzzed her in. As soon as I saw her I knew something was wrong. Her eyes were wild, her expression frantic. She rushed into my arms.

"Geoffrey . . ."

"Hey . . ." I stroked her hair. "Hey, calm yourself. Calm."

"I'm scared, Geoffrey. *Really, really* scared."

"Why?"

"Some men are after me."

"What men?"

She stared at me. "I don't know."

For a moment I thought she was stoned. "Are you on something?"

"*No!*"

I believed her; she wasn't spacey, just terrified.

"Pull yourself together. You're not making sense."

"There's this powerful man. It's people who work for him, I think. But I don't know for sure. I only know he's had people killed."

"Hey, now . . . slowly. Who're you talking about?"

"I don't *want* to talk about it. Do you have Valium?"

"What?"

"*Valium.*"

"Yeah. I think so. Sure."

"Get it for me." I hesitated. "Please. I'm so scared, Geoffrey. All screwed up inside and scared. . . ."

When I brought her the Valium, she grabbed the bottle, and before I could stop her she gulped down thirty milligrams. After that I couldn't get her to tell me anything. She hugged me, buried her head in my chest, murmured again about how scared she was, and dropped off to sleep.

I cradled her for a while, worrying about her, trying to make sense out of what she'd said. I think I felt some omen then that what we had was vulnerable and could be shattered. But the thought of that was too upsetting; I needed her too much. After a while I blanked out too, to protect myself, I think, from the pain of such a loss.

In the morning when I awoke she was still sleeping, breathing heavily in my arms. I got out of bed carefully, so as not to wake her, and went into the kitchenette.

I was out of coffee—bread and juice as well. I wrote up a shopping list, dressed and went out to shop.

A few years ago they closed Nassau Street to traffic, turning it into a pedestrian mall. On weekdays it's a river of people moving between Wall Street, City Hall, the courthouses and various subway stops along the way. But early on a Sunday morning it's as lonely as an empty canyon in the desert.

When I came out that morning the only other human in sight was a homeless old wino asleep on the corner by the Edgar Allan Poe plaque. All the shops were closed, and the grill of the Isaac Mendoza Book Store was padlocked shut. Though it was not yet 8:00 A.M., the street thermometer read out 80 degrees.

The nearest delicatessen, at Battery Park City, was a fifteen-minute walk away. I paused, pondering whether to leave Kim alone. I wasn't as concerned about her alleged pursuers as I was about her waking up, thinking herself abandoned and going into another panic.

I decided to chance it, make the trek, figuring she'd taken enough Valium to keep her calm even if she did wake up. I reached the deli, bought the groceries, and, when I returned, found her curled up on my couch, wearing one of my old shirts.

"Hi, loverboy." She certainly didn't look desperate; rather she spoke with her usual sultry confidence.

"Feeling better?"

"What happened last night?"

"You don't remember?" I carried my newly bought provisions to the kitchen. She followed, stood behind me as I started to make our breakfast.

"I remember coming here."

"That's nice. Do you remember you were scared?"

She smiled mischievously. "Scared?"

"Come off it!"

"Of course I remember. I was putting you on."

"Don't give me that."

"*I was.*"

"You wouldn't."

"Shouldn't," she corrected me.

I switched on the coffee maker. "You were panicked."

"Just an act." She clung to my back. "Honest, Geoffrey—an act, that's all it was."

I turned to her. "You're saying last night was all pretend?" She nodded. I was outraged. "How could you do that? How could you be so cruel?"

"Had to. No, really, Geoffrey. Please hear me out."

"I'm listening."

"Mr. Lorenzo, my acting coach—he gave us all an assignment. Call a friend or lover late Saturday night, say you're afraid for your life. Convince the person you're in real trouble." She stood back from me. "Honest! That was it."

"I don't believe you!"

"*It's true!*"

"Disgusting!"

"Maybe. But wasn't I good?"

"Yeah, you were good, all right." I looked straight at her. I wanted to believe her. I think she sensed I did, because she stared straight back to assure me she was telling me the truth.

"I'd like to have a little talk with your Mr. Lorenzo," I said, "about a funny little thing called ethics, and a quaint old saying, 'Don't cry wolf'!"

She flung herself into my arms. "Oh, Geoffrey, I really can act. You forgive me, don't you? Please, Geoffrey—please forgive." She planted kisses on my chest.

I forgave.

After breakfast she cleaned up the dishes while I went out to buy the *Times*. When I returned, she was dressed, in her slinky disco outfit of the night before. I found her facing the bathroom mirror, putting the final touches on her makeup.

"Don't you want to stay and read the paper?"

She shook her head. "We still have a date for brunch?"

"Two o'clock. Windows on the World."

"Sounds great." She came close, whispered in my ear: "I'll make you happy afterwards."

"How about now?"

"I'd love to, Geoffrey. You know me. But there're things I've got to do." She came close to me, played her fingers on my chest. "Sorry about last night. I know I was a bitch."

She kissed me, then broke away. At the door she turned. She stood there a moment, as if posing for a photograph. I thought I caught a glimpse of sadness in her face, and sensed, in her hesitation, a desire to tell me something and then a change of mind.

"Kim!"

" 'Bye, Geoffrey. . . ." She flashed me a smile. And then she disappeared.

The view from Windows on the World is terrific. On a good day it takes your breath away. But like any romantic restaurant, it's a lousy place to sit alone. By 2:45 I began to feel bad.

At 3:00 I couldn't take it anymore; I left the table, went out to the lobby, found a phone booth and dialed her number at home.

The voice on the answering machine was pure Southern honey: "Hi! This is Shadow. We're not here at the moment, but we'll be back real soon. So, please, *cher*, leave your name and number and we'll get back to you [giggle], you can bet on it!"

I left my message: "Geoffrey for Kim. I've been sitting here an hour. Am I being stood up?" Then I went back to the table, ordered a Bloody Mary, and stared out across the scorched flatlands of New Jersey, a hundred and seven floors below.

At 3:30 I'd had it. I summoned the waiter, ordered a club steak rare and a half bottle of wine. Then, determined to enjoy myself, I ate and drank in solitary splendor.

I was feeling pretty high when I finished. Moody, too. Outside I wandered around for a while. Though the heat was crushing, there were the usual Sunday crowds. At Battery Park I found a place on a bench, stared out at the gleaming harbor and watched the boats pass back and forth. Then I wandered over to the Vietnam War Memorial, raised my Leica and took some photographs.

I walked home through the empty financial district. I found the same wino I'd seen in the morning by the Poe plaque, shirt off now, taking in the rays. When he saw me walking toward him with my camera around my neck, he held up an imaginary camera of his own.

I took his picture. He took mine. "Gotcha, Shutterbug!" he said.

Back in the studio, I lay down on my bed. I must have fallen asleep. At 7:00 P.M. I woke up, suddenly feeling scared.

When she didn't show at the restaurant, I had assumed it was deliberate, an act of calculated contempt. Now I realized that instead of thinking of myself, I should have been worrying about her.

Had something happened to her? An accident? Or, and the question finally emerged from the shadows, had her explanation for her panic the night before been an attempt to cover up some actual danger she had faced and now had met?

I phoned her apartment again, and this time, when I heard the message, Shadow's mellifluous delivery rang false. Appropriate perhaps for a downtown disco girl, but a little slick for a serious model. Kimberly, I knew, would never have left a message like that. Kimberly, I knew, had too much class.

No point in going up to their place—if no one was home there'd be no one there to let me in. I decided I'd have to keep calling until someone finally answered the phone.

I called again at eight, and then every hour after that until eleven o'clock, meanwhile watching a movie on TV. It was a thriller about cops investigating a pair of bizarre homicides in New York. The lead detective's girlfriend was a photographer; at one point the psychotic killer began to track and terrorize her. The closer the detective came to catching the bad guy, the closer the bad guy came to killing the detective's girl. By the time the show was over I was wild with anxiety. Meantime my messages became increasingly frantic: "Even if you want this sour old photographer out of your life," I told the machine, "*please* call to let him know you're safe."

Later, lying in bed, not knowing what to feel, I decided to give her number a final try. I got the same recording, but this time, after Shadow said ". . . you can bet on it," I found I had no words to say. So I just breathed into the receiver, the way a telephone heavy breather might, and then, I don't know why, I got this feeling there was someone at the other end smiling smugly to herself.

I woke early, dialed the number, and this time there was no recorded message. I let the phone ring and ring, and, when there was still no response, dialed again to make sure I'd dialed right. Still no answer. There was only one thing to do. I gulped down my coffee, dialed one last time, then dashed downstairs and up Nassau to the subway, where I grabbed an uptown express.

Though I'd never been inside her apartment, I knew her building well. It was similar to a thousand other anonymous dirty-white-brick monstrosities that dot the cross streets of the Upper East Side. There was no doorman; you had to buzz your way in. "Stewardess buildings," a friend of mine calls them—buildings where a gang of flight stewardesses will rent a unit for between-flight shack-ups and rest.

I found the buzzer marked "Devereux/Yates," rang it, waited, then rang again. No answer. I was sure they were up there. The machine was off, which meant one or both of them were home, probably asleep with the phone unplugged. I gave the button another push, and this time held it down. I doubted anyone could sleep through a blast like that. But still there was no response.

I stepped back to the sidewalk. The sun was beating down furiously. I was thinking I might locate their window and throw something at it that would wake them up when I saw a man in the inner hallway moving toward the door. I went back to the lobby. If he opened up and came out, I would try to slip past him pretending I was a resident.

But he didn't come out. He stood in the doorway, looking directly at me.

"Hey, buddy? You ringing three-A?" He was husky, bearded, dressed in fatigue pants, with a big ring of keys hanging from his belt. He wore a dark green Marine Corps T-shirt wet under the arms, and his biceps sported nautical tattoos.

"Yeah, that's right," I said.

"Ain't home," he said. "Just up there myself." He was staring at me in a peculiar way. "I'm the super," he explained.

"I think they *are* up there," I said. "Their answering machine's not on."

"That's 'cause I turned it off. They cleared out most everything, 'cept for that."

"*You* turned it off?"

"They're gone, mister. Flown the coop."

"Impossible," I said. "Kim Yates—"

He smiled. "She's a friend, uh-huh. . . ."

I didn't like his intonation, or the way he smiled either. "What do you mean—*you* turned it off?"

He studied me a moment before he spoke. "They took a powder. Pulled out yesterday. Left the furniture, TV—all rented stuff. But the clothes are gone. And so are all the shoes. Those girls had lots of shoes." He shrugged. "They're like that, you know. Here one day, gone the next. And no forwarding address neither. Case they owe you money, you want to find them again." He grinned and showed his teeth.

He was waiting for me to say something, but I was too stunned to reply.

"Want to see the apartment?" I nodded. "Cost you some." I pulled out my wallet, peeled off a ten. He sniffed. "Quick look-see's all you get for that."

I gave him another ten, his grin grew a little wider, and he beckoned me through the door.

We rode the elevator up in silence. At the third floor he motioned me down the hall. The walls were covered with a cheap green flock. The row of identical doors, each bearing a number and a peephole, reminded me of a dormitory corridor.

The door to 3-A was open. The moment we walked in I knew he was right. The place looked like an empty motel room. The living room furniture, knock-down Scandinavian type, was set awkwardly at one end. There were no books in the bookcase. The wall-to-wall carpeting was beige and nondescript. A small TV, of obscure Korean manufacture, sat beside a cable decoder, a phone and an answering machine in the corner on the floor.

"Couple days from now, after I paint her up, we'll have this place rented out again. Higher rent too. They'll pay anything these days, girls will, just to be in a nice safe neighborhood."

He led me through an archway to the bedrooms. Each one contained a queen-sized bed, mattress exposed and bare. All the bureau drawers were cleaned out, and the closets were open and empty. I stepped into the bathroom. Half a bar of soap was melting in a soap dish and a couple of damp towels lay in a tangle in the tub. The toilet seat bore one of those fuzzy pink covers. The medicine cabinet was open. There was a crushed tampon box on the shelf.

"Cleaned out pretty good," the super said. "Swept up most of the garbage myself." He walked me back through the bedrooms. "See those?" He pointed, chuckled. "Couldn't take those with them, could they?"

I think I was in a kind of daze because it took me a while to figure out what he meant. I looked at him, and he pointed again, first at the closet doors, which were faced with mirrors, and then at the ceilings above the beds where mirrors were mounted too. He laughed.

"What's so funny?"

"Hey, buddy, I'm the super. My job's keep the building neat and clean. They pulled out over the weekend. Neighbors seen one of 'em moving suitcases and crap, yesterday and Saturday too. You gotta expect the old quick exit with girls like that." He looked at me. "They come and go—"

The guy was starting to annoy me. "Girls like *what*?"

"Professionally speaking's what I mean."

"Kim Yates is an actress."

"Sure. Suit yourself. Miss Kimberly and the colored girl, one who calls herself 'Shadow' . . . Well, they're *all* actresses, ain't they?" He laughed again. "Listen, maybe you wanna talk to the neighbors. Three-C's seen them moving. And the fairies in three-H, end of the hall—one of them knew your Miss Kimberly pretty well. . . ."

I knocked on 3-C. The door was opened by a middle-aged man who reminded me of a Saint Bernard. He was red-haired, heavyset, unshaven, with hooded watery eyes.

"Yeah?" He wore a navy blue terry-cloth robe, open to the waist, exposing a heavy gold link chain nestled in curls of coppery hair that carpeted his upper chest.

"I understand from the super you saw the two girls moving out of three-A," I said.

He scratched at his stomach. "So?"

"I'm a friend of one of them."

"Which one?"

"Kim Yates."

He nodded. "White girl? Yeah, saw her yesterday. The other one, the black—haven't seen her since Friday P.M."

"What time did you see the white girl?"

"Late morning, I think. She came out of there with suitcases. Then later I saw her coming out of three-H." He shook his head. "Won't miss them, I can tell you that. Don't mind a couple of pretty girls want to make an honest living. But those two . . ." He shook his head and leered.

I went down the hall to 3-H. A lean young man, preppie type, with nice even features, opened up the door. He wore jeans and a ribbed black tank top. A hank of light brown hair hung across his forehead.

"Hi." He smiled at me, but something in his smile struck me as forced.

"Sorry to intrude," I said. "The super suggested I talk to you. My name's Geoffrey Barnett. I'm a friend of Kim Yates down the hall."

"Kimberly—sure. But she's gone. Left yesterday. I'm Brent." He offered his hand.

"One of your neighbors said he saw her coming out of here."

"That's right. She stopped in to say good-bye to Jess. Jess Harrison, my roommate."

"Is he here? Could I talk to him?"

"He's here." Brent lowered his voice. "But I don't know—"

"I'd really like to talk to him," I said.

Brent studied me for a moment. "All right, I'll check." He motioned me inside.

While I waited I looked around the living room. A potted plant, leaves starting to brown, stood before the window. A framed Diane Arbus exhibition poster was mounted on the wall. A pair of ballet slippers, signed by Heather Watts, hung beside the light switch from a hook. There was a handsome rosewood stereo system and a large collection of compact discs.

Brent reappeared. "Jess isn't feeling all that good, but he'll talk to you a little anyway. He's got AIDS. Wanted me to tell you. If you change your mind, he'll understand."

"I haven't changed my mind," I said.

Brent nodded. "One thing I ask, seems like he's getting tired, please excuse yourself. He had a pretty rough night last night."

Jess, older than Brent and starting to bald, waved to me from the bed. He lay on top of the sheets wearing a pair of gray gym shorts and a T-shirt that bore the faded words "West Point." He held a damp washcloth to his forehead and he looked pretty sick.

"You're the photographer?"

I nodded.

"Kimberly mentioned you." He gestured toward a chair.

"I appreciate your seeing me," I said, "because right now I'm pretty confused. Kim and I had a brunch date yesterday afternoon. She didn't show, so I called and called. Now her apartment's empty and the guy down the hall says he saw her moving out with suitcases yesterday before she and I were even supposed to meet."

"Was around noon when she left," Jess said. "She stopped in to say good-bye."

"You say she mentioned me?"

He nodded. "Not yesterday. But she spoke of you several times. Said you were taking these fantastic pictures of her. I know she liked you a lot."

*Liked me!* "That's nice to hear," I said. "But apparently she didn't like me well enough to say good-bye."

"I'm sorry. . . ."

"Didn't even call."

He looked at me. "What can I say?"

I stood, then started to pace. "Look, you don't know me, Jess. No reason you should care. But Kim and I, we had something going. Something serious—at least that's what I thought. Now she's stood me up, no reason I can think of except we had a fight on Friday night. But we made it up on Saturday. Meantime she's cleared out her place. And now the slob super and the jerk in three-C, they talk about her like she and Shadow, like they were . . . I don't know—"

"What?"

"Hookers. Or something like that."

"They said that?"

"No. But they made it pretty clear."

He turned away. There was silence in the room. When he spoke again it was in a whisper. "It's true, I'm afraid."

I stared at him. "Now, what the hell, Jess! I mean, how the hell can that be?"

"It's awkward for me to be the one—"

"I understand." I sat down again. I felt as if I'd been kicked. "Please, you got to tell me what you know."

He shook his head, as if to clear his brain. "Kimberly told me she and Shadow did tricks. She also told me they'd been lovers once. I assumed they still were. At least sometimes. Of course there's nothing wrong with being gay."

"Of course not. But 'tricks'?" He shrugged. I could see the word made him uneasy. "She told me they were actresses, models—"

"They *are*. Shadow's a very successful model, and Kimberly's extremely serious about her acting. She didn't talk all that much about herself, even when we dished the dirt. I know she's from Cleveland, upper-middle-class family, and that she quit college to come here and study. She met Shadow in one of her classes. Shadow introduced her to a lady who ran an escort service. Shadow was working for the woman, so Kimberly started working for her too. Just to make extra money. Part time at first. Then, I gather, she and Shadow—they became sort of famous as a team."

*Jesus!*

He shook his head. "I know it sounds bad. But maybe not as bad as you think."

"I think it's pretty bad," I said.

"Well, it's not like she was out hooking on the street." He removed the washcloth from his forehead and carefully wiped his brow. "Look, I know guys . . . I mean I used to hustle occasionally myself when I needed the bread. At least her way was safe. Prescreened clientele. Rich guys, tycoons, big-shot attorneys. Not sleazy salesmen from out of town."

"Jesus, Jess! Was she really so goddamn desperate?"

"It wasn't like that. I don't think desperation had anything to do with it. Way she explained it to me, she did it for the experience."

*"Experience!"*

"She told me she liked the acting part, that was what turned her on. Also the novelty, and what she called 'the risk.' But what she liked best, she told me, was the whole notion of sex for money, that there existed this marketplace where, if you did it well, you could sell it very high. She took great pride in the price people paid to be with her, even for a little while. 'I'm very expensive, Jess,' she said. She and Shadow, as a team, she told me, they could earn up to fifteen hundred dollars."

I sat down. "She actually told you that?"

He nodded. "Like I said, we were pretty close. Maybe because she knew with me she didn't have to pretend, me being ill the way I am." He paused. "I'm really sick. Doubt I'll make it through the fall. Brent's been great. Stuck by me. Sleeps in here right by my side." He pointed to a sleeping bag rolled up on the floor. "But Kimberly was special. Having her in my life, dropping by when she could, that meant an awful lot. Maybe it's because I was never really close to a girl before. And, I like to think, I also meant something to her."

"I'm sure you did."

He nodded. "When I got sick, she started coming around. Not much lately, though. Lately she's been pretty busy." He stared at me. "Guess she's been with you."

"Yeah."

"Anyway, she used to come by and talk. She was very loyal that way. Month or so ago she told me she might have to leave suddenly, and she wanted me to know so I wouldn't worry if one day she disappeared. Yesterday she came in. 'This is it. I'm off,' she said. Wanted me to know she'd be thinking about me, even if she didn't write. When she left"—his voice broke—"she kissed me on the lips. . . ."

• • •

Back out on the street I felt dizzy—hurt, confused, furious too. I felt the anger grow as I walked up Lexington Avenue in the heat. Kimberly Yates had been a liar, a fake—and me . . . well, it was pretty clear what I'd been: the biggest fool in all New York.

I think that's what angered me the most, not just her deception, or the way she had disappeared without a word—though those things were crushing enough. No, what infuriated me was the knowledge that I, a photographer, who prided himself on his ability to unmask and see, had looked at her so closely, gazed at her so deeply, and had failed so utterly to see what was there.

How she must have laughed, I thought, at all my talk about revealing character, when I had failed to penetrate even the most shallow layer of her disguise.

# Two

There I was holding a photograph and looking at it. And so far as I could see it didn't mean a thing. I knew it had to. I just didn't know why. But I kept looking at it. And in a little while something was wrong. It was a very small thing, but it was vital. . . .

—Raymond Chandler, *The High Window*

**A**S THE DAYS PASSED I FELT INCREASINGLY HAUNTED. I stayed inside, in my studio, surrounded by my images of her, spending hours contemplating them, trying to read her face.

There were times when I wanted to tear those prints off the walls. Times too, I think, when I wanted to be tortured by them. One thing I knew—I had to work her out of my system. If I could find a trace of her falseness in any of my pictures, then, I thought, I could begin to deconstruct my pain. But the pictures did not reveal her; they revealed me. They told me nothing . . . except that I had loved her.

Finally, in an attempt to relieve my stress, I called Frank Cordero in New Mexico. I told him everything. He listened sympathetically.

"It's like first she built you up," he said, "and then, almost deliberately, she tore you down."

"I know. That's what's so awful. It's as if she were two completely different people. So here I am pining for her. Am I crazy, Frank? Or what?"

"No, I don't think you're crazy," he said. "But I don't think you're going to be free of her—not until you find out who she really is."

"*Who is she?* Jesus! I ask myself that almost every hour."

"If your pictures can't tell you, Geof, you'll have to find out some other way."

"Like how?"

"You've been a journalist. Check out her story. She gave you leads. Track them down."

I spent that evening considering Frank's advice. There was a side of me that wanted to let her go, be done with her forever. She'd misrepresented herself, which, as far as I was concerned, was among the worst forms of betrayal. To lie to me, her lover, for whatever reason, and then to disappear without coming clean—by any rational standard she deserved no further attention or concern.

But I wasn't rational. I was hurting. I was obsessed and I was confused. Frank's advice sounded right: follow up on my leads, track her down if possible, and then confront her. If I could do all that, then I might be able to rid myself of my obsession and get on with my life.

There was another reason I wanted to find her. I wanted a conclusive parting. I've always been one for final ringing curtain lines. For all her deceptions, she had helped me break through my block. So, as much as I wanted to cut her, I also wanted to thank her, express my gratitude along with my contempt.

And there was still another reason, which, with a certain amount of shame I confess, had to do with sex. I longed one last time to look into her eyes, stroke her skin, feel her touch, breathe in her incredible scent. . . .

The next morning I began to work the phone. I called every acting school in New York. Not one had a teacher named Lorenzo, nor a student actress named Kimberly Yates.

I called directory assistance in Cleveland. There were three doctors named Yates. I called them all. Not one had a daughter named Kimberly. Not one had a wife who played the viola. Not one knew of any other person who filled that description.

I called the dean's office at the Cleveland Institute of Music. The school did have a female instructor in viola. I got her name, called her, and though she did not have a daughter named Kimberly, she was kind and tried to help. She said she knew almost all the serious violists in northern Ohio. She described several women to me. None fit Kim's description of her mother.

I called the registrar of Oberlin College. There was no record of a Kimberly Yates ever having been a student at Oberlin.

She had lied, it seemed, about everything. I felt as if I'd been turned inside out.


That morning I walked up to Spring Street, and rang the buzzer to the Duquaynes' loft. The maid gave me a suspicious look, then had me wait at the door.

Amanda Duquayne finally appeared, slender and stunning in tan pants tucked into soft black riding boots. Her white silk blouse, open wide at the throat, exposed a galaxy of freckles.

She slowly and blatantly looked me up and down. "This *is* a surprise," she said, in her best Social Register voice.

"Sorry to intrude," I said. "You're unlisted or I would have called."

"We have to be unlisted," she explained. "Too many cranks around."

She didn't offer me her telephone number, but she did invite me inside. As I followed her to the sitting area, I admired her straight and haughty back. She spread herself on one of the leather couches, then casually crossed her legs.

"Now, what *can* I do for you, Geoffrey Barnett?" For the first time in our acquaintanceship, I actually saw her smile.

"Kim has disappeared," I said.

She raised an eyebrow. "Kimberly? Has she? Really?"

I nodded. "No forwarding address."

She did some upper-class thing with her mouth to show feigned concern. "Oh dear," she said.

"I thought you might help me find her."

"*Me?* Whatever made you think of me?"

"Since you know her, since you're friends, I thought—"

"But really we aren't, you see. I really hardly know her at all."

I looked at her quizzically. "The other night, when we came in, the way the two of you kissed—I just assumed—"

"A social kiss, Geoffrey. That's all it was."

I peered into her eyes. "Maybe I shouldn't have come, Amanda. Maybe you're not supposed to talk to me."

She smiled. "I'm very sorry, Geoffrey, but I have no idea what you're talking about."

We gazed at each other, with frozen smiles. Then I had the feeling she wanted to hear me beg, that it would turn her on to sit coolly with her legs nicely crossed while I squirmed in my seat.

It isn't my style to importune, but that particular morning I was desperate for information.

"I really need your help," I said. "If you know anything, or know somebody who might know something, or can help me in any way—I'd be grateful, I really would. . . ."

A sudden coldness in her stare told me this was not the way to her heart, so I shut up and gazed at her, woefully and imploringly, and as soon as I did the ice began to melt. She studied me with such a searing intensity that I felt forced to lower my eyes. The moment I did, she spoke to me again, her way of telling me that silent submission was what she'd wanted all along.

"Can you sit a moment, Geoffrey, while I go and hunt up Harold?

He hates being disturbed when he's painting. But I think the two of you should talk."

While she went to search him out I examined the "investment collection" of photographs. Among the classic images, several unusual ones caught my interest. There were two excellent and kinky Mapplethorpes, and a curious work from the late twenties by Man Ray, showing a woman, head encased in a tight-fitting mask, whose gloved and handcuffed hands were suspended by a chain above her head. Another extraordinary and very rare carbro-color print by Paul Outerbridge showed a woman in high heels wearing nothing but a top hat, a domino mask and a single black fishnet stocking.

"Barnett!" Duquayne pranced across the wide expanse of floor, his paint-spattered sweatshirt catching the late morning light. We shook hands while Amanda watched us coolly from the side.

"Now, what's all this I hear about a disappearance?" He enunciated the word with relish.

"Kim's gone. Her roommate too."

"Roommate too! Oh ho! The plot thickens!"

"Except for you and Amanda, I never met any of her friends."

"But I'm sure Amanda's told you—we barely knew her. She was more like an acquaintance. Friend of a friend. That sort of thing."

I looked at Amanda. "I remember your mentioning that she brought around other men. I thought for sure—"

Duquayne turned to her. "Wasn't that at our big drink party, darling? Who ever meets anyone at a thing like that?" He turned back to me. "Want a drink, Barnett?" He headed toward a built-in bar. Since I couldn't read his eyes, I glanced again at Amanda. She was studying me in an aloof and pitying way, the way I imagined she might gaze at a cripple on the street.

"Perhaps you'd tell me the name of the friend."

"Who's that?" Duquayne handed me a gin and tonic.

"You just said Kim was 'a friend of a friend'?"

He glanced at Amanda. I looked toward her too, just in time to catch an exchange of complicity. I had suspected her of lying from the first; now I was certain her lies were calculated.

"Really, Barnett—people don't want to be involved. Not in a thing like this."

"Like what?"

"Whatever."

"But, you see, I don't know what kind of thing it is. All I know is my girlfriend's missing."

He sipped from his glass. "Is she? Or did she walk away? See, that's what's bothering us. Now, if you think she's actually missing, in the 'missing person' sense, my advice would be to go to the police."

Of course she'd walked—I knew that already. I had no claim on her; I only wanted to find her for myself. I stared at him. "So that's your advice?"

"We really don't know anything, Geoffrey," Amanda said.

I turned to her. "Of course you do. You knew Kim pretty damn well. Otherwise you wouldn't have invited her to your intimate little dinner party, and when we arrived you wouldn't have greeted her the way you did. Now, if there's some special reason you don't want to own up to that—fine, just be straight enough to say so. But don't feed me any more crap. 'Barely knew her.' 'Friend of a friend.' Spare me more of that."

Duquayne put down his glass. "You don't want to talk to Amanda that way, Barnett."

"Don't I, Harold? I think I do."

"Hey! You're out of line here, guy!"

"Am I? I know this much. Kimberly was bisexual. She also liked to have sex for money. That wouldn't be how you two met her, would it? Hired her through an escort service? Paid her to get into bed with you? Played all kinds of kinky games?"

"Why, you vile little shit!" Amanda said.

"Well, well—Miss Perfect loses her cool!"

"Get out!"

I laughed. Their anger told me I was right. I moved to the door. "Know something, Duquayne? Your paintings suck."

He shrieked after me: *"Loser!"* But I was already on the stairs. Descending, I heard something smack, then break; I think he threw his drink at the wall.

I went back to my studio, brooded awhile, then started looking through my proof sheets, searching not for portraits that explored or revealed character, but for shots that were just good likenesses.

I selected three, separated out the negatives, then hand-carried them to a lab on Church Street. I ordered fifty commercial 8 × 10 blowups of each. Then I headed back uptown.

This time, when Brent let me in, his young face was creased with concern.

"Another bad night," he said. "But he refuses to go to the hospital."

"His choice, isn't it? Is he well enough to talk?"

Brent motioned me toward the bedroom. "Five minutes tops, okay?" I agreed not to stay any longer.

Jess lay beneath the sheets, the same wet rag across his forehead, his chest hair curled and wet against his skin. At first I thought he looked smaller, as if he'd shrunk in the past three days, but then I realized it was his eyes that were enlarged.

I told him what I'd discovered: that all the background facts Kim had given us were false. As I described my various telephone calls he began to show concern.

"Can't imagine why she'd lie," he said. "She had no reason to lie to me."

"Maybe like a lot of people who move to New York, she wanted to re-create herself."

"Maybe. So who is she, Geoffrey?"

I shrugged. "At this point I don't even know if Kimberly's her real name. But I have to find her, Jess. There was too much between us to let it just end like this."

He nodded. "How will you find her?"

"By finding out who she is. I was hoping you could help me. Was there some little thing she let slip in your talks, something that didn't fit? A revealing detail? Anything?"

Jess shook his head.

"What about that escort service? You said Shadow introduced her to a woman."

"Mrs. Z."

"That's her name?"

"That's what Kimberly called her: 'So then I went to work for Mrs. Z.' That's about all she said."

He was getting tired. I checked my watch; I'd overstayed my time. "The first time I saw her she was with a bunch of kids. Did she ever mention any friends?"

"No one except Shadow. And you, of course."

I suppose, if I'd been in a different kind of mood, I might have taken some comfort in that.

I found the super in the basement, sitting in a swivel chair. He was dressed in camouflage fatigues and a khaki undershirt, and there was a hunting knife in a scabbard on his belt.

He had carved out a little office for himself down there, from a mess of old beds, trunks, broken bicycles and bins of light bulbs and spare plumbing parts. There were centerfolds from *Hustler* taped to the wall, and, to complete the executive motif, a battered desk that looked as if it had been scavenged off the street.

He glanced at me over his copy of *Soldier of Fortune* magazine. "You again?"

"Didn't think I'd come back?"

He shrugged.

"Because she was a call girl?"

"What do you want?"

"Information."

He grinned. "Ain't got no information."

"Look, they lived here. You must know something about them."

"I keep to myself. Don't pry into other people's stuff."

I laid a twenty-dollar bill on the desk. He glanced at it, stared at the centerfolds on the wall. Then he shrugged again. "They didn't have no bank account."

"How do you know that?"

"They told me. When I asked why they always paid the rent in cash."

"See—you *do* know something." He didn't reply. "When I was here the other day, you told me you cleaned out the apartment."

"Garbage—that's all there was."

"No papers, letters?" He shook his head. "No clothes? Books? Records? Not even an envelope?" I stared at him. "What was there to clean?"

"Few empty bottles. Carry-out containers from the Chink joint down the block."

"I don't believe that," I said. "I don't believe Kim Yates could pack up everything she owned in just a couple hours."

He glared at me. "You saying I stole something?"

"I'm saying there was a lot more than empty bottles and Chinese food containers that you 'cleaned up.' "

"Suit yourself," he said, showing me his best thousand-yard stare. "Now, get lost. I got work to do."

I placed my card on top of the twenty-dollar bill. "Change your mind, *comandante*, I'll make it worth your while." He didn't look up, just grunted and turned back to his magazine.

On my way home I stopped at the lab to pick up my blowups. My plan had been to circulate them, leave them at Lil's and the other clubs, at the modeling agencies, acting schools, any place she might have frequented or been known. But when I got home, I started dealing them out on the floor like giant playing cards. Then, staring at this huge rectangle composed of my images of her, I grew dizzy and crawled into bed.

I got up in the middle of the night, thinking I'd go out with my camera and work the streets. But as I stepped gently on my carpet of photographs I was seized by a different idea.

I got out my paper cutter and a pot of paste, and set to work. I mounted one of the portraits in the left upper corner of a big piece of mat board, then began to slice up other blowups of the same shot. Soon I had a serialized image of her, one frame of her full face, then a row of strips of varying thicknesses showing her eyes, lips, ears and cheeks. I used the second photograph for the second row, the third for the third, then started again with the first. By dawn I'd constructed a mural-sized montage, the face of the woman I knew as Kimberly Yates fractured into a thousand pieces and then recomposed. Standing back from it, I saw forms and rivers shaped by the ebb and flow of tones.

The piece was a portrait and a construct, both real and abstract. I liked it so much that, first thing in the morning, I went to the lab with twenty more negatives to be blown up. Then I went to an art store, bought a stack of mat boards and a gallon of paste. Then for three days I worked with slivers of my portraits, constructing more murals. Finally I set upon the nudes, cutting them up and serializing them too.

It was exciting work and I was possessed by it, the same way I'd been possessed during those first nonstop days when I'd tried to take her portrait. But, strangely, there were times when I didn't think about her at all, when I forgot whose face and body had provided my raw material. Taking her apart, cutting her up, turning her into something new—as I worked with pieces of her the patterns became ends in themselves. The huge murals composed of fractured and reconstructed images suggested a whole new direction for my photography.

But still there were times when I paused, gazed at my montage-constructs, and tried to puzzle them out. Knowing that these images had been stenciled off her filled me with a fierce yearning. No matter that she had lied, played false, made me feel the fool, I wanted her desperately, and prayed that she'd come back.

I'm not sure when I first noticed him. I probably saw him several times before it registered that I'd seen him before. It was only then that I realized that there was indeed a secret hidden in my photographs.

The first place I became consciously aware of him was in the background of a casual shot I'd taken of Kim at the South Street Seaport. I couldn't see him very well; he was slightly out of focus. His face was half concealed by a camera too, and it was that camera that caught my interest. It was a Pentax 6 × 7, a heavy medium-format professional instrument, not the kind of equipment the average person carries around.

The camera registered on me, and then I forgot about it, until, a few minutes later, looking at other frames from the series, I found him in the background again, and then again. I began to feel uneasy. This man with the camera—what was he doing there? For a while

I couldn't put my finger on what was wrong. Then I grew excited.

Yes, it actually seemed that this man, who for some reason I'd always caught holding his big Pentax to his eye, had been photographing in our direction at the very moments that I'd been photographing Kim. And that was either an extraordinary coincidence, or it meant that he had been photographing *us*.

I recalled the afternoon. It had been Kim's idea to go to Seaport. As always when we worked outside, I tried to accommodate her; for me the exterior sessions were not for serious photography but an excuse to get us out of the suffocating tension of the studio.

It had started out as an overcast afternoon, but then the late summer light broke through to play exquisitely on the river. There must have been ten thousand people milling around, the regular yuppie contingent from Wall Street and a vast number of summer tourists, including many foreigners. A lot of these out-of-towners had carried cameras. So why had this particular man, with his professional Pentax 6 × 7, decided to fasten upon us? And if I was right, if that was what he had been doing, had his interest been casual, or had we been under his surveillance?

It was several hours before I found the answer, and, when I did, I stared at my evidence, hardly believing it could be true. Three facts were indisputably clear: the man with the big camera appeared in the backgrounds of shots I had taken on several different days; he nearly always appeared facing me with his camera to his eye; he only appeared at places that Kim had suggested that we go. This last fact shook me the most.

*Who was this man?*

I examined all the shots in which he appeared, searching for one that was clear. There were several in which I could make out his left eye, a couple of good views of his hair and ears, one that nicely caught his chin and nose. But no single shot gave a decent impression of his face.

I decided to use the Identi-Kit method. I made blowups of all the best angles I had of him, then cut up the prints until I had a collection of his features. I then reassembled the clearest of these, creating a composite.

It was a difficult task. That damn Pentax was always blocking out one of his eyes. But then it occurred to me that the camera itself could be a clue to his identity: if he was a professional photographer, a picture of him, camera up, would be characteristic and therefore, I hoped, recognizable.

The portrait I finally created looked a little strange, assembled from pictures with different points of perspective. But strange or not, I had no doubt I had revealed him. A person who knew him should be able to identify him upon looking at my composite.

I rephotographed it, then made up some 8 × 10s to show around. When I was finally finished and staring at my handiwork, I was seized by the notion that I had seen the man before.

Had I? I wasn't sure. After all, I'd been staring at bits and pieces of him for an entire day. Familiar with the torments of puzzling over a half-forgotten face, I gave up trying to place him and took a break.

But later that evening, glancing at the composite again, I was struck by the fact that I was now on the track of another photographer, a kind of double of myself, who, apparently in collusion with Kim, had engaged in movements parallel to my own.

All I had to go on was the cryptic name of an escort-service madam ("Mrs. Z"), and the cut-up face of a photographer. I decided to start with the photographer—I thought he might be easier to find.

New York is full of camera stores, big, small, fancy, basic, a few where the salesmen are helpful, a great number where they're hideously rude. There're used-camera stores where you are likely to be taken, and places, owned by Hasidim, where you get big discounts buying "gray market." But in the entire city there's only one store professionals really like. You pay full price at Aaron Greene Photographic, but you get good service and you don't get hustled.

Aaron has sold me many cameras over the years. In my photojournalist days, when I used them up fast, he sold me a slew of Nikons and Leicas. Later, when I went into art photography, he found me my battered Deardorff and my Sinar.

I went to see him early in the morning, just minutes after the store opened. Already there were people inside, buying, selling, trading. Aaron was busy with a gentleman looking at old twin-lens Rolleis—there were half a dozen models lined up on the counter.

I caught Aaron's eye, signaled that I wanted to talk, then prowled among the showcases, excited by the displays of shiny black-and-chrome equipment. If you have money in your pocket, and are aroused by the sight of beautiful machines, Aaron Greene's is a dangerous place to go.

After a while, Aaron found me. He embraced me. "Hey, boychik!"

He's a stocky man in his mid-fifties, calm, good-humored, with a kind of permanent half smile that turns his lips. Practically nothing fazes him, which is why, he says, he'll never be better than a middling photographer. But he doesn't care, he loves fine cameras, loves the look and feel of them, the precise craftsmanship with which they're made. As he told me once, he's found himself a perfect job: he gets to handle cameras all day long, open them up, demonstrate them, turn people on to them. "I'd pay to do it," he told me. "But miracle of miracles—doing it has made me rich."

Now he was staring at me. "You don't look too good. What's amatter, Geoffrey?"

"How bad do I look?"

He appraised me. "Like a guy who's broken up with his girl."

"That's pretty close."

His smile turned compassionate. "What can I do for you? What do you need?"

I showed him my composite. "Ever seen this guy before?"

He looked at my picture, then handed it back. "You doing surrealism these days, Geoffrey? Huh?"

"Please, Aaron, look at the picture. Have you ever seen him?"

"Not that I can think of. Who is he?"

"A photographer."

"I see the monster Pentax. So?"

"So I need to know his name."

He stood back, then peered at me quizzically. "Last I heard, there were six hundred thousand of you guys going around calling yourselves 'photographers.' "

"Has he been in here?"

He examined the portrait again. "If he has, I didn't wait on him."

"What about the other guys? Could you ask them, please?"

"Sure, Geoffrey. Later, though. We're kind of busy here just now."

"Thanks, Aaron. By the way, who repairs the Pentax?"

"There's Sid Walzer in the West Forties, and there's this Japanese kid around the corner. Lot of district people use him. They like the monster. Ever hear the damn thing go off?"

He edged me down to the Pentax case, pulled out a used 6 × 7 with pentaprism, set the shutter speed to one second, then cocked and tripped the release. There was a loud clunk as the mirror flipped up, then crashed back down. "Crash like that, I wouldn't take this jobbo mountain climbing. Might start a little avalanche."

"Who likes these things?"

"Advertising photographers. Centerfold shooters. You name it, they use it. It's a terrific device."

"What's so terrific?"

"The six-by-seven image, and still you can handle it like a thirty-five."

"I need a favor, Aaron." I handed him my composite. "Check around for me. The repairmen too. See if anyone knows this guy."

"This is important, Geoffrey?"

I nodded.

"Okay. Call me in a couple days."

On my way home I stopped at the big newsstand at the City Hall subway station. As usual, the tabloid headlines were screaming murder. When no one was watching, I bought a copy of *Screw*, "New York's premier sexually oriented newspaper." I folded it under my arm, exited the subway, then walked home down Nassau Street. I knew *Screw* contained ads for escort services. My plan was to call them all and ask for "Mrs. Z."

Stepping off the elevator, I heard voices in the hall. When I turned the corner in the corridor, I saw two men standing by my door. They turned to me. Both were in their mid-thirties. One was heavyset, with a drooping mustache and greased-up wavy hair. The other, Italian and cadaverous, seemed more of a friendly type.

"What's going on?"

"Who are you?" the fat one asked.

"This is my loft."

"Barnett?"

"That's right."

"We want to talk to you."

The thin Italian guy smiled at me then, a sick-sweet kind of smile. "Good timing, Geoffrey. We were about to leave you a note."

"About what? Who are you guys?"

But even before they showed me their badges, it occurred to me

that they were cops. The fat one was named Ramos, the thin one
Scotto. It wasn't hard to discern their roles: Ramos was the tough
guy who called me "Barnett"; Scotto was the nice one—he called
me "Geoffrey."

"Always leave your door unlocked?" Ramos was playing with
my doorknob.

"It's locked," I said.

"No it isn't. We already tried it," Scotto said.

They stood aside while I tried the door. It was open. I was
shocked.

Scotto examined the lock. "Wasn't tampered with. Maybe you
forgot to lock up when you went out."

"I never forget. I've got cameras inside."

"Better see if they're still there."

"And if they aren't, we are." Ramos snickered. "Always around
when you need us, right?"

Scotto turned to me and rolled his eyes, his way of saying: I
can't help it if my partner's a schmuck.

I pushed my door open, caught sight of my Sinar and started to
relax. At least they hadn't taken that. But then when I looked
around and saw the damage, I started feeling sick.

Someone had attacked my wall. The glass over the framed print
of my Pietà was smashed and the print had been torn to pieces.
But worse was the damage to my big montage murals of Kim. They
were still on the walls where I'd tacked them, but the vandal had
slashed them and worked them over with spray paint. The word
"CUNT" had been scrawled across them several times in an angry
graffiti writer's script.

"What's the matter? Ripped off? The big camera's here."

I pointed at my murals. Ramos shrugged. "Who do you think
did this, Barnett?"

"How the hell should I know?" I was angry now, enraged by

92

the vandalism, pissed off too at the cops for their lousy dumbbell attitude.

"Take it easy, Geoffrey," Scotto said. "Dave just asked a question, that's all."

I turned away, and then, worried about what else might have been done, began methodically to check around my loft.

"You're doing right," Scotto said. "Make sure nothing's missing. And if there is something, tell us now. That way we can make you out a report, and you can collect good on your insurance."

The first thing I looked for was the negative of my Pietà. It was where it was supposed to be, and the rest of my negative files appeared untouched. I started to feel better then, and the further I looked the better I felt. My Deardorff and my two Leicas were safe, as were all my lenses and meters. As far as I could see, nothing was missing, and I could find no further evidence of vandalism. It seemed implausible, but, so far as I could tell, the only damage was to the Pietà and the murals.

Ramos and Scotto meantime had helped themselves to seats. They sat quietly, watching me. By the time Ramos cleared his throat I'd almost forgotten they were there.

"Not too bad, huh?"

I turned on him. "Think it feels good to find your place broken in?"

"Damage is what Dave meant," Scotto said.

"There *is* damage! Plenty of damage!" I pointed at the murals.

"Just doesn't seem likely—" Scotto said, as if speaking to himself.

"What's that, Sal?" Ramos asked.

Scotto nodded toward my murals. "Go to so much trouble just for that."

"What do you mean?"

"His lock wasn't drilled out. Which means it was picked. Or someone had a key."

"Nobody's got a key," I said.

"So, like I said, someone went to a lot of trouble. . . ."

Ramos nodded as if he understood. Then they both stared at me. There was an inference in their stare I didn't like: that there'd been no break-in, that I was the one who'd defaced the murals.

I decided right then I didn't like them. I sat down and faced them. "What do you want with me?"

"We're here about the Devereux homicide," Ramos said.

I stared at him blankly.

"Pretending you don't know what I'm talking about?"

I shook my head.

Scotto squinted at me. "You don't know Cheryl Devereux?"

"You mean Shadow? Sure, I know her."

Ramos glanced at Scotto with disgust. "So you're saying you didn't know she was killed? That it, Barnett?"

Suddenly it hit me. *"Oh, no!"*

"Don't you read the papers, Geoffrey?" Scotto asked.

"What happened to her?"

"She was found the day before yesterday in the trunk of a car at Newark Airport. Car was in the long-term lot. It had been there at least a week."

I felt a tightening in my throat. "What about Kim?"

"That'd be Kimberly Yates, the roommate, right?"

I nodded.

"Don't know nothing about her," Ramos said. He glanced at my defaced murals. "Except, of course, assuming that's her—someone thinks she's a cunt."

I stared at him. "You're really a piece of shit. Anyone ever tell you that?"

He rose from his seat. I tightened up, certain he was going to attack me. Actually I was hoping he would. I felt like a fight. But then Scotto stood and made gentling motions with his palms.

"Take it easy, guys! Calm yourselves!" He turned to me. "Dave was just talking. He didn't mean nothing by it. Don't act so touchy now."

"Kim's all right, then?"

"We have no idea. We're here about Cheryl. Hard to believe you didn't know she was dead."

"Been all over the papers last few days. 'Model Torture Slaying.' TV too."

"I've been busy. I haven't been reading the papers."

"That's all right," Scotto said. "No law says you gotta read them. Now before we start, couple things I gotta say. You don't want to talk to us, you wanna consult a lawyer, say so, that's all you gotta do. But seeing as how you claim you didn't know Cheryl was dead, I can't imagine you not wanting to cooperate."

"Of course I want to cooperate," I said. "I don't know anything. I hardly knew her. Where'd you get my name?"

"You've been sniffing around where she lived, asking questions."

"The animal super told you that?"

"Never mind who told us. It's true, isn't it?"

"No! It *isn't* true."

"You're saying you *didn't* go around there asking questions?"

"I'm saying I asked questions about Kimberly Yates. I didn't ask about Shadow."

They exchanged a look, then Scotto shook his head. Then, for some reason, I started to apologize. I told them the break-in had upset me and the news about Shadow had been unnerving. While I spoke they both gazed at me, as if to determine whether I was telling the truth.

"You say Shadow was found in Newark?"

They looked at each other, then Ramos shrugged. "Go ahead. Tell him, Sal. Been in all the papers anyway."

Scotto leaned forward. "Like I said—airport cops found her in the trunk of a rented car. New York plates. The renter used a phony credit card. She was in bad shape. Beaten up. Lots of broken bones, fingers, toes . . . like that. Still not clear exactly how she died. But one thing's clear—she was tortured first."

"Jesus!"

"Been dead at least a week. We know that from the condition of the body. And of course we know from the parking lot just when that car was driven in."

"When?"

"You're asking us *when*?" I nodded. Ramos seemed amused. "Tell him, Sal. Tell him when."

"Week ago Sunday. In the afternoon. Which is an interesting point in time. Because, according to what we hear, the next day you were all over her building knocking on doors asking when she and her roommate were seen moving out."

They looked at me then, both of them together—two sets of eyes focused on me at once. And then at last I understood: they suspected me of involvement in the murder.

That did it. I woke up, stopped feeling punchy and sorry for myself. I started talking, as fast as I could, describing everything that had happened, how Kim had been my girlfriend, how she'd told me she and Shadow had a modeling session that Saturday evening, and then how she'd come to me in the middle of the night, saying she was scared, babbling about agents of some "powerful man." Then how, Sunday morning, she had denied her story of the night before, and then had stood me up at Windows on the World. I told them about my inquiries the following day, my discovery that they'd moved, and also what I'd learned from Jess, about the escort service and Mrs. Z.

They didn't seem too interested in that. They were much more interested in a detailed accounting of my movements on Sunday afternoon.

I felt pretty confident as I told them again about the restaurant. I described the waiter and how I'd finally eaten lunch alone. I found my credit card receipt and showed it to them. Then I told them how I'd walked back to my loft, stopping first to take some pictures at the Vietnam Memorial in Battery Park. Finally I mentioned the shot I'd taken of the wino on the corner.

I took them to the window, pointed the wino out. He was still there, as he'd been all summer, ensconced near the Edgar Allan Poe plaque.

"Go down and ask him," I said. "Pretty sure he'll remember me."

"Guy like that, whatever you ask him, he'll say he remembers it," Scotto said.

Ramos asked to see my photographs.

I went to my files and fetched the proof sheets. I even dug out the shots I'd taken of Shadow. I pointed out that some of the tourists at the Memorial were carrying newspapers, which, if blown up, might show the date. And I pointed out a big public clock in the background that showed the time to be 4:25.

As I told them all this, scurrying about, bringing them the documentation, Ramos studied me while Scotto wrote in his notebook.

". . . so," I said, "depending on what time that car was driven into the parking lot, it should be clear I didn't have anything to do with it."

"We never said you *parked* the car, Geoffrey. One person could have killed Cheryl, and another ditched her body."

"So I'm not off the hook?"

"Never said you were on it," Ramos muttered. "Course we'll be checking out your story with the restaurant and looking close at all the pictures you took. But I got to tell you now, there's one thing bothers me."

"What's that, Dave?" Scotto asked.

"Fact that Barnett here's even got these alibi photographs."

"I never called them that," I said. "I'm a photographer. I take pictures. That's what I do."

"Maybe so," Ramos said. "Thing is, if we're sure a guy did something, all the alibis in the world don't mean squat." He gave me a hard stare. "See, most people, they don't have alibis. They aren't out conveniently photographing people carrying dated newspapers with a big clock in the background at A, the same time a car with a body in the trunk is being stashed in a parking lot at B. What I want to know is why you think you *needed* these pictures."

"Now, wait just a minute!" I said.

"No. *You* wait!" Ramos rose from his chair. "You wait, and see what happens. 'Cause I got to tell you, there's something weird I feel coming off of you, and it don't smell all that sweet."

"What are you saying?"

"I'm saying how I feel. First I see you striding down the hall holding a copy of *Screw*. Then you tell me your apartment's been broken in, even though there's a good ten grand's worth of cameras sitting around in here untouched. Then you say the only thing that's different is someone's scrawled 'cunt' on these strange cut-ups you made of your girlfriend. And all around the place what do I see? More photos of the broad. Everywhere I look, pictures, pictures, pictures, a fair percentage of them in the nude. Now, what does that tell me, Barnett? Maybe that you're"—he snickered—"a sex pervert. Which isn't inconsistent with the pictures you show me of the homicide victim, strutting around here in her nifty black underwear. You think maybe I don't think that's a little strange? I'm not sure I believe a word of it. So let's leave it like this: Cheryl Devereux has been killed and her roommate is missing, and you've been involved with both of them in some kind of kinky way I haven't figured out yet. When I do figure it out I'll be back. Meantime my advice is get yourself a good attorney."

He motioned to Scotto that it was time to leave. Then he strutted out. Scotto smiled weakly at me from the door, but this time he didn't roll his eyes.

After they left I set to work on the murals, trying to clean them up. I couldn't. The spray paint was indelible. Then I lay down on my couch and started thinking about Shadow, about her bones being broken. Then I thought about Ramos and what he'd said, and I decided that though he was undoubtedly a slob, and his speech was uncouth, and he was definitely wrong in his assumptions, he could not be called a fool.

I was in my darkroom, making up a new print of the Pietà. The smell of the chemicals relaxed me. I knew the exposure and dodging and burning program for that negative by heart. I got several requests for prints of it every month. It was my bread-and-butter negative, my sinecure, my capital.

I had just finished the exposure and had put the paper in the developer when the telephone rang. Using one hand to agitate the solution, I picked up the darkroom extension.

"Like the damage, Barnett?" The male voice on the other end sounded tough.

"Who is this?"

" 'Who is this?' " He mimicked me in a nasty falsetto. "Who the fuck you think it is?"

I dropped my print into the solution. "You're the bastard who broke in."

"Yeah, I'm the bastard, you're the pigshit, and you-know-who's the *cunt*."

There was something horribly aggressive in his tone that scared the hell out of me. "What do you want?" I asked.

There was a pause and then he spoke. "Next time I come I hope you're there. Then instead of tearing up your shitty picture, I'll tear *you* up." The phone went dead.

I called Scotto, told him what had happened. He said I shouldn't worry about it, that it sounded like a freak acting big.

"One thing I'd suggest though—if you were really broken in."

I was incredulous. "You *still* don't think I was?"

"What Dave and I think are two different things. Meantime my suggestion is get a locksmith up there and have him put in something unbreakable. Like a good bar lock, something like that. Then you won't have to worry anymore."

"Fine. I'll do that," I said. "But you're not getting my point."

"Which is?"

"This creep's focused on Kimberly. He gets off calling her names. I say he's the guy who killed Shadow, now he's after Kim, and he thinks he can get to her through me."

"So who is he?"

"I think it's the super in their building," I said. "He's animal enough."

"You recognized his voice?"

"No. But it could have been him. He made the same kind of tough-guy grunts."

"Not enough, Geoffrey. Can't accuse just because of that."

"I'm not accusing. I'm suggesting you check him out. The guy's got some kind of macho complex. He reads *Soldier of Fortune* and keeps pin-ups on his wall." There was a pause. I could hear Scotto breathing on the other end. "What's the matter, Sal?"

"Like Dave says, Geoffrey—*you* read *Screw* and *you* keep pin-ups too."

"I don't believe I'm hearing this. Why are you looking at me? What about Kim's 'powerful man'? What about the super and 'Mrs. Z'? Why don't you check on them."

"Let us worry about all of that. Just stay away from that super, and do something about your door."

I took his advice. I called in a locksmith and spent three hundred bucks on a bar lock. Then I ordered new prints of Kim, and, when they came, set to work making up new serialized murals, using the damaged ones as my guide. This time the work went quickly. I finished the first mural at 11:00 P.M. I liked it even better than my original. It seemed sharper, more unified. I hung it, admired it awhile, then pulled out my tape of *Touch of Evil* and put it in my VCR.

I originally collected my *film noir* videos so I could study their brilliant photographic effects and their vision that extended beyond mere night photography into deeper "darknesses" of character. But as I watched them together with Kim, I began to appreciate their stories too. Now, with her gone, I found myself playing them again and again, a kind of substitute, perhaps, for wandering the streets at night.

*Touch of Evil* is a special favorite for the way it seethes with an almost palpable corruption. I'd seen it half a dozen times, and was enjoying this latest screening when, just at the point where Janet Leigh was being terrorized by the motorcycle gang, my buzzer sounded from downstairs.

I left the VCR on while I answered the intercom.

"Western Union. Telegram for Mr. Geoffrey Barnett."

I buzzed the messenger in, then checked the new lock on my door. I waited behind the peephole, still enjoying the screams issuing from my TV. A couple of minutes later a young black man appeared in the hall, a can of Pepsi in his hand. I watched him approach. He looked all right, dreamy and spaced-out, but I wanted to be sure.

"Show me the cable," I said through the door.

He shrugged and held a yellow envelope up to the hole.

"Okay. . . ." I slid open the bar lock and opened up.

As soon as I saw him I knew I'd made a mistake. He'd moved back against the far wall and now there was something bright and tense about his face. He was holding his Pepsi can in a strange way too, as if it were a weapon.

I started to shut the door. But I was too late. With a vigorous upward motion he thrust the can toward me, heaving out its contents. Then he turned and ran toward the stairway, so fast I'd have stood no chance of catching him. A moment after the attack I heard the fire door slam, and then my nostrils caught the smell of lye.

The fluid hadn't touched me, but it was a near miss. Noxious fumes was rising from the wall. The lye had hit at face level not a foot from where I'd stood. I watched, horrified, as the paint curled and peeled, then boiled off in a thick foul-smelling smoke. Then I heard my phone ringing, over the screams of Janet Leigh. I shut the door, barred it and picked up the receiver. I recognized the voice.

"Maybe next time he won't miss. Could happen on the street, in the subway, or when you're taking one of your pictures late at night. Think about it."

"What do you want?"

"Who do you think you're dealing with? You're making a big mistake. These kind of people—they don't pay money to sleazebag crook photographers. So think about this: next time we send a boy, we'll send one who'll pitch the juice right in your eyes. You won't be taking many pictures after that. Will you, pigshit?" He chuckled, then hung up.

The cops arrived minutes after I called them. Not Ramos and Scotto, who were home asleep, but two regular officers, a leggy blonde who looked terrific in her uniform and her male partner, soft-spoken and black.

"This is definitely an assault," the blonde announced. "Seems like someone wanted to do a hit."

"You see them throwing lye around up in Harlem sometimes," the black man said. "Usually they just throw it on your car. Makes a statement the way it messes up the paint."

"So who wants to hit on you, Barnett? Got any enemies?"

"The man on the phone. But I don't know who he is."

She shrugged, filled out her report, advised me detectives would be around in the morning. When she was done, she looked at my wall.

"Nice stuff. I like photography."

*Someone had tried to blind me.* To be made blind was the worst thing I could imagine. As I lay in bed, sweating from the heat, my mind kept returning to the image of the lye eating away at the wall beside my door. Another foot and it would have hit my face, burned pitilessly through the delicate tissues of my eyes.

It was all connected, of course, this latest attack, the desecration of the murals, Kim's disappearance, Shadow's torture and murder. People were after me, they wanted something from me, and now they had shown me several samples of their power.

It had something to do with my being a photographer, and with their not wanting to pay me money. But there was something else about that threatening phone call that bothered me profoundly. The man had phoned not a minute after the attack, and he had known the boy had missed. Which meant the boy had been *told* to miss. Which meant he would have hit me if he'd been ordered to. And if his hand had slipped, or if he'd lost his nerve, or if he'd just gotten his orders screwed up, I'd already be blind—that was how close I'd come.

I was awakened by pounding on the door. I checked my watch. It was 8:00 A.M. I had a fierce headache. Rubbing my eyes, I suddenly remembered the lye attack.

"Open up, Geoffrey. It's Sal Scotto."

There was more furious knocking while I stumbled to the door. I peered through the peephole. It was indeed Scotto and Ramos. My two favorite detectives.

"Go away," I said.

"We ain't going away. We're here about the assault."

"What difference does it make," I said. "Ramos doesn't believe anything I say."

"Come on, Barnett. Open up." Ramos's eyes were serious.

I opened the door. "Excuse the underwear," I said. "I wasn't expecting visitors."

"We're not visitors. We're detectives," Ramos said.

I motioned them in. "Regular Kojak, are you, Ramos?"

"What's with this guy, Sal? Why's he so fuckin' hostile?"

"Why shouldn't I be hostile?" I said. "I already know what you're going to say."

"Read minds, do you? What *am* I going to say?"

"That I threw the lye at myself."

"Funny, that's just what I was thinking. Since not a drop got on you, wise guy."

"Hey! I've had it!" I said to Scotto. "Somebody wants to call me 'pigshit' over the phone, nothing I can do. But I don't have to take insults from cops."

Scotto looked sternly at his partner. "Why don't you lay off him, Dave." He turned to me. "He's a good detective."

"And I'm a good citizen," I said. "I'm also a good photographer. Someone's doing a number on me. I nearly got blinded last night. The reason the lye didn't touch me was because it was a warning.

All of which I told the cops. So why don't you read their report? Meanwhile I'm going to take a shower."

I took my time cleaning up and getting dressed. When I came back out they were waiting for me, ensconced in the chairs they'd used the day before.

"We're going to be checking out that super like you suggested," Scotto said. "We don't think it'll take us anywhere, but we'll do it to show good faith."

I started feeling better. "I appreciate that," I said. "What about Mrs. Z?"

"You actually think there's someone called 'Mrs. Z'?"

"No," I said, "but maybe someone whose name begins with a Z. See, if it were just some woman and Kim didn't know her name, I'd think her natural instinct would be to call her 'Mrs. X.' "

"Very shrewd," Ramos said.

"If she really runs an escort service, it shouldn't be too hard to track her down."

"All right," Ramos said. "We'll look into that."

I nodded to him, and he nodded stiffly back. I gathered we were starting afresh.

"What else?"

"I'd like protection."

"You mean round-the-clock bodyguards like we give the Mayor?" He laughed. "Forget it."

"What about tracing my calls?"

"Unlikely to work and difficult to do. But you can buy yourself a phone tape device. If he calls again, you tape his voice. That way you got evidence when and if he's caught."

"Sure, why not?" I said. "Three hundred bucks for a bar lock. Another hundred or so for an on-the-line tape machine."

"What did he say exactly?"

I told them, then told them what I thought it meant. That for some reason I'd been confused with another photographer. A photographer who was trying to hold up some people for money.

"And who is this 'other photographer'?" Ramos asked.

I showed him my composite of the Pentax man. "Maybe him," I said. "I'm trying to find out who he is."

Ramos nodded. "When you do, let us know."

"Yeah, I'll do that," I said.

There was a pause, and then Ramos leaned forward, as if there was something important he wanted to say. "Look, Barnett, you and I, we got off on the wrong foot. But the thing you got to understand, I've worked a lot of homicide investigations, and there wasn't one of them there wasn't some trouble with the photographs. The angle, the depth, the perspective, whatever—the photographs were always off. So I've learned something: photographs lie; diagrams tell the truth. So, maybe, I saw you were a photographer, I took it out on you. I apologize."

I was touched. He was sincere. "It takes a big man to apologize."

He nodded, we shook hands, then they got up to leave.

Sal stopped me at the door. "No question you got yourself a problem, Geoffrey. Throwing lye—that isn't funny. Dave and me, we're agreed—we're going to try and help you best we can. But understand: we're working on the Devereux homicide. We don't know if your stuff is connected yet."

After they left I thought about what I ought to do. Usually, when I'm feeling bad, I go out and take pictures—the concentration usually straightens out my brain. But now I hesitated. My caller had warned me I might get blinded while shooting on the street.

I'd been a tough guy once. In my photojournalist days I hadn't been afraid of anything. So maybe, I thought, becoming an artist has turned me into a wimp. I considered that awhile and decided that if I wanted to I could be just as tough as I'd ever been.

· · ·

I spent the afternoon clearing papers off my desk. I owed letters to several friends, there were gallery invoices to send, and lab and other bills to pay.

08/7 07:55AM S Cleveland OH 216 734-3684 14.0 3.44

The phone charge didn't register as unusual when I first saw it on my long-distance bill. It was listed right after a call I'd made to Frank Cordero a couple of days before. But then I took a second look, and then it hit me: At 7:55 A.M., on Sunday, August 7, someone had used my phone to call Cleveland.

The call had lasted fourteen minutes. Kim claimed Cleveland as her hometown. August 7 was the day she disappeared. At 7:55 I was out buying groceries for our breakfast. When I returned, Kim told me that her story about being in danger had just been an acting exercise.

I was excited. Actress or not, she really *had* been scared. The way I put it together, even while I was sleeping she'd been planning her escape. As soon as I went out she used my phone to see if it was all right to come home. When I came back she told me her story was just a story. Then after confirming our date for brunch, she went back to her apartment, did some fast packing up, said a quick good-bye to Jess, and left. But her escape hadn't been so clean. The Cleveland number was on my phone bill. Wherever that phone was, that was where she was staying. I was positive. All I had to do was call.

Rapidly I punched out the number. Then I settled back and listened. I let it ring twenty times before I gave up. Then I called the phone company business office and complained about my bill.

"I never made this Cleveland call," I said. "I wasn't even in town."

"It's an automated charge, sir. The call was made from your telephone."

"But I didn't make it."

"Very good sir. We'll investigate and correct your bill."

"Can you tell me whose number it is?"

"Sir, you just said you weren't home that day."

"But—"

"Sir, if you weren't home you will not be charged for the call."

"Could you at least give me the address?"

"I'm sorry, sir. We cannot give out that information."

"But surely, with the reverse directory—"

"There is no public access to that directory, sir."

I tried the Cleveland number every twenty minutes. Finally, a little after six, I got an answer.

"Hello?" It was a woman but it wasn't Kim. The voice sounded older, tougher, more working-class. I hesitated. If I asked for Kim I could scare her off. "Sorry, wrong number," I said, then hung up.

It was Thursday. The Public Library was open late. I took a taxi to Sixth and Forty-second, stopped at a newsstand, bought a *Post*, then walked around toward the main entrance on Fifth. It was a hot August evening. People were milling about. A drug dealer whispered "Smoke, smoke" as I passed the entrance to Bryant Park.

The main reading room was filled with scholars. Homeless people too were dozing in the seats. I went to the far end where the out-of-town phone books were kept, found the Cleveland book, found a free seat at a table, and set to work.

I expected to spend hours, but I was lucky—I found the number in fifteen minutes.

Arnos G 32231 W Loraine. . . . . 734-3684

Arnos: Could that be Kim's real last name?

I went out to the corridor, found a pay phone, then used my telephone credit card to call Cleveland again.

"Hello?" It was the same woman.

"May I please speak to Mr. Arnos?" I said.

108

A short pause. "There is no Mr. Arnos." And from her tone I gathered that if there ever had been one, she'd as soon not be reminded.

"Sorry," I said. "Am I speaking to the lady of the house?"

"Who do you want to talk to, mister?"

"Mrs. Arnos."

"No Mrs. Arnos either. This is *Ms.* Arnos. What do you want?"

"Very sorry, ma'am—I'm working here from a list."

"Selling something?"

"Yes, ma'am."

"Take my name off the list, and don't bother me again." She hung up.

At least I knew I had the right name.


Back home I thought about what I ought to do, whether I should drop the whole thing now, let Kim go. Now that there was a homicide involved, going after her would be a major step. If I did manage to track her down I just might land in a lot of trouble.

But Frank had been right when he'd told me I'd never be free of her until I found out who she really was. So, in fact, there was no choice. I *had* to go after her.

I phoned American Airlines, booked a morning flight to Cleveland, then packed a bag. I took along my best Leica, three lenses and six rolls of TMX-400. Then I sat down with the *Post* to read the latest news on the Model Torture Slaying.

There wasn't much. Numerous police detectives from both New Jersey and Manhattan were working on the case, but so far no progress had been made. Meantime a designer I'd never heard of had given an exclusive interview to the *Post*, in which he said that Cheryl Devereux, known in the profession as Shadow, was as much of her time, the late 1980s, as the famous model Twiggy had been of hers.

I loaded *The Big Sleep* into my VCR and tried to lose myself in the plot. It wasn't hard, the story was labyrinthine. When I got to the scene where Bogart finds the blackmail camera hidden in the Oriental head, I remembered Kim's feeling that the blackmail material in the movie wasn't very strong. Which made me think, in turn, of people who "don't pay money to sleazebag crook photographers." What new threat, I wondered, did they now have in store for me?

After checking in at La Guardia, I phoned Aaron Greene to ask how he was doing tracking the Pentax guy. He said he was still working on it and he'd let me know. Then I flew to Cleveland.

What can I say about that rust-belt town? From a purely photographic point of view I found it fascinating. The very qualities that once made it a talk-show joke were the traits that spoke to me.

The air, for instance. It was thick and smoky. Even driving out of the airport in my rented car, I felt oppressed by haze and stickiness. But I've always liked that kind of oppression. It gives a special quality to light. And the light in Cleveland was extraordinary. All those shimmering particles of industrial waste, catching the sunlight, made the city seem to burn.

I liked the hard look of the people too, the ones I saw outside the plants and mills: men whose eyes were devoid of mercy; young blacks with scornful mouths. And the mills themselves intrigued me, the way they were clustered along the Cuyahoga flats. Here a hundred chimneys spewed out smoke, each trail its own shade of gray or brown. These trails hung in the windless air and were reflected in the molten river. Beyond lay Lake Erie, its steel-gray surface reflecting nothing, a hard, still, clouded mirror.

I'd bought a city map at the airport. The Hertz girl had marked it up for me, the block where G. Arnos lived, and the location of a nearby motel. I found the motel first, a stark two-deck sickly green box, fifteen units to a deck. A sign out front identified it as THE DEVORA. When I drove up, a pale old man in an undershirt was trying to mow the lawn.

Inside the office, I was caught in a cross fire between two electric fans. The clerk, a teenage boy with a bad case of acne, explained that the air conditioning was out. "But we expect it on by tonight," he assured me. Meantime the nightly rate was twenty-six dollars. The place was dismal, but my finances weren't in the best shape, so I signed the register, got my key, brought my car around to my door, and moved in.

The word "depressing" merely begins to describe my room. The air was stale and muggy, the rug was worn through on either side of the bed, and the bed itself was covered by a thin gray bedspread textured with even grayer ribs. The only wall decoration was an old Eastern Airlines calendar. The TV set, bolted to its table, wore a film of dust. The easy chair was cracked. The closet wasn't deep enough to hold my jacket. In the bathroom the shower curtain was ripped, the stall smelled dank, and the toilet coughed like a dying fish.

It was awful, but I almost liked it, perhaps because it suited the way I felt, bespoke being on the run and down and out. The Devora motel was a place where the terrible people who wanted me blind would never find me. Here, for a time, I would be safe.

I changed my shirt, then went out to my car. I was on the south side of the city, on the edge of a working-class area of Poles and Greeks. I drove around for a while, slowly, absorbing the feel of the place. Then I went to a supermarket, bought an egg salad sandwich, got back in my car, drove until I found a grade school, parked across the street, and ate.

Though it was summer and school was out, the playground was crowded with kids. I tried to imagine Kimberly Arnos, if indeed that was her name, playing here too when she was a girl. I imagined her skipping rope in this schoolyard, or striding up and down the corridors inside. I even had a vision of her furrowing her brow, worrying over a word on a spelling quiz.

I found the Arnos house, circled the block several times, then parked inconspicuously across the street. I arranged my car so that I could watch the door through my adjusted rearview mirror.

It was an ordinary house among other ordinary frame houses, each with a small lawn in front and a narrow driveway leading to a detached garage in back. The houses varied in state of upkeep and each had its own distinctive feature—a larger than ordinary TV antenna on one, a basketball hoop set above the garage door of another.

Something about the Arnos house, a lack of movement behind the curtains, and the fact that all the downstairs windows were shut, told me nobody was home. So I just sat in my car absorbing the sounds and sights of the neighborhood, willing myself inconspicuous.

Occasionally a child appeared, riding a bike, or carrying a baseball glove and bat, moving toward the school. Several times I saw women leave their homes, get into cars, drive off and then return with bags of groceries. At 3:30 a UPS truck appeared, and slowly worked the block. Then a patrol car drove by; I didn't pay any attention to it, just buried myself in my newspaper like a man waiting patiently for his wife.

After five there was more traffic as the men started coming home. Burly and barrel-chested, dressed in stained and sweaty clothes, they looked as if they spent their days doing hard physical work. With their arrival the sound level started picking up. I heard radios, TV sets, people talking, arguing too. One man came out and began to water his lawn. Another brought out a set of wrenches, and, after setting his car radio to a Cleveland Indians baseball game, threw open the hood of his Pontiac and began working on the engine.

A little after six a blue Chevrolet with a dented fender entered the drive of the Arnos house. It didn't go as far as the garage, but stopped parallel to the front door. A woman got out. She had short hair, wore sandals, slacks and a blouse. She went to the door, unlocked it and disappeared inside.

Five minutes later she came out again, this time in sneakers, close-fitting shorts and a khaki tank top. A yapping little Yorkshire on a leash tugged her toward the lawn.

The dog must have been cooped up all day; it took a long piss against a tree while the woman lit a cigarette, inhaled deeply, then distractedly surveyed the street. She looked right at me, but she didn't react—the setting sun was in her eyes. When the dog was finished she gave the leash a yank, and started walking down the block.

Through the mirror I watched her walk to the corner, then cross the street and start back toward where I was parked. She was following the sidewalk that ran right beside my car, was moving up on me at a steady pace. I stopped watching the mirror, afraid of catching her eye. I just sat, pretending to read my paper. Then, just as she strode by, I turned to look.

She was moving too fast; I didn't catch her face. But she didn't look at all like Kim from the back. She had a good figure, maybe a little stout, but shapely and defined. Her bare arms looked strong and her legs were good. I had the feeling she worked out—she carried herself that way. Her short hair, dark brown and thick, was brushed back, butch style, on either side. She was far too young to be Kimberly's mother. I estimated her age at from thirty-three to thirty-five.

I watched her cross the street, mount her lawn, then allow the dog a final piss. She lit another cigarette, took a couple of puffs, then, pulling at the dog, reentered the house.

Nothing happened for an hour. The sky darkened. I could see the flicker of TV sets through windows up and down the block. Finally a TV went on in the Arnos house. I was getting pretty tired of sitting in my car, but decided to wait the situation out. My hope was that Kim would drive up just in time for dinner. If she did, I wasn't sure what I'd do. Probably nothing—but at least I'd know that she was there.

I ended up waiting until 10:30 P.M. Very little happened. At 9:30 the woman came out again with the dog, waited just long enough for it to piss, then pulled it back inside the house. Lights went out in the downstairs rooms, and then finally in the bedroom on the second floor. I was hungry and tired, and everyone in the neighborhood seemed to be going to bed, so I found my way to Buckeye Road, then found a White Tower restaurant at the edge of a parking lot. I used the men's room, then ate alone at the counter, listening to the cook, thin and pasty-faced with bad skin and a broken nose, tell me how AA had saved his life.

I was exhausted when I arrived back at the Devora. The vacancy sign flashed vigorously on and off. My room smelled musty, and the air conditioning wasn't working as promised. I took a quick shower, crawled naked upon the upper sheet, then lay sweating in the hot night air asking myself what I was doing in this dreadful place.

I was back on the block at 7:00 A.M. It seemed a smart move to vary my routine, so I parked a little farther away this time, facing the house instead of setting myself up to watch it in the mirror.

The woman emerged with her dog a little after nine, and this time I was able to see her face. She wasn't ugly, but wasn't handsome either. She had tough squat Slavic features that seemed to go with the tough tone she'd used with me on the phone.

Still there was something attractive about her. I tried to put my finger on what it was. Perhaps it was "presence." She walked with confidence, like a woman at ease with herself. She was not at all sultry, nor in any other way did she resemble Kim. But still, in her moment of need, Kim had called her. I wanted to know why.

I also had the feeling she didn't care much for the dog. She handled it as if it were a nuisance. She always lit a cigarette when she exited the house. Then she stood taking deep draws while the dog took its pee, giving me the impression her thoughts were far away.

She came out again at 10:30, and this time she was dressed in a blouse and slacks. She seemed irritable as she gave the dog a quick perfunctory walk. Then she put it back in the house, shut the door, got into her car and drove off down the block.

No question in my mind that Kim wasn't living in the house, so there seemed little point in continuing to stake it out. When the woman left, I waited until she reached the corner. Then I started up and followed.

We drove for about ten minutes to a shopping mall not far from my motel. She parked in the lot, walked to a building and entered a door between two shops. There was a big glass window on the second floor, and a sign that said SOUTH SIDE HEALTH CLUB. I parked, got out of my car, and walked to the door. It opened directly onto stairs that led up to the gym.

I went back to my car and repositioned it. I wanted to see what was happening on that upper floor. The light was perfect—the sun poured directly into the front part of the room. After a few minutes I saw Ms. Arnos, dressed in exercise clothes, working out on a Nautilus machine.

She must have done a standard Nautilus circuit, for she emerged, her hair wet from a shower, slightly more than an hour after she'd gone in. She got back into her car and drove out of the mall. Again I waited, then followed.

This time the task was a little more difficult, for she turned onto a busy street, congested with buses and trucks. Soon we were out of the residential area, moving rapidly toward downtown Cleveland.

As I followed her I kept back as best I could: it would be better to lose her than have her recognize my car. But again I was fortunate. When she drove into a parking lot on East Ninth, I found another lot directly across the street. The attendant at her lot greeted her like a regular customer. We both parked and emerged at the same time. She strode by me, then turned and started walking toward Euclid Avenue. I took off after her on foot.

She was walking fast, glancing occasionally at her watch, like a woman with an appointment to keep. It was nearly 12:30. The lunch-hour crowds, office workers and shoppers, thronged the broiling streets. Catching up with her, trailing her by three strides, I could see that sweat now bound her blouse against her back.

She turned off Euclid, walked a block along a side street, then turned again onto a short sharply angled alley. There was a porno shop there, and, across and a little farther on, a lounge with a blue-and-white neon sign above the door that announced GIRLS*TOPLESS*GIRLS.

She paused outside the lounge, glanced at her watch, then took a final drag on her cigarette. Then she threw the butt on the sidewalk, crushed it with her heel, and entered.

I didn't want to follow her in, not until I knew if she was going to stay. I walked to the end of the block, turned, leaned against the building at the corner, and brought my Leica to my eye.

A deep shadow cast by an office building cut diagonally across the bend in the alley. I liked the composition; it was strong and architectural. I took three shots, bracketing my exposures, then walked back toward the lounge.

Had she met someone there for lunch? The windows were blocked, I couldn't see inside, but it didn't look like a place that served food. I still had a problem about going in; if I ran into her face-to-face, a later approach could be difficult. I decided to wait inside the porno shop.

It was, I imagine, like most other sex shops around, not that I've visited all that many. Racks on the walls displayed books and magazines, organized by proclivity. There was a small display of intimate items: dildoes, black silk panties, stuff like that. The cashier sat behind a register on a raised platform beside the door. Fat and bored, the butt of a dead cigar clenched between his teeth, he glanced at me, then turned his attention to a fish-eye security mirror mounted at the far end of the room.

There were half a dozen men in business suits breathing heavily, studying the merchandise. A black man wearing a coin apron stood before a darkened room in back. Behind him I could see a row of video booths. Moans, issuing from the various sound tracks, merged into one miserable low-pitched sexual growl.

I walked back to the front of the store. I wanted to keep my eyes on the door to the lounge. I flipped through a couple of magazines. As always when I look at porn, I was struck by the poor quality of the photography.

The pictures said nothing, the models looked embarrassed, and their poses were awkward, as if the photographer had commanded them to freeze. Occasionally I saw a pretty face, or an attempt to frame a scene, but there was always something wrong: the lighting was too harsh, the content too blatant, or there was no passion or feeling in the shot. Porn is about skin, and yet, curiously, the skin in porn invariably looks bad.

I spent fifteen minutes in the store. Customers came and went, and several browsers moved to the video booths in back. Finally I went to the counter and looked up at the cashier. He slowly lowered his eyes.

"I'm from out of town," I said. "Do you have a local guide?"

"What kind of guide?"

"Guide to the action," I said.

He rubbed his sleeve across his nose. "Nothing like that here." He looked at my camera. "Like to take pictures? That what you like to do?"

"Yeah," I said. "I like to take pictures. Know where I can take a few?"

"Intimate poses?" I nodded. "They got girls in the joint around the corner. They'll split their beavers for you, but they stay behind the glass."

"What about that place across the street?" I asked.

He turned to look. "Topless joint? So it's tittie you're after. Yeah, they probably let you shoot in there you tip 'em well enough."

At first, when I entered the lounge, I could barely see; the room was dark except for a small well-lit stage in the center of the U-shaped bar. Two girls were at work, a white girl and a light-skinned black, naked except for scanty G-strings, halfheartedly bumping and grinding in time to an electronic throb. There was the faint aroma of girls' sweat in the air. Drawn in by this and by the light, I took a seat. Fifteen or so men were seated around the U, some watching the dancers with bored blank faces, others gazing at them with fascinated eyes.

"Drink?"

I looked down. The bartender was standing just in front of me. It was Ms. G. Arnos, and she was stripped to the waist, bare breasts jutting out from her torso, a pair of firm hard cups like the kind you used to see on the fronts of Cadillacs.

"Beer, please."

"What kind?"

"Light."

"Draft or bottle?"

"I'm from out of town. Don't know the local brands."

"Erin Brew is pretty good," she said.

I smiled at her. "Make it Erin, then." She didn't smile back. When she turned, I noticed the muscular definition of her back.

Though I wasn't prepared for it, it seemed an ideal situation— I'd yet to meet a bartender who wouldn't talk. But when I gave her a lavish tip for my beer, she pocketed it with a brisk nod and walked away.

There was a certain surliness about her that belied her topless state. If being topless meant one was reduced to being a sex object, she was doing everything possible to neutralize the erotic effect. The girls on the stage might flaunt their boobies, wiggle them in a customer's face, but as far as she was concerned, if you ogled hers, you'd get nothing but an icy stare.

I slowly drank down two beers. After a while the place thinned out. At 2:30, when the dancers took a break, G. Arnos appeared again and asked if I wanted something else.

"Sure," I said. "I'd like to talk." She looked at me with disgust. "Another beer, then, please."

She brought me another beer, but this time, when I tipped her, she nodded in a more appreciative way, and, instead of retreating to her sink, stood facing me, waiting for me to speak.

"As I said—I'm from out of town."

"Yeah, you did say that."

"Name's Jim Lynch."

She looked at my offered hand, took it and gave it a shake.

"Grace Arnos," she said.

"Hi, Grace."

"Hi, Jim."

"Buy you a drink?"

"Don't mind if you do." She reached under the bar, pulled out a bottle of Erin, opened it and poured it into a mug.

"Well, here's to Cleveland," I said, clicking her mug with mine.

"Isn't that a joke?"

"Don't know," I said. "The town doesn't seem so bad. Not half so bad as you hear."

"Where you from, Jim?"

"Boston."

"Never been there myself. Salesman?"

I nodded.

"What's your line?"

I didn't even have to think about it. "I sell cameras," I said.

She glanced down at my Leica. "Noticed that when you came in. Nice little piece of hardware. Said to myself: 'Grace, that's no Kodak. Not that.' Have a look?"

I took it from around my neck, and placed it on the bar. I could tell by the way she picked it up that she wasn't used to having a camera in her hands. But I was impressed by the confidence with which she held it; she wasn't intimidated by it at all. She brought it up to her eye, then pointed it at me.

"Hey! Smile!" She made a clicking sound with her teeth, then handed it back.

A couple of seconds passed before it hit me: the way she said "Hey!" was just the way Kim said it, exactly the same. I must have been staring at her because she looked unnerved. "Something the matter?" she asked.

"Nothing. Just wondering—"

"What?"

"Whether you'd let me take you out to dinner."

She looked at me hard, as if she was trying to read my mind. I met her eyes straight on.

120

"Just 'cause I work this joint, that shouldn't give you any ideas."

"No ideas, Grace. Just a lonely guy in a strange city looking to make a friend. I can buy a bottle tonight, go back to my motel, drink and watch TV. Or I can take a nice lady out to a restaurant, have a couple drinks and talk. I'm not thinking of anything more than that."

She studied me awhile longer. "Lot of guys come in—they're not all that nice. I look them in the eye, they're staring at my boobs. But you—you strike me different. I thought that since you walked in. Had this feeling you were looking at my face. Nothing wrong with my tits, mind you. But they're not for grabs—not in here they're not. And not later neither . . . unless I put them in your hand." She grinned. "Now, if all that's all okay with you, you can take me out. I could use a decent restaurant meal. Where you staying?"

"Devora Motel," I said.

"I know the dump. Not far from mine. I'll be leaving here around 5:45. I do some errands, go home, change, walk my dog, that kind of crap. So suppose I pick you up around seven? We'll go to a lounge I know. If it goes good, we'll go on to eat."

Walking back to the parking lot, I couldn't believe my luck. Not only had I met her, I'd actually gotten myself a date. I congratulated myself on my approach: lonely salesman, low key, persistent and polite.

She wasn't at all what I'd expected. A topless bartender at a topless bar—that in itself was bizarre. But there was more that interested me: her working-class style, her direct no-nonsense manner, the morose distracted way she smoked and walked her dog, and the searching way she looked me in the eye.

Grace radiated strength and confidence, which might explain why Kim had turned to her when things got dangerous in New

York. Did Grace know where Kim was now? If I was clever enough I might find out.

Some of my ebullience left me, however, when I drove up to the Devora. There could be a problem if Grace came to the office and asked for "Mr. Lynch." I hadn't given her my real name just in case Kimberly had mentioned me. I'd felt the camera around my neck was bad enough.

I sat in my car pondering what to do. Finally I made up my mind. I walked to the office, where, despite the fans, the clerk's shirt was wringing wet.

"If it's about the air conditioning," he said, "expect to have it on by five."

"I hope so," I said. "I nearly suffocated last night."

"I'm sorry, sir."

"That's okay, but now I've got a little problem you can help me with."

He was all ears as I outlined my difficulty. A newly met lady friend would be visiting, and, being married and discreet, I'd given her another name. When she came by and asked for "Mr. Lynch," there was twenty dollars in it if he'd ring me in my room.

"Twenty dollars?"

"Make it thirty." I laid the cash on the counter.

He stared down at my three tens. "Yes, sir, Mr. Lynch!"

Grace arrived right on time. She was wearing an attractive linen blouse, which made it all right, I figured, to stare a little at her chest.

"Seen much of Cleveland?" she asked as she pulled out of the motel.

"Not much," I said. "Haven't had the time."

"Think your wallet can stand it if we go a little fancy?"

"Sure. Where do you want to go?"

"Shaker Heights."

We drove for almost half an hour. She did most of the talking. She described what it was like to live in Cleveland—though she'd been born and raised there, she didn't like the city much. She felt trapped, she said, but didn't have an alternative, at least for now. If she could have her way, she'd live in a warm tropical place. She'd spent a year in Florida once, but then she'd moved back when things had soured for her there.

She liked being a bartender—it was a job she knew how to do. Normally she worked the night shift, but this was summer, vacation time, so this particular week she was filling in days. As for being topless, that was the required costume for the job. Personally she didn't care. She had nothing to be ashamed of, and it was actually comfortable, what with all the heat and humidity the last few months.

The ambience at the bar where she took me was a far cry from the place where she worked. An attractive young woman, in a long evening dress, sat at a white piano playing Cole Porter tunes. The air conditioning worked, the lighting was subdued, and the customers looked affluent and relaxed. A buzz of lively chatter and the tinkle of cocktail glasses and ice played against the music and filled the room with a sophisticated hum.

"What do you think?" she asked, after she ordered a champagne cocktail.

"Pretty nice," I said.

"Yeah. And special for me too. I feel real nostalgic whenever I come in here. Fell in love here once. In this very room."

"What happened?"

"The usual."

"What's that?"

"Oh, you know—it lasted awhile, then it ended." She pulled out a cigarette. I lit it for her. She inhaled, then pensively stirred her drink. She looked at me. "You're a nice guy."

"Thanks. I try to be."

"Which is why I'm going to tell you something personal, which you may not be too happy to hear."

"Go ahead."

"I like all kinds of people. But romantically speaking it's different. Given a choice between a guy and a gal—I'll usually take the girl."

"No problem," I said. "I already figured that."

"You did? Really? That's because you're from the East."

"I told you, Grace—I wasn't looking for sex."

"Appreciate that. Always feel better once that's settled." She took another long draw, then stubbed out her cigarette.

"The person you fell in love with here—was she a girl?" I asked.

"Yeah, that she certainly was." Grace grinned and shook her head.

"Hard being gay in Cleveland?"

"Little bit. But people don't mess with me."

"They accept you."

"Don't know if they 'accept' exactly. But they know I don't take any shit."

The girl at the piano was playing "I Get a Kick out of You."

Grace nodded to the music. "Love this tune. Makes me feel, I don't know—kind of squishy inside. . . ."

We ate dinner at a little Italian place in the Murry Hill section just above Western Reserve University. It was the kind of inexpensive graduate-student joint you don't find easily in New York these days—small, friendly, with Neapolitan cuisine, dishes like chicken cacciatore and eggplant parmigiana, and that wonderful old cliché, a candle stuck in a Chianti bottle on a red-and-white checked tablecloth.

I was pleased with the way Grace had opened up; all she needed, it seemed, was a good empathetic listener. So I worked hard playing that role, lavishing her with compassion, telling her about an imaginary lesbian couple I knew in Boston, wonderful creative women, trying for years to adopt a child, but people were intolerant. Wasn't it ridiculous? But that's the way people were. They always hated what they didn't understand, and sometimes they hated because they understood too well.

She looked up at me as she was spooning up the last of her spumoni. "I may not have sex with guys, but I give a hell of a mean massage. Worked as a masseuse for a couple of years. Still do it a little on the side to make extra bucks." She winked. "Interested?"

"Sure, I'm interested," I said, "so long as we don't have to do it at my motel."

She laughed. "Course not. Got a room specially set up for it at the house. No charge either, not for you. You've been real nice. Fair exchange, seems to me, for a good evening on the town."

We stopped first at my motel, so I could pick up my car. I rather liked the idea of openly following her, without having to worry about being spotted. She fascinated me: a brassy balls-up dame tending an emotional wound. Had Kim played sultry "femme" to Grace's earthy "diesel"? I couldn't imagine two women more opposite.

Even while Grace was unlocking the door of her house I could hear the dog yelping inside. When it saw me, it stood up on its hind legs and barked.

"Heidi! Stop that! Don't bark at the nice man!" Heidi lowered herself and sniffed suspiciously at my shoe. "She's into feet." Grace smiled. "Heavy crotch worship too."

Grace quickly attached a leash to Heidi's collar, and headed for the door. "Be back in a minute. Make yourself at home. Bathroom's upstairs if you need it." Then she took the dog outside.

Heading up the stairs, I prayed Heidi had a very full bladder, full enough to allow me a good look around. As it happened, I hit pay dirt as soon as I entered Grace's bedroom. There was a collection of framed photos nicely arranged on the dresser. One of them, a color shot, showed Grace and Kim sitting together cross-legged on a boat, smiling and gleeful, arms buddy style across each other's shoulders.

I trembled a bit as I picked up the picture. It appeared to have been taken in Southern waters. There were palms on the shoreline and the kind of waterfront condos one finds all up and down the Florida coast.

But the most striking thing about the shot, the thing that made my heart beat fast, was the curious position of their hands. Not the hands they used to cup each other, but the hands that lay free in their laps. The forefinger of each was pointed directly at the other's ankle, which seemed to be the source of all their glee.

"Jim?" It was Grace, returned with Heidi, calling to me from downstairs. I set the photograph back down on the bureau.

"Up here."

"When you're ready, come down to the cellar," she yelled.

I picked up the picture again, squinted at a section of it, trying to make it out. Grace seemed to be pointing to the very spot on Kimberly's ankle where she had that curious tattoo. Kim had told me it had been done in Florida by an Oriental woman. Grace had told me she'd spent a year in Florida. The initials were right too: *K* for Kimberly, *G* for Grace.

.   .   .

126

I found her in the cellar in a kind of workout room. There were free weights, an exercise bicycle and a set of arm pulleys attached to the wall. She stood before a professional massage table, covered with dark brown vinyl. Heidi sat quietly panting by her feet.

"Strip down and get on," she said, giving the table a slap. "Be with you in a sec. Going upstairs to change."

I must have known instinctively what I was going to do, because even as I undressed I started making friends with the dog.

"Nice Heidi! Good Heidi!" I patted the little monster on the head. "Good little girl! We're going to be friends. Aren't we? *Aren't we, girl?* Yes we are. *Oh, yes we are!*"

I could hear Grace moving around upstairs, so I still had a little time to check around. I took off everything but my shorts and shoes, and then explored the cellar.

There was just one other room, a cavernous space that contained the furnace and the washer-dryer. There was a window in this room, a typical cellar window, narrow but big enough to crawl through. I found a stepladder, set it in front of the window, mounted it and undid the latch.

I tried the window. It opened easily. I undid the latches on the exterior screen, then closed the window, leaving it unlocked.

I was back in the massage room in plenty of time. I could hear Grace beginning to descend the stairs. I quickly slipped out of my shoes, set them on the floor in front of Heidi, and then, while the dog began to sniff, hid my watch behind the barbells. When Grace walked in I was in my shorts playing with Heidi on my hands and knees.

"What's going on?" she asked.

I glanced up. "Getting friendly."

Grace knelt to pat Heidi's head. She was barefoot, and had changed into a tank top and shorts. I could clearly see the tattoo on her ankle—entwined initials, *K* and *G*, identical with Kim's.

I think it really hit me then. Of course I'd known that they'd been lovers from the moment I'd seen the photographs upstairs, so seeing the actual tattoo was merely confirmation. But there's something about a shared tattoo, an irreversible engraving upon the flesh, that far transcends a brief affair. To have been tattooed together, to decide to go through life bearing each other's initials, was not some kind of casual choice. It was serious commitment.

Grace placed an Ella Fitzgerald record on the stereo, then motioned me onto the table. I mounted it, and when I was lying face down, she asked me how I liked to be massaged.

"What are my choices?"

"Light, medium or hard."

"What's best?"

"How about a taste of each?" she said. And then without nonsense she pulled down my shorts.

She was a talented masseuse; I doubt I've been in better hands. She began on my shoulders and neck, slowly worked her way down my back, kneading and chopping until she reached the soles of my feet, then turned me over and started up my legs.

All this was done in time to Ella Fitzgerald singing scat, just about the sexiest vocal music I know. By the time she reached my thighs I was pretty excited. She flicked my hardening cock with her finger, then hoisted herself upon me and wiggled against me so the material of her shorts caressed my groin.

"Hung, aren't we?" she asked, working me beneath her buttocks.

"Well, I do like to think so," I said, gasping. "I like what you're doing . . . very much."

"That's the idea. For a massage like this, I usually charge forty bucks. Manual release is fifteen extra. If that's what you want I'll give it to you for free."

That was *not* what I wanted. To get a hand job from Kim's old lover—the idea horrified me! But how to decline without hurting Grace's feelings? Quickly I thought of a way.

"Tell you, Grace—I appreciate your offer, but that's really not what I want. The reason, if you're interested, is because I don't think it's what *you* want. So why don't we just keep it straight."

She nodded. "Know something, Jim? You're a real nice guy." She lifted herself off me, then continued the massage. When she was finished, she motioned for me to pull on my shorts. Then, while I dressed, she lit a cigarette.

"You're a lot more considerate than most of them, I can tell you. If more men were like you I might just change my preference." She laughed. "Well, I don't really mean that. I think I was born this way. I like girls far too much to ever want to switch to guys." Her eyes sparkled. "But then, who knows? I mean, sex is such a weird thing, isn't it? Yeah, I think it's just about the strangest weirdest thing there is. . . ."

The air conditioning was finally working at the Devora; my room was now excessively chilled. I lay in bed, huddled under my grungy blanket, trying to come to grips with the day's experience.

Following Grace, meeting her at the topless bar, seeing the picture of Kim—all that had been extraordinary. But the massage had been the strangest part of it, for a reason that was only clear to me in retrospect. Conscious that Grace's hands had also many times touched Kim, I felt that being massaged by her had somehow closed a circle. It was as if Kim and I were now linked through the medium of Grace, as if Kim herself had been with us in that cellar room.

First thing the next morning, I went to a five-and-ten and purchased a cheap quartz watch. Then I drove to Grace's neighborhood and parked on a cross street a block from her house.

I waited there until she drove by, let her go a block, then followed. I was particularly careful this time, since now she knew my car.

When I saw her drive into the shopping mall, I turned and drove back to her house. I knew it would take her an hour to complete the Nautilus circuit, and it was likely she would drive on to work from there.

But there was always the possibility she would return home first, so I gave myself forty-five minutes of safe time. If she came back unexpectedly or a suspicious neighbor called the police, I'd claim I was looking for my watch. A pretty thin story, but it would have to do. I was taking a chance, but it would be worth it if it led me to Kim.

Deciding against a surreptitious approach, I drove aggressively into Grace's driveway, parked parallel to her door, went to it, tried it, shouted "Good morning" to the dog, then shrugged and walked around casually to the back.

Here I removed the basement-window screen, pushed the window open, and, being careful of my Leica, crawled into the laundry room. I went to the workout room, retrieved my watch from behind the barbells, replaced it with the cheap dime-store watch I'd bought, then ascended to the ground floor.

By this time Heidi was going bonkers. I greeted her and started to play.

"Hi, Heidi! Remember me? I'm the *nice* man you met last night. Yes, Heidi! Yes, good girl! *Yes! yes! yes!*"

I soon had her in bitch heaven, wasting five minutes of my forty-five. With Heidi at my heels, I bounded up the stairs and into Grace's bedroom, where I snatched the photograph off the dresser, removed it from its frame, took it to the window, then brought out my camera and took its picture. Then I sat down at the bedroom desk and began to make a search.

It didn't take me long to find the two letters from Kim. They bore recent postmarks, and a Key West, Florida, post office box number as return address.

I didn't stop to read them, just took them to the window, lay them down carefully in the light, and photographed them. Then I returned them to their envelopes, returned the envelopes to the proper drawer, returned the photograph to its frame on the dresser, and checked to make sure everything looked the way it had.

I glanced at my watch. I was surprised: I'd used only fifteen minutes of my allotted time. So far so good. Now it was time to go. But downstairs in the laundry room I panicked.

The window was too high. I couldn't climb out of it directly from the floor. Which meant I'd have to use the stepladder, which meant I'd have to leave it below the window, which meant that when Grace found the window unlatched, she'd know someone had broken in.

But why, I wondered, should I exit through the window, when I was now in a position to use the door? I'd noticed that Grace never bothered to double-lock—she just shut the door when she left.

I pulled in the basement-window screen, latched it shut, shut the window and locked it too. I returned the stepladder to its rightful place, and then, followed closely by Heidi, went up to the main floor of the house.

So easy. Just open the door and leave. Too easy, as it turned out, for when I opened the door, Heidi gave a shrill little bark, wagged her tail and scooted out.

For a moment I stared after her, disbelieving this ridiculous turn of events. Then, knowing I was now in very big trouble, I grabbed her leash off the coatrack, and rushed outside myself.

Heidi was squatting in the front yard taking an unexpected mid-morning pee. When I came out, her eyes engaged with mine, and a cheerful expression lit up her hairy little face. I crept up on her, but she jumped away just before I could catch her. Then she squatted again, and eyed me cannily. She thought I wanted to play.

"Come here, Heidi, damnit. Come here, goddamnit!"

She peered at me strangely, confused by the displeasure in my voice.

"Here, girl. Here, little girl . . ." I urged and coaxed. She approached me warily, suspicious of my intentions. When she was close enough, I grabbed her by her collar and quickly attached her leash.

*Thank God!* But when I looked back at the house, I was filled with new despair. The front door was shut. I was now locked out. When I looked down at Heidi, she cocked her head. Oh yes, she was quite amused.

I was worried. This was a lot worse than leaving the stepladder by the basement window. I'd been lucky with Grace, I'd found out where Kim was living, but now I'd bungled the job.

"Locked out, are you, mister?" Dread ran through me as I turned. A woman, hands on her hips, was observing me from the porch next door. She wore a powder-blue terry-cloth robe, and her unruly hair was streaked with gray.

"I sure am, ma'am," I said, smiling, trying to make light of the situation. "Grace is going to kill me for this."

The woman made a kind of disgusted face, then pushed out her lips. "I know where she keeps the extra key."

"You do?"

"Seen her use it. It's in one of them potted plants by the door."

"Oh, that's great," I said. "I was thinking I'd have to call a locksmith."

"The big pot in the center. One with the ferns, I think."

Heidi started yapping while I ran my hand through the topsoil around the ferns. Soon my fingers felt something smooth and metallic. I held the key up and turned back to the neighboring house.

"Thank you, ma'am. Awfully grateful for your help."

She stared at me, curious. Is this the point, I wondered, when she asks me who I am?

"Poor little doggie," she said, shaking her head. "Cooped up all day long with the windows shut. Doesn't get nearly enough exercise. Not *nearly* enough." She stared at me for emphasis, then sniffed and withdrew into her house.

I got Heidi safely stowed away, closed the door, returned the key to its hiding place, and got into my car. Then I hesitated. The neighbor woman would tell Grace about the incident, and as soon as she described me, Grace would know who the intruder was. Then Grace would look for me at the Devora, and then she'd find out my real name.

That was something I couldn't risk, so I decided to take another chance. I mounted the neighboring porch and rang the bell. The woman appeared. We spoke through the screen door.

"Sorry to bother you again, ma'am," I said. "I sure would appreciate it if you wouldn't tell Grace I locked myself out."

She shook her head. "Haven't spoken to the woman in six, seven years—not since she and my husband had the row. So don't worry, mister—I won't be talking to her, not just 'count of this. But I do feel sorry for that little tyke. It's a crime the way she leaves him all alone. Please come back again, if you can, and give the poor little thing a walk."

"I sure will try," I promised.

It was only while driving back to the Devora that I considered how one crime can lead to another, how a real criminal might have killed that woman just because she'd seen his face. But I wasn't a real criminal—I was just a guy searching for a girl. And now, thanks to some daring and ingenious housebreaking, I'd found out where that girl was.

My plan was to check out of the Devora, then fly direct to Florida. But first I called my number in New York, and activated my answering machine.

There was a message from the man with the threatening voice. "How you doing, pigshit?" he asked. Detective Scotto had also called; he wanted me to call him back. But the message that caused me to change my plans was the one from Aaron Greene: "Call me, boychik. Got your photographer." I immediately phoned him at his store.

"Yeah, we found him, Geoffrey," Aaron said. "Sid Walzer, the Pentax repair man, recognized him from your composite. His name's Adam Rakoubian. 'Dirty Adam.' Sleazeball, from what I hear."

"Name sounds Armenian. What's sleazy about him?"

"The way he operates. Approaches young women on the street, teenage, underage—he doesn't care. Claims he's this famous fashion photographer, then lays on the charm. 'Hey, gorgeous!' 'You're beautiful, sweetheart!' 'How 'bout you pose for me, darling?' That jerky line. But funny thing—about fifty percent of the time it actually works. He gets them up to his studio, and once up there they're dogmeat for his lens."

"What does he do? Rape them?"

"In a way, I guess, it is a kind of rape. He loosens them up, breaks them down, then talks them into taking off their clothes. Has them sign an airtight release, gives them fifteen, twenty bucks, then poses them cutie-pie style, split beaver, like that, claiming he'll get them a *Playboy* centerfold."

"Lots of guys promise that."

"Yeah, but at least they try. He doesn't. He sells the stuff direct to hard-core porn collectors."

"Charming," I said.

"Oh, he is, Geoffrey. Scum of your illustrious profession. Sid says he works out of a district studio, somewhere on West Seventeenth. So that's it. Hope it helps. Gotta go now. Come see us when you get back."

After he hung up I called the airline and booked the next flight back to New York. Then, for a moment, I thought about phoning Scotto. But it was me, not the cops, who'd tracked Rakoubian down. And the matter of why he'd been surreptitiously photographing Kim and me was something I thought I'd do better settling with him myself.

I had a couple of hours to spare before check-in time, so I drove downtown and went into the topless joint. The clients looked the same, the same two girls were dancing on the stage, and Grace, bare to the waist, greeted me with a smile from the bar.

"Well, look who's here. Get you a beer?"

I ordered one for each of us, then told her I was leaving in an hour.

"Something wrong? Thought you were staying a couple days."

"Some nonsense at the home office," I said. "Have to go back and straighten it out."

"So you thought you'd come by and have a final look-see at my tits?"

"Sure, Grace. And yours are great. But I won't insult you by telling you to waste them on a man."

"Don't worry, I won't."

"I know you won't. You're your own woman. Look, I don't know you very well, but it feels like you're a friend. That's why I came— to tell you that, and also to say good-bye."

She gazed hard at me then, as she had the day before. I wondered if she saw through my hypocrisy. But of course she had no inkling why I wanted to graciously terminate our relationship.

"Well, thanks," she finally said, "that's pretty nice. I feel the same myself." She paused. "Guess this is it, huh? We probably won't see each other again. . . ."

I shrugged.

"Good luck, Jim."

"Luck, Grace."

Then I stepped back and took a picture of her, standing there topless behind the bar, looking butch and tough and in control, and also maybe a little lost and hurt.

There was some kind of air inversion over New York. The city was covered by haze. It hung so heavy and low, I couldn't see anything while we circled for thirty minutes in a holding pattern, and the stewardesses strode the aisle pouting, and the pilot made lethargic comments that made me think we were never going to land.

Finally we broke through and made our approach, and then we landed rough and after that everyone was irritable. We surged into the aisle, then stood restlessly like penned-up sheep, waiting for the door to open and grant us our release.

The airport was like a madhouse. Many flights were delayed and thousands of people were milling about, sweating, confused, hauling baggage, asking dazed airline employees what was going on. I fought my way out to the ramp where a harassed dispatcher was calling up taxis and loading people in.

The cab I got was a wreck, but I had no choice—it was either take it or go back to the end of the line. It was a bottom-of-the-barrel fleet job, dirty interior, split seats, no air conditioning and one of those plastic dividing screens that make you feel as if you're in a cell. When I asked the driver to turn the radio down, he pretended he couldn't hear. He took off like a rocket, but minutes out of La Guardia he ran into a massive traffic jam. Then, as I watched the meter tick, he inched his way through the fetid sulfurous air. Two hours and forty bucks later, he delivered me to the corner of Nassau and Ann, where the old wino, who made his summer residence there, waved to me as I paid the bastard off.

No break-ins this time, no notes under my door, no further indications of lye attacks. The mutilated murals of Kim were just where I'd left them, there was another message from Scotto expressing annoyance that I hadn't returned his call, but nothing from the guy who'd threatened me. Perhaps he was waiting for my return.

I pulled out my phone book and looked up the name Adam Rakoubian. Then I dialed his number and got his machine. Rakoubian's voice sounded slimy. He was out for the rest of the day, but he'd be back around ten, he said. I was invited to leave a message, but I declined. I had another idea.

I ordered in some Chinese food, then went into my darkroom and quickly developed my Cleveland roll. By the time the food arrived I had made up prints of Kimberly's letters. And even though the prints were wet, I read them while I ate.

The letters weren't long. In the first she thanked Grace for her support, and for wiring her money. It was off-season in Key West, things were slow, but she'd found herself a waitressing job. "Should tide me over till things calm down up North," she wrote.

The second letter was far more revealing:

". . . no remorse. Tried our best, but we were up against *devils*. Who could have predicted the way it turned out and that they'd do *that* to Shadow? God, I miss her! She took all the heat. As for the others—Adam's a skunk, with a yellow streak down his back. Knew that but didn't factor it in. And shouldn't have underestimated D. One day I'm going to stick it to him and Mrs. Z! You know me, Grace—you know I can hold a grudge. Have fantasies about that. Big bad fantasies. I'll get them both for what they did! I promise you. *I will!*

"Meantime, here I am, in 'paradise'—remember how we called it that? And being here, at 'the end of the line,' alone, without you, I think of all our happy times. There's a memory around every corner. The walks we took. The swims. The fishing and all the lying around. Especially that! The smell of Key West aloe on your skin. Remember the Southernmost Tip? Reeling by it at midnight on that crazy motorcycle, then circling back and kissing, then making love on the rocks below. And Mrs. Chang—I looked for her. Seems she moved to Tampa. Just going by her place reminded me of us and all our vows. Well, that's about it for now. I'll call you Sunday night. Take care of yourself. I love you. Always. Your loving loving K."

She'd drawn three X's and a little smile beside her name. I put down the still-wet prints, and then I began to shake.

She knew about Rakoubian! "Adam's a skunk," she'd written. And who the hell was "D," whom she'd so badly underestimated? What had she been up to, and why had she confided everything to Grace? I had been her most recent lover. Why hadn't she written to me?

The answer, of course, was obvious: she and I had had a liaison; she and Grace shared a permanent tattoo. All that lovey-dovey stuff about making love on the rocks in Key West—that tortured me, made me furious and even more determined to track her down.

At 10:15 I called Rakoubian again. The phone message started, then he broke in live.

"Yes—?" There was a high-pitched whine from the machine.

"Mr. Rakoubian."

"Let me turn this off." The whining stopped. "Still there?"

"Still here, Mr. Rakoubian. I have your name from Sid Walzer. My name's Jim Lynch. I've seen your work in several collections, and I was wondering if I might see you about buying some prints."

"You're a collector?"

"That's right. The thing is, I'm just passing through town. Leaving very early in the morning. I was hoping we could meet tonight."

"It's pretty late. . . ."

"I know. Sorry about that. I've been tied up in meetings all day."

"Tonight, huh? Well, since you know Sid. . . . Look, if you're serious—"

"I'm serious, Mr. Rakoubian. Very serious."

There was a pause. "Okay. Come over." He gave me the address. "And in case you see something interesting, my suggestion—"

"I know, Mr. Rakoubian. I'll bring my checkbook. Wasn't that what you were going to say?"

It was a typical photo district building, formerly industrial, now converted into studio apartments. You buzzed your way in through the front door, then took a freight elevator up. When you reached your floor, the elevator door slid open, but you still needed a key to unlock the second door that opened onto the corridor.

The normal procedure, when someone knew you were coming, was to unlock that outside elevator door for you, then wait for you in his apartment. I figured Rakoubian would do just that, but in case he didn't I got ready for him on my way up.

I had brought along my oldest Nikon body, an original F model I'd used in Vietnam. It was battered, the brass showed through at the edges, but it could still take a picture. In the elevator I carefully wrapped the strap around my hand. That camera had seen quite a few battles. It was about to see another.

When the elevator stopped I stepped out. As I'd anticipated,

Rakoubian had already unlocked the outer door, and he'd done even better than that: he'd left his own loft door ajar.

Normally I would have knocked before entering. This time I walked straight in. He was sitting on an overstuffed Chesterfield couch, a pudgy man, maybe ten years older than I, shorter but about the same weight, with thick gray hair and unshaven jaws. As I moved toward him, he started to rise. I could tell by the way his eyes enlarged that he knew who I was, and that he was afraid. I reached him before he could stand. Then I pushed him back into his seat.

"Dirty Adam's what they call you. Also shitbag, scumbag, creep."

Sweat broke out on his upper lip. He stared at me, then opened his mouth to protest. I could smell the fear coming off him, and then I recognized him, knew where I'd seen him before. At that crazy restaurant in Tribeca, the one with the souvenir-shop junk mounted on the pedestals, the place Shadow had taken us—Kim had spoken to him at the bar.

I got mad just remembering the way she'd laughed when I'd asked her afterwards who he was. "Just one of your own, Geoffrey. Another photographer."

I pulled back my hand and, with the back of my Nikon, hit him hard across the side of his face. He moaned and fell back. Then he tried to smile; he twisted his mouth into this weird kind of grin as if he expected to be hit again.

I looked down at him. I was shocked at what I'd done. His nose was bleeding, the side of his face was cut, and there was blood oozing from his ear. For a moment I was frightened. Had I really done this to another person? But then some new kind of energy had boiled out of me—I was thrilled. The violence, erupting from deep inside, made me feel good about myself, and clean.

Rakoubian was still groggy but he was trying to smile, as if to

140

show me he'd been hit before and the blow I'd just dealt him hadn't been so bad. So, since he wasn't suffering very much, I hit him again, this time harder than before. His head snapped back, he tried to smile but couldn't. For a moment he sat there immobilized. Then he slowly crumpled and fell onto his side.

I had a quick look around the loft. It wasn't at all like mine. It looked like a movie set Sydney Greenstreet could have inhabited while playing one of his pasha roles, filled with heavy carved furniture, chairs and tables with paws for feet, a lot of brass knickknacks, including a water pipe, and overlapping Oriental rugs.

I opened the front hall closet, found a wire coat hanger, which I straightened and used to bind Rakoubian's ankles, making sure to twist the wire tight.

At one end of the loft there was a section set up for photography. This, I presumed, was where he made dogmeat of the girls. Here I found a roll of gaffer tape, the shiny metallic stuff photographers use to hold up lights. I used this to bind Rakoubian's wrists behind his back, wrapping the tape around them again and again. Then, after checking that I hadn't broken his nose, I slapped a piece of tape across his mouth to keep him quiet while I made a thorough search.

It wasn't like the search I'd made that morning in Cleveland. At Grace's I'd been careful to leave no trace. This was different. I *wanted* to disturb Rakoubian, wanted him to be afraid of me. So I set to work methodically to tear his place apart.

I started with his closet, ripping up his clothing, at the same time getting a sense of who he was. His clothes disgusted me—shiny dark sweat-stained suits, heavy soiled ties, textured white-on-white shirts, black lizard shoes with gold metal clasps.

I found a heavy brocaded maroon silk robe hanging from the back of the bathroom door. It had padded lapels and a tasseled sash and smelled as if a dry cleaning job would do it good.

His medicine cabinet betrayed the same lush sense of self. An entire shelf was loaded with men's colognes. But when I went back to the couch to check on him, I noticed his poor personal hygiene. He was a man who tried to make himself presentable by wearing fancy clothing and slathering on perfume, when all he had to do was take a daily shower, shave and clean the black crescents from his nails.

He was conscious now; his eyes followed me as I walked from his bathroom to his desk. I made a big point of pulling out his desk drawers and turning them onto the floor, then prowling through his papers as if they were garbage—which, to me, of course, they were.

He began struggling, trying to attract my attention, when I started in on his negative files. I found drawer after drawer of Kodachrome slides. I put some on his light table and examined them. They were just as Aaron had described, sleazy soft-focus nudie-cutie stuff and the kind of hard-core beaver material they publish in *Hustler* magazine.

I turned to him. "Where are the pictures?"

He moaned and shook his head.

"The ones you took of me. Tell me, shitface."

He rolled his wounded eyes, then hung his head.

Every commercial photographer I know has his private stash, the personal obsessional photographs he takes for himself. Sometimes the pictures are violent, sometimes they're sexual and sometimes they bear a passing resemblance to art. The big compensation for being an art photographer is that though you make a lot less money than the commercial guys, you're free to work out your obsessions, because your obsessions *are* your work.

I didn't have time to search for Rakoubian's stash, so I thought I'd expedite the process by putting on a little stress. I emptied out several of his slide trays on the floor, then went into his darkroom, found a bottle of undiluted glacial acetic acid, brought it out and sprinkled half of it on top of the slides. I used a broom to stir around the mess. Foul-smelling fumes began to rise as the acid ate away at the chromes. Then I went back to Rakoubian and grabbed hold of his hair.

"Get the point? I'm just beginning. Now, before I make a bonfire of everything you ever shot, I'm going to break a few of your tools."

I got up, went to his equipment shelf, took a look at his cameras. I saw his 6 × 7 Pentax and two snazzy Hasselblads, a 500C/M and a 500ELX.

I scooped up the Pentax, all his Takumar lenses and also a toolbox I found. I hauled all this stuff back to the couch. Then I set to work.

I opened up the back of the Pentax, smashed it against the floor, then dug around inside it with a screwdriver, doing as much damage as I could. Then I took his seven Takumars, lined them up on the floor and attacked each one, front and back, with a hammer. Then I looked at him and grinned like a demon. Tears were gushing from his eyes.

"Going to talk now? Or do I start on the other two?" I grabbed hold of the piece of gaffer tape, and viciously ripped it off his mouth.

He shrieked with pain, then moaned, then struggled to catch his breath. Then he begged me to spare his Hasselblads.

"No bargains," I said. "Where are the pictures?"

He was ready to talk. The pictures, he blubbered, were hidden in the wastebasket under his desk.

"The wastebasket! Don't lie to me!"

"It's true," he screamed. "They're safe there. Last place anyone would look."

"Oh, you're precious, Rakoubian!"

He started to blubber again, begging me to please not kill him, promising he wasn't responsible, that it had all been Kimberly's idea. I taped his mouth again, to shut him up, then went to the desk, upended the wastebasket and searched around through the mess. Beneath a layer of old newspapers, I found a yellow Kodak polycontrast box. There were photographs inside, negatives and prints.

I spent a good twenty minutes studying them. In a way it was like finding the missing pieces of a puzzle. Here were the pictures Rakoubian had taken of me while I'd been shooting Kim. Several matched the pictures I had taken of her, in which Rakoubian had appeared in the background, Pentax to his eye.

There were other pictures of us too, covertly taken through the window of my loft with a telephoto lens. One, taken at night, showed Kim and me about to embrace, silhouettes behind one of the Japanese rice-paper shades I sometimes pull across my windows instead of lowering the blinds.

The problem was I didn't know what the puzzle meant, because I didn't understand the purpose behind Rakoubian's photographic stalking. And I couldn't put together his shots of Kim and me with the other photographs that were also in the box.

Among these were several I can only describe as deeply disturbing. They showed a person with an old man's body fondling himself through his underpants while sitting on what looked to be a throne. The subject's face could not be seen, for he wore a fencing mask. The huge masked head on the wrinkled hairless body suggested something decadent and evil.

There was another set of shots, taken from directly overhead, that showed this man in the process of removing his mask. In the final shot in this series, which I assumed was taken with a hidden camera, his face was fully revealed.

And finally there were shots of this same man, in normal street clothes, entering and exiting various buildings, getting in and out

of limousines and walking rapidly on the street. These also seemed to be candid, and taken on the run.

The subject of all this surreptitious photography looked vaguely familiar. He had thick close-cropped white hair, thin tight lips, an arrogant chin and sharp penetrating eyes. Although I was certain I'd never met him, I had definitely seen his face, perhaps in another photograph.

So, there were two sets of pictures in the box: pictures of me with Kim, and pictures that identified this familiar-looking man as the decadent naked person who wore the mask. But what I couldn't understand was how the two sets were connected.

I went back to Rakoubian and studied him awhile. I wanted to give him the impression I was determining his fate. When I thought I had him fairly well unnerved, I whispered in his oily ear.

"I'm going to take the tape off your mouth, carefully this time, so it doesn't hurt. Then you're going to answer all my questions. You're not going to plead, or blubber, or lie, because if you do I'm going to throw you out the window."

He blinked.

"I'll do that, you see, because now that I've got the photographs, I don't care whether you live or die. You're wondering: What if I tell him everything, and he kills me anyway—what guarantees do I have? You have no guarantees. You only have my word. Can you trust me? Let's put it this way: if you *don't* talk straight when I untape your mouth, you're going down to the street headfirst. Understood?"

When he nodded I took hold of the tape and carefully pulled it from his lips. It hurt him, but not nearly so much as when I'd ripped it off.

After he recovered from his pain, he looked at me as if I were some kind of maniac. And as this was just the impression I wished to encourage, and in fact was how I was feeling, I stared at him maniacally until he spoke.

"What do you want to know?"

"Everything."

"How much do you know already?"

"Assume I know nothing and take it from there."

He looked confused. "Where do I begin?"

"Begin at the beginning," I suggested not unkindly.

He glanced at me, nodded, and then stared out across the damaged room. The shards of his lenses were scattered all around. Perhaps it was the sight of them that finally inspired him to talk.

"It was all Kimberly's idea . . . ." he began.

Once he got going it wasn't easy to stop him. Even with his bloodied face and bound ankles and wrists, he behaved as if he were some kind of star. I didn't bother to disabuse him. I let him digress, elaborate, puff himself up with words, because always, in the background, was his knowledge that I was dangerous. Only a totally crazed photographer would deliberately destroy a fine set of lenses the way I had.

"Kimberly and Shadow—they were part of Mrs. Zeller's group."

"That's 'Mrs. Z'?"

He nodded. "The kids all call her that. She encourages it, no doubt because it makes her sound like a fascinating character. If you knew her, you'd probably agree she is. She's a powerful woman. Extraordinary."

"Way I heard it, she runs an escort service, which makes her just another bordello madam to me."

"She does *not* run an escort service." He was offended. "She's an acting coach, an extremely gifted one. She also offers unique performances for individuals and private groups."

"So it's not 'escorts'—it's 'performances' we're talking about?"

He nodded. "But *what performances*! They've been compared to *Oh! Calcutta!*—but they go much further and they're customized."

He began to tell me, then, about Mrs. Z. He wanted to make sure I understood just how classy a woman she was. I let him talk, meantime trying to cope with the notion of Kim not as call girl but as actress in bizarre little plays.

". . . it began with private parties. Mrs. Z had this group of young people. Kimberly, Shadow, Sonya, a few more, and an equal number of talented males. They were all studying with her, they were young, attractive, they needed money, and they were uninhibited exhibitionists. So, the way it started, she'd get them to work up these sexual vignettes for private dinner groups. Very discreet. To be invited you had to be introduced. Then, after word got around and people began offering her large sums if she'd only include their particular fetish or fantasy, she fixed up the top floor of the building she owns, making it a private little stage. She writes the scripts, rehearses the players, provides costumes and direction. Some of her clients are pretty famous. People you may have heard of. I won't mention any names."

"How do the names Harold and Amanda Duquayne grab you?"

He glanced at me, surprised. Then his eyes turned canny: he would have to be careful; I knew more than I'd been letting on.

"Yes, I've heard talk about them," he said. "That they're very much into that kind of thing. And other downtown people too. To them it's a species of—'performance art.' " He laughed. "That's what they call it. Of course it's only sex. But to justify it, they have to give it a fancy name."

"Anyway?" I said.

"Yeah, anyway. . . ." He seemed surprised at how bored I was. "Kimberly and Shadow were members of the group. And they were good friends too, with Sonya. Do you know about her?" I shook my head. "She was the girl who died."

So two girls were dead. "Died or was killed?"

He shrugged. "It was, as they say . . . 'unfortunate.' According to Mrs. Z, there was some kind of accident, the poor young thing died, nothing could bring her back, and nothing could be gained by pointing fingers or assigning blame. That's what Mrs. Z said. But when Kimberly and Shadow came to me, they said something else."

He paused to blow his nose, which he then wiped on his sleeve. That gesture and the smell of his sweat and the awful jaundiced folds around his eyes made me want to turn away. But I continued to stare at him to keep the pressure on.

"They said the Masked Man did it. And it wasn't the first time he'd done something like that. Kimberly knew about some other girls, real call girls, who'd gotten involved with him and had also been badly hurt. She and Shadow were afraid of him. They wanted to expose him. They wanted justice for Sonya, so they said." He smiled. "Maybe Shadow did want justice. But Kimberly . . ." He shook his head. "She just wanted money."

"I take it they didn't know who he was?"

"*Nobody* knew. Because of his rules. See, when he would appear, he always wore his big fencing mask. Nobody ever saw him without it. No one. *Ever.* Not even Mrs. Z."

He smiled again. He liked his role: the man with the saga to impart.

"The scenes were held in the gutted loft on the top floor of a rotten old building she owns down on Vestry Street. The rot and ruin are very much part of the mystique. Have you any idea of the kind of well-known people, society people and people prominent in the arts—how many of them have traipsed down there and gotten off on the dingy decrepit character of the place?"

Yeah, I told him, I *did* have an idea, then I told him to get to the point. He seemed unduly impressed by the social and celebrity aspects, but what interested me was how come no one had ever seen the Masked Man unmasked.

"Because of how things were arranged," he explained. "Now, the way you normally go in is through the front door. Then you climb four flights of dilapidated stairs. By the time you get to the top you're out of breath. That too is part of it—the entrance is the prologue, as they say.

"But there's a back door, too—a private entrance, which opens off a service alley behind the building. If you enter there you can take a private elevator to the top. That was the door the Masked Man used. He had his own key to it, and he entered only after everyone else was upstairs and the front door was locked. Then he'd come up in the elevator, change in a little dressing room, and make his entrance wearing the mask. When the performance was over, he'd leave before anyone else. We'd have to stay locked in until he was gone."

He looked at me. "To you it probably sounds grotesque. But it wasn't. Not at all. It was—I'm not sure this is the right word—to us it was almost awesome."

*Yeah, awesome.*

"We used to speculate about him. You would too, if you saw this scrawny old guy, practically naked, wearing this peculiar mask, but who seemed to have such an aura about him, to exude such power, command such deference and respect. Who was he? we all wondered. He was *somebody*—that much was sure. *But who?* We didn't know. That was the little riddle Kimberly and Shadow wanted me to solve."

"Let's go back," I said. "If Mrs. Z never saw him, how did they communicate?"

"Only by phone, according to her. No one even knows how he found out about what she did. The first time he was probably brought as someone's guest. And then when he saw what was possible, that, in fact, *anything* was possible if you had enough money and were willing to pay, he got in touch with Mrs. Z and made special arrangements for himself.

"The way she explained it to us, he'd call, outline what he wanted, she'd make some suggestions, they'd come to an agreement, then he'd commission a performance for a particular date. Then he'd come and go unseen, just the way I said, leaving the fee in cash in the changing room. We speculated about the amounts. The kind of things he liked and the fact that they were put on for him alone—for that kind of very private performance, we all thought he probably paid a lot."

"Fine, Rakoubian. Nicely told," I said. "Now, exactly what kinds of things are we talking about here?"

He grinned. "Special things. Sexual things. Call it 'violent theatrical sex' if you like."

"You mean orgies?"

"I do *not*. Performances, sexual performances. Very artistic sometimes. At least the ones I saw . . ."

I didn't argue with him. One man's art is always another man's trash, as borne out by his own split-beaver work, samples of which were still simmering in acetic acid on the floor. Yes, the fumes from my show of force were still in the air—a reminder of the menace I had brought into his sleazy little life.

Perhaps he sensed the menace again then too; when his eyes met mine, I saw loathing in them, which quickly shifted to obsequiousness, as he begged me to loosen the twisted coat hanger that was cutting so painfully into his shins.

He nodded when I refused. He was an Armenian; he knew how to accept a bitter fate. And yet this fat sad-eyed little perfumed man with the silly little airs, with blood caked on his cheeks and ears, was, in some awful sense, my double. I looked at him and he looked at me, two photographers eyeing each other with mutual contempt.

It was midnight, and I still had questions; the interrogation of the bound prisoner went on.

"So what did the Masked Man actually do?"

"Sat in his chair and watched."

"He didn't participate?"

"As far as I know, only one time. That was when the accident occurred."

He took a deep breath then and looked beseechingly at me, to indicate how greatly he would be in my debt if only I would loosen his bonds. I shook my head. He was the kind who probed constantly for a weakness, and, if and when he found one, would never relent. Better, I thought, to leave the wire cutting into his ankles, lest he think me merciful and begin to lie.

"I don't know much. As I mentioned, there were clients who did participate. But not the Masked Man—he seemed strictly the spectator type. He'd watch and then he'd leave. It was harmless. Just a special kind of private show."

According to Rakoubian, the Masked Man liked to see girls hurt. That was his thing, and so all the scenes constructed for him were built around that theme.

Kimberly was particularly good at it, Rakoubian said; she would wince and contort, so you were sure she was in terrible pain. But, he emphasized, a kind of ecstatic pain, a pain willingly accepted because it was erotically charged. There was this notion of sacrifice too, he said—that the girl would submit in order to please. A very old story, of course. But the beauty of it, the interest, Rakoubian insisted, lay in the variations and details.

Anyway, one night the Masked Man expressed a desire to join in. The evening had begun normally enough. That particular night

Sonya played the part of victim, which seemed to turn the Masked Man on. She was just the type of thin, proud, blond, imperious girl he liked to see victimized. And so he asked Mrs. Z if he could take her into another room to engage in a private scene.

At first Mrs. Z refused. Her interest was in artifice. Though there was violence in her scenes, and at times the violence seemed real, it was never extreme, no one was ever really hurt or marked.

But the Masked Man repeated his request, and this time Mrs. Z conveyed it to Sonya. And even though, like the others, Sonya found the Masked Man spooky, she agreed because she was hard up just then, and was looking to make enough so she could leave New York, move back to Europe and start over as a model.

Rakoubian was reaching the climax of his story. He checked my eyes, to be sure I was still under his spell. Then he began to speak with a quickness and an edge he hadn't used before.

"There was some dickering back and forth over the money. Then they finally agreed on a price. Then Sonya went with him into another room. And then something went wrong. The Masked Man got carried away. Sonya was killed, there was a great deal of distress, and Mrs. Z had to cover everything up.

"Things weren't the same after that. A couple of the kids quit and the Masked Man disappeared. But then one night he was back again, sitting in his old chair, doing his thing as if nothing had occurred. It was shortly after that that Kimberly came to me."

"Why?"

He squinted at me. "I don't know what you mean?"

"Why *you*?"

He addressed my question with a maximum display of dignity. "She knew me, that's why. I worked for Mrs. Z sometimes."

"What kind of work?"

"Photographic work. Stills, videotaping. Scenes her clients wanted captured on film. So Kimberly came to me, because she knew me as the house photographer. She said she wanted pictures of the Masked Man so she could blackmail him on the murder. She said she wanted to make him pay for what he'd done to Sonya. Pay heavily, she said."

"What was the deal?"

"Find out who he was. Get pictures of him, preferably ones that showed him putting on or taking off his mask. After I got them, we'd present him with a set of prints and make our demands. Kimberly was talking about asking for a million dollars. I thought that was grandiose. But we agreed, whatever we'd get, to split it down the middle."

"So you got the pictures?"

"I got them. I staked out the back entrance, and, using infrared, got some good shots of him coming in. Then Kimberly managed to get me inside one time when Mrs. Z wasn't there, and that's when I planted a camera in the ceiling of the dressing room that I could operate by remote.

"I got lucky, got the goods. The shot of him in the performance room was easy. Once I saw his face, and knew who he was, I followed him around, got more pictures of him on normal film. But the crucial picture, my tour de force, was the one of him taking off the mask."

I picked that photograph up, looked at it again. "Who is he?"

"You don't know?"

"I've seen the face, but I don't connect it to a name."

"The name's Arnold Darling."

The moment he said it I remembered: I'd seen him in a brilliant color photograph on the cover of *Fortune* a couple of years before. I recalled the picture well. Darling was posed before an intimidating black office tower. I could even remember the caption underneath: "Arnold Darling: The Corporate Buccaneer's Favorite Architect."

A ruthless man, a man to be feared—the article had been clear about that. Formerly a professor of architecture, he had made a mid-life career change from academic to master builder. He'd been phenomenally successful. With daring designs, based on an instinctive feel for the kind of secretive power and controlled menace the new generation of corporate raiders wished to project, he'd obtained several highly visible commissions. It wasn't long before he was regarded as form-giver for the takeover age, winning jobs away from more traditional favorites, such as Skidmore, Owings; Johnson and Burgee; and I. M. Pei.

But there was more to Darling than mere success. He was considered a major cultural figure. He had donated the design and construction costs of the Darling Auditorium at New York University, and had endowed the triennial Darling Prize, described as "a Nobel for sculptors." He was often cited too as one of the most aggressive collectors of Japanese scroll paintings and screens.

A powerful man, refined and generous, and now it turned out he not only liked to see girls hurt but he liked to hurt them himself. No wonder Kimberly had been scared.

"Okay," I said, "that was the blackmail scheme. Now, why were you photographing Kim and me?"

Rakoubian looked at me, hesitated, then lowered his eyes. "Insurance," he muttered.

"What kind of insurance?"

He turned cautious. "It was her idea. She said we needed another photographer."

"*Why?*"

He paused again. "We weren't sure how Darling would react. We didn't want the blackmail traced to us. So Kimberly came up with the idea that we should deal with Darling through Mrs. Z. She'd transmit our demands and act as conduit for the money, and for that we'd give her ten percent."

"What does all that have to do with me?"

"The plan was that after Kimberly approached Mrs. Z, she'd disappear. That way, if Mrs. Z was co-opted by Darling, Kimberly would be safe from any reprisals. But there was always the possibility that Mrs. Z and Darling would try and track her down. In that case Mrs. Z would logically go to Shadow, Kimberly's roommate and best friend, to find out where Kimberly had gone."

"Get to the point, Rakoubian. Why the pictures?"

"Documentation."

"Of what?"

"That you were a photographer and that the two of you were a pair. Kimberly left them around her apartment, and she even planted one in Shadow's wallet. That way, if Shadow was pressed, she'd have something to show. It was a diversion and also a way to do a dry run, to see how Darling would react."

"That's what you mean by 'insurance'?" I stared at him. He didn't answer. "I don't believe you. Kim and I met by accident."

"She told me. That's how she got the idea. She ran into you photographing on the street, and this light bulb went off in her brain—that there should be what she called a 'cover photographer.' So she went to work on you, got you interested in her, and then when the two of you went out to photograph, she had me take those pictures. Of course Shadow wasn't in on that. The idea was she'd steer them to you unwittingly."

Even as I listened to him I couldn't believe what he was saying. I think my mind glazed over to protect itself from the consequences of an enormous rage.

". . . Shadow didn't know anything about the blackmail. She thought the only purpose was to identify the Masked Man so he could be turned in to the cops. Kimberly felt that if Shadow was confronted, she'd tell Mrs. Z that her roommate was seeing a photographer, and then Mrs. Z would draw the obvious conclusions that Kimberly had helped *you* plant a camera in the changing room, and that *you* had taken the blackmail shots.

"Got to hand it to her. It was a terrific plan. First, because if things went wrong, Darling's attention would be diverted to you, and I'd have time to escape. Second, for the way it brought Mrs. Z into the plot. She, after all, had brokered the deal between Darling and Sonya that led to Sonya being killed. Since she was implicated in the death, and we were offering her a cut, we didn't think she'd hold back any of the money. The threat was clear—if she *did* hold back, we'd turn her in as well. But Darling wouldn't see it that way. He'd suspect Mrs. Z of acting for herself. For that reason, Mrs. Z would become a kind of fall guy too, who'd provide us with another layer of safety."

"*Fall guy!* Is that what I was supposed to be?"

He looked scared. "I'm just using Kimberly's words."

"She decided everything, according to you. Think I'm buying that?"

"Please! Listen!"

"I've *been* listening. And all I've heard is: 'according to Kimberly,' 'Kimberly thought,' 'Kimberly decided,' 'it was all Kimberly's idea. . . .' You want me to believe a twenty-five-year-old kid thought all this up by herself? Meantime a slick old phony con man of a photographer was just doing what he was told?"

He grinned at me then, the same shit-eating grin he'd showed me earlier. That time I didn't hit him. There would have been no point. The trick was to keep him on his toes so his lies wouldn't get out of hand. So far he'd been useful: he'd given me a coherent explanation for most of the things that had had me confused. The story was coming together. But the part about my being their 'cover photographer'—had Kim really used me that way? The thought was devastating, almost unthinkable. Still, I had to know.

"Kimberly felt that if Shadow was confronted, she wouldn't name you right away," Rakoubian said. "They'd have to frighten her a little to get her to talk. But eventually she'd tell them about the two of you—if only to save herself."

"But things didn't work out that way. Your plan, which you keep insisting was so terrific, ended up getting Shadow killed."

He hung his head. "It never occurred to us Darling would kill her."

"Why not? He'd killed Sonya. You knew he was a sadist and a freak."

"That was an accident. It happened in the throes of passion. Killing Shadow was cold and vicious. We just didn't anticipate . . ."

He was wrong. From what Scotto had told me, Darling had gotten carried away with Shadow too. But I didn't interrupt; the story, mercifully, seemed finally to be coming to its end.

"Darling and Mrs. Z had formed an alliance. They'd shown us they'd rather kill than pay. Even so, Kimberly wanted to keep pressuring them for money. But once I heard what happened to Shadow, I wanted out."

He paused, wiped his nose on his sleeve again. This time I looked away. He waited until I faced him. Then he showed me a weak smile and went on. "We had a fight. Kimberly said we had to continue. But I was the one who had the photographs, and I said no. That was it. She disappeared. I have no idea where. And you, you're all right now, because we dropped our demands. It's all finished now. It's over."

"Not quite," I said. "Kimberly's gone, you're sitting here holding the pictures. But guys are coming around to my place trying to throw lye in my eyes."

"I don't know anything about that, Barnett. We never antici-pated—"

I focused on him with total scorn. "Yeah. So you say. Maybe I ought to go to work on your Hasselblads and finish off your slides."

"Go ahead, if it'll make you feel better. But it's Kimberly you want to punish. Sure, I was her partner. But I was a patsy too. The whole scheme was hers. She's the one who brought you into it."

After I untied Rakoubian, he massaged his repulsive hairy wrists, complaining that they'd gone numb. Then, when I got up to leave, he begged to show me some of his pictures, nudes he'd taken of Kim.

They were exactly what I'd have expected, cheap second-rate pin-up stuff. I tried to be polite, but when he complimented me on the nudes *I'd* taken of her, I told him to cut the collegial shit. I told him, as far as I was concerned, we had nothing in common as photographers.

He was offended by that, and even tried to protest when I started toward the door with his box of blackmail pictures under my arm. But he acquiesced when I pointed out that since I'd been set up to take the blame for them, the pictures now rightfully belonged to me.

It was two in the morning when I finally stepped out on the street, feeling wasted, desolate, utterly destroyed. I walked all the way back to my place, and as I did I thought the whole time about the awful way that I'd been used.

Kim's betrayal of me, as described by Rakoubian, was so monumental, it seemed beyond belief. To have set me up that way, to have left me there to take the rap, to have latched on to me just because I was a damn *photographer*—a scheme like that, so calculated and heartless, was something I could barely comprehend.

I played around with it awhile, trying to minimize her role. Supposing, I asked myself, I discount Rakoubian's assignment of the blame? Even then, if I believed the whole scheme had been his and she'd been only *his* confederate—even then, because of its awful logic, she'd still helped to set me up and throw me to the wolves.

Well, I didn't care about Rakoubian anymore. Or Mrs. Z. Or Arnold Darling—I didn't care whether he'd gotten carried away with Sonya, or what kind of a perverted sexual monster he might be. All I could think about was Kim, and the rage I felt against her. Better that she'd been just a call girl; at least there was a particle of degraded honor in that. I could find no merit in her having been a member of a kinky performance group.

Was this woman whom I had loved and held and kissed—was she really so cold, false, cruel and corrupt? Had I really been so unimportant, so insignificant in her life? Had she really held me in such contempt?

I had to know.

And I knew where to go to find the answer.

Three

If your pictures aren't good enough, it's because you aren't close enough. You must be
part of the event.

—Robert Capa

*T*HE FOLLOWING MORNING AT LA GUARDIA AIRPORT, I
stopped to call Sal Scotto from a phone booth.

"Where you been?" he asked. "Trying to get hold of you."

"I got your messages," I said, "but I've been out of town."

"We need to talk."

"That's why I'm calling. I'm at the airport, about to leave again."

He hesitated. "Don't think you should leave just now, Geoffrey.
Dave and me, we need clarification on a couple things."

"Like what?"

"That super over in Devereux's building—we've been looking
into him. There're a few little items that don't quite add up."

"Forget about him."

"What do you mean 'forget about him'? You're the one steered
us to him in the first place."

"I was wrong. He didn't do it."

"How do you know that?" He paused again. "If you *do* know
something, Geoffrey, you'd better tell me right now. Way I've gone
out on a limb for you, wouldn't want to think you're jerking me
around."

"You didn't go out on a limb for me, Sal. My life was threatened. I asked you for protection and you refused."

"Protection! That's in the movies! I did everything I could."

"Doesn't matter. Forget it. When and if I have something to tell, I'll tell you, okay? Meantime, my regards to your charming partner. 'Bye, Sal."

"Hey! Don't hang up. . . ." He was still sputtering when I did.

It's a three-hour flight from New York to Miami. Any month between December and March is a good time to go, and October and May can be okay too if you're not a nervous sweaty type and don't like to walk too fast.

But if you make the trip when I did, on the last day of August, and arrive a little after noon on what the natives tell you is the hottest day of the year, and if you haven't lived all that perfect a life anyway, and it's occurred to you you may deserve a little stint in purgatory for your sins, you will, upon arrival, have the opportunity to know just how hot the furnaces of hell are going to be.

Actually at first it didn't seem so bad. I stepped off my air-conditioned plane into an enormous air-conditioned airport full of congenial happy people, most of whom were speaking Spanish. From there I took an air-conditioned minibus to the parking lot of the car rental company of my choice, and there transferred into my rented air-conditioned car.

It was the few moments in between when I was in the open air that I'll remember all my life. I'm talking about a dank humid oven-hot heat that hits you like a fist. I've photographed in the tropics, been baked and broiled and smelled the smells, but I never experienced such a scalding hotness as I did that August day. It was composed of torrid wind, coming off the Everglades, tainted with decay, then made noxious by aircraft and automobile fumes.

And I was about to drive a hundred sixty miles deeper into the fire.

In retrospect, I'm glad I did. It would have been too simple to take the plane. It wasn't that the drive to Key West was all that difficult—I was one of very few maniacs braving the road that sweltering August afternoon. But those three and a half hours on the highway gave me a chance to rest and think, and also a sense of the distance I had to go. If Key West is, as they say, "the end of the line," then it may be necessary to literally travel a little of that line in order to fully appreciate the meaning of being at its end.

The turnpike led me through the southern suburbs of Miami, then on to the fringes of Everglades National Park. The divided highway ended at Florida City, and from there on it was one long commercial strip of Long John Silver's, Captain Bob's, Bojangles, boat rental agencies and live-bait shops.

Once on the Keys I started to move: Key Largo, Islamorada, Long Key, Conch Key, Grassy Key, Boot Key, and then the interminable Marathon, after which the honky-tonk gave way to the empty road, an asphalt ribbon crossing the islands, rolling across the bridges. There was hardly another car in sight.

My eyes began to smart as I drove into the sun. Colors were bleached to tones. The roots of the little mangrove islands looked like snakes poised to strike, and the water off the reef took on the flat purple-gray color of a bruise.

A pickup truck passed, going ninety-five. There was a rifle in the window rack, and two shirtless men in back with ragged beards and billed fishing caps, sipping beer from the can. They gave me a sinister wave, a silent greeting that said, We'll be seeing you later, bub, and, when we do, don't mess with us. Then they were gone, and ahead there was only the empty road again, the black baked-out ribbon, rolling south toward heat and emptiness.

Big Pine Key. Ramrod. Sugarloaf. Torch. The scrub-encrusted islands called Saddlebunch. Then Boca Chica and Stock Island, a huge automobile graveyard, and then—finally and at last—Key West.

At first it didn't look like any kind of paradise I had ever seen. There were gas stations and fast-food joints and a couple of shopping malls and an enormous flat-roofed Sears. But when I got off the highway and drove deeper into town, a breeze blew forth, the sky began to darken, and I found myself in another world.

There was a special texture to the quiet shady streets, lined with old wooden buildings—shacks, houses, mansions all mixed together, some rotting, others superbly restored. Magnificent tropical plantings too; I counted banyans, jacarandas, sapodillas and palms, hibiscus, oleander and fountains of bougainvillaea pouring off balconies. And surrounding everything was a beguiling scent, the warm sweet aroma of night-blooming flowers.

As I wound my way through this section (which, I learned from my map, was called Old Town), I began to decompress. I passed a young black girl skipping rope, a group of laughing Cubans clustered on a veranda playing cards. And then I spotted a truly beautiful woman of a certain age, sitting alone on a second-story balcony. I slowed my car, our eyes met, then, slowly, she smiled at me and waved.

I checked into a motel called the Spanish Moss, a little shabby, but a veritable Ritz Carlton compared with my lodgings in Cleveland. Then I took a walk.

I wanted to get a feel for the place, and so headed for the main street, Duval, to join the throngs. Here I merged with sailors, gay couples, bikini-clad adolescents carrying fishing poles, all headed toward Mallory Pier for the famous ritual of Key West—bearing witness to the sunset.

The pier was crowded, with circles formed around various human and animal acts. There was a juggler, and a jazz combo and a bagpipe player. There was a lady hawking cookies, and a sinewy youth, stripped to the waist, cracking open coconuts. I also saw examples of a type I hadn't seen in years: tall, thin stooped young men with gentle eyes and wispy beards, escorting stout young women, in tie-dyed clothes, with waist-length tresses and beauteous smiles.

There were whistles and cheers as the sun sank into the Gulf, and then the mob broke up. I was exhausted. In thirty-six hours I'd traveled between four cities, broken into a house, terrorized a man, and had learned crushing things about the woman I had loved. And so, even though it was only 9:00 P.M., I ate a quick dinner at a cheap Cuban restaurant, then went to bed.

I woke ten hours later, refreshed and eager to stalk my prey. On my way to my car, I ran into my motel-room neighbors, a friendly retired couple from Arizona with Mount Rushmore faces, struggling with two odd-looking machines.

I gave them a hand. The machines were metal detectors, which they were going to use to scour the beach for coins and rings. After I helped them load the contraptions into their car, the woman took hold of my hands.

"Thank you and God bless you, son," she said. "May you have good luck with your quest here too."

The Key West Post Office, on Whitehead Street, is a modern building with a normal enclosed section, and also a long grilled-in open-air arcade. It is in this later portion that the P.O. boxes are situated, in easy view of the parking lot. The only trouble is that occupation of spaces in the lot is limited to fifteen minutes.

I found Kim's box and peeked inside. Nothing there. I certainly didn't expect to find it loaded with mail; she was in hiding, after all. But if Grace Arnos was the only person who knew where she was, and if she and Grace spoke regularly on the phone, it could be as long as a week before she showed up to check her box. Could I mount a watch that long?

I had no alternative. Though I knew she was a waitress, it would be madness to track her down aggressively. The moment I started asking questions she'd hear about it, get spooked and run.

The hours for the arcade were 7:00 A.M. to 7:00 P.M., but since I couldn't possibly maintain a twelve-hour-a-day surveillance, I needed a control for the times I wouldn't be there.

I entered the Post Office, bought a prestamped envelope, then returned to the arcade and started riffling through the contents of a trash container. It didn't take long to find what I was looking for, a discarded advertising flyer. I folded it neatly, sealed it inside the envelope, wrote "Boxholder" and Kim's box number on the front, then pushed the letter through the slot for local mail.

Once that envelope was in her box, I could check on it whenever I renewed my watch. If it was gone, or in an altered position, I'd know she'd been there while I was away.

That first morning I established my routine. I found a parking space on Whitehead, with a sight line to the arcade. But since the boxes were too far away to observe with the naked eye, I mounted a 135mm. telephoto on my Leica and used it as a telescope.

Even in the best cop movies I've yet to hear a character adequately describe how tough it is to man a stakeout. It's not just a question of physical discomfort, though being cooped up in a car is excruciating enough. For me the most difficult part was the strain of keeping alert while watching a specific spot for hours at a time.

I had to constantly fight off the wanderings of my mind. I had to avoid moving around too much lest Kim appear from an unexpected direction, notice me and run. I dared not play the radio too long, lest I run down the battery, and although Key West in late summer is *very* hot, if I ran the engine, in order to run the air conditioning, I also ran the risk of running out of gas.

I coped by varying my position from time to time, and rationing myself to ten minutes of radio and air conditioning an hour. I also ate large quantities of unhealthy food, with the result that the backseat of my car was soon covered with crumpled bags.

I tried every kind of crisp and salty snack, even purchasing a twenty-bag sampler pack—Corn Twists, Cheese Doodles, nacho and plantain chips, and, of course, plain old potato chips. I tried them "Hawaiian style," "kettle-crisped," "thick cut," "wavy," "with 'tater skins," and fried in every sort of oil. It was the need for things that were starchy, salty and crunchy to keep my concentration sharp.

I had another problem too: sitting in a parked car all day would sooner or later attract attention. All I needed was for some Post Office employee to ask, "Why's this guy waiting around out front? Better call the cops."

By the end of my first day of surveillance, I had an upset stomach. I also dozed off twice. My back was sore and my muscles ached, but my control envelope was now safely in Kim's box.

The second day was equally painful, even though I raised my ration of radio and lowered my input of chips.

The third day was so miserable I spent a good part of it wondering if I'd do better canvassing restaurants. I also spent some time thinking about how lucky I'd been in Cleveland, and then, with despicable self-pity, about how my good luck never seemed to hold.

It was just before noon, the fourth day of the stakeout, when I finally caught sight of her, and then it was only by a fluke.

I had turned my attention away from the arcade for a moment

when I caught a glimpse of someone familiar in my rearview mirror. It was a young woman riding a bicycle up Whitehead Street in the direction of the Southernmost Point.

A quiver of excitement ran through me, and also the thought that perhaps my luck still had a way to run.

I was afraid to follow her by car; I had seen enough of Key West to know there were numerous one-way streets and impassable narrow lanes. So I grabbed up my camera bag and started after her on foot.

At first I thought I'd lost her. I was devastated. But then I saw her standing astride her bike, talking to another girl on the sidewalk in front of the Green Parrot Bar.

I took a position in front of a motorcycle store across the street, where I could see them reflected in the plate glass. When I was sure they were too wrapped up in their conversation to notice, I turned and raised my camera to take a closer look.

No mistake. It was Kim. The wet place where my shirt stuck to my back suddenly felt cold. That telephoto brought her close, right against my eye. I tripped the shutter out of sheer perversity.

A funny thing about a single lens reflex camera: when you use it to watch a person, there's a certain distancing, no matter how powerful your lens. It has to do with the complex system of mirrors, the pentaprism, that stands between the subject and your eye. For this reason many photographers prefer a range-finder camera; they feel the viewing is more sensitive because it's more direct. But I have always liked the SLR; the distancing makes me feel safer and helps me cast a colder eye.

After I took that picture of Kim, my eye went very cold indeed. I was no longer just following her on the street; I was a photographer using my camera to inspect.

I focused on her hair. It looked different from when I'd seen her last. She'd cut off a lot of it, and it was lighter, streaked by the summer Florida sun.

I tilted down to her chest: her breasts heaved beneath a dazzling white T-shirt with the words "Key West" emblazoned on the front.

I tilted further: she wore matching cotton shorts. Her white clothes made brilliant contrast with her tanned skin. With my camera I caressed her bare legs and thighs. She looked good. But she'd betrayed me, suckered me. I'd been her "fall guy," her "cover photographer." Yet, for all of that, I longed to reach out to her and touch. . . .

The street conversation was over. The other girl went off. Kim started walking her bike along Southard toward Duval.

I followed. Would she turn around? If she did I'd raise my camera and use it as a shield. I almost smiled when I thought of that; that was what Rakoubian had done when he'd stalked us in New York.

On Duval she reversed direction, headed north. I let people pass, so there were bodies between us, then I too joined the parade.

She was moving less quickly now, slowed down by the crowds. I got her nicely framed between two young men in matching white tank tops. Then we marched along united for a block, she, the guys and I in lockstep, fifteen feet apart.

As I followed her I felt my excitement grow. Stalking Grace in downtown Cleveland—that had been cool, smart, passionless. This was something else.

I felt the bloodlust of a hunter on the track of a rare, seductive game. To follow or to kill—the choice was mine. That hunter's power made me heady; it also reactivated the hibernating photo-journalist inside. As we walked I twisted the telephoto off my Leica, mounted on a 35mm. Elmarit, then raised it to my eye.

Even as I followed I wanted to take a shot at her. But when I looked through the viewfinder, all I could see were the backs of the two guys in front. The place between them where she'd been was empty. My prey had disappeared.

It was twenty minutes before I gave up my search for her. Thinking she might have turned into a shop, I checked all the stores on the block. But of course you don't walk into a store with a bicycle, and her bike wasn't parked anywhere around.

There was a little alley she might have used; it was for pedestrians, but she could have ridden through. Or perhaps, in the instant when I'd looked away, she'd spotted me, mounted her bike, turned at the next corner and driven off.

All that seemed so unlikely that I began to doubt myself. Had I really seen her? Had she *really* been walking just ahead? Or had I gone delusional? Had the heat and all the salty starchy food clouded my brain?

I was standing on the sidewalk, wondering what to do, when suddenly I sensed a presence just behind. I trembled as I felt her breath upon my ear.

"Hello, Geoffrey," she whispered.

She said I should come with her, that she knew a quiet bar where we could talk. And so we walked in silent tension to the end of Duval, all my bitterness held tight inside.

She guided me into the compound of the Pier House hotel, where, the moment we entered, we were cut off from the rowdiness of the street. But the quiet there only added to my stress. By the time we reached a proper little bar called the Chart Room I felt I was about to burst.

Kim ordered a Bloody Mary. I ordered a Perrier. The waiter went away, and then our eyes finally met.

She peered at me. "You look fit, Geoffrey."

"Do I? I'm not feeling very fit."

She was studying me the way one might study someone one had wounded, to measure how serious the injury was.

"No," she said, "I don't imagine you are."

"You never said good-bye."

"Oh, God!" She shook her head.

"Didn't you owe me that?"

"I'm sure I did," she said gently. "I'm sure I owed you a lot of things."

The waiter brought our drinks. She smiled at him.

"I hope this isn't going to be one of those conversations, Geoffrey."

"What kind is that?" I asked.

"Kind where we talk about who owed what to whom, and all that sort of stuff."

"Sometimes," I said, pretending to be the soul of patience, "one has to talk about unpleasant things."

She sipped her drink, then picked up some peanuts from a bowl and popped them into her mouth. "I was in trouble—you know that now. Shadow was killed that Saturday night. I had to get away. So I left. What could I have said? How could I have explained? No, the best thing was just to leave, get out fast and clean. The less you knew the better. You see, I didn't want to drag you into it."

That did it. I felt a rush. "But I *was* in it. Right in the goddamn middle of it."

"No you weren't, Geoffrey. You were safe. Anything I told you, any good-byes I might have made—*then* you could have been implicated. But you weren't."

" '*Implicated*'? Of course I was '*implicated*'! Are you really pretending I wasn't?"

There must have been a vicious intensity in my voice; a group sitting at another table stopped talking and glanced nervously at us.

"Try and keep it low, Geoffrey. This bar's not tacky Key West."

"Oh, I can see that," I said, looking around. "It's just so fucking *civilized*. It tells me something, that you brought me here."

"What does it tell you?"

"That you're afraid."

"Of what?"

"Of me. My anger and what I might do."

"I'm not one to be afraid of things, Geoffrey. And I'm certainly not afraid of you." She gave my arm a gentle pat, as if we were lovers who'd been parted by nothing more than a weekend business trip.

I stared at her. "You're—incredible!"

She looked at me as if I were mad. Something was wrong, we weren't connecting, were talking about different things.

"It was all your idea, according to Rakoubian."

"You talked to him?" She snorted. "He *would* say that."

"Then it *wasn't* your idea?"

"What do *you* think?" she asked. "If I'd known you'd talked to Dirty Adam I'd have left you standing there on Duval."

"Then what would you have done?"

She shrugged. "Left town. Since this place is now obviously blown." She peered at me. "How did you find me here anyway?"

"I found you."

"How?"

"What difference does it make?"

"If you found me, someone else might find me. Someone who could hurt me. Do you know what I'm talking about?"

"Arnold Darling? Mrs. Z?"

She exhaled painfully. "Well, you *do* seem to know a lot." She squinted at me. "Why would Rakoubian talk to you anyway? Why would he tell you about them?"

"Because I *made* him tell me."

"*Made* him?" She smiled. It was an eager smile, so eager it made me a little bit afraid of her.

"I told him if he didn't talk, I'd throw him out the window."

Her eyes enlarged. "That's great, Geoffrey. Fantastic! Wow!" She looked at me closely again, then chuckled to herself. "I wonder—"

"What?" And when she turned cool and didn't reply: "Jesus! Please don't act like that."

"Okay, Geoffrey, if you really want to know, I wonder if I underrated you."

"Oh, you most *definitely* underrated me," I said caustically. "Was that what this was all about? Rating and underrating? Seeing who could get the better of whom?"

"That certainly was *not* what this was all about."

"Wasn't it? You get involved in a blackmail scheme—I don't care whose idea it was—you get yourself involved and part of the deal is to set me up as the 'cover photographer.' Then I show up here, find you, and all you can say is 'My, you're looking fit' and 'How did you find me here anyway?' What's with you? How do you hold up your head? Tell me, please. I really want to know."

She smiled. "Is that *really* what you want to know, Geoffrey? Did you come all the way down here just to ask me that?"

"What else is there to ask you?"

She shook her head. "If that's all you care about, you made a wasted trip."

"If you won't answer me, then I guess I did," I said.

"Oh, I'll answer, all right, when you get off that fucking high horse of yours. But if all you want to know is 'How do I hold up my head?'—go screw yourself, Geoffrey Barnett."

"Jesus," I said, "I can't believe this. *You're* indignant. *You!*"

"Yes! Because who the hell are you to track me down here and ask me crap like that?" She finished off her drink. "If you want to know what happened, *really* happened—that's something else. That might be worth talking about. But not this guilt trip you're running on me. That's crap."

"Yeah, crap . . ." I said.

We went quiet after that. It was as if we both wanted the anger to subside, wanted, each of us, to cool down and rethink our positions.

I looked at her closely. I felt confused. Clearly there was more to the story than Rakoubian had told me. Moreover, seeing her again made me realize how much I still wanted her, no matter what she'd done, what horrible lies she'd told.

I knew I mustn't give in to her, that seduction was her game and if I let her seduce me again I'd be a double fool.

*No matter what you feel, don't show it*, I thought. *Listen to her version, and then attack it. Show her up, if you can, for the fraud that she is. And then demolish her with your contempt.*

I don't recall the exact sequence that afternoon, just that we spent it together in a variety of places, and that each time we moved, my feelings toward her changed. We walked down streets, stopped at bars, drank, then walked again. Most of the time she talked.

She tried everything—pleading, anger, big droopy-eyed sincerity. She mocked and played humble and gave virtuous high-minded testimony. And all the time she did all that, I just let her go on.

It was excruciating to listen to her as she scrambled for a foothold. My stony silence urged her on to greater efforts. When I refused to grant her anything, she turned petulant and sulked. Then I'd say something to start her up again. And then she'd be off and running, again trying to persuade me. For the first time in our relationship, I felt I had the upper hand.

Wandering around in the tourist swarm at the bottom of Duval, heart of all the honky-tonk and rinky-dink, with the aroma of pot in the air, the smell of grease pouring out of the fast-food joints, the noise of amplified country music gushing out of the bars, and all the time Kimberly, eyes ablaze, swearing to me, pledging, promising, vowing that she absolutely did not know Rakoubian had been tracking us with his camera:

"Until this very moment, I did not know, I swear to you, Geoffrey, I absolutely *swear*, I had *no* idea. *None!*"

"Then how did he know where we'd be?"

"Followed us, I guess." She looked at me. "What's so funny?"

"Oh, just a little thing I didn't notice at first, that the places where he shot us were all places *you* wanted to go; places *you* chose. Like he was tipped off and waiting to ambush us when we arrived."

"*I* didn't tell him. I swear. That's just a coincidence."

"Is it?"

"Got to be. Tell me again—where did he take all these photographs?"

"South Street Seaport and Battery Park. Also in my loft. Somehow he got into a room across the street. Then he shot us through the window."

"Can't blame me for *that*, Geoffrey. He didn't need me to tell him your address."

"Who left the blinds up?"

"Who do you think?"

"Must have been one of us."

She smiled. "Well?"

"What about the other places?"

"Just two, Geoffrey. *Two*. That's no big deal. We went out

photographing maybe twenty, thirty times. Sure, most of those times I chose the locations, but you could have overruled me."

"I didn't."

"You *could* have." She shook her head. "You can't make a solid case against me, Geoffrey—not just because of *two*."

Middle of the afternoon at the Green Parrot, a roughneck motorcyclists' bar, with the kind of open-air windows that lift up and out and are then attached by hooks to the ceiling of the overhangs outside: Kimberly, gazing at me, waiting for me to acknowledge her, while I listened to the pool cues clicking against the balls in back, and the little shrieks of the teenaged girls passing by on the street.

"Knock, knock! Anyone home?"

I turned to her.

"Look, Geoffrey—what Adam told you doesn't make sense. Why would I need a 'cover photographer'? What possible use could one be to me? *He* was the photographer. *He* was the one who needed the cover. Not me. *I* was already exposed."

"You were in on it?"

"The blackmail—sure. Mrs. Z knew. I went to her, laid it out for her, made all the demands. What she *didn't* know was that Dirty Adam was stage-managing me from the wings."

"And she never asked you who took the pictures?"

Kim shook her head. "I didn't tell her either."

"Pretty obvious, wasn't it, since Rakoubian was the 'house photographer'?"

"I don't know if it was obvious. But yes—I suppose in his mind it was. I guess what happened was he wanted to protect himself, so he stalked us and took those pictures of us, and *I had no idea. No idea at all*."

I looked at her skeptically. "How come you didn't see him then?"

179

"He was clever. He stayed back. You said he used a telephoto. And remember: I was posing for *you*, concentrating on *you*. He was in the backgrounds of your pictures, behind me."

She had a point—he didn't show up that many times. "But what about at the restaurant?" I asked.

"What restaurant?"

"That crazy place in Tribeca with the Madonnas and the Statues of Liberty."

"The joint we went to that time with Shadow? Yeah, I re- member—he was sitting at the bar. We said hello." She looked at me, shook her head. "You don't think I took you there to meet him, do you?"

I shrugged.

"Really, Geoffrey, if I was trying to set you up, wouldn't that be the last thing I'd do?"

"Maybe you're perverse."

*"That perverse?"*

I seesawed my hands.

"Still don't believe me?"

"I'd like to."

"What's the trouble, then?"

"There're a lot of troubles. For one thing, I think Rakoubian was too scared to lie."

"Maybe you didn't scare him all that much, Geoffrey. Maybe you weren't as forceful as you thought. I know you. You're not a violent man. You're a very gentle guy."

Perhaps she was right, perhaps I hadn't been that forceful. Though, in my memory, the violence I'd felt that night was real.

"What else bothers you?" she asked.

"The way we met. Rakoubian said when you saw me that night a light bulb went off in your brain. He said that's when you got the idea of using me. And then you started to pursue me."

She smiled. "And you believed him? Do you really think I was wandering around New York looking for a photographer, and I saw you, and I said to myself: Hey! There he is! Just what I need! Go for it, kid! Is *that* what you think?"

Of course she was right. That did sound unlikely. Suddenly I wished I could go off by myself someplace and think the whole thing through. But I was afraid to leave her, afraid that if I did I might never find her again.

"Well?" she said, waiting.

I shook my head.

"So?"

"He knew about it."

"*Because I told him*, dummy. Don't you see? You're both photographers. If I'd met Irving Penn on the street, wouldn't I have told you?"

"I suppose . . ."

"This was the same sort of thing. I told him after I started posing for you. I said I'd met you, and I was working with you, and then I asked him what he thought."

"What did he say?"

"He was interested. He asked a lot of questions. He said he knew your work and that you were good. Now that I think of it, he seemed a little jealous too, maybe because he's always going up to girls, trying to get them to pose, and there I was telling him how I'd chased after you, taken off my clothes voluntarily for you. Really, Geoffrey, talk about light bulbs going off in people's brains! That must have been when one went off in his. You saw what kind of creep he is. A born schemer. Later, when I told him you and I were getting into something serious—that's when he must have smelled an opportunity. He thought he could set you up to take the rap for him, just in case things went wrong."

"And he never told you about that little scheme?"

"Why would he? It was *his* insurance protection plan. He never told me about it because he knew I'd be furious. That I'd cancel everything. And then where the hell would he have been?" She stared at me, eyes big and innocent. "Well?"

"Well?"

"Makes sense, doesn't it? For his own reasons, Geoffrey. *His own purposes*. Can't you see—I had no motive to help him set you up."

I stared at her. "Oh, boy, you're good," I said.

At Land's End Village by the shrimp docks and tacky stores, we paused beside the Turtle Krawls, pools where sea turtles were kept in the days when Key West supplied turtle meat to the nation. Now the main holding pen has been turned into an old-age home for reptiles. A few ancient inhabitants paddled about listlessly near the bottom.

Kim pointed to a restaurant behind. "I waitress over there."

I turned, saw a sprawling low-roofed building with a glassed-in terrace set beside the water. It was long past the lunch hour but there were still cars parked in front. I'd heard of the place. "I hear it's good," I said.

"Wouldn't it have been a hoot if you'd wandered in, and I'd been assigned to be your waitress?"

"Most definitely a hoot," I agreed sourly.

She looked at her watch. "My shift starts at five. I want to stay with you, clear things up. I'm going in now to find someone to cover for me tonight."

I nodded, watched her disappear into the restaurant, then turned back to the Krawls. A fortyish woman with the bright eyes of a true believer was showering the turtles with hunks of squid. I peered down into the mossy-green water, saw one old monster attack a mass of tentacles with his jaws.

I thought about Kim. Was she lying? *Fifty-fifty*, I thought. But I hoped she was telling me the truth.

After Kim arranged things at the restaurant, we walked into Old Town. She took my arm as she talked:

"Rakoubian came to me. That's how it started. He knew Shadow and I were broken up over Sonya, but he approached me alone because, he said, he knew I wanted vengeance. He said he could see that in my eyes.

" 'So what makes you such a big expert on my eyes?' " I asked him.

" 'Years of experience. I'm a photographer, dearie. Girls your age, they're my stock-in-trade. I know girls and I know their eyes and I know vengeful eyes when I see them. And yours are vengeful. Am I right?'

"He *was* right. I *did* want vengeance. He smelled that out. He knew my type. So he said: 'Help me get pictures of this guy and you'll get your vengeance.' And since that didn't seem like such a bad idea, I agreed.

"We talked. After a while we got onto the subject of money. The Masked Man was rich—that much was obvious. He was a rich old man. 'Just the kind of man,' Rakoubian said, 'who can get away with murder.'

"I asked Adam what he meant. He said, you know, the usual stuff: the rich don't go to jail, they can afford the kind of lawyers who keep you out. They pay off the judge, or bribe the jury, or get a mistrial, whatever—he doubted even if we managed to get pictures, they'd amount to very much. Because what then, really, would we have? Just some pictures of some rich old guy putting on a mask. Big deal! So what? Who would care? And how would that tie him to a murder? Guys like the Masked Man, Adam said, they always get away with it.

"But then he became expansive. He said he had an idea. He asked me if it wouldn't be a much sweeter revenge if we used such photos, assuming he'd be able to take them, to make the Masked Man *pay*.

" 'See,' he said, 'that's what it's all about. In the end it's always money. That's the real revenge, dearie, because that's where it hurts them. The pocketbook—that's where they feel the pinch. Look, nothing's going to bring Sonya back. But we can hurt the guy for wasting her. What we have to do is get our pictures, then *threaten* him with exposure. Tell him we're going to turn him over to the cops. *Unless* he pays us a million bucks.'

"That's when the whole notion of blackmail first came up. And I liked it. I admit that, Geoffrey. I liked it very much. It appealed to me on all sorts of different levels. Yeah, I liked it. And Rakoubian could see I did. He had me figured right, didn't he? I was a tough little bitch. And he knew it. Yeah, he could see it in my eyes. . . ."

We wandered up and down Caroline, Eaton and Fleming streets and then through various lanes: Weaver, Finder, Love and Locust. As we walked the houses brooded over us; the sky began to darken, the great palms shivered and cast longer shadows. On one block we passed a porch where a parrot was tethered to a perch. It screeched at us: "Hi! Fucky-Ducky! Hi!" And then the crazy little bird cackled like a madman in the dusk.

"What's your name?" I asked her.

She looked at me. "You know my goddamn name."

"Yeah, I know your 'goddamn name.' It's your real name I want."

"Is it so important?"

"To me it is."

"What does 'real' mean?"

"Come off it, Kim. This isn't philosophy class."

"You know I'm no philosopher, Geoffrey. You know I'm just a blackmailing little bitch."

I stopped and peered at her. "Is that how you define yourself?"

"That's how *you* define me now, isn't it?"

"Maybe," I said. "But I want to know more. Your name, who your parents are, where you went to school, your past. I want to know all that. And I want to hear it straight."

She met my eyes straight on. "Oh, I could give it to you straight," she said. "We could go through all that crap, and then what would you know? And who's to say anyway what name is really real, the name you're born with or the name you give yourself? Is it 'Bob Dylan' or 'Robert Zimmerman'? 'Cary Grant' or 'Archie Leach.' Or take Lauren Bacall—you say I remind you of her. Well, I read she was born 'Betty Perske.' So is that her name? Or is her *real* name 'Lauren Bacall'?"

As we walked along Margaret Street a light tropical wind blew through Kimberly's hair. She looked good. *Maybe too good*, I thought. I decided to step up the interrogation:

"Why did you lie to Jess Harrison?"

"I don't know that I did."

"You told him you did tricks."

"That wasn't a lie."

"Rakoubian says you didn't."

"He's the biggest liar around."

"He said Mrs. Z never ran an escort service."

"She didn't. But some of us actresses made side arrangements with her clients."

"Jesus, Kimberly—do you know how hard you sound?"

"I never pretended I was soft."

"You did with me."

"No, Geoffrey. With you I didn't pretend."

God, I wanted to believe her! "Why didn't you tell me you liked doing sex for money?" My question came out almost like a wail.

From the way she looked at me, I think she understood my pain.

"Because you never asked me, and I stopped doing it before I met you, and what I did with you wasn't for pay." She caught her breath. "There was another reason too."

"What was that?"

"I didn't think you'd understand."

I shook my head. "I understand a lot of things. But not unnecessary lies."

"The only lies I told you were necessary ones."

"I see." I groaned. "What about the Duquaynes?"

"What about them?"

"Did you make it with them?"

"Yes."

"In performance? Or privately?"

"Both."

"*God damn you!* Why didn't you tell me?"

"Right . . . like: 'Gee, Geoffrey, I'm taking you to these people's home for dinner, and, by the way, I've had sex with the wife while the husband was tied up in a chair.' "

"Whose idea was *that*?"

"Harold's."

"Fun!"

"Actually it was."

"You like girls, don't you?"

"Sometimes. Don't you?"

"You and Shadow were lovers."

"We had been. Occasionally."

"Yet she knew nothing about the blackmail?"

"That's right."

"So she suffered for what she didn't know?"

"Yes, Geoffrey, she did. She certainly did. And that's the reason I'm not done with this yet."

At the intersection of Angela Street and Passover Lane, the city cemetery spread out before us. The white graves, as in New Orleans, were set above the ground, and the bordering palms arched high against the clouds.

Kim was panting. I grabbed her. Then I pushed my mouth hard against hers and kissed her viciously. She took it from me, even when I cut her lip with my teeth.

"Why did you do that?" she asked, breaking away to spit out blood.

"I felt like it."

"Good enough reason." She looked at me, smiled. "I liked it. You knew I would."

"I didn't give a damn whether you'd like it or not."

"Why then, Geoffrey?"

"I wanted to see how tough a little bitch you really are."

"And? Well?" She eagerly awaited my appraisal.

"You're tough enough," I said.

Walking south on Truman Avenue, the last stretch of U.S.1, the cars and trucks jammed up and honking, the leaves of the palms thrashing heavily in the early evening summer wind:

"Where do you live?"

"Catherine Street. I share an apartment with two other girls. Waitresses."

"Bother you—being a waitress?"

She shrugged. "No big deal. I've done it before."

"Why Key West?"

"Why not?"

"You knew the place?"

She nodded. "And I liked it too. It's a kind of refuge. 'The end of the line.' "

"Maybe that's the trouble with it."

"What do you mean?"

"One way in and one way out. It's like a box canyon. Not the best place to hide."

We walked in silence for a block. Then I turned to her. "You never really cared for me, did you?"

"No, that's wrong. I did."

"But not very much."

"A lot more than you think."

"But you weren't honest with me."

"I couldn't be."

"Damnit! You keep saying that. Every time you do, I feel like kicking you in the shins."

She stopped walking, stood still, then balanced herself on one foot and stuck out the other. "Go ahead," she said, exposing her shin. "Go ahead, Geoffrey. Kick!"

"I'd like to."

"Do. No one'll stop you. In Key West people beat up on people all the time."

"Put your stupid foot down," I said. "I wouldn't want to damage your precious tattoo."

"You remember!" She looked pleased as she lowered her foot. "I got it here, you know."

"Figures."

"This Chinese—"

"Woman did it. She's probably gone now too. Tattoo artists are always on the move."

She looked at me curiously. "You're a funny guy. I didn't realize it until today."

"You 'underrated' me, didn't you?"

She looked at me, then laughed.

Suddenly I wanted desperately to make love to her right there, most emphatically there in Key West, in the shadow of all the lush

188

decadence of that little island, with the hot stifling air carrying a hint of rot, while the palms thrashed and the gays cruised and the rednecks drove by in their pickup trucks and the six-toed cats in the Ernest Hemingway House shrieked and screwed violently in the night.

While I was unlocking my door at the Spanish Moss, my neighbors from Arizona pulled in from one of their metal-detecting expeditions at the beach. When they saw Kimberly, they turned to each other and smiled. I could read their minds: they thought I too had found a kind of treasure.

As soon as the door was closed and we were alone in my room, I grabbed hold of her T-shirt and ripped it open down the front.

"*Jesus!*" she said.

I reached through the torn flaps of cotton and seized hold of her breasts. They were warm and her chest was damp. I stared at her. "I'm going to fuck your brains out," I said.

She was amused. "Is that my punishment?"

"I'll be doing it for me, not you."

"Fine, go ahead," she taunted. "We'll see whose brains end up on the floor."

I shoved her roughly toward the bed. "Won't be mine."

She stumbled back upon it. "Nor mine," she said.

She gazed at me, smiled her most sultry smile, then undid the clasp of her shorts.

I watched. When she had them down to her knees, I grabbed hold of her ankles, flipped her over, fell upon her, and, placing my hand on the back of her neck, pressed her face down hard against the mattress.

"Geoffrey! Stop! I can't breathe!"

"You'll manage."

She turned her head to the side and gulped at the air. The down on her back sparkled wet. I pulled her panties to her knees. The smell of her body rose and filled my head. Then I fucked her as violently as I could. She came almost immediately. Then she came again.

I grabbed hold of her hair. "You're just a little whore. Aren't you? *Aren't you, bitch?*"

"If you say so, Geoffrey."

"Say it!"

"I'm just a little whore," she sneered. Then she looked back at me. "And you? What're you?" She gazed at me with mocking eyes.

I shook my head.

"You're a big manly rapist who uses his cock to make the girls scream. Right, Geoffrey? *Hmmm? Hmmm?*" Then she thrust herself hard against me, and then she came again.

I was shocked at the way I'd attacked her. But also I was thrilled. It was the same sensation I'd felt the first time I hit Rakoubian— letting go and then a feeling of being cleansed inside.

We settled down after that, screwed a little more, and then, when we were exhausted and our flesh was hot and damp, we broke apart and fell asleep.

When I woke it was dark. She wasn't in the bed, and for a second I was frantic. Then I saw her on the other side of the room, sitting in a chair beside the window, her face and breasts glowing from light cast by the streetlamps filtered through the restless leaves of the palms outside.

"Hi," I said.

"Hi."

"I didn't hurt you, I hope."

She smiled. "Of course you didn't. I loved every minute of it. Did you?"

"Yes. Unfortunately."

"Oh dear . . ."

"I want to hate you. I don't."

She stood and yawned. She was wearing just her shorts. "You called me 'whore' and 'bitch.' But still you must like me pretty well. You smiled in your sleep."

"Must have been dreaming."

"Of what?"

"A girl I knew."

"What did she look like—this girl?"

"Like you," I said.

She laughed. Then she came to me and kissed the center of my forehead. "Yeah, that's me, Geoffrey. Just an illusion, just a dream." She smiled and floated back across the room.

Her kiss disarmed me, it was gentle, not what I expected at all. I felt confused again, about her and us. *What's happening between us?* I asked myself. *What's our new relationship?*

"Neither of us has been totally straight with the other, Geof."

"What's that supposed to mean?" I asked.

"You concealed things."

"What things?"

"The reasons behind your block. Why you couldn't shoot people anymore." She turned to me. "You bullshitted me. The way I saw it that gave me the right to bullshit you a little too."

"What do you know about my block?"

She spoke softly. "I know plenty. Rakoubian asked around about you. He found out what happened in Guatemala."

I stared at her.

"You gave me this romantic phobia line, that it was deep and psychological, and you were just like some famous pianist who mysteriously loses the use of one of his hands. But that wasn't the reason. The real reason was much more prosaic." She looked at me, whispered, "Wasn't it, Geoffrey?"

I turned away, but she went on.

"At first, when Adam told me, I thought he was jealous, that he wanted me to think less of you so I'd think a little better of him. But today, when you told me how he set you up, I realized he'd had other reasons for checking you out. Why didn't you tell me? I'd like to hear about it. I really would, if you'd care to tell me now."

"What's this supposed to be, Kim? Truth night? We'll level with each other and henceforth never tell another lie?"

"Why not?" she asked. "You level with me, I'll level with you. What do you say?"

"Great," I said. "Except how will I know if you're telling me the truth?"

"How about if I pledge?" she asked. She raised her hand. "I hereby pledge. How's that?"

That sounded pretty good, so I told her about Guatemala, and, as I did, wondered why I'd held the story back.

I'd gone down there on assignment for the Sunday *Times* to shoot portraits of human rights advocates. It was a time when the government down there had been extremely repressive, and it took a special kind of bravery to speak out and protest. I photographed some very brave people, a surgeon, a lawyer from one of the wealthy Guatemalan families, and a housewife whose husband had "disappeared." Each of them had the composed features of people who hate injustice, eyes bright with indignation and fortitude. I worked hard to catch the common quality between them, and in the end I was pleased with my work.

Later, when my pictures were published, right-wing Death Squad maniacs clipped them out. They mailed them to my subjects with holes punched in the eyes, and later, when these same subjects were all killed on a single night, it was pretty clear my pictures had been used to draw up an assassination list.

My photographer friends tried to comfort me. They said the same thing could have happened to them, and from now on we'd all have to be more careful. Colleagues who disliked me said much meaner things. But in the end my worst enemy was myself.

I blamed myself for being naive, for forgetting that a camera can be a dangerous weapon. I imposed my own punishment: I would not shoot people for a while. A childish idea, but it made me feel better. Except that what started out as an act of self-denial soon evolved into a phobia. From the day of the killings until the day I started shooting Kim, I could not bring myself to photograph a human face.

"Oh, Geoffrey, you could have told me. I would have understood. I wouldn't have thought you were CIA, or whatever people said. I gave you lots of chances to tell me. But when you kept your secret, it seemed like . . . I don't know—like you *wanted* a dishonest relationship."

That did it. I actually felt embarrassed, which greatly softened the effect of her deceits.

"Anyway," she said, "I'm very proud that I helped you break through the way you did."

"You've been a powerful force in my life. My best friend thinks so. The first time I told him about you, he said 'Don't give that girl up.' "

"Then I gave *you* up. At least that's what you think, isn't it? One thing I want you to understand, Geoffrey, no matter what happens between us now: if, as you say, I've been a powerful force in your life, that's a power I won't ever abuse."

She held my eyes for a moment, then glanced at her watch. "Hey! It's late."

"Hungry?"

She nodded.

"Get dressed and I'll take you out."

She picked up her torn T-shirt and waved it gently before my face. "Love to, Geoffrey, but, unfortunately, I haven't a thing to wear."

I loaned her a shirt, then we walked a couple of blocks to a dark funky place called the Full Moon Saloon.

We took a corner table, ordered crabs, then Kim started pointing out the regulars. There was the happy-go-lucky sunburned shrimp-boat skipper who'd made a fortune smuggling marijuana, and the intense, shifty-eyed, young black dude who was the biggest coke dealer on the island.

She looked happy as she regaled me with all this Key West lore. Though she'd been in town for only a month, she knew a lot. I let her talk, and then I told her I was sorry, I knew she needed to relax, but there were still things I had to know.

"Don't apologize," she said. "Ask me anything."

"What happened that Saturday night when you came running to me at two A.M.?"

She paused, looked down at her food. "I think that was the scariest night of my life."

She started to talk, and as she did I felt this sickening feeling growing in my gut.

After Sonya was killed, Kim heard rumors about the Masked Man, stories that told her he was a lot more dangerous than the benign spectator he'd appeared to be. The stories concerned professional call girls. Kim managed to trace one of them back. She met the girl in a coffee house in the Village. The girl wore dark glasses and wouldn't give her real name. "Just think of me as your informant," she said.

She told Kim she'd been hurt. She'd known that she would be, she'd been told up front, and on that basis an extremely high fee had been negotiated and paid.

"What will happen exactly?" her informant had asked the call girl service manager, worried because the amount offered was so many times larger than what she usually received. The answer she got was candid and complete:

"You'll be tied up and gagged and mildly drugged, and then certain minor bones will be broken by a man who likes to hear them break. It won't be nearly so bad as it sounds; the drugs will alleviate much of the pain. But not all of it—don't say you weren't warned. Your fear and anguish are important. They're what this man is paying to see.

"Afterwards medical attention will be provided. Anything broken will be expertly reset. For a while you'll have to wear a cast; you can tell your friends you were in a skiing accident. Out of the dozen or so Hermès scarfs you'll receive, you'll be able to make a handsome sling. . . ."

During the recuperation period, there was an onslaught of gifts: not only scarfs, a different one sent each day, but also a matching set of Vuitton luggage, a little fur hat and muff, various and sundry earrings and pins, and finally a gold Cartier watch.

But neither the extraordinary fee nor the generous gifts could wipe out the memory of the horror. The girl told Kim that even if she were desperate and broke she would never go through such a scene again.

So how bad had it been? The pain was real enough—not severe, as promised, although the girl had definitely wanted to scream. No, it wasn't the pain she was afraid of, it was the terror—the sense of helplessness, of powerlessness, of being at the mercy of this person she couldn't see. Because he wasn't just some kinky guy who got off hurting girls; most of the guys who did that were rather sweet, once the session was done. The Masked Man was different. In this business one became highly sensitive to people, and the signals coming off him were very, very bad.

What signals? Kim asked her. After all, since he was masked, you never saw his features. Oh, but she did, the girl said, she caught little glimpses through the mask, a hint of the thin tight set of the lips and the sharp predatory eyes. And then there was the feel of him, his touch, his smell, the little sounds he made, the way he moved, like a mechanic fixing the motor of your car, whistling slightly under his breath as he worked, half humming this cheery little tune. . . .

There was—how to put it?—no consideration, no human connection, no sense that you were a human being. And he wasn't human either. There was something horrible about him that was impossible to describe. His touch was cold. He radiated malevolence. When he touched you it was like being touched by a snake.

Kim picked up a crab, sucked out the meat, wiped her mouth. All the time she was speaking she had stared past me at the room. Now her eyes met mine.

"Sonya was special," she said. "I loved Shadow, but Sonya was someone I adored. Everyone in our group felt the same way. All of us in Mrs. Z's 'ensemble.'

"She was a real beauty, you have to understand—a true live Nordic goddess. She was from Sweden, came to New York as an *au pair*, then decided to stay on. Precision-cut blond hair, cold blue eyes, she had this great little accent. She was nice too. She loved to joke and make us laugh. And onstage she was terrific, especially as a dominant. Cruel countess, pitiless equestrienne—Sonya loved those kinds of roles.

"And that was what the Masked Man liked to see: one girl being cruel to another. Mrs. Z spun all sorts of scenarios, including one in which Sonya played this empress who puffed on long gold-tipped cigarettes while her female rivals, and I played one, were tortured slowly before her eyes.

"Then one night Mrs. Z prepared a surprise. That was her method—to suddenly reverse the roles. She'd turn us regular submissives into dominants and make the dominants submit. It made for good theater, shock value, but there was something else working too, something we mentioned sometimes among ourselves. That Mrs. Z *liked* doing it. That she got off on it. That she liked to bring down the mighty and the proud. And that coincided with the Masked Man's fantasy, this thing he had about seeing haughty girls brought to their knees and made to beg.

"Look, for all I know, it wasn't a surprise. They could have discussed it on the phone. Maybe the Masked Man said, 'I'd like to see Sonya crushed.' And Mrs. Z replied, 'Oh, yes, that can be arranged. . . .'

"Which brings up my relationship with Mrs. Z. When I first came to New York, and I heard about her, I wanted desperately to join her class. She was a cult figure. She took very few students. It was extremely difficult to get in.

"I was on the waiting list, and when an opening came up I auditioned for it and she accepted me. The first year was great. Two full afternoons a week. I worked my ass off as a waitress to pay the fees, because I felt it was a privilege to study with her—a possible route to becoming a star.

"She had this idea about releasing the actor through uninhibited sexual play. There was a lot of that in class, and talk too of 'triggers,' nude work, stripped down psychodrama, the sacred ceremonial role of the actor as he who bares his naked self.

"She experimented with us. The sex stuff seemed to fascinate her, and we loved it—we knew it was daring and felt it put us on the cutting edge. Then one day she seemed to change, as if what we were doing released something dark inside. As if, in a single day, this fairly classy woman became, well . . . evil.

"Because, you see, a woman like her would never do what she did unless she enjoyed it."

"You're saying she got corrupted?"

"I think the corruption was already there."

"So suddenly the legendary acting coach became a sex-show impresario?"

"Yeah. And the shows were fascinating, Geoffrey. Very well done. Mrs. Z couldn't do them any other way. I loved being in them. There was this extraordinary feeling afterwards. Exhilaration and release."

She smiled, picked up her glass, slowly drank off her wine. For a moment there was a sparkle of lust in her eyes. Then it faded as she thought of something else.

"The first time the Masked Man asked for a private session with Sonya, Mrs. Z got very huffy, as if such a thing was too outrageous even to consider. Now I think it was a setup, that she knew from the start that Darling would make that request, and that her refusal, her huffiness, and the negotiations that followed were just a charade for Sonya's benefit.

"You know what happened—Sonya was paid ten thousand dollars. Cash! Incredible! Then the two of them went down to Mrs. Z's apartment on the floor below."

"What did Sonya agree to do?"

"The same as the call girl I told you about. Be tied up, drugged, then have a few bones broken. And because Sonya knew the threats were real, she expected to beg and cry and offer to do all sorts of awful things if only the Masked Man would relent."

"Sexual things?"

"More like degrading things, the more degrading the better. He wanted to see the Ice Maiden crawl. And she did—I'm sure of it. She spoke to me briefly before she went down.

" 'I'm going to do everything he asks,' she said, 'because I don't want to get messed up.'

" 'But you *will* get messed up. You know that. That's what all that money's for,' I said.

"She said she knew that, but still she thought she could avoid the worst of it if she conducted herself in a certain way. She had this idea that if she debased herself enough, she could satisfy him without having to be hurt. Poor Sonya! She thought she could wear him out. She didn't understand. She was going to have to pay for all the times she'd played the queen. The fact that he was accustomed to seeing her as dominant made her all the more valuable as a slave.

"While it was going on, Shadow and I waited upstairs to take her home. Mrs. Z just sat there playing solitaire. We never found out exactly what happened. God knows, Darling wasn't *touched* by her submissiveness. In fact, too much of it may have pushed him out of control. The way it ended up, he broke her neck."

Kim wept as she told me this; tears streamed down her face. And I felt the same hollow sickening feeling in my stomach. I pushed my food away.

"Which brings me finally," she said, "to that Saturday night when everything fell apart. I told you how Rakoubian approached me, what we agreed to do. After he got his pictures, I went to Mrs. Z. I was nervous, but I was a good enough actress to cover up.

"I laid it out for her: the Masked Man was Arnold Darling. I had proof, including a picture that showed him taking off his mask.

"She asked to see it. I showed it to her. She shook her head, pretended she was surprised. She'd maintained all along she didn't know who he was, but I knew she was lying; her reaction was so obviously feigned.

" 'So what do you want?' she asked. I told her a million dollars. She said that was absurd, that the material didn't justify anywhere near that kind of money.

"I told her the amount didn't seem so large to me, not with a homicide involved.

"She listened, and then she asked: 'What do you want of me?'

"I told her I wanted her to act as go-between, and for that she'd get ten percent.

" 'And if I refuse?' she asked.

" 'You won't,' I said. 'Because you're guilty too for Sonya's death.'

"She understood. She said she'd give it some thought. I told her not to think too long, because if I didn't hear from her soon, I'd take the pictures to the cops.

"She looked at me quite strangely then, and then she kind of smiled. 'Be careful, my pet. You're playing with fire.' Then she kissed me on both cheeks.

"The next week or so was pretty tense. Adam was calling me every day. I tried not to let on to you that anything was wrong. I brought Shadow down to meet you. I was glad you two got along.

"The only odd thing was the call from Amanda Duquayne, and that was only strange in retrospect. I told you we'd done these little numbers together. But I hadn't heard from her in quite a while. Anyway, you know what happened. We went there, quarreled, then I went home to discover someone had broken into my apartment.

"But not really, you see, because the lock wasn't broken. Someone got in with a key, then tore the place apart. Dresses slashed. Shoes clipped in half. Like he went through all our stuff with a gardening shears." She made quick scissoring motions with her hands.

"He must have been looking for the photographs."

Kimberly shook her head. "I'd given Mrs. Z the standard line: the pictures were 'deposited' with a friend, and if anything happened to me, such as an 'accident,' they'd be released immediately."

"They were deposited with Rakoubian, of course."

She nodded.

"Still, you must have been scared?"

"Out of my mind. So right away I called Adam and he said 'Stay cool,' we had to expect a move like this, it was just a negotiating tactic, their way to soften me up so they could whittle down the price. I asked him if he thought the Duquayne invitation was a ruse to get me out of the apartment. He said it probably was. Then he told me again not to worry, that it only meant they were getting ready to close on a deal.

"But I *was* worried, and when Shadow didn't show, I became very concerned. Sure, she stayed out sometimes, but she always called me when she did. I barely slept. Then, when you woke me up, I started cleaning the apartment just so I wouldn't have to think."

"You told me you and Shadow had a modeling session."

"What we had scheduled was a rehearsal."

"At Mrs. Z's?"

She nodded. "It was to be just the two of us late that night, preparing a scene for a new client, someone we hadn't met."

"What happened?"

"I always knew I'd have to leave New York, no matter how the blackmail turned out. I'd told Rakoubian, of course, and Shadow too, my explanation being that since Sonya's 'accident,' I'd grown so fearful of Mrs. Z, I was afraid to stay in town. I also told Jess Harrison, the guy down the hall with AIDS. But I never told any of them about Key West. And I was careful when I bought my ticket. Even though it cost me more, I bought one with open dates and used a phony name.

"I spent most of that day getting ready to leave. I finished cleaning out the apartment and packed up the few things that remained. I also spent a lot of time thinking about how I could explain it all to you."

"I thought you weren't going to explain it."

"I was. Later I changed my mind."

"Why?"

"Because of what happened, the trap I walked into later that night."

Shadow finally called late in the afternoon. Kim was relieved to hear from her. Shadow said she'd slept over at one of her friend's, and when Kim told her about the break-in and the damage to their clothes, Shadow sounded upset, but not so upset, Kim thought later, as she should have been.

Anyway, they had a normal enough conversation, and agreed to meet at midnight at Mrs. Z's. Then Kim went down to West Seventeenth to see Adam Rakoubian.

She told him she was scared, she was going to leave New York, hide out where she couldn't be reached. No more face-to-face meetings with Mrs. Z; from now all the dealings would have to be by phone.

"What about the money drop-off?" Rakoubian asked.

She assured him she'd be there for that. She also told him she thought it was time to lower their demand. If they cut it in half, she said, Darling would think he was getting a bargain.

They quarreled. Rakoubian stonewalled on the money. She, in turn, accused him of talking big while she took all the risks. Both of them got angry, and nothing was resolved. When she left she began giving serious thought to dumping the blackmail idea and going to the cops.

There was an actor's trick Mrs. Z had taught her: to really consider a certain option, so you can voice it with conviction on the stage. So she actually did consider that as she started downtown to Mrs. Z's. *I have to mean it*, she told herself. *Only by meaning it, will I be able to compel belief.*

When she arrived at the loft, Shadow wasn't there, just Mrs. Z alone. The acting teacher, seated in the spectator's throne, got directly to the point.

In the first place, she said, no intelligent person pays blackmail, because he knows, no matter how much he pays, it's only an installment against future demands. Furthermore he knows that even when pictures are turned over, copy negatives have invariably been made.

Therefore the Masked Man (she refused to acknowledge his name) had considered her proposition and refused. Yes, he had once tried on the mask, and yes, he had attended various performances. But he had had nothing to do with any homicide, and could alibi his whereabouts the night the alleged crime had taken place.

This having been said, Mrs. Z continued, the Masked Man wanted to rid himself of the nuisance. He was prepared, therefore, to pay twenty-five thousand dollars for the photographs, and (this was the most important part) a sworn notarized statement from Kimberly in which she would admit to having attempted extortion.

That was it, his final offer, and there would be no further discussion. It was a take-it-or-leave-it proposition. So, did Kimberly accept? Or not?

No, she most certainly did *not* accept, she said, but she agreed there would be no more discussion. Her offer to sell the photographs for a million dollars was hereby withdrawn. She would take them and her story to the cops.

Mrs. Z looked at her closely. "That is not a credible threat."

Kimberly responded that it seemed credible to her, as, at the very least, the performance loft would be closed, and the involvement of prominent people, such as the Duquaynes, would be exposed. Furthermore, Sonya's disappearance could easily be verified, and regardless of any phony alibis, there would be considerable interest in Kimberly's claim that Darling had murdered Sonya in a violent sex-for-money scene brokered by Mrs. Z.

As Mrs. Z began to show distress, Kim was feeling pretty good. She felt she was handling the situation well, and the time to strike a bargain was at hand.

But then Mrs. Z said quietly that she'd like to show Kimberly a videotape. She turned on a VCR and a monitor, and when Kim saw what was on it, she began to scream.


We were on Duval. It was 11:30, we'd finished dinner, and were walking toward the Post Office to pick up my car. The bars of downtown Key West, filled and boisterous, poured country music into the sticky summer night.

"It was awful, what she showed me," Kim said, clutching my arm. "They had Shadow naked and tied up. They'd grabbed her the night before; when she'd phoned me she'd been in their hands. The tape showed her writhing and terrified. It wasn't acting—I knew her too well to be fooled."

"Was the Masked Man there?"

"You couldn't see him. The camera was focused on Shadow. But you could see these hands moving in and out of the frame, doing all these awful things. I thought they were his. I felt they were, on account of the look in Shadow's eyes."

"What kind of look?"

"Total terror. The look of someone who knows she's going to die."

"*Jesus!*"

"After about a minute, Mrs. Z turned it off. 'She's halfway now to going the way of Sonya,' she told me. 'She'll go the whole way unless you do what I say.'

"I was to sign the extortion papers and then retrieve the photographs. If I didn't come back in a couple of hours, Shadow . . . well, she didn't have to spell it out.

"There was no choice. I signed, then left the building. My legs were trembling. I don't think I'd ever been so scared.

"My plan was to go to Rakoubian and make him give me all his negatives. If he refused I'd threaten to turn him over to Mrs. Z.

"There was a taxi waiting up the block. It started toward me, then something told me I shouldn't get in, that it was too convenient to find it sitting there in that deserted area that time of night.

"I ran across the street. That's when I noticed two men, one on each end of the block. They'd been waiting in the shadows. When I ran, they started running too. I darted down a side street, then through an alley, and then into that disco, Lil's, on Desbrosses, near where you and I met. No trouble getting in. They knew me there. I ran straight through the place, then out the fire door in back.

"I knew then I couldn't return to Mrs. Z's, no matter the threat to Shadow. Whatever I did, they'd kill us both. They'd have to, to shut us up."

"Why didn't you go to the cops?"

"You kidding, Geoffrey? I was up to my ears in it. I'd withheld evidence on a murder and I was party to a blackmail scheme. And even if I did go, I was sure I'd still get killed. That's how scared I was."

"So you came to me?"

She nodded. "There wasn't anyone else. I caught a cab coming out of the Holland Tunnel, rode it down to Park Row, then ran down Nassau to your corner and phoned." She took hold of my arm again, squeezed it, then brought my hands to her lips. "Thank God, you were home. You saved my life. And you were so damn nice. When you saw I didn't want to talk, you didn't insist. And then I did what I always do when I'm overwhelmed—closed my eyes and went to sleep."

"The next morning you decided to run?"

"Yes. But I couldn't tell you then. Now you see why, don't you, Geoffrey? *Don't you?*"

"Yeah," I said. "I guess I do."

I knew most of the rest of it, how she left my place, went back to hers, picked up her bags and said good-bye to Jess. Then she taxied to the airport and called Rakoubian while waiting for her plane.

She told him what had happened, that Shadow had probably been killed, and that she was getting out of it now, was going away.

He tried to persuade her to take another crack at Mrs. Z, or at least wait to see if Shadow reappeared. She hung up on him, boarded her flight, flew to Miami, then took a bus to Key West. In just two days she found an apartment and a job. She wanted to bury herself; she thought she had until I showed up that afternoon.

"Funny," she said, "now that I think of it, Adam should have sounded a lot more frightened than he did. Now, of course, I know the reason: he thought he was safe; he'd set you up to take the rap for him."

We found my car, and when she saw the mess in the back, she shook her head and smiled. She helped me clean out the discarded snack bags, then we drove to the Spanish Moss, where we fell asleep in each other's arms.

I think it was around three in the morning when I woke up and saw her sitting across the room. She was in the chair staring out the window, sobbing almost silently.

"Hey, what's the matter?" I went to her, put my arm around her, tried to wipe away her tears.

"Scared," she said.

"Why? It's over now."

"It's what you said about Key West."

"What did I say?"

"That it's like a box canyon, one way in and one way out."

"That was just talk," I said. "I think you're safe here, very safe."

She shook her head. "If you found me, they'll find me, and they kill people, don't forget. I think they're still looking for me and they still want to kill me and now I don't know where to go."

"They won't find you, I promise," I said. Then I tried to coax her back to bed.

"They *will* find me! Of course they will. *You* did! So why not them?"

"They won't," I said. "They can't. You see, I *really* missed you. And I had a clue."

"What clue, Geoffrey? What are you talking about?"

She looked so frantic then, so sad and desperate, that I thought it only fair to tell her what I'd done.

I went through it all: the unexplained number on my telephone bill, my research at the library, my trip to Cleveland, finding Grace, tracking her to the topless joint. Then our date, the massage, and how, the following morning, I'd broken into her house and found the return Key West address on the envelope.

Kim nodded at me through it all. She smiled at my surprise when I first saw Grace topless, and giggled as I recounted my misadventures with Heidi the dog. When I was finally finished, she shook her head.

"Did you know I was that girl?"

"Which girl?"

"The one Grace fell in love with," she said wistfully. "I was a waitress in that bar in Shaker Heights. . . ."

I looked at her. There was still something that knotted my stomach: the ever-loving tone in her letter to Grace.

"Are you still in love?" I asked.

Kim laughed. "Me and Grace?" When I nodded, she turned serious. "I think maybe she's still a little in love with me. And certainly I feel something for her, though I wouldn't exactly call it love."

"What would you call it?"

"I care for her. She launched me. Loaned me the money so I could go to New York, even though that meant I'd be leaving her forever. I feel about her the way you probably feel about your friend in New Mexico—that she's my closest friend, a sister almost. Did you read my letter to her?"

"It wasn't in the envelope," I lied.

We woke early, kissed, made love, showered, ate breakfast, then drove to Smathers Beach. There was hardly anyone on that southern crescent of the island, just a few joggers running along Roosevelt Boulevard and a couple of purveyors of soft drinks and tacos positioning themselves for the mobs that would descend later on.

I parked behind a van with a map painted on its side showing its owners were in the midst of a five-year drive around the world. Then we walked out onto the sand, actually ground coral, and strode along the water's edge.

"Oh, Geoffrey, Geoffrey. . . ." She spun around on her heel. "How the hell am I going to get myself out of this?"

I took off my shirt. Though it was only eight o'clock, the sun felt wonderful on my back.

"Seems to me there aren't too many choices," I said. "I'll call Scotto, tell him what happened, and turn over the photographs."

She stopped whirling. "What are you talking about?"

"I think that's the best solution."

"What photographs?"

"The ones of Darling."

She looked stunned. *"You've got Rakoubian's photographs?"*

"I took them from him. I thought I told you that."

"Where are they, Geoffrey?" Her voice was urgent.

"In my suitcase back at the motel."

*"Jesus!"* she said. "I can't believe this! You've got the pictures. *Oh my God!"*

She broke away from me, ran into the water, then high-stepped through it like a drum majorette. "We've got the pictures! We've got the pictures!" She sang out the phrase like the refrain of a song.

She must have noticed me staring at her because she ran back out of the water, and took hold of my hands.

*"Don't you see?"* she said as she pulled me along the sand. *"We've got them, Geoffrey. Now we've got them! Now we're really safe!"*

It took me a while to calm her down, get her to explain what she meant. When finally she did, we were sipping tea in the loggia at the Casa Marina Hotel, looking toward the gardens and the sea, and she was stone-cold serious.

"When Sonya was killed, they covered it up, made it look like an accident. The pictures of Darling don't prove all that much, just that he's a kinky guy who likes to wear a mask. But Shadow's different. She's a 'Model Torture Slaying.' There's a real police investigation going on. And the pictures tie into it because, really, they're the reason she was killed."

Ceiling fans slowly revolved above us, while elderly hotel guests, in straw hats and lime Bermuda shorts, shuffled by complaining of the heat.

"Fine," I said. "I know all that. Now what does my having the pictures have to do with us being safe?"

"Don't you see? We have something to bargain with. It's the pictures that made them hesitate. If they didn't care about the pictures they would never have let me go—they would have killed me then and there. And they would have killed you too, Geoffrey, since they think you were the photographer. But they didn't. They threatened you, broke in, threw some lye, talked tough to you on the phone, but they never harmed you."

"All right," I said, "so they care about the pictures."

She nodded. "A lot more than they pretend. Mrs. Z says, 'Oh, they're not important, you've probably made copy negatives, the pictures are just a nuisance.' But now that Shadow's been killed they're no longer *just* a nuisance. They're valuable because they're the motive. Give the cops the pictures and they start looking very hard at Darling and Mrs. Z. Eventually somebody talks or makes a deal, and then the two of them go on trial for murder."

"Which is why I want to call Scotto."

She shrugged. "That's one way to go."

"Is there some other way?"

"Yes . . . if we have the guts."

I knew then what she was about to say. "No way! Forget it, Kim. Absolutely not!"

She touched my arm, stroked it. "Think about it. In the first place, the way it looks, Darling isn't soiling his hands anymore. He's brought in pros. That guy who called you, the boy who threw the lye, the people who parked the car at Newark Airport—they sound like hired goons."

"Doesn't that worry you?"

"Sure. Because once you go to the cops, both of us are targets. The pictures don't mean anything without the story. And you and I are the only ones who know it."

"There's Rakoubian."

"He won't talk. He doesn't want to die."

"Neither do I," I said. "Really, Kim, haven't you had enough of blackmail? Your best friend was killed. You're stuck down here. Isn't it time to lead a normal life?"

She stared at me, then shook her head. "Not yet," she said. "See,

Geoffrey, this isn't finished yet. Darling and Mrs. Z—they have to pay."

We didn't talk about it anymore, just spent the morning lying lazily on the beach. Then I took her to her apartment, waited for her to change, and drove her on to her restaurant, as she had to work a double shift.

I spent the afternoon by myself, walking around Key West. After three and a half days of staking out the Post Office, I needed to break out and move.

Toward the end of the afternoon, I wandered up to the Southernmost Point. It was a curious place, a dead-end intersection with a large striped concrete buoy bearing the words: SOUTHERNMOST POINT CONTINENTAL U.S.A. Beside the buoy stood an old black man behind a display of shells and sponges. That was it, there was nothing else.

The understatement appealed to me. This was the tail end of the nation. It was pathetic, and there was no reason to make anything more out of it. I stationed myself there, then started taking pictures of people taking pictures of one another as they posed before the buoy.

It seemed to me that the premise behind their picture-taking was their conviction that by freezing selected moments from their lives they could somehow cheat aging and death. That seemed poignant to me, well worth trying to express. But it was an elusive idea, and, though it concerned photography, was perhaps too deep to be expressed in photographs.

Finally, as the afternoon waned, I strolled down to Mallory Pier to attend the sunset. I ate by myself at a Cuban restaurant, and then went back to my room to rest.

The moment I lay down I felt empty and forlorn. I'd found Kim, heard her story, and believed in her again. I had, moreover, held her in my arms, and I no longer felt the anger that had brought me to this strange tropical little town. I didn't even think it was important anymore to know her real name; she was who she was, authentic to her vision of herself.

But I was bothered greatly by her idea that we should continue with the blackmail. That she thought I'd even consider a thing like that disturbed me very much.

She came to me that night after she finished work. She used my bathroom to wash away the sweat and the smell of food, then crawled into bed beside me and molded her body against mine.

"Did you call him?" she asked.

"Scotto. No."

"Why not? I was sure you would."

"Maybe tomorrow."

"Tomorrow's a new day," she said.

"Are you working?"

"Yeah, but I'm free until five." She hugged me. "Would you like to go snorkeling out on the reef? It's really a lot of fun. One of my roommates has a boyfriend who has a boat. We can borrow masks and tubes."

It *was* fun. The roommate, Pam, a frizzy-haired blonde, was from South Carolina and spoke with a spunky Southern drawl. Her boyfriend, Doug, who owned the boat, was a genial beach-comber type.

With their lean bodies and gorgeous tans, Kim, Pam and Doug looked the embodiment of sun-worshiping American youth. But they were nice to me, didn't make me feel apart even though I was pale and middle-aged.

As soon as we were out on the water the girls took off their tops. Then Doug showed me how to snorkel. The reef was fascinating, the corals beautiful and delicate. I learned the names of different varieties: elkhorn, staghorn, pillar, flower, brain.

I liked the schools of tiny fish that darted between the corals, and the occasional moray eel that wriggled its way among the underwater trees. Doug pointed out sponges on the ocean floor and an encrusted cannonball from an ancient wreck.

The girls had brought along a hamper of sandwiches. We ate, I took portraits of them, and then we headed back. The whole trip, spent with attractive friendly kids, made me feel good—burned by the sun, washed by the sea.

After Kimberly went off to work, I returned to my room, stared at the phone and thought about calling Scotto. But I decided to put it off. I knew that once I called him, my life would be changed. I wasn't ready to break my Key West idyll yet.

The next day Doug picked us up in his ratty jeep and drove us up to Sugarloaf for flats fishing. Again the girls took off their tops. Kim's anointings of my skin with suntan oil finally began to take effect.

When Kim caught a bonefish, I immortalized her victory with a photograph showing her holding up her catch and grinning like Ernest Hemingway.

When we got back to Key West and she went off to work, I thought again of calling Scotto, and again I put it off. I studied Rakoubian's pictures for a while, to see if they contained something new. The shots of Darling in his mask were frightening, but the hurried pictures of him going into buildings seemed almost innocuous.

Several times on my various walks I'd passed the Key West Public Library. At two the next afternoon I entered the low pink-hued building, found a chair in the small reference section, and spent the afternoon researching the mysterious architect.

He appeared, from the pictures I found of his various homes, to be as rich as Rakoubian had said. In a spread on his Manhattan town house in *Architectural Digest*, I saw two paintings by Gauguin on the dining room walls and a portion of his priceless collection of Japanese scrolls and screens.

But it was his remarkable vacation house in Jamaica that intrigued me most, a building he had designed himself. In this elegant structure, made of bleached wood and great expanses of glass, he had tried, he said, "to combine the majesty of a Palladian villa and the austerity of a traditional Japanese house."

Each piece of furniture was a handmade original, every object exquisitely chosen, every flower perfectly arranged. Floating above the fireplace was a gilded medieval sculpture of an angel. It seemed improbable that a man who had created such a paradise could be so awesomely corrupt.

But as I read other articles I found subtle indications. "A tough boss, incredibly demanding, he doesn't suffer fools gladly," an associate said. "He's quite capable, when displeased, of treating you as if you don't exist."

Another architect, a rival, said, "We are what we build, and Arnold Darling's buildings reflect his soul. Sharp, hard-edged slashes against the sky, there is no comedy in them, no wink of complicity. His is a brutalism that conceals its brutality. Darling diagrams the cruelty of our corporate age."

I believe in the efficacy of photographs, that a well-taken picture can often tell you more about a subject than even a firsthand look. So I pored over photographs of Arnold Darling's work, searching for keys to the man, and by the end of the afternoon I began to understand a lot.

He was secretive. The articles told me that, but his buildings expressed it too. No question that he was an artist who channeled his feelings into structure and form; the buildings were strong, sometimes even magnificent, but there was also stealth and cunning in them, a clandestine rage and a taciturnity that matched his tight-lipped face.

Walking from the library down to Mallory Pier, I thought about Darling in his mask. Why, I asked myself, does he wear a fencing mask, instead of one made of rubber, or one of those fetishistic black-leather jobs you see in sex boutiques?

There was a reason he liked the fencing mask, and the more I pondered it, the more clearly I saw how that was connected to his designs. Such a mask does not cling to the contours of the face; rather, it acts as a second skin. Darling's buildings were like that, seamless, self-protective. Their vaultlike doors gave an impression of impenetrability and their deep-tinted windows hid their occupants from sight.

But there was more. A fencing mask, designed to protect the face from the consequences of combat, is, by its nature, aggressive. It's the mask of the warrior, the man who attacks, and who, while so doing, conceals his eyes.

At the bottom of Duval, I paused before a person I'd noticed several times before, an old man, sitting against a wall, quietly playing a harmonica. When our eyes met, he gestured toward a tin cup by his feet. I put five dollars in it and asked if I could take his picture. He nodded, then began to play again.

As I focused on his face I was struck by its vulnerability, the very opposite of what I'd seen in Darling's. There was pathos there, and pain, and the ravages of life. Nothing in his countenance was masked.

I think it was at that moment, the moment I took that picture, that all the anger I'd previously felt toward Kim was suddenly transferred to Darling. I hadn't cared about him before, but now, on my way to the sunset ritual, I began to care very much. This was the man who had murdered Sonya and Shadow, and had ordered lye thrown at my eyes. He was rich and secretive and evil, and now I too began to hate him.

The hatred seethed in me all that night, but if Kim sensed it, she didn't let on. When she came to me after work, she was gentle and loving. She stroked and fondled me and whispered endearments in my ear.

The next morning, when we were eating breakfast, I asked her what she meant by "pay."

She looked at me curiously.

"You said Darling and Mrs. Z 'have to pay.' "

She laughed. "Pay money, of course."

"Would that really do it for you?"

"It would be reparation."

"Does money repair?"

"Of course not, but it can help." She gazed at me. "If a person feels injured and sues for damages and wins and is paid, that helps to even up the score. That's why people looking for equity always ask for money."

"You sound like a lawyer."

"I'd have made a good one. I have a lot of indignation. I think you've noticed that."

"So you want Darling to pay us a million dollars?"

"That wouldn't be so bad now, would it?" She smiled.

Later at the beach, as she was oiling my back, I brought up the subject again.

"Why would he pay this time, when he refused before?"

"Because of Shadow. The case against him is stronger now."

"But he's made it clear he won't pay. That's what Rakoubian said."

"Rakoubian's stupid. He doesn't understand. Of course he'll pay if he's got no alternative."

The way she was sitting on me, rubbing in the oil, reminded me of the massage I'd gotten from Grace. I liked the feel of her weight on my body. Suddenly I felt aroused.

"We'd have to do it differently this time," I said.

"Yes, we'd have to be much more clever. And now that we know where Mrs. Z stands, we wouldn't be falling into any traps."

"What about that affidavit you signed?"

She played her fingers on my neck. "Who cares? It confirms my story. I signed it under duress. It was a fake anyway, just a way to make me think they'd let me go."

"Blackmail isn't all that easy, Kim. Sooner or later you have to show to collect your money."

"Between the two of us, Geoffrey, with all our brains, I'm sure we can figure out a way."

I turned, looked up at her. "Then what happens? What's to prevent them from killing us afterwards?"

"The same thing that kept them from killing us in the first place."

"What's that?"

"The photographs."

I turned my head back to the sand. "We wouldn't turn them over—is that what you're saying?"

"I wouldn't, would you? But even if we did, we'd keep back copies. They know that. Mrs. Z said as much."

"In that case, what would they be paying for?"

"Silence."

"You've thought this through."

"I've spent a month thinking about it." She bent forward, lay her face against my back, kissed my spine. "Do you think it can be done, Geoffrey? You know, done *properly*?"

. . .

The next two days, while I tortured myself over the problem, she acted as if she didn't have a care. It was as if, having transferred the burden to me, she finally felt she could relax.

We went about our routine, swimming and snorkeling in the mornings, then she would go to work, and I would walk around taking pictures and feeling agonized.

Though we spoke of many different things during our times together, our brief exchanges about the blackmail ran through our conversations like a thread:

"What do we do about Rakoubian?" I asked her. We were lying in bed in my motel. She was fondling me through my clothes.

"Ignore him."

"What if he wants a cut?"

"He gave up his right when he chickened out. Jesus! Why worry about him?" She stroked my cock. "Now, here's something *worth* discussing," she said.

Afterwards, resting together, my hands cupping her breasts, I asked her what I should say to Scotto.

"Tell him anything you want."

"I suppose we could take their money, then turn the pictures over to him anyway."

"Totally impractical. We'd have to give the money back." She crawled onto me and began to lay a line of passionate kisses across my stomach. "But, God, Geoffrey, I love you just for thinking of a thing like that!"

"Is the money really so important?" I asked her, as we dressed to go out to eat.

"It's the idea of making them hurt that's best. But the money helps, doesn't it? I mean it kind of softens the thing. It's like, I don't know"—she put her arms around me—"like getting a reward."

. . .

We spoke about it as we took a shower crowded together in my tiny motel shower stall. She was slowly soaping my back.

"If we *do* blackmail them, and they *do* pay us, and we get away with it—then what do we do?"

"My goodness, Geoffrey, what do you think?" She stopped soaping me. "We live high off the hog, on easy street. . . ."

"How dangerous is Mrs. Z compared to Darling?" I asked her. It was early in the morning. We were jogging along Roosevelt, on the northern curve where the houseboats are tied up.

She squinted. Her T-shirt was soaked through. Her forehead was flushed. "She may be even more dangerous," she said.

"Why?" I was panting.

"Because it's new to her. Because she's just discovering it. Because it's not clear yet just how far she'll go."

"She's already been party to two murders. How much further *can* she go?"

"I'm not sure, but I think there's always another level. The pit's always bottomless, don't you think?" She ran ahead. "Race you to the end," she yelled. I chased after her, but failed to catch up.

Perhaps she was right, the pit is bottomless, for I was then in a kind of pit myself. Art photographer turning blackmailer: that was the route I was on.

And, strangely, it seemed appropriate, as if photography, this fine and moral art I practiced, somehow led naturally to blackmail. There was a tradition to it—perhaps a thousand stories had been written in which people who possessed incriminating or disgracing photographs demanded payment from those who could be incriminated or disgraced. Blackmail, it seemed, had been an ignoble offshoot of the trade, ever since the invention of the camera.

. . .

That night, after dinner, as Kimberly and I walked through the quiet sweet-smelling streets of Old Town, I told her I'd come to a decision.

"Yes, Geoffrey?" I could feel her tension as she took my arm.

"I want to bring in my friend Frank Cordero, the one who lives in New Mexico."

I felt her grip tighten. "Tell me why."

"I don't think we can do this without him."

"Tell me about him. How did you meet?"

"We met in Vietnam," I said. "He was a lieutenant, Special Forces A-team commander. One night, when I was staying at his camp, we got to talking about photography. He was an amateur, modest about his work, but serious—he even had a darkroom set up out there in the bush. After we talked awhile he asked if I'd critique his pictures. I said Sure, thinking that was the least I could do. So then he brings out the most extraordinary stuff—pictures so sensitive that at first I didn't believe he'd shot them. But he had. This commando type, who killed and laid booby traps and ambushed enemy patrols, spent his spare time taking sympathetic pictures of Vietnamese kids.

"We became friends. He taught me about war, and I taught him about photography. He was with me when I shot my Pietà.

"Since he lives out West we don't get much chance to see each other. But the friendship's very close. He's become a professional photographer, he's married to a Vietnamese girl and he's got a houseful of terrific kids. I want to go out there now and see him. He's the only person I know who can tell me whether this thing can work. If he thinks it can, I'd like him to participate. Of course I need your permission for that."

She didn't say anything for a while. Then she asked me how good he was.

"The best," I said. "Straight. Fearless. First-class strategic mind.

If he joined us he'd be like a hired gun, which, considering Darling's resources, is something I think we need."

"What would we give him?"

"A full third share. I can't see offering him less."

"A third—that's a lot of money." She hesitated. "On the other hand, a hundred percent of zero is zero, isn't it?"

"What do you think?" I asked.

"I think you should go see him, the sooner the better." She stopped walking. "Hold me, Geoffrey."

I held her.

"Now kiss me the way you did that time at the cemetery."

I kissed her.

"Harder, Geoffrey. Please, as hard as you can."

I kissed her hard.

"Bite me."

I bit her.

"Oh, that's good," she said, "very good. Now take me back to your room and screw my brains out."

As we started back to the Spanish Moss the palms swayed wildly in the wind.

## Four

Is it not the task of the photographer . . . to reveal guilt and point out the guilty in his pictures?

—Walter Benjamin

I

T HAD BEEN TWO YEARS SINCE I'D LAST SEEN FRANK Cordero. He'd come up to New York with his portfolio of photographs looking for a gallery. He'd crashed in my loft, then made the rounds in his worn old boots and cowboy hat. People gushed over his work, oohed and ahed, told him his pictures were "fascinating." But in the end no gallery would take him on.

The night before he flew back to New Mexico we went out together and got quietly drunk. He wasn't mad or bitter, held no rancor for the New York dealers, and had no intention of changing his course.

"They don't think they can sell me here—fine, they ought to know. Meantime I'll keep on working, and sell what I can in Santa Fe."

Though he'd been badly disappointed, he showed more concern for my problem than for his own: "What are we going to do about this block of yours, Geof? How're we going to get you back on the track?"

He was the most loyal friend I ever had. And so, when I saw him smiling at me in the Albuquerque airport, tanned and lean, his short black beard beginning to gray, the crow's-feet around his eyes etched a little deeper than I remembered, I was moved to feel that at last I was with the one person on this earth I could truly trust. And that was a relief after the weird scenes I'd been through in the weeks since I'd met Kimberly Yates.

He embraced me, grabbed my camera bag, hustled me out of the airport. A few minutes later we were in his battered Land Rover heading east on the Interstate, the raised road that slices through the center of Albuquerque.

The city flew by below, a grid of endless commercial strips, while the sky arched above like a giant hemisphere of deep blue silk stretched taut.

It was a Big Sky—as they say out West.

We left the city, curled around the back of Sandia Mountain and there confronted an amazing pile of clouds, soft white bulbous billowy things, pouring into the valley.

"Good formation," Frank said. He glanced at me. "Red filter?"

We laughed remembering the days in 'Nam when I'd taught him how a red filter can turn a blue sky black, making a dramatic background for scenes of war.

He glanced at me again. "It's serious, what's brought you out?"

"Pretty serious," I agreed.

"We'll give you a day to get used to the altitude. Then we'll talk about it," he said.

It felt good to be in the West. I could get high on the pure rarefied air, so much dryer than the tropical haze that clung to the Florida coast. And the dusty desert tones were a fine relief from the hot saturated colors of the Keys. Perhaps best of all the faces of the people looked real. They were in touch with the land. For a while, driving in silence with Frank, I wondered whether I'd been corrupted by the hothouse atmosphere of Key West. Blackmail photographs of a sexual voyeur—suddenly all that seemed far away.

Past Sandia we turned north, past dry fenced fields crisscrossed by gulleys and sparsely covered with desert grass. Then we drove through the old gold-rush town of Golden, where piles of stones, ruins of buildings, were spread about on either side of the road.

We stopped in Madrid for a beer in the local saloon. Ten years before, when Frank had first brought me there, Madrid had been a ghost town. Now it was a thriving village. But still there were haunting visions: rotted-out old houses strangely illuminated by the dying sun, and the hulks of forsaken automobiles with cryptic slogans emphatically scribbled on their sides.

It was late in the afternoon when we reached Galisteo. Mai must have seen us coming. She emerged from the house when we drove up, wearing a faded work shirt, jeans and hand-tooled boots. She smiled at me, the same marvelous smile that had driven me to distraction in Saigon. "Howdy, stranger," she said.

I rushed to her, grasped her up, whirled her around in my arms. "Geof-Frey, Geof-Frey!"

Then a bunch of handsome Eurasian kids crowded around.

Frank introduced them, three girls, Ali, Jessie and Meg, and the smallest, a boy, Jude, who gazed at me shyly while clinging to his mother's waist. Ali, the oldest, had Mai's willowy Vietnamese figure and the swelling breasts of an American teenage girl. She stood against Frank, who placed his hands protectively on her shoulders, while I distributed the funky Key West T-shirts I'd brought them all as gifts.

When the kids had gone to their rooms to start their homework, Frank showed me the improvements he'd made in the house. It was an old adobe set in a two-acre field, a ruin when he'd found it and bought it cheap. He'd rebuilt slowly, adding rooms as the family grew. In the years since I'd seen it, he'd added one for Jude and enlarged the back building, Mai's studio and foundry. His own studio and darkroom were in Santa Fe, twenty miles to the north.

Mai had prepared a Vietnamese dinner: a rich beef broth called *phu*, crisp spring-rolls, *cha-gio*, and thin slices of barbecued pork served with mint, lettuce leaves and delicate rice-flour cakes. The accompanying *nuoc-mam* sauce perfumed the dining room and brought back memories of warm mellow evenings in Saigon.

"Mom usually cooks Mexican. Makes a mean chili," Ali said.

"But tonight, in *your* honor, Geof—" Frank gestured at the array of food.

After the girls had cleared the table and retired to their rooms, the three of us sat out on deck chairs in front of the house sipping beers and watching the sun sink behind the old Spanish cemetery on the hill.

"The girls are great. Beauties too," I said.

"Yes, they're great kids, Geof-Frey."

Mai had always divided my name into syllables. She'd been in the States for fifteen years, but she still spoke with the singsong accent she'd used when she was an art student in Saigon. She'd met Frank at the Vietnamese-American Association when she'd enrolled in his English-language class. We'd both fallen in love with her, but Frank had won her heart. I'd always envied him his marriage. That night, looking at her, I could feel a little of that envy still.

Several of her metal sculptures were set out on the field in front, angular black forms made of old iron Frank had stripped off a ruined steam locomotive he'd found in Gallop, then hauled piece by piece to Galisteo. In the fading light her sticklike constructions began to resemble the skeletons of dinosaurs.

"You guys have it made out here. Hope you know that," I said.

"I think so," Mai said. "But sometimes Frank doesn't." She turned to him, shook her head.

"Sometimes I wonder if we aren't playing in the bush leagues," he said.

I reminded him of the dreary hassles of the city, the meretricious charms of the big-league Art Scene in New York, and how fortunate he and Mai were that they didn't have to compete with superficially talented hustlers like Harold Duquayne.

"Sure," he said. "But there've been some times lately when I've wondered when the struggle's going to end."

"It will, Frank." Mai rose, kissed me on the cheek, then stood behind Frank's chair, leaned down, thrust her fingers into his beard and kissed the top of his head.

"It's a good struggle. I think so, Geof-Frey." She looked at me, kissed Frank's head again, then slipped inside the house.

Frank and I remained out long after the sky turned black, catching up on everything, his kids, Mai's sculptures, his and my ambitions in photography.

"Fame, success—I know better than to care about that," he said. "But I'd like just once to experience it, to know firsthand how it feels. I think then I'd have an easier time living out here renouncing it."

"The only trouble with that," I said, "you might find out that you like it."

"Yeah, Geof." He laughed. "Well, isn't that the risk you take?"

*The terrible splendor of the sunrise*: In northern New Mexico it comes out of the Sangre de Cristo Mountains, comes fiercely, firing up the cold dry shrublands, reddening the saltbush and the scrub. The yuccas, chollas and grasses begin to glow. The gullies, called arroyos, create the shadows, black slashes across the plain. Then, as the sun rises, you feel the first intimations of the heat.

By 6:30 the kitchen was busy, Mai presiding over the stove, supervising the frying of sausages, the turning of flapjacks by Jessie and Meg. When we all were fed, Frank piled me and the girls into the Land Rover and took off down a dirt road that followed the dry gulch called Galisteo Creek. He dropped the girls at the school bus stop near Los Cerrillos, then turned north toward Santa Fe.

His studio was situated on an upper floor of a restored warehouse on Guadalupe Street. Not the choicest area in that city of galleries, but, still, within walking distance of the Plaza. A sign on the door said: FRANK CORDERO, PHOTOGRAPHS. There was a big room, lit by track lights, where he exhibited his prints, a darkroom where he did black-and-white printing for two famous Santa Fe photographers, Leo DeSalle and Nelly Steele, and a small workshop where he kept the old cameras he found, rebuilt, then sold to collectors.

He was getting tired, he told me, of making more money from the cameras than from selling his own photographs.

"Sometimes I'm here the whole day, and no one comes in, not a single person. No need for anyone to buy anything—enough for me if they just come in and look."

He put a CLOSED FOR THE DAY sign on the door, then we got back into his car.

"Where're we going?"

"Old road to Taos," he said. "We'll talk as we drive."

I told him the story, all of it, every detail from my first meeting with Kim on Desbrosses Street, to her seeing me off for Miami the morning before. He nodded as I spoke, occasionally asked a question to clarify the sequence of events. Other than that, his only interruptions were the stops he made to show me the sites of famous photographs.

I welcomed these respites. It was stressful to tell my tale, and listening to myself recount it, I began to wonder about my role. Did I come off as hero or antihero, lover or fool? Frank didn't let on what he thought. But I could tell by his smile that he liked the way I'd handled Rakoubian. And I knew, despite his silence, that he was taking in everything I said.

Meantime I was thrilled to see the places where the legends of our profession had planted their tripods and created immortal images. We stopped before the old wooden cross that Eliot Porter had photographed on the outskirts of Truchas, and then the small grave marker Beaumont Newhall had found in the cemetery at Las Trampas. We visited the church in San Lorenzo Pueblo photographed so brilliantly by Laura Gilpin, and the Mission Church in Ranchos de Taos (perhaps the most photographed site in the American West) where Paul Strand had so gravely shot the buttresses.

In Taos we ate burritos, and all the while I continued to talk. Then Frank drove me around Mount Wheeler, past the D. H. Lawrence shrine, on to the ruins of "E-town," where Edward Weston had taken his famous series.

"Funny about these places," I said. "The spot where I took the Pietà—I doubt I'd recognize it today."

"Because that picture wasn't about a place. It was about people." He paused. "I'll say one thing for this Kimberly of yours—she's got you shooting people again."

He pointed out something else to me too—that I'd returned to the Leica, the camera of my youth.

"It's like you went into this slow phase for a while, Geof, when you needed to use a view camera. But now your life has speeded up and you have to react more quickly. Maybe Jim Lynch was right—maybe you still are a photojournalist. Maybe the quick incisive look *is* your thing, not the slow examining gaze."

There was something special Frank wanted to show me, more important to him and more vivid than the subjects of other photographer's famous images. It lay just a few miles south of Eagle Nest.

He didn't say much as we approached, but I could tell by the way he was handling the wheel that a special emotion was brewing inside. Then, when I caught sight of the place, a soaring modern structure that seemed to grow out of the earth, I recognized it as a building I'd seen in several of the photographs on the walls of his gallery in Santa Fe.

As we turned up the drive he told me what it was, a Vietnam Veterans' Chapel built by the father of a marine killed in the war. It had since been taken over by the Disabled American Veterans, who now maintained it as a permanent memorial.

There was only one other car in the parking lot, and not a single person inside the chapel. We both sat down on a semicircular bench that faced the tall narrow window at the high end. Then we stared at the only visible artifact, a tall cross bearing an eternal flame.

I was impressed by the purity of the interior, the opposite of the heavily decorated mission churches we'd been looking at. But what really moved me was Frank's reaction. He focused on the cross with enormous concentration, then his shoulders began to shake. After a time I decided to leave him alone. Later, when he rejoined me, his eyes were red.

"Gets to me," he said. "Don't know why. Feel it every time I come. It could be the design, the site. Maybe just the idea that a kid got killed and his dad wanted to make a chapel to remember him, and when it was built it became a place to remember all the kids who died. How many years has it been, Geof? Twenty since we met? Fifteen since I finished my final tour? And it still hurts, you know. Maybe because I got a Vietnamese wife, half-Vietnamese kids, it's with me all the time. Maybe too because I don't want to forget it, not a single brutal moment. . . ."

He was calmer as, walking around the exterior, he told me how much he wanted to take a picture that would capture all he felt about the place. But he found the chapel difficult to photograph. He'd tried many times, shooting in different seasons, and he'd even tried to put some people in his pictures, visiting veterans he'd posed against the stone.

"But that didn't work out," he said, "and anyway I'm no good at setting stuff up. Remember what you taught me, Geof? That basically there're only two ways to approach photography: you roam the world searching for images or you make your own."

"You like *film noir*, Geof. Remember *The Woman in the Window*?" I nodded. We were driving back to Santa Fe by the new road that runs along the Rio Grande. "Edward G. Robinson explains blackmail to Joan Bennett. He makes a nice little speech.

" 'There are only three ways to deal with a blackmailer,' he tells her. 'You can pay him and pay him and pay him until you're penniless. Or you can call the police yourself and let your secret be known to the world. Or'—and here old Edward G. pauses for effect—'you can kill him.' "

I remembered that nice little speech.

"That's what you're up against. I should say 'we'—because I want in if you'll take me after you've heard what I've got to say. I have some reservations. The girl bothers me a little. But even if she's not as straight as you think, I can deal with her unless she's very bad news."

"Whatever she is, she isn't that," I said.

"Trust her?"

"I do now—yes."

"But then you're not the best person to judge her, are you, Geof?"

I had to agree with him about that.

"Okay, I got maybe nine points I want to make. First, normally I'd say double the demand to show we mean business. But we can't do that here because the original demand for a million was way too much. Still, now, we've got to stick to it. Show the slightest sign of weakness and we're dead.

"Second, we have to enforce compliance by giving the enemy (and that's what they are, Geof, *the enemy*—don't ever forget it!) a whole array of unpleasant alternatives. Fine to threaten them with the cops, but that isn't enough. Murder rap's good, but not sure. Find their other weak spot, threaten them there. That's how we make them pay."

"So what's their other weak spot?" I asked.

"Exposure. The tabloids. That's what'll make Darling shake. Guy wears a mask, he's afraid of being *seen*. So we go for that. We got pictures, we can show the world what he is. See, there's our basic threat: disgrace.

"In this same area, call it point three, we exploit that weakness to unnerve him. I'd like to see you stake him out, then ambush him with your camera. Even money says he won't be able to take it, that you can make him cover up. Do that and you're in charge. Then you'll hold the whip."

"That means going back to New York."

"You're going to have to do that anyway. Thing is, Geof, if you shoot him like I say, he gets to look you in the eye and see you're serious. Easy for him to come to a meeting prepared to stare you down. But take him by surprise, and every shot will be like a blow across his face."

I smiled. I liked that. In fact I liked Frank's whole approach. He had a grip on the thing, which made me feel good, and that I'd been right to bring it to him.

"This Mrs. Z—she's another weakness. As are the Duquaynes, if they're as fashionable and well known as you say. They didn't do any murders, but they don't want to go down with people who did. If we approach them right, we can get them to pressure Mrs. Z. And that may help us divide her from Darling."

I didn't get what Frank was saying. "Darling and Mrs. Z are accomplices."

"Yeah, right now they are. But for how long? He's got money, she doesn't, which means he's got to pay for both of them, and that breeds resentment—on both their parts. If he hadn't whacked Sonya, she wouldn't be in trouble. If Kim hadn't gotten ideas, he wouldn't be getting blackmailed. Doesn't matter that they're allies, each has got a problem with the other. The more we can exploit that, the more we weaken them and increase our chances."

"What next?"

"Send them a message. They have to understand what happens if they don't comply. The best message is a demonstration—like sending that kid to throw lye at your door. We're going to have to do a violent act to make them see we're serious, something comparable to breaking Rakoubian's lenses. That was a stroke of genius, Geof. Best move you made."

"What kind of violent act?"

"We'll think of something."

I must have moaned, because, when Frank glanced at me, his eyes were a little sharp.

"This isn't a game."

"I know that."

"Intellectually maybe, but not yet, not in your heart. What old Edward G. said in that movie—that's the way they're going to think. They're going to give very serious consideration to killing you, Geof—to killing all of us. Which brings me to point number five: Play for keeps. I'm talking now about mental attitude. This is combat, and they're the enemy, and there's no middle ground— it's us or them. Go into this, you're going into lawless territory where you have to be prepared for treachery and also to kill. I mean really be ready to do it, Geof, because that split-second when you're thinking, Should I kill this guy or is there some other way? will be the split-second when, without compunction, he'll be killing you."

He went quiet after that, and I fell silent too. I didn't doubt that everything he said was true. I only wondered whether I had the character for it. I was a photographer. I didn't know if I had a warrior's blood.

"Actually," he said, "it won't be so bad. I'll always be there watching your back. I want you to take pictures too. The more you take, the more they'll fear you because photographs are their nemesis. And with pictures, if things go wrong, you'll have material to take to Scotto. The cops would rather put away a decadent killer like Darling than a one-time amateur blackmailer like you."

"Okay," I said, "what's number six?"

"Neutralize the cops. You've handled them pretty well so far, but you can't leave them hanging the way you did. From your description Scotto sounds good, but Ramos may be even better. Good cops are relentless—that's why they choose the work. They like the chase and they like the capture. So when you go back to New York, you're going to have to handle them with care.

"Another thing you're going to have to do is sacrifice Rakoubian. Sounds harsh, but the guy deserves it. He deserves whatever he gets."

"What do you mean—'sacrifice'?"

"Squeal on him. Have Kim tell Mrs. Z he took the pictures. They may kill him for that, which wouldn't be such a bad thing— you'll be rid of the one person who might try to extort from you later on. Also you'll give Darling and Mrs. Z an outlet for their rage. Once they do something to him they may feel a lot less anger toward you."

I thought about that, and, funny thing, the longer I thought about it, the better I felt. Rakoubian had been willing to see me killed. Whatever happened to him now came with the territory.

"Okay," I said. "What's next?"

"An idea I have about Darling. Normally a guy like that would insulate himself. If he wanted to get rid of Shadow he'd contract out the job. He didn't. He tortured her. Which tells you what a twisted animal he is. But there's more. See, it's pretty clear he had some help, someone to drive her body to Newark, and those two guys who chased Kim on the street. Which means there're people around who know what he did, and no matter what kind of goons they are, they probably don't like him for hurting girls and enjoying it. Guys like that, if they're caught, they'll spill their guts, and Darling's got to know that too. That has to keep him up at night, as does the prospect that under certain conditions Mrs. Z may very well squeal herself. Okay, what does that tell us? That he may have as his objective the liquidation of all these difficulties at once. I mean killing you, me, Kim, his associates, Mrs. Z, everyone who knows—*everyone*. Now, if he does decide to go that route, if he sees that as his only way out, he can't use surrogates, he'll have to do it himself. And that means exposing himself on the field of battle.

"Which brings me to my final point: choose the battlefield. Ultimately, in a deal like this, there comes the payoff-and-exchange when the parties have to meet. That's the most dangerous time, the time we're most vulnerable, the time we want to control the territory. Can't be the base. Key West's your base—the place you take the money and hide out. And New York's no good—it's their territory as much as yours. Which leaves New Mexico. Resolve it out here, my stamping grounds, and we'll have a big advantage."

I'd been listening so intently, I didn't notice that just before Santa Cruz he had turned off the road to Santa Fe and driven a mile or two along the route to Tierra Amarilla. He stopped the car.

"What's this?" I asked.

"Get out. Take a look."

I got out, looked around, didn't see much of anything.

"You can't tell now," he said, "but right here"—he made a mark with his boot heel in the dirt beside the road—"this is the very spot."

I looked at him. He was grinning. "Can't help it, Geof. I couldn't

238

resist. This is where Ansel set up his tripod." He motioned to some ruins in a field on the left side of the road. "That's what's left of the village." He raised his finger above the distant mountains. "The moon was just about there. . . ."

"Moonrise, Hernandez": Ansel Adams's greatest picture, a photograph swooned over by school kids and sophisticated collectors alike. The picture had been printed over nine hundred times, but still the prints were so greatly desired they fetched close to ten thousand dollars whenever they came up at auction.

"To take a picture like that—the thought of it!" Frank looked at me, then down at the ground. "Don't think you know, but for years I've been jealous of you. Guess most every photographer has. Jealous too of Ansel for 'Moonrise.' Jealous of Cartier-Bresson for the man leaping over the puddle. Of Kertesz for the man carrying the picture while the train passes on the bridge. Of Caponigro for the running deer. Those are the miracle pictures, the ones no matter how good you are, you can never find—they have to find you. I've thought about it a lot, why they come to some and not to others, and I've decided I shouldn't be jealous; they've enriched my life too much. I've also come to the conclusion that people don't just stumble into shots like that, that they come to the great photographers because the great photographers are ready. I was with you, remember, when you took the Pietà. You were ready. Were you ever. . . ."

When we reached Santa Fe, he called Mai, told her we wouldn't be back till late, then took me on a tour of the town. We strolled around the Plaza, then looked into the galleries on Canyon Road.

Most of what we saw was garbage: sentimental paintings of Navaho women and illustrator-type cowboy scenes. The prices shocked me when I considered the fact that the galleries wouldn't charge them unless they were what people were willing to pay.

After dinner at a Mexican place, Frank took me back to his studio. While he disappeared into his darkroom to finish up some work, the full force of what he'd said coming down from Taos suddenly hit me hard.

He was talking about killing or being killed, and sacrificing Rakoubian as if he were a pawn. I didn't know if I was ready for stuff like that. I picked up the phone on his desk and called Kim in Key West.

I caught her just as she was about to leave for work.

"Geoffrey, what a terrific time to call. I was starting to get depressed about tonight. How's it going? It's so humid here, you sweat from just thinking about going out."

The notion of her sweating turned me on. I imagined the gloss on her forehead, the faint aromatic flavor of her skin.

"Frank thinks we can do it," I said.

"Great! Is he willing to join us?"

"Yeah. Only problem is—it could turn violent, he says. I don't know if I'm up to that."

There was a pause before she spoke. "Don't worry about it."

"I *am* worried."

"Frank's our hired gun."

"Yeah . . . ?"

"So we'll let him take care of the violent parts." She paused again. "Hey! I miss you, lover-boy!"

"And I miss you."

"It's hard to sleep alone."

"Hard for me too."

"Come back soon, will you?"

"Looks like we'll be meeting in New York."

"All the better," she said, "'cause I'm really starting to loathe this place. I'd love it, of course, if I could lounge around the Pier House pool. But waiting on tables . . . Well, it won't be long now.

When you and I are done with this thing we'll *own* Duval Street. Got to go to work, Geoffrey. But I want to leave you with a thought. Instead of letting the danger scare you, see if you can let it turn you on. Go with it, the way you did with Dirty Adam. The way you did that first night down here. Remember how you ripped my clothes and left my brains on the floor?" She laughed. "Fun, wasn't it? Well, taking Darling's money can be fun for us too." She made a kissing noise. "That, Geoffrey, is a big sweet kiss. And please give a hug to Frank for me, even though I haven't met him yet."

After we hung up, I sat behind Frank's desk. Talking to her made me feel good. She was so vibrant, alive, and she was right about letting the danger excite me. All I had to do, I found, was just to think about it in a certain way.

When Frank came out of the darkroom he showed me the latest work of Leo DeSalle and Nelly Steele. He did all their black-and-white printing. Several times he paused to explain the pains he'd taken to achieve a particularly sensitive effect.

The two famous photographers made good strong pictures. DeSalle was the old master, working in the grand-view landscape tradition, while Steele, his young lover and protégée, made perfect tender little still-lifes.

"Leo doesn't bother with the darkroom anymore. He's done it all, and he'll keep doing it till he dies—climbing around the rocks like an old mule, setting up, then burying his head under the focusing cloth. But Nelly cares about everything, every tone, every nuance. Which is why, in time, she'll surpass him. And if she's smart, she'll leave him for someone else."

There was something poignant in Frank's observation that dovetailed with the comments he'd made on the site of "Moonrise, Hernandez." He was a master printer and a master analyst—he had the ability to see straight to the core of a situation. Looking again at his own work, I wondered why he tried to obfuscate what he saw. There was a density in his pictures that blocked access to their meaning. He showed the viewer something new, but he did not beckon him past the surface of the paper with his passion.

"Can't imagine trying to bring this off without you, Frank," I said. "But still I'd like to know why you want in on such a dirty deal."

He searched my eyes. "Money."

"Come on! It can't just be that."

"Why not?" He looked almost angry.

"Hey! Don't make me feel bad I asked a question."

"Sorry," he said. And then: "Your question cuts pretty close."

"I understand. Look—maybe you don't see it, but in a way you really *do* have it all. Great family. Great wife. You live in one of the most desirable places in the country. You and Mai are artists, you make your own hours. Maybe you're not as rich as DeSalle, but how many artists are?"

"Sure," he said, "I know all that. But it's not enough anymore. I'm forty-four. I'm tired of struggling. I'm sick of worrying—can I afford to have the car fixed? pay the grocery bill? send Ali to college? I'm sick of printing DeSalle's pictures, then reading articles about the superb prints of Leo DeSalle. I want to be a full-time photographer, take my shot, see how far I can go. And I want the same for Mai because I think her best work's still ahead. That's what it's all about, Geof—scoring the money to buy the time to pursue our own work for a couple years."

But after midnight, as we drove back to Galisteo, the scent of piñon trees heavy in the night air, he told me something else: "What I was saying up at Hernandez—sometimes I wonder whether I'll ever be ready the way you were."

"Ready for what?"

"To take the great picture when it comes."

"Come on, Frank!" His self-pity bothered me.

"No, Geof—I mean it. I know I'm a highly competent photographer. But maybe I'm better at something else?"

He went quiet after that, but a few minutes later, when he spoke again, his voice was different.

"Maybe this thing you've brought me, this blackmail thing— maybe this'll be *my* 'Moonrise,' " he said.

Again in the morning the fiery sun stoked up the cold dry fields. Mai drove the girls to the bus, while Frank and I sat outside working up a plan.

We plotted out the next steps: Kim's and my trip to New York, what each of us would do, who'd say what to whom, demonstrations we could make of our seriousness of purpose.

I phoned Kim in Key West twice that morning, and both times I put Frank on to speak with her. He asked her questions about Mrs. Z. Listening in to his side of the conversations, I could tell they were getting along.

"I think this partnership just may work out," Frank said after he spoke with her the second time. "She's a real live wire, this girl of yours."

"You told me, 'Don't let her go,' " I reminded him.

By noon we were excited; we felt we had a viable plan. We'd war-gamed the thing every which way, and though there were several points of danger, we couldn't find any major flaws.

Mai called us to lunch. The three of us ate at a picnic table in the back garden. Then Frank offered me his second car, a beat-up Volvo, to use while he went up to Santa Fe to tend his gallery. He gave me a map, marked some places he thought I might find interesting. When I was in the driver's seat ready to leave, he propped his arms against the door, leaned forward and spoke.

"You know you're going to have to pack iron."

I shook my head.

"You *have* to, Geof."

"I didn't carry a gun in 'Nam. I'm not starting now."

"Yeah, right—you only carry a camera. Well, we'll have to think about that," he said.

I drove to Lami, checked out the railroad station, then followed the Pecos River into the Sangre de Cristo range. There was a Benedictine monastery up there. I looked at it. But when I came to a settlement called El Macho, I did a U-turn and drove back to Galisteo.

I found Mai in her studio, an open-walled building set behind the house. She was wearing a welder's mask, cutting steel with an oxyacetylene blowpipe. She had an old stereo going full blast back there, Maria Callas as Norma, barely audible above the roar of her torch.

When she saw me she signaled me to stand back. For a while I watched her work. It was a strange scene, Callas singing her heart out while that lean little Vietnamese woman in the huge mask created showers of sparks.

Finally she turned off the torch and raised her visor. "Want to talk, Geof-Frey?"

I nodded. She pulled off her asbestos gloves, tossed them onto her worktable. Then she led me around the side of the house.

We walked out into the front field, where her sculptures were set amid the weeds. Again I saw, in the strong abstract forms, images of skeletons.

"Oh, yes, Geof-Frey," she said, "they are the icons of this country. New Mexico is crucifixes and bleached old skulls. Crosses, swastikas and bones."

She led me to her largest piece, took my hand, pressed it to the metal. "Caress, Geof-Frey. Feel the texture. The sun and the rain, how they mark the steel. Old wood, iron . . . they change here. Age. Adapt. In time they become . . . part of the land."

I looked at her. She had aged in the years since I'd met her, but there was still something youthful in her face, her eyes. There was a moment there when I felt a surge of love for her, as intense as the love I'd felt so long ago in Saigon.

"Mai . . ."

She brought her finger to her lips. "Don't say it, Geof-Frey."

"You know what I'm going to say?"

"What you're doing here. I don't want to know. Frank doesn't tell me. Better you don't tell me. Best keep it secret. Okay?"

"Okay," I said.

"Frank has changed. Do you see it?"

I nodded.

"He's more bitter now. Kids don't see it yet. He's so kind with them. But I worry. One day they will see. He needs luck, Geof-Frey. Before too long. Life is good here. I am happy. But Frank not happy. He wants more. We have everything. But for Frank . . ." She shook her head. "Not enough."

"He's an American, Mai. You know us, we're never content."

She smiled. We walked farther into the field. Some of her sculptures had rust on them, an effect, she told me, that she liked.

"You're sorry I came, aren't you?" I asked her.

"Always love to see you, Geof-Frey."

"You think I'm bringing trouble here. Trouble for Frank."

"Better not talk about this," she said. "Now I go back to work."

I watched her as she walked urgently back across the field, then around the side of the house to her studio.

Ali and Jessie cooked the dinner that night, a mélange of dishes that Frank called "Viet-Mex." Afterwards we retired to his shop to further refine the plan. I called Kim to coordinate our trip to

New York, and then, though it was only ten o'clock, I went to bed.

In the morning, I said good-bye to Jude and Mai, thanking her for everything. At the bus stop in Los Carillos I kissed the girls.

"So long, Geof-Frey," they said in unison. They broke up—they had rehearsed Mai's pronunciation of my name.

When we reached Albuquerque, Frank pulled off the Interstate, then into the empty corner of a parking lot at a shopping mall.

"Something I want to show you," he said, reaching to the rear seat, picking up a flight bag. He opened it, removed a camera. It was a Leica R-4, the model I use. "This is your gun," he said.

"Hey, Frank!"

"Hear me out, okay? You don't carry guns, you carry cameras, right?" I nodded. "So here's a camera. The fact that it contains a gun—well, so what? It's still a camera, isn't it?"

"Does it take pictures?"

"No."

"Then it isn't a camera."

"Okay, it's a gun in the shape of a camera. Satisfied?"

"Not quite."

"What's the matter?"

"It's a gun."

"Jesus, Geof. Going to sit here and split hairs?"

I started to laugh.

"What's the matter?"

"A gun-camera!"

"A gun concealed in a camera," he corrected me.

"Yeah. The point is—"

"*What?*"

"It's still a friggin' gun."

"Okay, it's a gun. It really shoots. Two shots. Twenty-two cal-iber. *But this is not an offensive weapon.*"

"It's such a cliché, Frank. I mean, Jesus! the gun hidden in the camera. It's like a cheap spy novel or something."

"You think this is like a cheap spy novel—is that what you think?"

"Don't act insulted."

"I *am* insulted. I was up half the night putting this together, to accommodate your delicate sensibilities."

I shook my head.

"Yeah, yeah, I know—no weapons. You only carry a camera. So when you went to see Rakoubian, planning to clobber him, you took along your old Nikon to do it with. Tell me something: What's the difference between using a camera as brass knuckles and using a camera as a gun?"

"You're shaming me, Frank."

"Good. That's what I want to do."

I looked at him and then I remembered Kim's advice, to let danger and the possibility of violence excite me, to go with it rather than resist.

"Okay, Frank," I said, "why don't you show me how it works."

He opened the back and showed me the mechanism. He'd chopped down the handle of a single-action Beretta semi so it could only take a two-bullet magazine. He'd installed the gun in the shaft of a 90mm. Leitz Elmarit lens, whose diaphragm closed to the very edges of the barrel opening. A piece of molded plastic, easily pierced by a fired bullet, acted as the concealing front "lens" element.

It was a clever little toy, especially the way the depth of field lever acted as the cocking mechanism and "trigger." I hung it around my neck beside my own Leica. The two camera bodies were indistinguishable.

"You start carrying this as a second camera. You're an old pho-tojournalist—nothing odd about that. You usually use a 35mm. lens, so carrying a second camera with a 90 is only logical."

"I wouldn't want to get the two mixed up."

"You won't," he assured me. "When you raise the gun-camera you can't see anything through the finder. But notice the little notch at the front of the accessory shoe. That's your sight. When you fire, don't hold the camera too close—it'll kick a little and you don't want to damage that million-dollar eye."

I tried out the sight. "Seems simple enough."

"It *is*. Just aim and fire. There won't be much recoil. The gun's fixed inside the body with a small version of a Ransom rest. That holds it in place and allows for recoil and muzzle lift. The springing's set so the barrel's brought back into alignment for the second shot."

"Is it loaded?"

"Not yet." He opened it up again and showed me how to load it. "If and when you fire it, you'll be amazed at how quiet it is. There's steel-wool packing between the gun barrel and the lens shaft, with just a little room left in the back for the first ejected shell. There'll probably be more noise when the bullet hits than from the powder explosion."

He watched as I played with it. "Well?" he asked.

"Well, what?"

"Still think it's corny?"

"Of course it's corny. It's also pretty goddamn ingenious."

"Will you carry it?"

"I'll think about it."

"Fine. You do that, Geof. Remember, you only use this up close, eight feet or less, and you only use it if you have to. It's awkward to fire. It's not very accurate. It won't knock anyone down or blow anyone away. But you can put a bullet into a person, and a bullet in the body isn't a treat. It's a last-ditch defensive weapon. People are used to seeing you taking pictures. So, for all its drawbacks, it'll give you one not inconsiderable advantage—the element of surprise."

He started up the car, pulled out of the lot, and drove me to the airport.

"I'd like you to carry this when you go after Darling, in case he tries anything, and because I think carrying it will help your confidence. But that's up to you. Naturally, you can't carry it past airport security, so if you decide to take it with you, you'll have to stash it in your check-through luggage."

"There're big penalties for carrying a concealed weapon in New York."

"The biggest penalty I know of is death."

"What happens if I'm caught with it?"

"Plead innocence. You didn't know you had it. Your buddy gave it to you, this crazy camera-gun freak out in New Mexico. Don't worry—I'll back you up."

I knew he would too. But still I hesitated.

"After a while you'll get used to it. Your camera and your gun-camera—they'll both be standard equipment. It'll be just like your credit card, Geof—you won't want to go anyplace without it."

I held the thing up to my eye again, aimed it at a taxi just ahead. It had a nice feel, a nice weight. It would make a good souvenir when we were finished.

I told him to pull over, and, as he watched, smiling, I wrapped the gun-camera in my dirty laundry and stuffed it in a bottom corner of my bag.

It was the middle of September, two and a half weeks since I was last in New York, but the city was still as hot and damp as it had been the day I left for Miami. I taxied from the airport to the Howard Johnson Hotel on Eighth Avenue and Fifty-first Street. We'd chosen the place because it was middle-class and nondescript, full of large groups moving in and out, the kind of place where they don't remember you at the desk, where they don't even look you in the eye.

I found the house phone, asked the operator to connect me to Mrs. Lynch.

"Hello?"

"Mrs. Lynch? This is Mr. Lynch."

A pause, then a throaty "Well, hello there, Mr. Lynch."

"May I come up?"

"I would surely love it if you would, Mr. Lynch."

She was waiting for me on the bed, naked and spread-eagled, surrounded by a scent of lemon and musk. "Geoffrey, Geoffrey! Come do me. Quick. . . ."

I tore off my clothes.

"Hurry," she said. Her arms, above her head, gripped the top of the headboard. As I lowered myself upon her she arched her back. "Yes, Geoffrey! God! Yes!"


We took showers after we made love, then sat in easy chairs and gazed at each other. Then I called Frank at his studio in Santa Fe, told him we'd arrived and were together. Then we got dressed, went out and walked.

I told her she looked great in her big-city clothes, with her Florida tan and her bleached-out hair. She said I looked pretty good myself.

"Weathered, kind of like a cowpoke," she said.

We walked down Eighth toward Forty-second. It was dusk and the whores were just coming out. The crack dealers had been out for hours.

"Great to be back," she said. "Feels like I've got this city by the hairs."

"The way you've got me, Kim?"

"The way we've got Darling," she corrected me. She smiled. "We're going to be rich, Geoffrey. *Rich!*"

We had a *feijoada completa* in a Brazilian restaurant-nightclub on West Forty-fifth. I ordered champagne, and after we ate we danced a few sets. She felt good in my arms.

"To getting even," she said, toasting me with her glass. "And to money," she added. "This time it's going to work. I know it. . . ."

At eleven o'clock we split up. She went back to our room to call Mrs. Z, while I went downtown to collect my mail.

I hesitated outside my building. Nassau Street at that hour was as deserted as it should have been, and I didn't notice anyone lingering about. I emptied my mailbox, stuffed to its top, then rode up in the elevator. Upstairs I checked around my door. The ruined paint from the lye attack was prominently visible, but the door itself looked to be intact.

When I opened up, there were two slips of paper lying on the floor. Messages from Scotto: "Urgent I talk to you. Call me when you get back." and "Still waiting to hear from you!"

I crumpled them up, locked the door behind me, then rewound my answering machine. I dumped my mail on my desk, and, as I listened to my messages, started to sort it, throwing away the junk.

In my wastebasket there were remnants of the Chinese carryout dinner I'd eaten just before I'd gone to see Rakoubian. The bag was swarming with roaches. I carried it to the hall and dumped it down the compactor chute.

My phone messages weren't all that interesting. One from my gallery, another from a collector who wanted to buy a print of my Pietà. Nothing, thank God, from the goon who'd threatened me before. But there were four messages from Scotto—the first two pleaded, the third was slightly irritable, and the last, left two days before, expressed considerable anger that I hadn't called.

I was deep into my mail, sorting the bills, when my telephone rang. The sound startled me. I switched on my machine to screen the call. It was Scotto, and the first words he said were: "I know you're there. Pick up."

I hesitated.

"Pick up, goddamnit!" He sounded mean.

I picked up. "Hi, Sal," I said. "Just got in."

"I know."

"How do you know?"

"Guy works for me saw the light go on."

"You've got my place watched? What the hell's going on?"

"A murder investigation's going on. When're you going to stop playing dumb?"

"Okay," I said. "Now, why don't you cool down?"

"I mean it, Geof—don't mess with me. I'll be there in half an hour. Buzz me in."

I considered calling Frank for advice, but he'd warned me not to call him from the loft. Kim was only to make her initial calls from our motel; after that we were to use public phones.

Well, I thought, maybe it's better this way, since I have to deal with Scotto anyhow. But he sounded pissed off, which made me wonder if there'd been developments and if I was in some kind of trouble.

It was over an hour before he showed up, and when he did he came on like a bully.

"Where have you been?" he snapped.

"I don't think I have to answer that." He glared at me. "All right, I've been hiding out."

"Someplace pretty nice, looks like to me. Nice dark tan you got."

"What's the trouble, Sal?"

"I already told you."

"You told me there's a murder investigation. I already knew about that."

252

"Dave Ramos wants to go to the D.A., have you designated a material witness."

"Which means?"

"You go before the grand jury. Then you talk or else."

"Fine. I'd like to talk. I'll tell them what I told you: my girlfriend's missing since the night her roommate's murdered. In the meantime my life's threatened, and someone throws lye at my eyes. When the investigating officers refuse me protection, I feel I have a right to leave town and hide out."

"Guess what, Geoffrey? You're annoying me."

"And you're bugging me, Sal. So why don't the two of us cut the shit."

"Tell me where you've been."

"I don't want to tell you."

"I know you've seen her." He gestured toward my reconstructed serial portraits of Kim.

"What makes you say that?"

"I smell it."

"Maybe your nose is off."

"Maybe it's not. Maybe I smell her all over you. Maybe you've been eating out her snatch and the fumes are still coming off your face."

I gave him a severe look of disgust. "I thought you were a classy guy."

"You thought wrong—I'm a cop."

I hesitated. I knew I had to give him something. "If I did decide to tell you anything, Sal, it would be that she doesn't know *who* killed Shadow."

"How about *why* Shadow was killed?"

"She doesn't know that either."

He went quiet, just stared at me. When he spoke again it was with confidence. "We found that Mrs. Z you told us about."

That worried me, though I tried not to show it. "What did she have to say?" I asked.

"You won't tell me nothin'. Why should I tell you?"

"Let's trade."

"I'm a cop. I don't have to trade."

"Suit yourself," I said. "Now, if you don't mind I've got mail to answer here."

He groaned. "You're acting like a real asshole."

"That's the story of my life."

"Don't be a sucker."

"What do you want?"

"Kimberly Yates. I want to talk to her."

"She won't talk to you. Anyway she's out of state."

"Which state? Okay, forget it. I won't ask you that. I'll ask this: last time we talked you were sure about one thing, that her building super didn't do it. Tell me why you were so sure?"

"Just a hunch."

"A hunch, huh? You know, you really are a jerk." He knew something—I could tell: he had an I-know-it look on his face. "Everyone thinks we're stupid. Stupid cops. Thick heads. Lugs. Who else would go into this kind of work? Got news for you, pal. A few of us are bright. Dave Ramos, for instance. He gets interested in something, he starts looking around, and when he does he's very methodical. Ever hear of VIA?"

"What's that?"

"Visual Investigative Aid. An approach to criminal investigation. A way to chart what you know and what you don't, useful when you have a complicated case. You chart this stuff, then you draw lines in between, and sooner or later you start to see connections. You see what you need to know to put the thing together. Knowing what you need to know—in police work that's half the battle."

He smiled at me, and that made me nervous. He *did* know something, I was sure of it.

"Okay, you call me from the airport, that means you're going someplace. So Dave and me, we listen to the tape—yeah, we tape everything. We listen and figure out you're calling from La Guardia. So we check on what flights are going out of there around the time of your call, we get the passenger lists, and, lo and behold, we find your name on a flight to Miami." He smiled again. "Shakes you up a little, doesn't it?"

"A little," I agreed.

"So we make some calls, check around Miami, hotels and stuff. And car rental companies. Don't want to forget those."

I didn't say anything.

"Seems there's this fella, Geoffrey Barnett, he's rented this nice little Toyota Corolla. Guy rents a car, guy returns a car. When he returns it to the airport we start checking on flights again. And guess what? We find his name, this time on a flight to Dallas with a connection to Albuquerque. So, using deduction, we're more or less sure the little honey pot's in either Florida or New Mexico. Maybe she's back here now. Not a bad suppose, since you're here and you follow the honey. Course, we can check with the airlines, run her name through their computers. Or you can tell me now and save me the time."

I knew Kim had used an assumed name on the plane, but still there was a moment there when I thought about telling Scotto the truth. We'd have to forget the blackmail, we wouldn't get rich, but maybe we'd see some justice. It might even feel good to go on to the law-and-order side.

But the thing had taken on a life of its own. Kim wanted the money, Frank needed it, and I'd brought him in. It would be hard to let them down.

There was something else too: my fascination with the game, which is the way I'd begun to think of it. A three-cornered game, with three teams of players: Kim, Frank and me; Darling and Mrs. Z; and Ramos and Scotto. The object of the game was to outsmart the other two teams and carry home the loot. And the prospect of doing that, the anticipated high if we won, was, I was beginning to understand, as important as the actual winnings.

I think something had changed in me those last few weeks. I think I gave up my gloomy view. And the possibility that we might really force something out of those monsters had become a lot more exciting than any photograph I could visualize.

I was also, I discovered, as I talked to Sal, finding it easier to lie.

"Okay," I told him, "you're a good detective. I never thought you weren't. I'm going to tell you something now so you don't waste your time. Kimberly's not in New York. As for where I went, yes, I was in Florida and New Mexico, and the reason was to take pictures—which happens to be my profession. As for Shadow, you say you located Mrs. Z. In my opinion that's the place to look. I'll tell you another thing. There was a Swedish girl named Sonya who also worked for Mrs. Z, a friend of Kim's and Shadow's. I never met her, but I hear she disappeared and there're people who think she was killed by someone close to Mrs. Z."

Scotto had been writing in his notebook the entire time. "That it?" he asked when I finished.

"One more thing, and I swear to you it's all I know. There're some fancy people who live in Soho, a painter named Duquayne and his rich-bitch wife. I think they know something. Before I left I tried to talk to them. They threw me out. Maybe you and Ramos'll have better luck."

Scotto put down his notebook. Then he stood. "Okay," he said, "you've told me a couple of things, maybe helpful, maybe not. I think you've been straight with me. If I ever find out you're not, I'm going to sic Dave onto you, Geof. And with Dave there's no mercy. None."

After he left I thought about his threat: he'd turn me over to Dave; Dave would have me designated a material witness. It didn't sound all that bad. More like passing the buck.

Meantime, I thought, I'd tied some good knots. Tomorrow Sal would pressure Mrs. Z, which, added to the pressure Kim was putting on her tonight, should propel her into a state of panic. And if the Duquaynes could be made to panic too, then Darling would soon feel the force of our attack.

An hour after Sal left, I slipped out of my loft. At first I thought about leaving my lights on, in case his lookout was still around. But it occurred to me it would look more natural if I turned them off—it was getting late, time for the itinerant photographer to go to bed.

Once outside I strode swiftly toward Broadway, hailed a cab, and asked the driver to drop me at Forty-second and Eighth.

It was 1:30 in the morning, but it could just as easily have been noon—the action at that sleazy intersection was still that heavy and fast. The tang of pot, sweat and cheap perfume hung upon the air. There were throngs of tourists, camera-toting Japanese, assorted teenagers, beboppers and a man, dressed in a horned helmet like a Viking, regaling the crowd on the subject of fleshly sin. Pimps, prostitutes and drug dealers cruised, and a mad shopping-bag lady, with bulging eyes, shouted a string of mindless obscenities to the wind.

As I walked toward Seventh I ran a gauntlet:

"Going out?" a girl asked.

"Date?" asked another.

"Smoke? Coke?"

"Smack? Crack?"

"Grass? Ass?"

"Love for sale," I heard a throaty voice whisper in my ear.

I merged into the crowd on Seventh, paused before a three-card monte dealer, then looked back to see if I was being followed. There was no one lingering, so I walked back to the corner, then quickly descended the subway stairs. I bought a token, passed through the turnstile, found a pay phone and dialed the hotel.

"Mrs. Lynch? This is Mr. Lynch."

"Geoffrey! I've been worried. I was afraid to call the loft."

I told her about Scotto and the hints I'd dropped. She especially liked my insinuation about the Duquaynes.

"I, meantime, have spoken with Mrs. Z," she said. "It got pretty hairy there for a while. I told her the photos were back in play and she'd better get the money and pay up. I told her Rakoubian had taken the pictures, then had tried to pin them on you. I told her you were in the thing now, you and I were partners, that someone had tried to burn out your eyes, you didn't like that, and next time any lye was thrown, you'd be doing the throwing. I told her if she didn't think you had the balls, she should check you out with Rakoubian."

"Jesus!"

"Yeah, I really hit on her. She stayed quiet the whole time. I told her she may have thought the business was finished but as far as I was concerned it had just begun. I didn't give her time to answer. Just told her she and Darling had forty-eight hours to make up their minds. She thought little Kimberly was out of her life. Now here I am, back again, talking like a bad-ass too." She paused. "I'm feeling good, Geoffrey. Real good. Why don't you come on up and see old horny Mrs. Lynch?"

"Nothing I'd rather do," I said. "I have to call Frank first."

"I'll be waiting," she panted.

I had no trouble getting hold of Frank; it was only 11:00 P.M. in New Mexico.

"Good moves with Scotto," he said, when I'd told him everything. "Of course, now you can't go back to the loft."

"What about the hotel?"

"Probably okay. But be careful. Take the subway shuttle to Grand Central, get off, then get right back on. Anyone else does the same thing you'll know you're being followed. But I don't think you are. I think what happened was Scotto slipped a twenty to someone in your neighborhood to watch your windows and call him when the lights went on. I doubt he has the manpower to follow you, and I doubt he has the motivation."

That was pretty much what I'd been thinking, but it was nice to hear it confirmed.

"How do you like the way they traced my airline tickets?"

"They're methodical guys. We should have thought of that. When you come back out you'll buy your tickets under another name. And no connecting flights. Spend the night in Dallas, then fly Dallas–Albuquerque the following day under still a third name. Pay cash, of course."

"Maybe there's other stuff we should have thought of, Frank."

"Maybe. But things are breaking good. Feels like we're on a roll."

"What do I do about Scotto?"

"Keep your contacts to short calls from public phones."

"He won't like that."

"He won't mind so long as you keep in touch. Hey! Relax, Geof! The best part's still to come. Round-trip the shuttle, then get yourself back to that lusty girlfriend of yours. But not too much excitement. You still got big things to do. . . ."

Mrs. Lynch was lusty indeed. She was all over me the moment I entered the room.

"Don't know what's wrong with me," she said, pressing herself against me. "I must be high on the excitement." She kissed me. "The power too." She unbuttoned my shirt, lightly clawed her nails down my chest, then slowly ran her tongue across the red lines she'd made. "I think it's you, Geoffrey. The way you smell, taste. You know how I love your skin." She licked at me again. "Can't get enough." She stroked my arms with her thumbs. "I'm crazy for you. You know that. Your . . . hardness." She fell back upon the bed, pulled up her dress, spread her legs. She wore no underwear. "Geoffrey, I'm so wet down there. Put it in me. *Please*. . . ."

Arnold Darling lived on upper Fifth Avenue in an old apartment house just north of the Metropolitan Museum. It was a Stanford White building famous for its high ceilings, well-proportioned rooms and celebrity residents, including two rival talk-show hosts, and the sister-in-law of the former dictator of Indonesia.

When I arrived a little before 8:00 A.M., there were two Cadillacs and a Bentley double-parked in front. It was a beautiful morning, the first decent one of the season. For three straight months the city had suffered through one of the great heat waves of the century. Now, at last, the air was clear and there was a cool autumnal breeze.

I stationed myself across the street, on a stone bench built against the wall that defines the eastern edge of Central Park. From there I watched the entrance to the building through my old Key West Post Office spying device, my R-4 mounted with a 135mm. lens. My second "Leica," the one with the barrel of the Beretta concealed in the lens housing, hung from a strap around my neck and rested just below my heart.

At 8:15 a distinguished-looking gentleman with wavy gray hair and a crocodile attaché case exited the building and got into one of the Cadillacs. I recognized him as the former CEO of a major aerospace manufacturer, indicted and awaiting trial for bribery and conspiracy to defraud the government.

A few minutes later a genuine celebrity came out, the Italian-American film star Tony Demarco, known for his stupendous physique, sad spaniel's eyes and winsome groans while undergoing torture. Interrogation scenes, during which he hung half naked by his wrists while being tormented by one or another evil Soviet military officer, were the inevitable centerpieces of his movies. People went to see a Demarco picture as much for the pleasure of watching him suffer as for the stunning brutality of his revenge.

I watched him get into the Bentley, then was distracted by the arrival of a tall skinny young woman, easily six feet two, who wore a Knicks T-shirt, a Mets baseball cap backwards, and held eight leashes attached to an equal number of dogs.

She was that peculiar creature of Manhattan's Upper East Side, a professional dog walker. Each of her dogs was of a different size, shape and breed. There was a wrinkled-faced boxer, a proud poodle, a high-strung Dalmation, and the star of the pack, an elegant Afghan, who, prancing, led the others, all panting and slobbering, forcing their walker to lean backwards as she pulled them to a halt in front of Darling's building.

She had stopped, it was clear, to pick up another animal. The doorman recognized her and retreated to the lobby. She stood ramrod-straight as she waited, her wards settling down before her in various postures, some sprawling on the sidewalk, the boxer sniffing lasciviously at her crotch, the Dalmatian snapping viciously at the legs of an innocent passerby.

A few moments later the doorman emerged, holding a leash attached to a russet-coated English setter. The walker took the leash, joined it to her others, then flicked them together like a cat-o'-nine-tails.

Suddenly all the dogs stood, poised to proceed with their walk, and, at that same moment, through a welter of leashes and canine flesh, I spied the figure of Arnold Darling as he stepped out of the lobby into the brilliant morning light.

He was wearing a sober dark pin-striped suit and a shirt so white it glittered as he paused outside the door. He stared curiously at the dogs, muttered something to the doorman, then took off fast walking south.

By this time I'd twisted the telephoto off my camera, slapped on a wide-angle, and was making my way through the gridlocked traffic across to the other side of Fifth.

My plan was to get ahead of him, then turn and confront him before he reached the corner. I was just stepping between a stalled commuter bus and a Jaguar when the light changed and the traffic began to surge.

The bus driver honked, I leaped, then was nearly run over by a taxi. Plunging forward to avoid it, I tripped and skinned my knees on the curb. When I recovered and looked up, I found myself not three feet from Arnold Darling, under inspection by his penetrating eyes.

Even as I knew I had bungled my entrance, some old instinct from my photojournalist days took over. I had stumbled up to subjects before, had many times assumed awkward positions to obtain a vital shot. So by sheer rote I raised my camera and started firing away, and the moment I did that I regained my poise: my camera, analogous to his fencing mask, protected me from his scrutiny, and my big Leitz lens had a power his naked eyes did not—it could eat him up alive.

*Whap! whap! whap! Whap-whap! Whap-whap!* The whir of my motor-drive drove him back. Take that! And that! And that! it seemed to say, and even as it did his cheeks began to flush.

I moved closer, thrust my camera at him, shot him five more times. When he continued to back off, I pressed my advantage,

262

and the feel of my gun-camera swinging back and forth against my chest didn't harm my confidence.

"My name's Barnett," I said, "I'm a photographer. You tried to have me blinded. I'm here to show you I still can see."

"Get away from me! Get away!"

"Fuck you, Darling. I've got you cold. I didn't take those nasty pictures of you, but I've got them now, and you're going to buy them back."

*Whap! whap! whap! whap!* I hit him four times hard, noting he had no eyebrows. Then I lowered my camera and smiled at him over its top.

"You're dead meat, sucker. Because before I take those nasty pictures to the cops I'm shopping them around to the press. *Star. National Enquirer.* Whoever'll pay the most. Imagine the headlines: 'Famous Architect Likes to Make Girls Scream.' 'SM Sex Parties at Mrs. Z's.' 'Sonya and Shadow Slain by Prominent Architect.' 'Architect in Deep Shit!' "

All the time I was speaking he'd been looking around, meantime using his hands to protect his face. I liked that. It told me I was getting to him. I pressed on. *Whap, whap, whap, whap, whap, whap!*

And then, as he was staggering backward, I saw my opportunity. The dog walker was approaching fast, her nine dogs fanned out in front. A perfect trap: he was caught between my relentless camera and that ninesome of frothing beasts. *Push him forward*, my best instinct told me. And so I did, thrusting my camera at him, not even looking through it, just shoving it into his face as I pressed the shutter to make the film whir through.

*Whap! Whap! Whap! Whap! Whap! Whap! Whap! Whap!*

He panicked, stumbled, lost his balance and fell. The timing couldn't have been better—the dogs were just behind. As he dropped they parted into two groups, and, when he was down, closed in. He was flat on his back, his head at the feet of the dog walker. She, meantime, had yanked back on her leashes, bringing her dogs to a chaotic halt.

A moment later they were all stepping over Darling, sniffing at him, pressing at him with their snouts. They panted and drooled on his pin-striped suit. It was a very pretty sight.

I knelt and continued to shoot, finishing out my roll. I got several great shots of him slithering up against the dog walker's knees, writhing to escape the muzzles of her dogs. He had by then lost all his dignity. And I had the shots to go with the ominous ones taken by Rakoubian.

"Call Mrs. Z," I told him. "From now on we'll be dealing through her."

My last memory of the scene was of the tall girl in the backwards baseball cap trying to help him to his feet, while her barking wards, all high-strung and overbred, tangled their leashes into a Gordian knot.

It was 2:00 that afternoon when Kim and I hit the Duquaynes. Kim had their private number—the three of them had had, after all, a very private relationship—and so we stopped at a phone booth on the corner of West Broadway and Prince so she could call and make sure that they were home.

As soon as Amanda Duquayne answered, Kim hung up.

"I know Harold's there. He always paints in the afternoons," Kim said.

We walked down to Spring Street, found their building. Kim pushed the buzzer.

*"Yes? Who's there?"* I had no trouble recognizing Amanda's fancy whine.

Kim grinned at me, then brought her mouth to the intercom. "Hi, Mandy. It's me—Kim."

There was a pause and then an intake of breath. "Oh, dear!" Amanda moaned.

"Buzz me in, Mandy. It's important."

"I don't know. This is so . . . unexpected."

"Mandy! Push the goddamn buzzer!" Kim spoke as if she expected to be obeyed. And sure enough, after an involuntary sigh of resignation over the intercom, the buzzer gave a long and splendid sigh of its own.

Harold, unshaven, in his paint-flecked sweatshirt, was standing beside Amanda when we walked in. She, in her at-home equestrian outfit, looked the perfect spoiled little wife.

"You didn't say *he* was with you." Amanda glared at me. Again I noticed her freckled chest.

"Geof and I are partners now, Mandy."

"I think you'd both better leave," Harold said.

Kim didn't bother to look at him. "Pretty hard to take you seriously, Harold, considering I've had you licking the bottoms of my shoes."

Harold recoiled like a man who'd been slapped, while Amanda tried valiantly to regain control.

"You can't just burst in on us like this!" she sputtered. "You have no right! And to come with *him*!" She motioned toward me. "He insulted Harold. Said awful things to both of us."

"Oh, can it, Mandy!" Kim used the dominant tone again. "Stop playing the offended party."

"But we *are* offended," Amanda whined.

"We're old friends. Don't be silly." Kim turned to me. "Did I tell you Harold likes to play doggie? And little Mandy here has drunk deeply of my—how do you call them, Mandy?—'vital juices'?"

Even as I felt for them in their moment of humiliation, I couldn't help admiring Kim for the way she'd taken command. Suddenly both Duquaynes were docile. Harold hung his head, and Amanda, who'd played proud princess last time I'd seen her, wore an expression of deeply injured pride.

"We didn't come here to insult you, Mandy." Kim's tone was soothing again. "We came to give you some advice. There's bad stuff going down, and the two of you may be involved. We wanted to talk to you before the police. But if having us here upsets you so much—"

"They already called," Amanda said. "They didn't say what it was about. Just that they wanted to come over here and talk."

While Harold showed a pained half smile, Kim gave me an emphatic look.

"I know what it's about," she said. We all moved to the couches and sat down. "It has to do with Mrs. Z. One of her clients killed an actress." The Duquaynes recoiled. "Remember Sonya?" They nodded. "It was her. When I threatened to expose this client—it's safer for you if I don't mention his name—they kidnapped Shadow to find out where I was. And when she wouldn't talk . . ." Kim drew her finger across her neck, then sadly shook her head.

The Duquaynes were starting to show signs of extreme distress.

"But why us?" Amanda asked. "We had nothing to do with any of that."

"Of course not, darlings. But now the whole thing's coming unwound. You were clients too. You had private sessions. Harold's a celebrity. A famous painter. He's been on the cover of *Art News*. You've both been on the cover of *New York*."

"But still, Kimberly, I still don't see . . ."

"Now everything's going to come out. All the glittering names. Yours too. Unless . . ."

"*What?*"

266

"Mrs. Z comes to her senses and agrees that reparation should be paid."

Harold squinted at Kim. "You're talking about money?"

"What else, darling? What other kinds of reparations are there in this world?"

"Money from us?" Amanda was tense.

"Not from you, silly. From the client."

As the Duquaynes looked at each other, I observed their relief—this was not going to cost them any cash.

"But then how—" Harold asked.

"How are you involved?" They both nodded. "You're not. Except that the cops have got your names. They won't be able to prove anything, of course, not unless certain evidence comes to light. Only Mrs. Z and her client can prevent that. That's why we think one of you should speak to her."

"What should we say?"

"You could say, very simply, very frankly, that you understand a situation has arisen that could be embarrassing to people who have supported her over the years. And that your advice is that she do whatever has to be done to see that the injured parties in the affair are satisfied. Anyway, darlings, this is just a suggestion. But, you see, if this *does* go to the cops, all the trees in the forest will fall, and that, I'm afraid, includes the two of you."

"We'll make the call," Harold said.

"What about the police?" Amanda asked.

"Refer them to your lawyer."

"Shouldn't we talk with them?"

"That's absolutely the last thing you should do. But I'd talk to Mrs. Z pretty soon, this afternoon if possible. Darlings, you don't want to leave this hanging. Not a thing like this."

Kim nodded to me, we rose, then the four of us moved to the

door. Harold and I shook hands, Amanda and Kim exchanged a kiss, Kim whispered to her, giggled, whispered something to Harold, giggled again, and then we left.

On the street I asked her what all the whispering had been about.

"A jest," she said. "I told Mandy we'll get together when this is over, have ourselves some fun. I told Harold next time we played I was going to tie up a very intimate part of his body. He loved it! He adores being tied. I suspect he even likes being hit."

I laughed.

"Geoffrey!" She kissed me. "You're really amused."

"I guess I am," I said. "They were so awful to me before, it was kind of a pleasure to watch them squirm."

"Well, that's wonderful," she said. "Progress in a way, because a couple of weeks ago I think you would have been appalled. It's all part of the gig, you see. We come on tough with them, tell them what we want, then offer them a little fun. They're sexually driven people. Kinky obedience training—that's their thing. But the poor darlings are too chicken to admit it. God forbid that the intimate desires of such an Exalted Couple should ever be divulged!" She grinned. "Carrot and stick is the way to control them. Sex is the carrot. Exposure is the stick."

At 5:00 P.M., while Kim was off seeing Rakoubian, I picked up my proof sheet of the Darling shoot from a photo lab on West Twenty-fourth.

The proofs looked good. There were a couple of shots of Darling covering his face that showed just the degree of panic I'd hoped to instill. Maybe Frank was right. Maybe we were on a roll. Certainly everything was clicking along. But I was wary. It just didn't seem possible that we could extort a million dollars without having to pay some horrific price ourselves.

I stopped at a Spanish *tapas* joint where there was a quiet phone booth between the men's room and the bar. I dialed Scotto, the phone rang several times, and then Ramos picked it up.

"Sal's out," he said. "But I wanna talk to you. Couple things I wanna go over. Come down to the precinct we'll sort them out."

"I'm busy," I said.

"*Busy?*"

"Pressed is what I mean."

"Isn't that nice? The man is 'pressed.' He doesn't have time to help the cops. We're only trying to solve a homicide here. But let's put that on hold 'cause the man is *pressed*."

"Your sarcasm's withering me, Ramos. Anyway, I already told Sal everything I know. If you want, we can go over it all again, but I don't have time to come down there now."

"What's a matter? Afraid to face me, let me see your eyes?"

"I think I work better with Sal," I said. "I'll call back later on."

"Sal's soft on you, Barnett. But I'm not. You're playing games. I don't like games."

"What kind of games do you think I'm playing, Dave?"

"You got your own thing going here. They got a word for that. 'Hidden agenda.' I aim to find out what yours is." I didn't say anything; I couldn't. His smart cop's instinct was telling him I wasn't straight. "Well?" he asked.

"Well, what?"

"What do you have to say for yourself?"

"Is this when I'm supposed to break down and confess?"

"Watch it, sucker."

"Is that a threat, detective?"

"Take it any way you want. But hear this: I don't buy your story. I think you know where the roommate is. Sooner or later I'm going to find missing Missy Kimberly, and when I do I'm going to find out about you. Turns out you've been lying, I'm going to fry your ass. All I gotta say for now. Sal'll be back in an hour." He hung up.

I started walking uptown. My conversation with Ramos had shaken me up. *What am I doing wrong?* I asked myself. *How am I giving myself away?*

Frank was right. The cops were going to be a problem. Even if we brought off the blackmail and collected the money, Ramos and Scotto were not conveniently going to go away.

I stopped at Penn Station to call Frank at his gallery.

"Better get back to the hotel quick," he said. "Kim's waiting for you. They wasted Rakoubian."

"*What?*"

"I just got off the phone with her. She was on her way to see him when she noticed patrol cars in front of his place. There was a crowd on the street. She edged in and asked what was going on. Seems your fat friend fell or jumped out of his window. My bet is he was pushed."

"Frank!"

"Steady, Geof. And save your regrets. I told you this could happen. They're playing hardball. After what you did this morning, I'm not at all surprised."

"Kim told you?"

"Yeah. Poor Arnold. Pissed on by all those fancy dogs. She also told me about the Duquaynes. You guys played them great."

His compliment was nice, but I was still thinking about Rakoubian. Suddenly I wished I were out of the whole goddamn mess.

"What if they'd come for him when Kim was there?" I asked. "They'd have heaved her out the window too!"

"Point is, they *didn't* run into her. Like I told you last night, we're on a roll. Last night Kim taunted Mrs. Z. This morning you taunted Darling. Rakoubian caused them a lot of trouble. If you were in the same spot, you'd have killed him too."

I was quiet.

"Wouldn't you?"

"No," I said. "No, Frank, I most certainly wouldn't."

"Look, Geof, I don't condone what they did. But there's one plus here—I predicted how they'd behave, which tells me I've got a good handle on them, which tells me the plan is working, and we should proceed without delay."

Back at the motel I found a badly shaken Mrs. Lynch.

"Sure, Adam was awful. Slime. A real piece of crud. But to waste him like that . . ."

She was pacing while I lay on the bed. Her hands were nervous and she was dripping sweat. Strangely, seeing her so upset actually reassured me. She and Frank talked casually about "wasting" people; now, at least, she was expressing pain.

"I mean he couldn't *do* anything to them," she said. She stopped, turned to me. "He wasn't *threatening* them. He didn't have the pictures *anymore*."

"He could identify Darling. I guess that was the reason," I said.

"I know." She started pacing again. "Like that's what this is all about. Shows of force and all that kind of crap. God, I hate them. I hate them more than—" She stopped. "I'd like to see them die, Geof. I really would. Rolling on the ground, you know, in the dirt, their bellies split open, their hands grasping at their guts, trying to keep them from spilling out. Crying, whimpering, dying painfully. That's what I'd like to see."

She became calm then, as if that thought, that awful vision, satisfied her rage. Her shaking stopped. The sweat dried on her forehead. Her fingers were cool when, a few minutes later, she sat beside me and began to stroke my neck.

We made love, showered, then went out to look for a place to eat. On Tenth Avenue Kim spotted a Cuban restaurant. She wanted to go there, wanted to be reminded of Key West.

It turned out to be a strange hybrid, Chino-Latino or Cuban-Chinese. We ordered dishes from both sides of the menu, ate pork asado with chopsticks and poured black beans over our Cantonese rice. For five minutes we were amused, then the joke began to pall.

"Why are we putting ourselves through this?" I asked her. "Why don't we go back to Florida and forget it? Just forget it."

She gazed at me, her eyes pinning me down. I felt like a rabbit caught in the headlights of a car.

"It's getting too rough," I told her. "I don't know if I can handle much more."

She nodded. "I know what you mean. I feel awful about Adam too."

"Maybe we shouldn't have turned him in, Kim. Oh, I know it might help us marginally. But to turn him over, set him up for slaughter . . ." I put down my chopsticks, shook my head.

"Listen, Geof"—her voice was tender—"you're a sensitive guy and I love you for that. But we're both going to have to toughen up." She smiled. "Know what your problem is? I think you give up hatred too easily." She patted my hand. "Anyway, there's nothing we can do for Adam now. We can only go forward and hope for the best—do what we have to do."

After dinner we wandered down to Forty-second Street, merging with the crowds. The neon flashed, the porn stores were open and the hustlers worked the mob. Kim grasped my arm. I looked at her. We listened to their propositions, laughed them away. Then at the apex of Times Square she broke free to face the empty intersection alone. She stood there on the sidewalk, staring at the signs. As she spoke she seemed to glow.

"I love this cesspool. Makes me feel good. Triumphant almost. As if places like this, which people say are so degrading, are the only places I feel I'm really alive. Know what I mean, Geoffrey? It's so damn human down here, like there's nothing phony, no false front. Here you can feel what it means to be a human being. It's the opposite, isn't it, of sitting in a church?"

The moment she said that I felt that she was right. The city swirled with criminality, and we were part of it, part of the great greedy grasping mainstream, competitors in the endless struggle for gain.

She was right about another thing too, the feeling she described of triumph. You could be predatory and sexual and still hold your head high because you weren't pretending to be anything else. You were only human, as she said, stripped of all hypocrisy. There was something wonderful about that, liberating, clean. I began to glow myself.

And so, as I strode with her amid that overheated crowd, my cameras bobbing against my chest, I no longer felt like an observer, a photographer, but like a player in the game.

I woke up in a sweat, disoriented, confused. But when I opened my eyes the room was dark. I reached for Kim. She wasn't there. I called out her name. No answer. I sat up.

She wasn't in the bathroom either. *Has she left me? Deserted me again?* Maybe I was still asleep, trapped in a nightmare. But of course I wasn't. And her suitcase was still in the room. But not the set of clothes she'd worn the day before. I looked at my watch. It was 5:35 A.M.

Maybe she's gone down to the lobby, I thought, to buy a newspaper, or get some aspirin, or munch on something in the coffee shop. I picked up the phone, dialed the desk, asked the clerk to page the lobby and restaurant for Mrs. Lynch. He said the restaurant was closed and there wasn't anyone in the lobby, and he'd been on since five and the only person he'd seen go out was a man in jogging clothes.

He promised he'd page her anyway and call me back if he saw a woman around. I waited ten minutes by the phone before I realized it wasn't going to ring.

Maybe, I thought, she went out for a walk. She was overexcited and couldn't sleep. I dressed quickly, went downstairs, checked in with the clerk. He told me where to find the all-night eating places in the neighborhood. I thanked him and stepped into the street.

There was a slick on Eighth Avenue—it must have rained, though I'd had no sense of that inside the hotel. The air was sticky. The autumnal flavor of the day before was gone. The yellow glow of the streetlamps was reflected in the pavement. I could hear the wail of distant sirens downtown.

No whores around. They'd long since gone home, or were out on dates, or wherever they went. The transvestites and pimps and dope dealers were all gone too. Only a few homeless people remained, a man curled in a doorway down the block, another sprawled across a grating in front of a discount movie house across the street.

I made the round of coffee shops, but didn't see her. And then I wandered aimlessly. After a while I found myself beside the river. No trucks around, everything closed, and the damp air stagnant without a trace of wind. The sirens still shrieked far away. I watched the oily water lapping around the rotting piers.

*She went somewhere, somewhere specific. She had a destination.* The only thing I could think to do was go back to our room and wait.

275

The sun was well up by the time I returned. There were people on the streets and the traffic had begun to build. A big air-conditioned bus was double-parked in front of the hotel. The lobby was choked with baggage. The desk clerk didn't notice me. A group was in the process of checking out.

As I rode up in the elevator I felt depressed. I told myself she shouldn't have deserted me this way. She should have left me a note, an explanation. But that wasn't her style. I'd learned that before. She came and went as she pleased.

I knew she was back the moment I opened the door. Her clothes were piled in the center of the room. There was an odor in the room too that didn't belong—something harsh and resinous.

I could hear water running. She was in the bathroom. I moved to the doorway and looked in. She was taking a shower, singing to herself, an old Cole Porter tune:

> "It's the wrong game with the wrong chips,
> Though your lips are tempting, they're the
> wrong lips,"

I leaned against the doorframe, waiting for her to finish, watching her perfect body in silhouette against the plastic curtain.

> "They're not her lips but they're such
> tempting lips. . . ."

She pulled the curtain, saw me, and then, for the briefest instant, she looked scared. A moment later she flung herself upon me, naked and wet. She hugged me while planting kisses on my face.

"Thank God, you're back, Geoffrey! It was terrible."

"What happened?"

276

"I had to take a shower to wash away the smell. My clothes stink of it too. I'm going to throw them out."

"Stink of what?"

She was trembling. "Varnish remover."

I stood back from her. That accounted for the resinous odor in the other room. "Why varnish remover? I don't understand."

She shook her head. "That's what I used. Hold me, Geoffrey. Please." Her eyes were wild. She had the same on-the-edge look the night she'd come to me after running away from Darling's men.

I held her. "Used for what?"

"To set the fire."

"Jesus, Kim! What are you talking about?"

"The message—remember?" I shook my head. "Come on, Geoffrey. Of course you do. Frank told us to send them a message, demonstrate that we were serious. Well, that's what I did. It was a big message too. It said, Don't mess with us, do what we say."

I could feel her body shaking in my arms. "My God, what did you do?"

She looked up at me. "I was so furious about what they did to Adam, I guess I got carried away." She stood back. Droplets clung to her body. Her hair looked great, wet and tangled. She looked so good I wanted to screw her then and there.

She pushed her mouth against my shirt, spoke against my chest. "Early this morning I torched Mrs. Z's building. Firebombed it. When I left, it was in flames. The whole rotten place was burning up." She looked up at my face again. "God, how I wish you'd been there, Geoffrey! To see the *flames*! To see them *dance*!"

# Five

I want to photograph what is evil. . . .

—Diane Arbus

*T*HERE'S SOMETHING I HAVE TO TELL YOU, GEOFFREY. Wanted to tell you in the car . . . but I was afraid."

It was 1:00 A.M. We were lying naked in a huge double bed in the Seek And Ye Shall Find Motel in Santa Fe. It had been thirty-six hours since we left New York. We'd spent most of the evening in the room eating carryout food and watching TV. I'd just turned off the set. I was bone-weary, about to close my eyes, when Kim announced she had something to say.

"Mrs. Z was in the building when I burned it. There wasn't any way to get her out." And then, when I didn't react: "Don't you hear me, Geof? She got burned up."

She spoke in a monotone, tired and subdued, as if recounting some ordinary little fact. "Poor Mrs. Z—she's just cinders now," she added wistfully.

"Sounds like a very bad dream," I said, all my denial mechanisms running flat out.

"Prettier to think so, isn't it?" She settled back, stared at the ceiling. "She double-crossed me. I had to see her. I had to protect myself. Then . . . things got out of hand." She paused again.

"Starting that fire—I thought it would be difficult. But it wasn't. It wasn't hard at all."

I couldn't think of anything to say to that, so I stayed silent. Then, to make the time pass, I looked around the room. It had the sorrowful quality of most motel rooms—schmaltzy framed prints on the walls, ruffled lampshades and other mawkish touches meant to make it seem like home, but which, because they spoke of the anonymity of the person who had chosen them, made me long for my Manhattan loft.

She turned to me. "Don't you want to know why, Geoffrey?"

"Sure. Tell me why," I said quietly.

She started to speak, then caught her breath; perhaps she feared the effect of what she was about to say. When she finally spoke it was in a rapid stream, as if blurting it out, like removing a bandage fast, would somehow hurt me less.

"I lied to you in Key West. Rakoubian told the truth. The blackmail *was* my idea. Except it wasn't. He just *thought* it was. I brought it to him—that much was true. But the original idea came from Mrs. Z."

The room started to feel cold.

"She came to me after Sonya was killed, said we could blackmail Darling and make a fortune. That all we needed were some photographs and for that we could use Rakoubian. She told me to propose the idea to him without telling him she was part of it. I did. I even helped him set up his camera in the changing room. Mrs. Z gave me the keys. Now the poor creep's dead and he never knew she was behind it all."

"And the 'cover photographer'—who was behind that?" I asked, suddenly on a knife's edge between fury and helplessness.

"Oh, Geof, believe me: Rakoubian thought that up on his own. I swear to you, Geoffrey, I didn't know. I had absolutely nothing to do with that."

I got out of bed, went to the bathroom, knelt on the tiles in front of the toilet and began to heave. I wanted to throw up. When nothing came, I moved to the sink and splashed cold water on my face.

Later I stood against the bathroom door and studied her. Our sheet covered her to her waist; she was bare above. Her hands were linked behind her head, her hair splayed on the pillow. The spaces beneath her arms were dark. I couldn't see her eyes.

"You *do* believe me, don't you, Geoffrey?"

I shook my head.

"I swear!"

"You swore to me before."

She looked up at the ceiling. "That was in Key West."

For a moment I didn't know what she was talking about. Then I thought I did. "Oh, I get it. Everything you said down there was false. But that doesn't matter because Key West is—what? A liar's paradise? Is that what you want to say?"

She didn't answer, just continued staring at the ceiling. I watched her awhile longer, waiting for her to speak. When she didn't, I broke the silence.

"I take pictures of you. We talk, sleep together, make love. But for all of that, after all these weeks, I have no idea who you are."

She shrugged. "I'm just a girl you met who got you shooting people again."

"Yeah. An ordinary girl."

"Go ahead, mock me. But I want you to know—"

"What?"

"Know *me*, Geoffrey."

I laughed.

"What's the matter?"

"Everything," I said.

We'd left New York the day she burned down the building, traveling under assumed names. I'd flown to Dallas on one airline, she to St. Louis on another. We'd each spent the night in our respective city of transit, then continued to Albuquerque, where we'd met that morning at the airport. We'd rented a car, eaten lunch at the Sanitary Tortilla Factory, then had driven up to Santa Fe.

Frank had been adamant: the three of us must not be seen together. So Kim and I had cruised Cerrillos Road looking for a suitable motel. We chose the Seek And Ye Shall Find because of its pink-and-white façade, and because the name appealed to Kim— it was, she said, pretty much the story of her life.

What *was* that life? What had she been seeking? And what had she managed to find? What was she seeking now from me? That's what I wanted to know.

She'd told me so many different stories I couldn't keep them straight. At least one of them, I figured, had to be true. But then, I thought, that might not necessarily be the case. Perhaps all of them were lies.

I was thinking about that, and what I was going to do about her, when finally she began to speak, in a strange emphatic way I'd never heard her use before.

"*She* thought up the whole thing, brought me into it. Then, when the crunch came, she chickened out. Maybe she thought Darling would find out *she* was the blackmailer. Maybe he accused her, so she had to give him *proof* that he was wrong. Whatever the reason, she switched sides. Didn't say anything, just *switched*. One day I was her *dear accomplice*, next I was good as *dead*. She sold me out to save her *ass*. Only reason she let me get away was she knew I'd tell Darling the whole rotten scheme was *hers*."

"Yeah, Kim. But the bottom line is she didn't kill you, did she?"

She shook her head furiously. "She *would* have! She *lured* Shadow to be killed. That was the night I ran to you. And you were *there* for me, Geoffrey! You were the only one I could trust. Now, isn't it funny? You don't trust me at all. Even now, now, while I'm telling you the *real truth*, you don't believe a word I say. Not a solitary word."

"Is there a difference?" I asked. She stared at me confused. "Between the truth and the 'real truth'—is that a distinction I should know about?"

"All you do is mock me, Geoffrey."

"Want me to feel sorry for you?"

"That's not what I want!"

"What *do* you want?"

"*I want you to believe me! I want you to love me!*"

I retreated back into the bathroom, sat down on the edge of the tub. *Oh, Christ*, I thought. *Jesus Christ!*

Later, sitting in the motel-room easy chair, feet stretched out on the matching ottoman, I tried to get her story straight. Kim faced me, attentive, straight-backed and cross-legged on the bed, her perfect bared breasts thrust forward, harbingers that she would speak the naked truth.

"Now, let's see if I've got this right," I said. "First, Mrs. Z double-crossed Darling."

She nodded.

"Then the two of you set up Rakoubian."

She nodded again.

"Then he got the idea on his own to make me look like the blackmail photographer."

"So far you've got it right."

"Then Mrs. Z got scared and double-crossed you. She lured in Shadow and turned her over to Darling. Under torture, Shadow inadvertently pinpointed me. So they came after me, thinking I'd taken the photographs."

"Couldn't tell it better myself."

"Meantime, after you and I got back together, you decided to take revenge. But before you got around to it Rakoubian was killed, because you told Mrs. Z he was the real blackmail photographer."

She shook her head. "She already knew that. It was Darling who didn't know. You told him when you ambushed him on the street."

"So I signed Rakoubian's death warrant—is that what you think?"

She thought about it for a moment. "I suppose you did . . . in a sense."

*Yeah. In a sense.*

"Which brings us," I said, "to the night before last, when you slipped out after I fell asleep. Was it your idea you were going to send Mrs. Z a message?"

"Not *send* her a message, Geoffrey. She was going to *be* the message."

"You went there to burn her?"

She looked appalled. "Absolutely not! All I wanted to do was turn her around, make her see things our way. Also I wanted my extortion confession back. It was a loose end. I didn't feel comfortable with it floating around."

"And then?"

"Like I told you—things got out of hand."

"Out of hand! You're incredible! You burn an old lady to death, and you talk about it like it was just some freak accident or something, like you were at a dinner party and by mistake you spilled some wine on the damask!"

Her eyes closed down to slits. "Old lady! That's what you think she was? She was *evil*, Geoffrey—*totally evil*. She was a *witch*. You've got to *burn* a witch!"

She told me what happened. When she called Mrs. Z, after she discovered Rakoubian had been killed, her old acting coach begged to see her. That morning the cops had come around asking about Sonya, and a little while later Darling had called her in a rage. My ambush had gotten to him; he wasn't used to being on the receiving end. Then the Duquaynes called, and they were the final straw. Everything was falling apart.

So Kim told her, sure, they could probably work something out, she'd stop by to see her later on. She didn't say when, just suggested Mrs. Z leave the key to her back door beneath a garbage can in the alley, and sometime in the night she'd drop in.

"I woke up around three o'clock. You were snoring away." She smiled. "Guess all our lovemaking wore you out. You looked adorable in your sleep. Adorable. . . ." She giggled. "Anyway, I got up, dressed, taxied downtown, found the key, crept in and took the elevator up. She was waiting for me in her bedroom. I sat down on the bed and we talked.

" 'You double-crossed me,' I told her calmly. 'The whole thing was your idea, then you sold me out.' 'But I had to, my dear,' she said. 'You don't know Arnold. He's ruthless when he's angry. It was me or you. I chose myself. You would have done the same.'

"She wasn't humble or scared the way she'd been on the phone. No, she was haughty and arrogant. She said the time had come for the two of us to make peace, and that we could still do a deal if I was interested. She said Darling was furious because of what you'd done to him that morning. All his fury was now focused on you, Geoffrey. *You!* There was only one way I could set things right, and that was to betray you. If I did that the slate would be clean. Darling would relent. I'd be off the hook." She glanced at me. "You look skeptical."

"I guess I am," I said.

"Don't you want to hear what she wanted me to do?"

"Sure. Tell me," I said.

"You speak so casually, Geoffrey. It's as if you don't believe anything I say."

I didn't know what to believe, but I was curious. "Why don't you tell me," I said. "Then I'll let you know if I believe you or not."

She nodded. "I was to bring you around in the morning to a certain address. Darling's people would be waiting for you there. I wouldn't have to come in. I only had to deliver you to the door. They'd snatch you right inside." She turned and stared at me, directly into my eyes. "They were going to blind you, Geoffrey. Hold you down, then slowly drop acid into your eyes. Drop by drop, and Darling was going to watch them do it. He was going to stand over you with a camera and take photographs of the whole thing. Pictures of your pain, your fright. *That's* what he was going to do, Geoffrey. *That* would be his revenge!"

I started to shudder. My pulse began to race. All the terror came back to me from the night the boy had come and thrown the lye. I didn't think then about whether she was telling the truth. All I could think about was blindness. A little bottle of acid in someone's hand. The liquid moving slowly to the bottle's lip. The first drop trembling slightly, reluctant to depart the glass. Then falling, falling slowly toward me. Darling leering. The flash of his strobe. I shut my eyes to make the vision disappear. And Kimberly talked on.

"The moment she said that I went into a fury. I picked up this coffee thermos she kept beside her bed, and brought it right down on her head. When she went limp, I turned her on her belly and looked around for something to tie her with. There was a coil of rope we used for our bondage scenes. I knew just where it was. I ran and fetched it, and then I tied her up."

She paused as if to catch her breath,

"That was the weird part, Geoffrey. I'd never touched her before. In class she always had us touching each other, but she always kept aloof. So there I was, handling her, tying knots around her limbs, and doing that got me excited, like finally I had this *power* over her—*I* was in control.

"When I had her hog-tied, I went to the kitchen and found the varnish remover. She woke up while I was pouring it around. 'Going to burn me, Kimberly?' 'Yeah, you got it, Mrs. Z!' I said."

Kim rolled her head across the pillow, as if she were suffering some sort of delirium. "She started blubbering, begging me to spare her. But I felt no pity, none at all. I couldn't forget how she'd played solitaire while Sonya's bones were being broken. And the way she'd smiled when she'd showed me the video of Shadow being tortured.

" 'No deals,' I said, 'it's your turn now.' I smacked her again, untied her, and started all these fires around the room. I stayed until the flames caught the bedding, then waited across the street until the fire engines came. I left when I heard a fireman say the smoke was so thick he couldn't check if anyone was trapped."

She stopped rolling her head. "I hurried back to our hotel. I remember I sang to myself in the shower there, just an old song to help me forget. But I was glad I'd done it. And I haven't regretted it since. I figured that since killing Rakoubian had been their message to us, killing Mrs. Z would make a good message back. And it turns out I was right too. Darling heard us loud and clear."

I must have looked at her strangely then, because she smiled back.

"Yeah, I've talked to him, Geoffrey. I phoned him from St. Louis last night. Told him to get his ass out here, and don't forget the cash. Told him if he didn't show day after tomorrow, the same thing was going to happen to him."

"Jesus! You *called* him! Where did you get his number?"

"Out of Mrs. Z's book before I lit the fires. I'm glad you weren't with me, Geoffrey. It wasn't pretty. Not at all. But like I said, maybe you have to burn a witch. Maybe that's the only way to get rid of one. . . ."

Her eyes closed not long afterwards, as if her act of confession had made it possible for her to sleep with impunity. But I lay awake beside her, more frightened than I'd been since the night of the lye attack. She was a killer. I'd seen joy in her eyes even as she'd admitted that. Now I was entangled with her. We were lovers and partners in a blackmail scheme. For all I knew, I might also be accessory to a murder. And more frightening than any of that was my conviction she had still not told me the entire truth.

A little before dawn I stole out of our room, took the car, and drove down to Galisteo. The house was quiet when I drove up, so I sat in one of the deck chairs in front and waited for the sun.

It rose out of the mountains, triumphant light, burnishing Mai's sculptures, turning them into images of broken dinosaurs. By the time Frank sat down beside me I was starting to wonder if things were as bad as I'd thought.

He surprised me: he already knew Mrs. Z was dead.

"Kim phoned from St. Louis, told me everything. I told her to call Darling and what to say. After she spoke with him, she called me back and we talked for quite a while."

"About what?"

"You, mostly, Geof. I told her she had to tell you the truth. Told her if she didn't, I probably would. She said she'd think about it. Thanked me for my advice."

I looked at him. His eyes were spectral, fracturing the rising sun. "I'm frightened of her, Frank."

"She's crazy about you."

"Is that what she says?" He didn't answer. "What the hell am I going to do?"

"Wait till this is over, then decide."

"Let's get the money first—right?"

"We're close now. You don't want to mess up the deal."

"Two more people are *dead*, Frank."

"Two *very bad* people." He shook his head. "Look, Geof, you didn't 'kill' Rakoubian. He was always going to get killed. As for Kim's little bonfire, if you look at it a certain way, it was a pure act, a justifiable act of revenge."

"Does that make it okay?"

"Maybe not 'okay.' But human. Very human."

"You don't think she's a monster?"

"What's a monster? I don't think you have to be afraid of her, if that's what you mean."

I turned to him. "Why wouldn't you see us yesterday? You didn't want to meet Kim. Why?"

"I'll meet her eventually."

"But not now. This idea the three of us can't be seen together— that's bullshit." He shrugged. "Why?" He didn't answer. "Don't you trust me, Frank?"

"Course I trust you. And now I want you to trust me. Sometimes, in this kind of an operation, it's better to keep a few things compartmentalized."

I didn't quarrel with him, but I was upset, which is why, when he urged me to stay for breakfast, I turned him down. Also, I wasn't in the mood to face Mai and the kids. Our parting was cool when I left to drive back to Santa Fe.

In our room at the Seek And Ye Shall Find, I found Kim breathing heavily, evidently asleep. When I got into bed she reached out for me, then molded herself against my flank.

I don't know how long I slept or what I dreamt about; I remember only that I was awakened by a harshly ringing phone. Groping for it, my eyes still closed, I could feel she was no longer in the bed.

"It's Frank. I'm at the studio."

I opened my eyes. Kim was gone. The room was filled with blinding light. I looked at my watch—it was almost one in the afternoon. Kim probably woke up, saw I was sleeping, then walked down to the Plaza to shop, I thought.

"What's up?" I asked Frank.

"Developments. I think you should come over here."

"Developments?"

"Better get your butt over here, pal." He hung up without saying good-bye.

I splashed cold water on my face, threw on some clothes, then noticed that the keys to the rental car were gone. The car wasn't in the motel parking lot either. Kim had obviously taken it.

I walked a mile down Cerrillos to Guadalupe Street, then another half mile toward the Plaza. Traffic was heavy, the trucks spewed out fumes. A teenage girl, in a Los Alamos T-shirt, leaned out of a car window and snapped my picture with a "point 'n' shoot."

I was sweating by the time I reached Frank's gallery. And then I was annoyed—the door was locked. I knocked and peered in through the glass. No sign of Frank. And no note telling me when he'd be back.

I was about to give up when he came out of his darkroom, saw me and let me in.

"You said get over here. Then you lock me out."

"Hey! Calm yourself." He motioned me toward the darkroom. "You're just in time to watch me print."

He hustled me inside, closed the door, shushed me when I tried to speak. He had an excellent darkroom. There were three enlargers, including a monster 8 × 10 loaned to him by Leo DeSalle. At the moment he was working with a Beseler. He had a strip of

35mm. negative locked in the negative stage. He motioned me back, checked his focus, set his grain magnifier aside. Then he slipped a sheet of paper into his easel and fired off an exposure.

I followed him as he removed the sheet, carried it across the room to his sink.

He glanced at me, then dropped it facedown into a tray of developer. He poked it with a pair of tongs, flipped it over, and then, as he began to agitate, we both bent forward, waiting for the image to emerge.

It didn't come quickly. Frank didn't use rapid developing papers; he liked only the heaviest most silver-laden varieties. And so it was a good minute before I was able to see that the subject of his picture was Kim.

She wasn't alone. I couldn't make out the other woman. But I could see they were conferring in what looked to be a garden. As the print grew clearer I saw a numbered door in the background. It wasn't our door at the Seek And Ye Shall Find.

"When did you take this?"

"About an hour ago."

"Where?"

"A motel called the Alamo, half a mile from where you're staying. I shot it through the bushes from the other side of the pool. Rooms that border on the pool have these secluded patios in front."

I understood then why he'd avoided meeting Kim—he'd wanted to be able to watch her without being recognized.

I turned back to the print, looked closely at the second woman. Her features, tough and Slavic, were finally coming clear.

"Who is she, Geof?"

I recognized her—though I couldn't quite believe my eyes. "That's Grace Arnos."

"Yeah." Frank sighed. "I thought so. But I needed to be sure."

I looked at him. "What's she doing here? What the hell's going on?"

He picked up the print, ran it through the stop bath and then into a tray of fix.

"I think something pretty bad is going on," he said.

I stayed with him while he printed out his surveillance shots, waited patiently until he developed each sheet. It was a tortuous way to find out what he'd seen, but for me, that afternoon, a slow tortuous way was best. I could have inspected all his negatives at once; I preferred to watch the situation unfold.

And unfold it did. The sequence of shots, which he'd grabbed very cleverly from a concealed position beside the motel pool, showed Kim and Grace talking, embracing, then kissing. The last shot showed them disappearing into Grace's room, arms wrapped about each other like lovers.

"Blackmail wasn't Mrs. Z's idea. And it wasn't Kim's. Grace was the brain behind everything. She had to be."

We were in Frank's Land Rover, driving south, on our way to inspect the payoff site. I was still in a daze, reeling from the darkroom, but Frank kept calling our destination "the battlefield," and, like a warrior anticipating combat, spoke in sharp clipped phrases while clenching a cheroot between his teeth.

"I even think it was Grace's idea to set you up as the 'cover photographer.' She had Kim plant it with Rakoubian, and he fell for it—of course. Got to hand it to the dyke. She had a terrific plan. Get Rakoubian and Mrs. Z to do the dirty work, and you to take the blame. Get Darling to kill off Rakoubian, then have Kim kill off Mrs. Z. Not hard to figure out what they've got in store for us, once we get the money out of Darling. Get rid of us, scoop up the loot, then go off hand in hand into the sunset. Shit! It's so fucking Byzantine, Geof. Double crosses within double crosses within one enormous fucking double cross."

I stared out the window. The shrub grass was starting to redden; autumn was coming to New Mexico.

He laughed. ". . . always worried about Grace. The trail to her was just too slick. You see that Cleveland number on your phone bill, fly out there, find the house, follow her to the topless joint, manage to wangle yourself a date. She offers you a massage, giving you just enough time first to find the photograph of Kim upstairs. Then there's the friendly neighbor woman conveniently posted next door to help you get the little doggie back inside—the neighbor woman who hasn't spoken to Grace in years, but knows in just which particular potted plant she hides her extra key. See: they made it seem hard, but it wasn't hard at all. And diverting you through Cleveland was a brilliant stroke—it gave Grace the chance to look you over, see if you were right for what she had in mind."

Crazy as it sounded, it made sense. "But why me?" I asked.

"They needed a photographer."

"There're plenty of photographers."

"Sure, but you're special, Geof. Somehow they found out about you, that you were a portraitist who couldn't take portraits anymore. That's how they got to you. And you didn't see it happening because they came at you from your blind side. That's what they counted on—that you *wouldn't* see."

*My blind side*. Sure. I'd have been a sucker for anyone who'd have come along and helped me overcome my block. There'd been several times when I'd been ready to stop chasing Kim, when I knew I'd been a fool. But still I kept coming, afraid that if I didn't find her again I'd slip back into the hole she'd found me in.

Frank paused to relight his cigar. "It's Grace who's been pulling the strings. Everyone's, including ours. She works through Kim."

"But why? Why does Kim do it?"

"Oldest reasons in the world, Geof. Love and money." He laughed again.

We drove on in silence for a while. "What happens now?" I asked.

"No way are we going to let them take away that money! We've come this far, we're not tossing in our jocks."

He had it figured out. Darling was due in Santa Fe the following morning. Assuming he showed up, and Frank was sure he would, we'd proceed with our original plan. Kim would contact Darling, arrange the pickup out to the payoff spot. Then, while Kim and I made the exchange, Frank would confront Grace. They'd have, he said, a little talk.

"What kind of little talk?" I wanted to know.

"Sufficient to discourage her."

"And if she doesn't get discouraged?"

"She'll get neutralized."

"How?"

"That's my problem. Yours is keep hold of the money."

"What if Darling tries to kill us?"

"He probably will. So we'll have Kim do a little wetwork."

"*Wetwork*—what the hell is that?"

"Hey, Geof! Don't go soft on me. I told you up front there could be killing in a deal like this. Anyway, it's Kim you should worry about. Once that money's in her hands, things'll get dangerous. Whatever you do, don't turn your back on the lying little bitch. . . ."

He turned off the highway, then drove along a dirt road. He followed a stony track, then cut cross-country. He pointed ahead as we came around the side of a hill. I looked, saw a cluster of half-finished wooden buildings.

"There's our battlefield."

But they weren't buildings, they were façades, the ruins of an

old movie set. Low-budget Westerns had been shot there years before. Now the place was abandoned.

"These days, when they make a Western, producers want an entire town," Frank explained. "Not just Main Street, but side streets too, a hotel, a second saloon, a courthouse, a big white church with a steeple. There's no water or electricity here, and it's hard to get to. No one's shot a movie here in years."

Frank, however, had shot many still pictures there. After he found the site he'd been haunted by it, and had come back numerous times to photograph. One day when he was shooting, a couple from Albuquerque drove up. They turned out to be the owners, who'd recently inherited the land. When they found out Frank liked the place, they asked if he'd be interested in buying it. He offered them thirty-five hundred dollars, they haggled for a week, and finally sold it to him for four.

He showed me around, and, as he did, I understood why he liked it for the payoff. It belonged to him, he controlled the access, so if Darling brought along goons and they tried to follow him in, we'd spot them in time to get out.

Also, the set was remote. The tracks that led into it didn't appear on maps. There were no farms around, or ranches, or Indian burial grounds—nothing to attract a stranger or a tourist.

But its best quality was the special mood created by those rotting old façades. Set up in the middle of nowhere, they constituted a kind of ghost town (a false ghost town, to be sure, since there had never been a human settlement there)—haunted, otherworldly, and thus psychologically intimidating.

Frank sketched out the scenario:

"Say you're a guy who's never been out here before. You've brought your cash, you're ready to deal, and late in the afternoon this gorgeous babe picks you up at your hotel. She takes a look at your money, gives you a quick weapons search, then drives you out into the countryside. It's almost twilight, you're thinking you're driving into wilderness, then she turns off the main road, hands you a blindfold and tells you to put it on.

"Okay, you can tell by the feel of the car that she's driving along on dirt. But you don't know which direction she's going, and when she finally stops, and you take off the blindfold, you find yourself in this weird environment.

"There're these strange deserted storefronts behind you casting long shadows on the dust. Could be armed men behind them ready to shoot you if you make any fancy moves. Meantime it's getting cold and dark and you can't see all that well. And, on top of everything else, no one's there—you have to wait.

"After a while, a good long while, this guy steps out through the creaky old saloon doors. He's this photographer guy who ambushed you a few days before in New York, and now he's walking toward you, confident, taking your picture as he comes. You show him your money, he shows you his incriminating photographs, you make the exchange. He walks back into the saloon, you get back in the car and the girl drives you back to your hotel. So"—Frank looked at me—"how do you like it so far?"

"So far it's fine. What happens to me?"

"You walk right out through the back of the set. Come on, I'll show you."

I followed him to the saloon doors, he pushed them open, then I followed him through. They creaked as they swung closed behind us. In back the façades were unpainted wooden walls, held up by a network of supports.

"You walk through here carrying the money, then you follow the path around to the other side of the hill. My old Volvo's parked back there. You get in and follow the back road out. Kim doesn't know about the Volvo or the back road. She only gets one dry-run ride out here with me tomorrow morning. She won't have time to come back and check around. Plus she'll have no reason to suspect you."

"What if I run into her on the road?"

He shook his head. "You'll be driving the opposite direction. You go back to the Madrid road, then follow the track along Galisteo creek. You stop at my place, drop off the money, then drive back to Sante Fe, where the three of us meet to split the loot."

"And by that time, hopefully, you'll have persuaded Grace to leave."

Frank nodded. "One way or another."

"And Darling? What about the 'wetwork'? When does that take place?"

"We'll leave that up to Kim."

We approached the Volvo. I got in, turned the ignition switch. The car started up. The gas gauge showed the tank was full.

"Okay," I said, "it's a good plan. So tell me: what's the flaw?"

"The only flaw is Kim may be tempted to kill you after the exchange. Darling too, of course."

"Both of us?" That sounded impossible.

"To make it look like you killed each other," he said.

"Jesus, Frank!"

"It's a possibility."

"What's my defense?"

"First, she doesn't know I'm not behind the storefronts covering you. Second, she likes you. Third, she's not afraid of you. She's only afraid of me."

"Why only you?"

"Because I'm ex-Special Forces. I'm a mercenary. I'm in this deal for the cash. You're not likely to go on the warpath if she and Grace steal the money. But I am, so I'm dangerous. When we're together for the split—that's when I figure they'll try and take us out."

"And if you're wrong, if she tries to take me out right here?"

"You have your gun-camera, Geof. If she tries anything—use it. Don't even hesitate."

I nodded, then turned away, waiting for that idea to sink in. Such a thick aura of treachery had come to surround the enterprise that at that point no betrayal seemed impossible.

Betrayal: the word was in my mind the rest of the afternoon, as I walked about Santa Fe.

"You need time to think it through, put it together in your head," Frank said, as he dropped me off at the Plaza.

I wandered the central part of the city, the area of expensive galleries and boutiques. Everywhere there were tourists gawking at Navaho rugs, Santa Clara pottery, necklaces, rings, belts embellished with silver and turquoise. And all the while two phrases echoed in my brain: *I've been used; I've been betrayed*.

Over and over I asked myself how I'd fallen into such a vortex. Did she love me? Apparently not. Had she ever? I doubted it. Had I loved her? I definitely had. Did I now? I couldn't.

When, weeks before, back in New York, we had lain in my bed watching *Double Indemnity*, Kim had told me she was sure Phyllis Dietrichson decided to use Walter Neff the minute he walked into her house.

Had she known she was going to use me from the moment she spotted me on Desbrosses Street, and then with a sultry confidence asked, "Are you an alien creature?"

It seemed she had, that that meeting between us might not even have been an accident. And the irony of it was that though she'd apparently known all about me from the start, I still knew nothing about her. Not even her real name.

The next twenty-four hours were extremely tense.

That night Kim and Frank met for the first time, when the three of us had dinner in the atrium of the Villa Linda shopping mall. It was a perfect spot for such a meeting. There were a dozen fast-food outlets ringing the walls, with tables and chairs set under a skylight in the middle. People walked by, but no one lingered. The place was totally anonymous.

Frank was highly attentive to Kim. She couldn't possibly suspect he knew her secret. Watching them together, listening to them talk and plot, I still couldn't quite believe what he'd uncovered.

But he'd shown me photographs, and generally speaking photographs don't lie, no matter what Dave Ramos thinks. Grace was in Santa Fe. She and Kim had met. They'd conducted themselves like lovers. And the feeling I'd had very early that morning—that Kim had still not told me the entire truth—was well borne out by Frank's analysis.

He was right about another thing too: the trail through Grace in Cleveland to Kim's hideout in Key West had been much too easy to follow. I'd congratulated myself on what a shrewd detective I'd been. Now I understood I'd been a fool.

I made love to Kim that night. I had to. I was afraid that if I didn't she'd suspect that I knew. At first it was awful. Her lies were so abundant, calculated and ensnaring, I quivered at each caress.

She misunderstood my trembling, mistook it for passion. And when that seemed to arouse her, I played along. Then I actually started to enjoy it. It was so easy to play false, revel in deceit. Perhaps I was beginning to understand her.

Was Frank right? Was she motivated only by love for Grace and money? Or was there something more—some actual pleasure she took in perfidy? I tried to put myself in her place, understand how it felt to have done what she had done, to plan the things that she was planning—as if life were a game in which to play was to cheat, to speak was to lie, and the only purpose a lover had was to be used and then betrayed.

Frank came by early in the morning, first to show Kim the way out to the battlefield, then to drive her to Albuquerque to see if Darling came in on the plane.

I stayed in our room at the Seek And Ye Shall Find, trying to make sense out of what was happening. I even considered walking up to the Alamo to have my own little talk with Grace. But what could I say to her, when, it seemed, I had totally misinterpreted our encounter? And then it struck me that even as she had pretended to be my friend, I had betrayed that "friendship" when I broke into her house.

Lies, lies . . . everywhere mendacity. And now all our individual lies, reaching a critical mass, were about to converge and to explode.

The phone rang a little after 1:00 P.M. It was Frank, calling from the airport.

"He's here!" he said.

Not only had Darling arrived, but he was exerting an especially tight grip on an oxblood leather attaché case.

"It's even got brass corners," Frank said. "That's where the money is."

There was, he said, no sign of accompanying goons. He was sure the man had come to deal. And Darling hadn't spotted Kim. After she'd pointed him out, Frank had kept her in the background. Even if Darling suspected he was being watched, he had no knowledge of who his watcher was.

He put Kim on the line.

"God, it's exciting! I've been dreaming about this for weeks. Just a few more hours, Geoffrey. . . ."

"Yeah. Then easy street," I said.

They returned to the motel a little after 3:00 P.M. to give me their report.

Darling had rented a car and driven to Santa Fe. As instructed, he'd taken a *casita* at the posh Rancho Encantato. As soon as he'd checked in, Kim had called him on the house phone, told him to present himself at the front gate at 5:45. She'd pick him up no later than 6:00. If anyone was with him, or if he wasn't carrying the money, or any attempt was made to follow her car, the deal was off. He had only one shot at buying our photographs. Blow it, she told him, and he'd be out of luck.

Now she wanted to rest until it was time to pick Darling up.

"Got to come down from the high," she said. "See you on the battlefield." She kissed me at the door.

Once we were back in Frank's car, he turned to me. "Play kissy-pussy games with Grace—that's what she means by 'rest.' " I asked him what he thought of her. "Attractive and seductive. Can't blame you for falling for her, Geof."

"But you wouldn't have—is that what you're saying?"

"No, I'm not saying that. I might have fallen for her too."

"So, I haven't been a total fool."

"The only fools in this game," he said, "will be the guys who end up dead."

Out at the site we went over everything, walking through the exchange three times. I played Darling's part, Kim's, and then my own. I understood my most important task was to give Kim and Darling the impression that Frank was hidden behind the storefront watching my back.

When Frank thought I was sufficiently rehearsed, he presented me with a chocolate bar and a thermos of water. He suggested I take some pictures. He thought using my camera would help me pass the hours until Kim and Darling arrived.

He wished me luck with Kim, and I wished him luck with Grace, then he got into his car.

"So, now it's just the two of us," I said.

"Yep. Just like a buddy picture, Geof."

I didn't use my camera to pass the time. At that point photography seemed irrelevant. There were two cameras around my neck, one of which wasn't a camera but a gun. But, on that particular afternoon, it was the phony camera that seemed most real.

I strolled about, the afternoon wore on, the shadows lengthened and the light started turning sweet. When I sat down on the saloon porch to eat my chocolate bar, I heard a sound that made me jump. A rattlesnake slithered out from beneath the steps. After that I kept clear of the set.

At 6:15 I started watching the valley, alternately looking at my watch. By 6:30, when our rental car had not appeared, I began to worry. Had something gone wrong? Maybe Darling had changed his mind, or maybe he'd pulled a fast one in the car. What if he'd decided to take Kim hostage, only agreeing to release her when we handed over the photographs?

Finally, on the verge of despair, I spied a trail of dust. It was the car. The sun was behind me; its rays caught and glittered off the chrome. If it was Kim, she was driving extremely fast. I watched awhile to be certain it was really she, then retreated to my position behind the saloon doors.

She drove straight to the place where I'd been standing, then stopped hard, creating a little storm of dust. I saw Darling sitting beside her wearing his blindfold. He didn't look animated. Then, when I saw her leave the car clutching his brass-cornered attaché case, I realized something was wrong.

She set the case down in the dust, then continued around to the passenger side. I remember thinking how curious it was that she was wearing an evening dress. Then, when she opened the door and Darling fell out, I knew right away that he was dead.

I rushed out of the saloon. By that time she was backing the car away. I stared down at Darling, then pulled his blindfold off. Even in death his tight thin lips were pursed and his chin tilted up with arrogance.

Kim had parked a hundred feet away. Now she rushed toward me, looking radiant.

"Geoffrey! I did it! It's over!" She plunged into my arms.

"What happened?"

"I shot him as soon as he put on the blindfold. It was spooky driving out here sitting beside him, but I couldn't just dump him on the road. Open the briefcase, Geoffrey."

I stooped and opened it. It was stuffed with neatly arranged bundles of fresh currency bound by rubber bands.

"See! I got it! Frank's idea. I mean, why go through that whole dumb payoff routine? Just see that he had the cash, then let him have it. He said you wouldn't do it, you'd hesitate. 'Do your wet-work as soon as you can,' Frank said. So that's just what I did."

I believed Frank had told her that, that there'd been more than one part of the plan he'd kept compartmentalized. I was angry with him for that, but not half so angry as I was afraid. For now I was truly afraid of Kim. If she was capable of assassinating Darling as he sat right beside her in a car, she was perfectly capable of killing me.

"What did *Grace* tell you to do?" I whispered.

"Grace? What are you talking about?"

I exploded: "Don't try and fake with me, Kim! Frank spotted you. He took pictures of the two of you kissing in her patio."

"Pictures! Why, that prying little sneak!"

"You're the sneak. Whose idea was it anyway, hers or yours?"

She shook her head and glared at me. "Fuck you, Geoffrey! Whose do you think?"

"Tell me!"

"Hers, of course. She thought up the whole thing."

"Yeah. So now that you've got the money, what does she expect you to do about me?"

She lowered her voice. "Kill you, of course."

"Of course. Then make it look like Darling and I killed each other, right?"

"Oh, Geof!" she moaned.

"What about Frank? He'd follow you to the ends of the earth if you pulled a stunt like that."

"I know, I know. . . ."

"So? Are you *going* to kill me?"

Tears formed in her eyes. "Do you really think I could?"

"I can't be sure. Can I, Kim?"

She nodded, as if to acknowledge that was true. Then she hugged me. "I'm a bad person, Geoffrey. I make my own laws. Sometimes I think . . ." She lowered her voice—"Sometimes I think I'm really evil."

She pulled back, placed her hands on my shoulders, then linked them behind my neck. "We'll have to kill Grace. We won't be safe until we do. She'll want the money. She'll come after us. We'll never breathe free with her alive."

"What about Frank?"

"Kill him too. Then there'll be more for us."

"He's my friend!"

She squinted at me as if I were some kind of fool. "Fine, Geoffrey, if you feel that way, you can split your share with him."

"So long as you get half?"

"That's my deal with Grace."

"And I'd better match it. How can I ever trust you now?"

"I don't know, Geoffrey. I don't suppose you really can." She pressed herself against me, forced her mouth against mine. "I want you, Geoffrey. I want to make love with you—right here. Now. In the dust. With Darling's body on the ground. And the money . . . the money very close. The light playing on us, spotlighting us. How do you call it, Geoffrey? The 'splendorous failing light.' That would be great. The look of it, I mean. The splendor of it. The baroque effect. With the shadows long and ominous. Like the end of an opera. Or those weird *film noir* movies you like. Wouldn't that be something? Wouldn't it?"

She kissed me again, then rolled her tongue across my lips. Then she burrowed her mouth into my shoulder and nibbled on my skin. I could feel the bite of her teeth, smell the lemon-and-musk scent of her hair.

"There's something I have to tell you," she said, speaking softly against my chest. "Frank's dead. Grace killed him, walked into his studio an hour ago and shot him in the face. It was fast. Frank never even knew. But she's crazy, you see. That's why we have to get rid of her."

I felt something go weak within me then—my best friend dead, Mai a widow, four kids orphaned on account of me. This was worse than Guatemala, worse than anything. Now the whole enterprise was meaningless.

"Where's Grace now?"

"Back at our motel."

Grace was waiting back in *our* motel, because she knew Kim was coming back alone. I took a step backwards. I knew then what I was going to do.

"What's the matter?"

"I want to take your picture," I said.

"You always want to do that when you're afraid. Think I'm going to kill you, Geoffrey? That I'm a black widow spider or something? Are you really still afraid of me?"

I raised my camera. "Sure. Maybe a little bit."

She brushed my camera aside. "Later."

"Now, Kim. While there's light. Before we make love. A shot of your . . . eagerness."

She smiled. She liked that. She stepped back from me. We stood six feet apart.

"Afterwards we'll make love in the dirt. Promise?"

I promised.

She stood looking at me. "How do you want me to pose?"

"You're fine the way you are."

"Isn't there some special thing you want me to do?" She placed a hand on her hip, stuck out the other and assumed a self-mocking sultry pose.

*She should do something.* "Tell me you're evil, Kim. Whisper it just the way you did."

I raised Frank's gun-camera to my eye, cocked it by pulling the depth-of-field lever.

"How did I say it?"

"Softly. You smiled at me in a way I'd never seen you smile before."

She smiled then, that same special way, and, when she did, I plugged her. There was a little pop, nothing loud at all, and simultaneously a neat little hole appeared in her throat. She raised her hand instinctively to protect herself, but she was a good two seconds too late. She looked at me surprised, then fell to her knees, then rolled onto the ground. The setting sun painted her red. I watched as the blood spurted from her wound.

"I'm going to die," she said.

I stood and watched her. She was pressing her fingers against her throat.

"I'm afraid, Geoffrey. Help me. Help me. Please . . ."

I looked down at her. She was still pressing the wound, trying to stop the flow.

"Find a phone. Call an ambulance."

I shook my head.

"Please," she begged. She was trembling and her eyes were clouding up with pain. "Going to watch me die, that what you want to do?" She looked over at Darling's attaché case, then smiled knowingly. "The money. You did it for the money. Sure."

"I never gave a shit about the money, Kim."

She tried to laugh at that, but she was too weak and could only smile.

"You really *were* going to kill me after we made love," I said.

She nodded. "You got me first. Didn't think you had the balls for a move like that." She swallowed hard. I could hear the blood gurgling in her throat. "I always underestimated you."

She looked at me curiously then, as if she were seeing me for the first time. Then another wave of pain swept across her face.

"Finish me off. Please, Geoffrey."

"No more bullets," I lied.

"My gun. In my purse in the car." I didn't move, just watched her. "Please, Geof. *Please*. It hurts so bad."

I knew it hurt, but I wasn't going to shoot her again. Instead I let my gun-camera drop, picked up my working Leica and focused in on her eyes. She didn't turn away, stared straight at my lens. She looked truly evil then, like a dying reptile. *Maybe this time*, I thought, *I'll get her right*.

I took her picture.

Afterwards I picked up Darling's attaché case.

"Please," she whimpered, "stay with me. Don't leave me alone."

I didn't stay with her. When I left she was still alive. The sun

was sinking, and there wasn't anything I could do for her, no purpose I could serve.

Walking to the car, I saw a pair of vultures, black forms circling slowly against the darkening sky. When I reached the car, I turned for a final look. The sun was gone. I couldn't see Kim; she was lost in the shadows cast by the set.

I looked up. Four more vultures were perched on the roof line of the movie-set façade. That old rattlesnake will finish her off, I thought. And then those ugly birds will have their dinner. She and Darling will be white bones in a couple of weeks.

You find bleached-out bones and skulls all around New Mexico.

# Six

There are no tears in *film noir*.

—*Foster Hirsch*

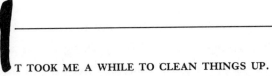

I T TOOK ME A WHILE TO CLEAN THINGS UP.

The night I killed Kim, I drove down to Mai's house in Galisteo, then phoned my room at the motel. Grace picked up. I told her I'd executed Kim, was going to give the money to Mai, and that if she ever bothered me or Frank's family again, I'd kill her too. Then I ordered her out of Santa Fe.

There was a pause after I said all that, as if she was thinking out a reply. But she didn't say anything, just breathed into the phone for a while. Then she hung up. Which was just as well, I thought.

The following morning Frank's body was found. The police speculated he'd been shot by a robber. There were no fingerprints or clues of any kind. Anyone with information was urged to contact the authorities.

Two days later there was an article in the *Santa Fe Register*, a small item near the bottom of the second page. The well-known New York architect Arnold Darling had checked into the Rancho Encantado several days before. His luggage and clothes were still in his *casita*, but he had disappeared. Again: anyone with knowledge, etc.

Darling's disappearance was worth a mention, but things like that had happened before. It seemed that people often choose New Mexico as a jumping-off point when they decide to disappear or change their lives.

After Frank's burial, I stayed on with Mai for several weeks. She was a strong woman even in her mourning. Every day she went out to her studio behind the house, put on her welder's mask and worked on her sculpture.

Jude and the girls took Frank's death hard, so I spent a lot of time with them.

Two weeks after the killings I bought a sturdy shovel and a pair of rubber gloves. Then I drove back out to that rotting movie set.

Kim's and Darling's faces had been pretty much pecked away, but the bodies lay just where I had left them. I put on the gloves, tied on a bandanna to cover my nose, then stripped the clothes and jewelry off them both. I dug a pit and buried them together. Then I burned their clothes, and scrubbed out the rental car just in case any of Darling's blood had gotten on the seats.

When I thought it was about time to go back to New York, I had Mai drive me out there again to pick up the Volvo. I followed her back, and, when we got to the house, I presented her with Darling's money.

I had counted it, of course, and was surprised to find there was only a hundred thousand dollars in the attaché case. Evidently Darling had thought he could bargain us down to 10 percent. He had no idea of the kind of vipers he was dealing with.

At first, when I told Mai it was Frank's share of our venture, she was hesitant about accepting it. She still refused when I told her it was "reparations," but she finally accepted when I persuaded her that she had to ensure the children's educations.

.  .  .

A week after I got back to New York, Sal Scotto came by my loft. We talked for a while. He told me he and Ramos were about to give up on the Cheryl Devereux case.

"Funny thing," he said, "this Mrs. Z you sent us to—evening of the day we talked to her, her place caught fire with her inside. Fire investigators think it was arson. My guess is it was self-immolation. She had some kind of weird cult thing going down there. Must have been what the killings were about."

"What about the Duquaynes?" I asked. "Did you ever talk to them?"

"Tried, but they wouldn't talk. Had these fancy lawyers warn us off. If we'd had something on them we would have hauled them in. But all we had was your hearsay."

So—all the killings explained themselves, and none appeared to be connected. Rakoubian "jumped" and Mrs. Z "self-immolated," and Darling "disappeared" in New Mexico. Frank Cordero was killed by "a party unknown," and as for an obscure actress named "Kimberly Yates," no one missed her, because no one knew who she really was.

"I'll tell you something," Scotto said to me. "The first time we met I told Dave Ramos afterwards: 'This guy's in over his head.' I think I was right. Except you got out clean." He looked hard at me. "Least you say you did. . . ."

He asked me if I'd be willing to swear out an affidavit stating everything I knew about the case. I told him I didn't much feel like swearing out anything, at least not until I consulted with a lawyer.

"Figures." He nodded. "I always knew you knew more than you told me. Wanna know my opinion, I think you were up to your ears in it. Maybe even a member of the cult. But like I said, you seem to have got out clean." He looked hard at me. "Funny. You're different now. Can't quite put my finger on how. Like you're more clearheaded. Focused, directed. Like you know what you want out of life. You were pretty weird before."

"Hey, Sal—I told you everything."

"Forget it, Geoffrey. Nobody gives a shit. Cheryl Devereux, a.k.a. Shadow, victim of a torture slaying—little splash in the media that's all that was. I can't even find anyone who's heard of this Sonya you told me about. Girls like that, they disappear all the time. Which doesn't mean I'm giving up. Figure they'll pull Dave off in a couple of weeks. But not me. I'll ask to stay on it for a while. I need the free time. Some personal stuff I've been wanting to do. Being a lone detective on a dead-end case like that—you can spend your time pretty much the way you want."

So Sal and I made an agreement—I wouldn't tell anyone he was goofing off, and he'd keep his suspicions of me to himself. It worked out pretty well for both of us. Gave me the peace of mind I needed to get back into the game.

I sold my view cameras to Aaron Greene. Once I was rid of them I felt relieved. I decided to give up fine-art photography and go back to photojournalism.

I phoned Jim Lynch to give him the news.

"Hey! Great, Geof! Now how about Beirut?"

He was so ecstatic when I told him I'd go, he invited me to lunch.

I flew out to the Middle East two weeks later, took a lot of pictures, and, strangely enough, had a fairly pleasant time. There were bodies around most everywhere, and, when I happened to be near when a big car bomb exploded, I was able to get to the site and shoot three rolls before they picked up the dismembered limbs.

Bloody stuff, brutal stuff—but I'd seen it all before. And thanks to the reflex viewing system of my Leica I was able to cast a cool eye. Frankly, I don't think I caught much that was new, but Jim was thrilled when he saw my proofs.

"Just like old times," he said. "You want the goods, you send Barnett."

I started taking portraits for magazines again, serious portraits of athletes, actors, people in the arts. The editors who hired me liked what I gave them, said my stuff had an intensity, a penetration, that they hadn't seen in my earlier work.

"It's like now you pin your subjects right to the wall," one guy told me. I shrugged, but he was right.

Last month *Vanity Fair* offered me a contract, and then so did *Rolling Stone*. So far I've opted to stay free-lance. I've got a cover idea I want to talk over with *Elle*.

Late this past winter, after I got my career securely back on track, I had a new piece of molded plastic made to fit the lens shaft of my gun-camera. I cleaned out the barrel of the Beretta inside, stashed the device and a box of ammo in a corner of my check-through luggage, and flew out to Cleveland under the name of Frank Cordero.

At the airport I rented a gray Buick with the kind of heavily tinted windows that appear opaque when the sun shines hard. Then, just for old times' sake, I checked into the Devora.

The following morning, I trailed Grace from her house to the shopping mall where she did her Nautilus routine. I watched her enter the gym, then parked beside her car, with my Buick facing in the opposite direction.

I opened the back of the camera, loaded two bullets into the Beretta, then munched on potato chips while I waited for her to come out.

When she came, hair wet from her postworkout shower, I cocked my weapon and held it ready. When she opened her car door, I suddenly opened mine, creating a little pen that would keep her from getting away.

"Grace?" I said. She turned. "Remember me?"

She stared hard at me, frowned. "What the hell do *you* want?"

"Came to take your picture, Grace."

She looked at me curiously. I shot her twice, fast and neat in the chest.

She died, I think, almost instantly. After she fell, I picked her up, placed her in her car, and locked her inside. I looked around. No one was near and no one, as far as I could tell, had seen. I was lucky. I'd killed her cleanly. Afterwards I just drove away.

I didn't kill her because I thought she might come after me. I killed her because of Frank. If it had been me who'd been killed out in New Mexico, he wouldn't have rested until he'd tracked my killer down. He would have called what I'd done "a pure justifiable act of revenge," and I think he would have appreciated the fact that I committed it with the special weapon he'd made, the disguised gun he'd created to accommodate my refusal to carry anything but a camera into war.

I learned something firsthand too from that little escapade, something Frank had told me once: though it's fairly hard to kill the first time around, it is a lot easier the second.

As for Kim, the memory's still vivid, but in time, I know, it will fade. I took so many shots of her over the weeks of our acquaintanceship, they all seem to run together now. At each stage I saw her the way I wanted to, and when we finally got to the end I saw her dead.

Every once in a while I look at my last picture of her—the one I took just after I shot her. I looked at it again last night. I must have studied it for at least an hour.

Like every other picture I ever took of her, it tells me nothing about her, nothing at all. But it does tell me something about Geoffrey Barnett. It fixes the moment he knew he could be merciless.

Which, I've begun to think, is the case with almost every kind of photograph. A photograph, you see, may or may not tell you much about its subject. But if you look at it closely, and you were the photographer, it can tell you a great deal about yourself.

WILLIAM BAYER is the author of the bestsellers *Switch* and *Pattern Crimes*, the Edgar Award winner *Peregrine*, and other novels. He is also a screenwriter and photographer. He and his wife, food writer Paula Wolfert, divide their time between New York City and Martha's Vineyard.